THE
Cardinal's
MAN

M·G·SINCLAIR

BLACK & WHITE PUBLISHING

First published 2017
by Black & White Publishing Ltd
29 Ocean Drive, Edinburgh EH6 6JL

1 3 5 7 9 10 8 6 4 2   7 18 19 20

ISBN: 978 1 78530 109 4

A CIP catalogue record for this book is available from the British Library.

Typeset by Iolaire, Newtonmore
Printed and bound by Nørhaven, Denmark

THE
Cardinal's
MAN

For Shula

It was the Prado where he first caught my eye. I was intending to visit the famous 'Black Room' by Goya, the paintings which were found surrounding the artist's body upon his death, too grotesque to be allowed beyond the confines of his studio. Unsure where to go, I made my way to the first floor. Then almost immediately I saw him. He was out of the way, positioned in the corner alongside a far more magnificent picture of Philip V.

Instantly he struck me like no person before or since. A court dwarf dressed in a red and yellow cape, painted by Velazquez in the mid-seventeenth century, his name Don Sebastian de Morra. Painfully proportioned, with stunted arms and legs, he was sat against a bare wall, crookbacked, his knuckles pressing into his thighs, his drip chin concealed behind thick beard. And yet this poor creature was fixing me with a stare of rapacious intelligence, his black eyes demanding my attention. And I realised at that moment how many great minds have been born in the wrong body at the wrong time – that for every Archimedes or Shakespeare, there have been other seeds which have had the misfortune to fall on stonier ground.

Escape

(1608 – 1632)

Sebastian Morra was born in Camoches, a village in the hinterlands of Normandy. Forty miles from Caen, it lay on an outcrop facing five thousand miles of open Atlantic, clinging to its spur like some barnacle to a whale. It was the ocean that brought the whiting, the bass, the mackerel, the bream and the crab. But it was also the ocean that brought the wind. A hard easterly that stung the eyes, that blew away the earth and left only sand and rock behind; that brought clouds and driving rain from September to June, an incessant wetness which made its way through every wall, roof and into the damp logs which sputtered in every fireplace. Dark and unrelenting months as the air tugged and squalled, wearing the people down as they protected their soil behind low walls, binding it as best they could with beans, beetroot and turnip, or else braved the water, with its currents and rip tides – moods that answered only to the earth and the sun.

1

The only release came with summer, both a blessing and a curse, a momentary respite from the scrabble and toil, a few weeks to revel, drink and forget. But always too brief and always with the same bitter ending, when the wind returned and the sodden cycle began all over again.

The village was a quarter of a mile from the shore, a straggle of no more than sixty dwellings, all in varying states of disrepair. Sebastian's was no exception. Like its neighbours, it was walled with mud and stone. Timber was avoided, the fishermen knowing all too well how their boats suffered in the salt and the breeze. But while rock could resist the elements, whatever the mortar, the wind would pick it out, leaving the loose stones to crumble – particularly high up, near the thatch. And no matter how much his parents tried to repair the seaward side, they could never seal all the cracks or keep out the chill which followed every setting sun.

The inside was divided into two. One room for his parents. The other, larger, was used for everything else – a place to eat as well as a bedroom for him and his brothers at night. It was dark. The only light came through the open chimney and a door on the landward side, and Sebastian was to remember it more as a burrow than a home. A life of shadow. All of them packed together like a litter of newborns. Evenings spent crouched tight round the fire, with its familial stench of smoke and sweat that made its way into their clothes, skin and nose until everything they drank or tasted was overpowered by it.

Both his mother and father shared the local physiognomy, flat faces that had been ground to the nub, though it was there the similarity ended. His father was black-eyed, sullen and lean, dressed in his dark tunic, either away at sea or staring into the fire with a drink in his hand. She was the opposite. Blue-eyed, always around and busying herself in her dress and shawl, nudging and cajoling, a whirl of good humour and chat. They squabbled incessantly but seemed to fit each other's absences well enough. She found comfort in his silence while he found sanctuary in her warmth. And each seemed content in their role, she taking care of the children, he fetching the water and catching the fish.

Sebastian was their first child, and as such, his birth was celebrated. However, by the age of three it was obvious something was wrong. While his chest was normal enough, his back, limbs and jaw remained of infantile proportions – the skull outlandish on his tiny body. Consequently, many of his earliest memories were of distorted faces: the expressions of horrified relatives, visitors flinching as they caught his eye, the stares of unfamiliar children peering round doorways.

Revolted, his father avoided him whenever possible. Instead the boy took sanctuary in his mother's company. Pitying him, she swaddled him close, at first within the confines of the crib, and then when, aged five, he was able to escape it, she still kept him close to her skirts – safe from his two younger brothers Charles and Audrien who rampaged through the gloom, a pair of clumsy giants oblivious to his presence. And there he remained for his earliest years, secure in his orbit. A speck in infinite space, yet safely revolving around a single star.

Cocooned from the outside world, Sebastian remembered those years as a dream. His mother was omnipresent, always watching over him. There was no one else, nothing to separate one day from another – no school or playmates, barely a glimpse of his brothers or father. It was as if he had never left the womb – until two months after his ninth birthday, when his life took a more unwelcome course.

* * *

Sebastian was first aware something important had happened when, during the usual breakfast of beans and crab, his mother began crying for no apparent reason. She had been unusually silent that morning, though he hadn't noticed anything unusual beyond the absence of his father (a habitually late riser as a result of the drink). When he asked what was wrong, she first looked bewildered, then sat him on her lap and explained that his father was sick. He hugged her but it didn't stop the tears. Later, unfamiliar relatives arrived at the house and whispered together, glancing across with peculiar expressions which made no sense to him. And when he tried to go to his parents' room, he was instead turned away or given his wooden blocks to play with.

As the weeks passed, he became convinced that something of great significance lurked inside and he would obsessively watch the curtain and those who emerged from behind it, barely able to hold their features in place. They seemed horrified by what they had seen and he came to dread the day when he would be called on to take his turn. Naturally, when he and his two brothers were finally lined up to pay their respects, he took one look at the murky entranceway then scurried for freedom, only to trip over almost immediately – the first of many occasions his legs were to disappoint him over the years. And it was only after being helped up and shushed by his mother that he finally ventured inside.

4

Sebastian had happy memories of his parents' room, of wriggling beneath the bed sheets and warming himself beside his mother when it was pitch black and cold outside. But now, looking in, he saw nothing comforting whatsoever. It was dark, the only light pricking in through a strip of hessian hung over the doorway. Indeterminate forms lined the walls, lumpen shadows from sacks of animal feed being stored for winter. Otherwise, apart from an outline of the bed and a rude-cut chair beside it, the room appeared to be empty. Peering through the gloom, he was unsure what to look for. Then he heard a rasp ahead of him. Mistaking it for an animal, he retreated to the doorway, yanking the curtain aside to reveal a gaunt head upon the pillow, withered by disease. Two yellow and bloodshot eyeballs immediately swivelled to look at him. Reluctantly he inched towards the bed, trying to hold the creature's stare, before slowly reaching towards it. As he did so, a claw emerged from the blanket and clutched at his wrist. Its grasp was surprisingly strong. He could feel the throb of agony and the urge to live. Sebastian waited for the creature to speak, but there was only silence as it stared back at him. He wanted to say something, to offer a word of comfort or a recollection of something shared. But he knew nothing about his father. There were no memories to reminisce over. Instead he sat, waiting for the grip to slacken and the moment when he could finally leave. For the remainder of that day and all the next, he often found himself absent-mindedly rubbing his wrist, trying to remove the prickle of death on his skin.

*　*　*

Sebastian didn't miss his father. The man had never been much more to him than a distant, pacing figure with angry eyes and a permanent scowl. Even so, he felt sorry for his mother Julienne. For the first few days after the funeral, she was a muddle of gulps and tears. He tried to console her, and while she would pull her face into a smile and thank him, it never seemed to last.

In desperate need of coin, Julienne took on work picking shellfish and gutting, which left her with no choice but to send him and his brothers to their aunt Collette's. There he was abandoned to her five offspring, aged between seven and fourteen, who, after a lifetime of scuffling and shouting, were little more than indistinguishable boulders of ruffled hair and bruised skin. The moment he saw them, he sensed danger and ran for the safety of his aunt's leg. However, Collette would have none of it and brushed him away, too busy to spend time with her own children, let alone her sister's. With nowhere else to go, Sebastian gazed at the rabble in front of him and ventured a weak smile.

One of the larger boys – a stringy, blue-eyed youth – returned a grin. 'We're going outside. Come.' He motioned Sebastian to follow.

I am not moving one inch, *mon ami*. He hid the reply behind a fixed smile. 'I think I'll stay here for the time being, if you don't mind.'

'What? Don't you like us?'

'Of course I like you. I'm just cold, that's all. It's warmer here, by the fire.'

'Oh, we can help with that.' The boy turned to Collette, hands clasped, his mother's little cherub. 'Maman, poor Sebastian has a chill. Shall we put him in the bed next door?'

6

Naturellement – and suddenly they were all around him, jostling him out of the room. He tried falling to the floor, but it was no use. They simply carried him around the corner, and there introduced him to reality, first verbally and then with their fists. He screamed, cried, begged – anything to make them stop. Charles and Audrien were too young to protect him and when he called for help, they looked on dumbly, powerless against the pack. Indeed, there was fascination in their eyes, satisfaction even, the pleasure of seeing him discover how it felt to be cast out of the light.

And so Sebastian's education began. He pleaded with his mother not to send him back again – but it was no use. All she could do was sob apologies while looking at him with a mixture of horror and shame, overwhelmed not so much by what was taking place as her inability to end it.

*   *   *

Necessity is a quick tutor and Sebastian soon acquired a feral, rat-like intelligence, grasping the best places to take cover and how best to scuttle between them. From his hiding holes, he watched the pack assiduously, learning their patterns as they moved from room to room. Above all he learned to fear their silence. Noise meant they were busy, squabbling amongst themselves. It was only when the uproar subsided and they had run out of things to do that their attention turned to him. Even then he found ways to defend himself – always keeping a handful of stones in his pocket to fling at pursuers or hiding on the roof and stamping on any hands unwise enough to follow. And when they did catch him, as they invariably did, he found there were advantages to his size. He was difficult to hit and nature seemed to have blessed him with thick ribs and bones that resisted even the worst beating – that moment when there was nothing to be done except to curl into a ball and retreat within.

They also called him names, among them 'flea', 'runt' and 'changeling'. Most popular was 'shrew', a moniker that was cruelly apt. It wasn't just his size, but his whole demeanour. The battering had left marks both without and within, burdening him with nervous habits that made themselves particularly apparent when he was in groups. Ill at ease, he would paw at his face or shuffle his feet, forever glancing round in search of escape. Even in later life, he would sometimes find himself flinching instinctively when people reached toward him, and suffering bouts of melancholia for no apparent reason beyond an innate distrust of his fellow man.

* * *

Having never seen another of his kind, Sebastian had no idea what to expect, and it wasn't until adolescence that his condition became fully apparent. Previously, he had sustained himself with hopes that he would catch up, that some dormant part of his body would awaken and propel him to the height of his peers. But the world continued to grow around him, as he stubbornly remained the same. It was a problem that only became worse with time. His body felt like a prison cell – the bones like bars through which a larger man was trying to escape. Certain parts grew to adult size: his skull, spine, palms and teeth. Others remained childlike: the jaw, fingers, arms and legs. Every moment of the day he was reminded of his abnormality, from when he woke to find himself engulfed in a sea of blanket to his evening meal, when what seemed a simple spoon in others' hands became a ladle in his own. Above all, he could see his deformity reflected in the eyes of others – the way they looked at him with ugly, rude expressions, midway between fascination and disgust.

His brothers, by comparison, flourished as the years went by. Despite their youth, they were far larger than him and he was only able to keep out of their constant fights through a combination of bribery and threat. It frustrated him how they advanced through life with such insufferable ease. Whenever he looked at them he could see himself but improved in every way. So tall, precisely proportioned, effortless in movement and thought. Not that it was their fault. They had no way of giving him the life they led, no way of freeing him from an existence eked out in tiny spaces, safe from the teeth of the outside world.

Desperate, he battled against his situation, trying to do what nature couldn't. For the whole of his twelfth year he kept to a meticulous routine. Every day at five in the afternoon he would walk to the tumbledown barn that lay half a mile outside the village, all the time struggling not to trip over his own unwieldy feet. After walking inside, he began by measuring himself against the doorframe, etching his height into the wood with a sliver of flint. Then, retrieving a coil of rope from the corner, he tied up his legs, tossed the rope over a beam and hoisted himself upside down. Next he would knot the rope tight so he was hanging freely before finally grabbing a heavy bag of stones and stretching himself for as long as he could bear. After a brief rest, he would start again, until, an hour or so later, the pain became unendurable and he would topple home as best he could while trying to force back the agony of burning limbs.

In spite of all his efforts, nothing changed. What little growth there was only came with age. Each cut in the door-frame simply overran the last, leaving an ever-deeper scar in the wood. He persevered nonetheless, long after his situation became apparent, until the day came when he could lie to himself no longer and finally hurled both bag and rope into a nearby field. In desperation he tried a more direct approach, breaking his leg with a shovel in the hope it might somehow grow back longer. But all he ended up with was an infection, a month in bed and the remainder of the year with a hobbling gait.

Momentary release arrived with Sebastian's thirteenth birthday, when he and his brothers were finally allowed to stay at home. It was summer and most days they would escape from the house to the fields inland, climbing trees or swimming in the local pond. Usually Sebastian observed from a distance, preferring to watch the wheat ripple in the breeze as the afternoon gave way to dusk. With no one to teach him, he named the trees and birds himself, or guessed them from the names he knew: woodcock became nightingales, rooks became blackbirds and beech trees, oaks – a private language that was his and his alone.

* * *

Despite having always wanted to support his mother and work beside her along the shore, Sebastian had to wait until he was fourteen before he was deemed large enough to try his hand with tools. There were already enough people to harvest the beach, so he and his brothers took a cart to the local farm where they were lined up in front of the owner and each presented with a spade and scythe. Then, after a few minutes' instruction, they were shown a strip of ground to reap and till. Naturally Charles and Audrien completed the task with ease, reducing their plots to naked earth within a few minutes, the barley piled in a neat stack alongside. Sebastian, meanwhile, struggled to lift, let alone use, either tool. Nevertheless, what he lacked in ability, he made up for in effort, planting his scythe in the ground before slashing wildly and ineffectually at the crop. His limited success only spurred him on and he had to be forcibly stopped after losing his balance and nearly decapitating himself.

Undeterred, he next tried cobbling and tailoring, only to find his misshapen hands too clumsy for needles or nails. And after equally unsuccessful attempts at smithing and carpentry, it soon it became apparent that ambition could not always make a substitute for size. Journeys lasted longer, loads were heavier and bulkier, tools were cumbersome, carts were higher, tables out of reach – every object seemingly designed to frustrate and impede, making even simple tasks a challenge.

Consequently, Sebastian was only fit for occasional work, such as scattering grain or picking berries. Instead he spent most of his days alone in the house, observing his brothers become ever more remote as they joined the world above. Every evening they would come home and recount the day's events, each time a little more foreign. And each time he would sense himself becoming a little more removed, the world around continuing to rise as he remained submerged

11

below – a barrier that lifted ever higher, obscuring him from view and forcing him to bellow to be noticed. His brothers were still polite, of course, but Sebastian found no comfort in that. And when they spoke to him, he could see the pity in their faces as they looked down, grimaces twisting their otherwise perfect features. They were listening to him out of duty, nothing more, and he would play along, wanting to be part of things, while always being aware of the distance between them. They shared the same surname, nothing more.

* * *

Now completely alone, Sebastian was confronted by his own insignificance, a life that seemed to grow smaller with every passing year. In desperation he took to sitting beneath the solitary cleft yew that marked the end of the village. Bent double by the wind, it provided some shelter from the elements, deep-rooted and ancient enough to draw life from the stone and the grit. A thin crust of salt had accumulated in the ridges of its bark and the various initials graffitied around its trunk. There he would wait in hope of a rich passer-by who might spot his potential, or a merchant in need of an apprentice. But it soon became apparent that he lived in a village that was close to nowhere of significance, too parochial to interest anyone rich or powerful, too small even for a market or church. The only people he ever saw were farmers, most of whom reacted with either laughter or abuse, though he did manage to talk a few of them into taking him to nearby towns, on the condition that he agreed to help unload the cart and not cause any trouble.

In the first week he travelled to Créances and Lessay; a

fortnight later, Geffosses; and soon after Anneville-sur-Mer. Over the next few months, he managed to visit everywhere of any interest within a twenty-mile radius, a few twice or three times. Despite his initial enthusiasm, it became dispiriting as the weeks passed by. Each village or town seemed no different to his own. The people's reaction was always the same: curious, they would point and mock, and every enquiry for employment would be met by polite refusal or rank contempt. And no matter how far he went or whom he spoke to, he always seemed to find himself back in the same place, sat under the same time-riddled tree, staring at the same muddy track and sodden fields.

Alone with his thoughts, Sebastian began to question his existence. He had no work, no friends, and no hope of change. And every day it became harder to withstand the jeers of passers-by. The truth was that they were right. He was no more than half a man, an insult to God and a mockery of nature.

Until one day the inevitable. After a particularly miserable day of intermittent rejection and abuse, Sebastian simply stood up and began the slow plod down the road in front of him, determined never to come back. Following it mindlessly, he walked like a wind-up doll running down the last of its spring, each step barely carrying to the next. Nevertheless, he jolted forward, staring at the horizon as the bare ground gave way to trees and fields, the wind at his back fading as he travelled inland. Afternoon became dusk and dusk became night until, unable to ignore his growing thirst, he was distracted by the glitter of a nearby lake.

After scrambling down the bank, he drank his fill, then stood up, sated. Looking down at the dark water, he could see his reflection staring back. Wavering in the ripples, it seemed more a child's drawing than a real person – a ridiculous creature, short-backed and barrel-chested with too many teeth for its mouth and no jaw to speak of. It appeared perplexed, unable to comprehend what it was, neither man nor animal but something in between, something not meant to live. He could feel the image pulling him towards it and sensed his weight pitching forwards. For a moment he remained on the brink, in perfect equilibrium, weightless. And then the lake enveloped him.

Barely thawed from winter, the water froze him on contact, his muscles drawing tight and expelling the air from his lungs. He clenched himself tight into a ball as the pain subsided from a bite to an ache. Then slow descent and thickening darkness until he reached the soft, cloying mud of lake-bottom. Prone in the silence, he choked back the urge to breathe and waited out the black and the cold. The gloom began to redden and he could sense blood; first a metallic taste at the back of his throat, but soon everywhere, throbbing in his nose and eyes, his ears beating to the ragged thump of his accelerating heart as the need for air became desperate and overpowering. His body began to rattle as he entered the final spasms and he could feel himself losing consciousness, the red deepening as the mud sucked him down. At that moment he knew he was going to die. Fear took hold. Suddenly death didn't seem comforting, instead painful and lonely. He wanted to live and not knowing up from down, he kicked wildly, sucking at empty lungs. Everything was slewing in different directions and his legs had become limp, as if already dead. The blackness began to pulsate, followed by a stab behind his eyeballs, unbearable, as though his head was about to crack open. Certain it was the end, he managed a final thrust for escape.

Abruptly the silence broke and Sebastian felt the chill of the world on his face then sucked in a backward scream of air. He continued to paddle and catch his breath before recovering enough to make his way to the rushes and haul himself onto the bank where he lay, too exhausted to care whether he was alive or not.

* * *

Arriving home, near blue with cold, Sebastian was confronted by his mother. As she caught sight of him, a look of horror crossed her features and for a moment he couldn't recognise her. Then her everyday face returned and she rushed him inside. After stripping and drying him, she wrapped him in a blanket then laid him by the fire with a caudle of wine, eggs and honey. She barely spoke the whole while, but he could see she was in fragments, and all night he lay awake, terrified at what the morning would bring.

He expected rage, tears and tantrums but it turned out to be nothing of the sort. In truth she had no idea what to do and simply responded in the manner of any other church-going, law-abiding woman of her time. She marched him straight to the local priest.

The church was in the next village, a mile-and-a-half by foot, but the whole way she didn't slow her pace or turn her head, except to occasionally check Sebastian was still behind her. He shambled along in tow, struggling to keep up. Forced into a jog, he made a ludicrous sight: a collection of mismatched pieces loosely sewn together and trying to move as one. But he said nothing, aware that any complaint would be met by a sharper reply.

* * *

Before Sebastian's mother appeared, Père Jean was cogitating as he lazed in a quilted armchair overlooking the sun-dappled greens and greys of the churchyard. It had taken twenty years' hard work to gain the respect of both bishop and flock. Now was the time to enjoy what he had earned. Having already written his sermon, he was debating with himself which reading best complemented his theme of love: Paul's first letter to the Corinthians or Luke, chapter VI. Eventually deciding on Corinthians, he was about to pay a visit to the abbey for a glass of calvados when she arrived, her eyes wide with animal panic. Realising it would not be a short visit, he pursed a smile before welcoming her inside. Then, after the briefest of thank yous, she emptied herself in a torrent of words, begging him to look after her son, to take him on as a student and help him make something of himself.

Père Jean had no intention of educating Sebastian. Aside from his deformity, the boy was a peasant and doubtless a halfwit too. All he wanted was to silence the woman and get her out of his vestry. His plan was simply to glance at the child, pronounce him too old, then buy her off with a few sous, while of course offering to pray on his behalf. However, looking down at the misshapen creature, he found it staring directly back at him. It seemed to have registered the importance of the situation and its eyes glittered, hard and unsettling. The pupils were varnish-black and he could sense himself in their reflection, smiling uneasily. Below, its mouth was crinkled in disgust and he had the feeling it knew exactly what he was planning to do. Embarrassed, he opened his lips to speak but the words were so inadequate and hypocritical that he couldn't bring himself to say them. Besides, the child appeared intelligent, or at least extremely resilient – either way the making of an interesting mind. On top of which, perhaps the woman was right. He was the boy's last hope, and he did seem to have potential, however raw.

It wouldn't be difficult adding him to the class. He had taken a new group of pupils only three months before. All he needed to do was keep the child well out of sight. Textbooks he could provide, and the boy could complete his exercises once the lesson was over. The only extra work would be a few minutes' marking each week. So, with a stiff nod to both mother and Sebastian, Père Jean invited him to return at ten o'clock the following day.

*　*　*

The church was a small Norman affair with a square tower of rough-hewn, grey stone. Classes took place between ten and three each day, with the exception of the Sabbath. Due to his low birth and general appearance, Sebastian was required to sit behind a curtain and remain invisible throughout, never speaking or moving when others were present. Instead he would observe proceedings through the slit between the material and the wall, asking questions during the few minutes after each lesson, once the other boys had left. He didn't mind. For the first time in his life, his size was irrelevant. Instead all that mattered was his memory, spelling and diction – and he approached his studies with the deranged enthusiasm of an infant, repeating each lesson like a mantra, trying to remember everything he could.

Despite starting behind the rest of the class, he accelerated past them within the year. It wasn't hard. He shared none of their distractions: no friends or toys or pets to amuse himself with. Besides, he was fascinated to finally be able to put a name to things, to tell a coot from a moorhen at a glance, or see a leaf and instantly know which tree it came from. Within eighteen months, he had learned enough to read and write basic Latin, and within two years he was proficient, even when presented with the demotic. After that, intent on taking his vows, he began to work his way through the ecclesiastical texts from Augustine and Jerome to Anselm and Aquinas. He found inspiration in their stories, most of all Augustine's, of people overcoming adversity and finding strength in their faith. In idler moments, he even dreamed of joining their ranks as a doctor of the Church.

Père Jean assisted as he could, letting him take home old pamphlets and circulars to read, though it was all the same fare – the rise of Cardinal Richelieu to principal minister and the alliance of the perfidious English with the Huguenots at La Rochelle. And the day his mother presented him with a copy of *Gargantua and Pantagruel* by Rabelais, he knew it could only be Père Jean's suggestion. The paper was cheap and without illustrations, but knowing the sacrifice she made to buy it, and despite being given far more expensive gifts in later life, he always treasured it above all his other possessions. Years later he could still quote large sections by heart, which he would often recite in times of distress.

* * *

The students were granted one break from their studies each day, at lunchtime when they were permitted a meal and half an hour to release their energy in the churchyard. Most often they went tousling for birds or else played tag amongst the gravestones. Consequently, they didn't pay a great deal of attention to their surroundings and some days passed before they became aware of the small figure observing them from a nearby stump. To begin with they assumed it was one of the local boys, come to eat his lunch or simply curious, perhaps. It was only later, during a game of hide and seek, that one of them came rushing back, reporting that it wasn't a boy but a goblin. Naturally the others mocked him, telling him such things belonged to fairy tales, but he would not be dissuaded. So another pupil was despatched to prove him wrong, only to come back swearing that if it wasn't a goblin, then it was certainly the strangest child he had seen in his life. The figure now became a source of immense interest, doubly so when it was spotted hiding behind a curtain during one of their classes. Intrigued, they developed theories – that it was Père Jean's secret love child or some form of homunculus or even a changeling, switched at birth.

Nevertheless, it was a full two weeks before they dared make their approach. Whatever it was, the creature kept out of sight for a reason, and none of them were keen to find it out. However, curiosity eventually got the better of them and lots were drawn. The loser – a gangly and pockmarked boy by the name of Olivier – was sent to speak to the creature and discover what he could. Forced onward by the eyes at his back, he advanced slowly towards where it was watching him, crouched on its usual stump. As he drew closer, he hoped it might become alarmed and flee. However, it seemed unconcerned by his presence and inspected him thoroughly, all the while consuming an apple with an oversized hand.

Up close, it was a strange beast, inspiring more pity than fear. Not so much one body as two fused together. The head, hands and chest seemed of normal size, while the back, arms and legs were those of an infant. Its face seemed perfectly normal, albeit small-chinned, and was looking at him with a curious squint.

'Do you speak?' He pronounced the words slowly and distinctly to ensure it could comprehend.

The creature appeared confused by the question.

'Of course I do,' it replied in flawless French.

'Sorry for asking. It's just that I didn't know if you were one of ...you know ...them.'

The query seemed simple enough, but again gave the creature considerable pause for thought, and it took a final bite of its apple before tossing it aside. 'I don't know what you mean by *them*.'

'You know ... one of the forest folk.' It seemed a kinder word than goblin.

The creature sighed with an air that implied it was not the first time it had been asked this question. 'I'm studying to be a priest. Just like you.'

'But you're a ...' The sentence trailed off. He didn't have to finish it. It wasn't just height that separated them. The dwarf, and it clearly was a dwarf, was dressed in peasant clothes, a hooded jerkin of coarse cloth – patched on the elbows and knees – his hair as unkempt as broken thatch.

'Serf?'

'I meant to say you're a commoner.' Olivier realised this didn't sound a great deal better and hastily redirected the

20

conversation. 'My friend was wondering if he might touch your hump.'

'What? He thinks it'll bring him luck?' The dwarf snorted contempt.

Olivier looked at the ground, unsure of what to say. Every word that fell from his mouth seemed to cause offence. Better to keep silent. Observing his unease, the dwarf appeared to warm to him, venturing a smile.

'Very well then. But don't expect much. If it's good fortune he wants, I'd advise he try elsewhere.'

After being introduced to Olivier's peers, Sebastian was soon allowed to join in their games – principally interminable rounds of tag and pig-in-the-middle, during which he proved to be both a terrible runner and near unable to catch a ball. Consequently, he resorted to all manner of ruses and deceits – most often distracting his rivals or else losing apparent interest in the game before making a dash the moment his opponent's back was turned. It made for entertaining company and they came to be acquaintances of sorts. He learned their names: Julien de Monville, Charles de Rigal, Olivier Letournier, Alain Veuville. Over time they even came to entrust him with their secrets, above all Olivier, who suffered a dreadful fear of a life of celibacy, and Julien, who was consumed by his desire to become pope. He couldn't help noticing how at ease they were in his company, perhaps even more than with their own friends, and how his appearance – for all its drawbacks – made them lower their guard. Slowly the class came to seem a less solitary place and often one of his fellow students would notice him behind the curtain and they would acknowledge each other with a smile or nod of the head. Not, of course, that there was ever any suggestion that he might join them.

*   *   *

It had never occurred to Sebastian that he wouldn't take his vows. All the boys entered a seminary upon completing their studies. The only difference was the vocation: most became pastors, some monks, a few Jesuits. Every summer, the eldest class would be called on by God, each member receiving a sign from the Almighty, an exhortation to serve His will. Drawn to the silence and seclusion, Sebastian desperately wanted to be a monk, safe from the intrusive eyes of the outside world. Determined to make up for lost time, he finished the required texts and then kept on reading. Rather than going home, he would often sit in a corner of the nave and study, forgetting himself in the empty space as he watched the stained-glass splinter across the floor and inhaled the incense, its smell an old world perfume – a musty spice redolent of Etruscans and Phoenicians, of trading ships and faraway places. Only with the coming of dusk would he remember the time, as he saw the shadows arch across the floor and the candles pricking out of the gloom like the first evening stars. Then, stowing away his books and pen, he would put on his cloak and cross himself at the door before making the two-mile walk back to Camoches and a plate of cold crab.

By twenty-one he had worked his way through all of Père Jean's limited library and mastered most of the areas he would need to learn: principally theology, biblical Greek and Hebrew. Now all he could do was await the word of God.

*   *   *

Just before Sebastian's twenty-second birthday, his studies officially ended. All that last day, Père Jean had observed his pupil's distraction. Sebastian's answers were still correct, but delayed, as though there was an obstacle between his ears and brain. Then, as they were discussing a passage from Boethius, Sebastian asked if it 'was possible if someone such as me could be called on by the Lord'.

Père Jean stopped and grimaced. Ever since the day he'd first taken Sebastian under his wing, he'd known the question would come. The idea was so ludicrous that he had never considered it seriously. Indeed, he only realised the depth of the boy's feelings after wandering into the vestry one morning to find him putting on a cincture and alb. They were grotesquely oversized and in almost any other circumstances the scene would have been laughable. Instead it was pitiful, and he always recalled the incident with a sigh. What made the situation even worse was that Sebastian was the best student he had ever had – not just able to read Greek but compose it as well, articulate and with a brutal logic that would have put Loyola himself to shame.

'Sebastian, I appreciate your desire to go to the seminary. But there are other, more worldly requirements.'

'Worldly? What do you mean?'

'I mean money. It costs a great deal to buy a benefice or endow a monastery. I'm afraid ecclesiastical life has changed somewhat since the Lord Jesus' day.'

'How much?' Père Jean saw that same determination in Sebastian's eyes that he had observed when they first met. He flinched, fearful of crushing closely held dreams.

'Sebastian, I'm sorry but I have to be honest. There is no possibility whatsoever of you joining the Church. For a start there's the cost. It's hundreds of livres – more than you'll ever earn. Then there's your ancestry. You're no fool; you must have noticed everyone else here is of noble blood. Even then I doubt they would admit you.' He paused, tiptoeing his way through the next sentence. 'It's just … well … that a priest needs to project a certain gravitas … to be a representative of God … and I'm not sure how easy it would be for you to deliver a sermon when you can barely reach the lectern. I truly am sorry.' He sighed out the apology, watching Sebastian struggle to hold his features together, the strain warping an already unnatural face. 'I don't know if it's any consolation, but had the circumstances been different, I think you would have made an excellent priest.'

'Thank you for informing me. I would like to leave now.' The reply was abrupt, as Sebastian clenched a smile, the corners of his jaw bulging from the tightness of the lock. Père Jean nodded, watching as he placed his books, inkpot, and quills back on their shelves, then folded his papers before stowing them in his bag, even remembering to cross himself before leaving and bow at the doorway as he bade his farewell.

'Wait…' Père Jean motioned him back. 'Maybe there's something I can do. I mean it's not much and you'd be taking a chance. There's someone I know in Paris … a Viscount Turenne. He said he had need of a clerk and I'd be delighted to give you a letter of recommendation.'

Warming to the idea, the priest stood up, elated to have found some way to ease his conscience. 'Yes … yes … there's enough in the poor box to get you to Paris … and a little left over for lodgings too. I'll write the letter now, and there's a daily coach from Coutances. You can make it there yourself, I presume … yes, very good.'

Sebastian agreed, of course. It wasn't a difficult choice: to spend his days working for a noble house or else trapped in some cramped shack on the outer rim of nowhere. The doubts didn't arrive until later.

* * *

Before leaving, Sebastian made his farewells, beginning by taking Charles and Audrien to the local tavern for an ale. He hoped they would be impressed, maybe even a little envious. But they weren't. All he received were a few grunts and a 'good for you'. They found him an embarrassment, seating him in the darkest corner and barely acknowledging him as he spoke. Not that he cared. As he'd grown through study, so they seemed to have regressed by comparison. Six years had passed and for all their intelligence and opportunity, nothing had changed. They were living in the same village, working the same fields, still dreaming their way through life.

Now they were determined to make their fortunes as wool merchants in Caen, and after a few mugs of ale they seemed to forget him entirely and began animatedly discussing plans to raise enough money for a part-share in a boat. The fact they knew nobody in the trade nor anything about wool or how to sell it didn't seem to concern them. Instead, they sat spread-legged, imagining how they would spend their eventual profits, intoxicated with their own grandeur and puff.

Sebastian tried to make a few suggestions, that maybe they might consider working for someone else first, just to learn the business, or find out the risk of capsizing or losing a cargo, perhaps. They didn't listen, nodding with rictus sincerity before explaining that they had already considered his point or else dismissing it as an irrelevance. Eventually he realised there was no point arguing and spent the remainder of the evening concealing an ever-growing desire to leave. It seemed odd to him that they had once appeared such vast figures. Now they seemed far smaller than him.

* * *

On announcing his departure, Sebastian expected his mother to be pleased, but she wasn't. Instead, she jerked back in her chair as if slapped, and stammered out a multitude of reasons why not to go: that he would lose his money; that he had no understanding of the real world; that he would be abandoned in the wilderness of Paris, unable to return home. There was desperation in her voice, and for the first time he realised she had never truly considered he might leave. It seemed like betrayal – that for all her words of encouragement, she never really believed in him. Not that he let her know. Instead, he gave the warmest smile he could muster and tried to calm her, promising to be careful.

'Besides, Maman, there's no changing the fact you're getting older. You won't be around forever. I'll have to look after myself one day.' She nodded but he could see she didn't mean it. Her eyes and mouth were skewed with pain. Even so, neither of them wanted to sour their last hours together and they spent the rest of the day reminiscing as they prepared for the journey: washing clothes, darning holes and packing food. Despite his mother's veneer of normality, Sebastian could see the strain in her movements, tight and stiff-jointed, as if she was struggling to keep her body under control. For a moment he considered staying, but one look at the narrow walls of the cottage and the sodden grey outside was enough to banish any doubts. Even at the last, as they hugged goodbye, she struggled to release him, clamping him to her so tight that he could feel the impress of her body, her warmth remaining on him long after they waved goodbye.

*　*　*

Leaving Camoches for perhaps the final time, Sebastian felt more excited than afraid. He remembered his childhood years spent staring up the muddy track, determined to escape. From the cart he could see boundless countryside: grey shale and rock giving way to distant fields and scattered villages, the peaks and forest of Swiss Normandy a tangle of faraway green to his left, patched by vast shadows from the cloudbanks above. Overwhelmed by the view, he felt like an explorer surveying the unknown. The border was forty miles to the south, beyond it Maine and Brittany. Some four hundred miles further lay Arles, then the Mediterranean. From there he could find boats travelling the trade routes, or journey by caravan along the Silk Road. He imagined landscapes and civilisations: red desert set against a flaming sun, the great Khan's imperial palace at Shangdu, high mountains shearing tattered cloud – and it wasn't until dusk that his imagination gave way to deep and untroubled sleep.

*　*　*

Paris was like nothing Sebastian had ever seen, an entire world crammed into three square miles. In the battle for space, everyone built up, out, under, in between, any way they could. Buildings overflowed the bridges, their backs hanging over empty air, supported by flimsy brackets of struts and beams. Wooden tenements, erected to absurd heights, twisted into knots under their own weight. High stone walls pressed out from the great houses and churches in an attempt to keep the world at bay. Cellars flanked the roadsides, tunnelling down into candlelit murk, while hovels were squeezed into chinks only a few feet wide. Between them, the people scrummed through the needling streets, trying to navigate their kinks and jags, never stopping, always hurrying. Humanity gushing in all directions, orderless – a river that had broken its banks and was simply trying to find the fastest way down, spilling through side roads, alleyways, in a churn and tumble of chatter and colour. Far above, flocks of starlings lived off the mess, roiling in clouds that folded through themselves into chaotic forms, mirroring the jostle below.

As he approached the heart of the city, the space continued to tighten. The buildings closed in and the crowds became thicker, the sky ever-narrowing. Lost in the crush, Sebastian soon lost all sense of where he was. The tide was overpowering and, unable to fight, he allowed himself to be carried along. All he could see were legs: stockinged, knickerbocked, bare, in hose – pounding, thumping, stamping legs. Giant centipedes advancing from all directions, cutting in and out of the shadows. He tried to navigate between them, but found himself caught in a clatter of knees and hips. Senseless, there was no order or pattern to the movement, that same milling of penned animals circling for escape. Occasionally the jostle would be interrupted by some piece of human flotsam littering the street, a beggar with a seamed face or a drunkard peering up from the gutter with a single fiery eye. But no matter the shock, he could never stop or stare – the crowd bustling him ever forward.

*   *   *

The Place de Seine was a narrow cul-de-sac off the main thoroughfare with a high terrace of stone on either side. Remarkably it was paved, unlike the dung-trampled tracks which surrounded it, and Sebastian immediately had a sense both of wealth and of not belonging. Nearby, a ginger dog did not appear quite so impressed and was relieving itself by a doorway, the liquid following a jagged course down the cobbles. Nevertheless, he was glad of the quiet and took a moment to collect himself. Of all the houses, the viscount's was the most impressive. It stood at the end, flanked by its peers. Built in the baroque style with a pediment, it was walled with Oise stone, the balconies and high windows of leaded glass a testament to its owner's position.

Pausing to check Père Jean's introduction was still safe in his pocket, he pulled the bell and waited to be let in. A servant appeared, who seemed bemused by his size but after taking his name and examining the letter ushered him through nonetheless. Inside was a palace in miniature: hung with portraits and chandeliers, flagged in marble, with a carved staircase and hammer-beam ceiling. What struck him most of all was a contemplative silence which took him back to long afternoons in the transept studying Saint Jerome.

Once the master had been informed of his arrival, he was led into the main room where the viscount was waiting. Sebastian had never met a nobleman. He expected solemnity, jewels and ermine, and was taken aback to see a dishevelled figure stamping around the room in a stained robe, unwigged and muttering to himself. The man was middle-aged, with thin lips and pinched features that looked starved of comfort or rest. Absorbed in his thoughts, he didn't notice Sebastian at first – though when he did, it was with familiar disbelief.

'What's he doing here? I didn't ask for a dwarf,' he barked at the footman, ignoring his visitor completely.

'He's a clerk, Your Lordship. He has a letter of recommendation.'

'Hmmm ... Give it to me.'

Sebastian presented the letter, proffering it like some holy text. The viscount showed no such reverence – plucking it from his hands, taking a brief glance and returning it in a crumple.

'Yes, the name, it's familiar ... that priest, what was he called again?'

'Père Jean, Your Lordship.'

'Yes, Père Jean. He says you are an educated man.' He spoke with an air of distaste that had taken many years to cultivate. 'Are you?'

'I'd like to think so.'

'We'd better find out.' And with that, he glanced over at a loose pamphlet on a side table.

'This should suffice. I want the front page copied. You have an hour.' He handed it over before turning to the footman. 'Show him to my study. And give the man a quill and ink.'

After responding with a bow, the footman led Sebastian

30

up a carved oaken staircase into a panelled study – dark-lacquered, its air heavy with the scent of burnt cedar from the hearth. Then, after laying out the materials as instructed, he informed Sebastian he would be returning in precisely one hour's time and expected the copy to be complete.

It was a straightforward task, no longer than forty minutes at most and Sebastian worked confidently, intent on rewarding himself with a quick look though the viscount's library once he had finished. Then, just as he was beginning the final paragraph, he spilled the inkwell. It was an innocent mistake, merely a nick on the lip as he pulled out the quill, but impossible to contain. A moment later there was ink everywhere, streaming a gush across the desk. Despite his best attempts to daub away the damage with a handkerchief, it was futile. The copy was ruined, smeared and scabbed with black crusts. The footman didn't even bother to look at it, observing the stain on the top of the bureau with horror and immediately shouting for assistance. Ordering the house-maids to *clean up this godforsaken mess*, he promptly marched over, grasped him by the arm and escorted him straight to the back entrance. Then, with a slam of the door, Sebastian found himself abandoned to the street.

*　*　*

Sebastian never made a conscious decision to beg. He was an educated man and thought such things beneath him. But it wasn't long before Père Jean's money ran out and thirst and hunger took their toll. His first steps were tentative, simply asking for a little food and drink as he knocked on doors in a futile search for work. Another week went by before he started asking for a few sous to pay for lodgings for the night. After that it was only a short step to requesting passers-by for a little assistance as he made his rounds. A week or so later he stopped bothering with the doors at all. Oddly, the hardest part wasn't the beginning but the end, the moment when he couldn't delude himself any longer and finally walked out to join his peers on the streets.

Most of his early successes came through perseverance, people paying simply to be rid of him. Masquerading as a poet, he would perform verses for whatever people could spare. But he was no rhymer. He coupled 'you' with 'blue', 'star' with 'afar', while his lines lacked metre and were little more than cliché. Nevertheless, he slowly rediscovered that feral intelligence – dormant since childhood – as he progressed from shrew to rat, learning to fend for himself and seize whatever came his way. He soon discovered how entertaining a child would always earn a coin from its mother, or playing a pipe was a good way to draw attention – while always being aware of the dogs it would also attract. He learned to sift the good person from the bad with the quickest of looks, and to see the opportunity in every glance and casual 'good day'. He took care to work in the mornings and on Mondays when wallets were full, and never bother with a Saturday, when the poor box would inevitably receive whatever pickings were left. And most often he would ply his trade near an almshouse or a church, because the poor gave more than the rich, perhaps because they better knew the pain of going without.

His favoured tool was the rancid scrap of bread. After placing a crust on the road, he would wait for the approaching footsteps of a passer-by, then rush out of an alleyway and pretend to consume it. After which and most importantly, would come the moment of realisation, when he would look up at the horrified stranger before trying to conceal the tidbit beneath his jerkin. It was always this final act – the embarrassment of the man fallen on hard times – that drew the sympathy and then the coin.

Naturally he made use of his size. The first time was an accident, a simple bump on a street. Used to collisions from passers-by, he barely gave it a thought. It was only when the man asked if he was hurt that he had the wherewithal to limp and was rewarded with three sous for his pain. After repeating the trick a number of times, he would hold a tray of stale buns for effect – favouring the dusted variety due to both their whiteness in the mud and the way the flour concealed the hard rind beneath. After a while it came so instinctive that even in later life he would feel the knock of a hip or elbow and struggle not to throw himself to the ground.

Over time he came to learn the city. The great arteries that quartered it, each named after its saint: Denis, Martin, Jacques and Antoine. The crammed Marais and Notre Dame which lay at its heart, along with a number of the muddy, nameless trails in between. He even came to take a certain pride in his work. The country was suffering and Paris too, the people burdened with taxes as Richelieu tried to buy his way out of war with Spain. Life was becoming harder and hungrier. Pitches that had once been plentiful were now long dry, and the competition was growing more bitter by the day. Many had simply given up, lying in doorways or down side streets, waiting for a death that was sure enough to come. But in spite of it all, Sebastian endured, grinding out the days with as much humour as he could manage. And when he looked at the misery around him, it was with grim pleasure, his achievement magnified by the failure of so many others greater and stronger than him.

However, he knew it was a life that couldn't last. Despite his nose for danger, it hadn't been enough to keep him entirely safe. There had been incidents – thugs slitting his clothes for the coins sewn into the seams, numerous tramplings beneath the crowd – while his tongue had got him into more than enough trouble. The final straw came one evening when he spotted a soldier weaving across the street, clearly the worse for wear and an easy target. Having exhausted his buns, he improvised with whatever items he had to hand, thrusting everything into a sack and scurrying into the man's path. While the fall wasn't his best, it was passable enough and he lay on the ground, clutching his ankle, awaiting the usual voice of concern and helping hand. Hearing nothing, he assumed he had somehow failed to catch the soldier's attention and let out another groan. But instead of assistance, he received a boot in the ribs that had him clutching his side in pain.

'Think you'll fool me, little man.' The voice was angry and drunk.

Looking up, Sebastian could see the soldier above him, red-faced and steadying himself for another go. Noticing some passers-by had gathered, he glanced round desperately for help.

His efforts proved successful. 'Damn you, aren't you going to help the man?'

'I would if he hadn't done the same to me last week. You will not take my money a second time. Gentlemen, this man is a thief.'

It took Sebastian a moment to realise what was happening, as he saw the expressions of those around him change first to confusion and then anger. However, it was only with the first cry of 'get him' that he thought to move. He looked around. There was no escape, only a palisade of shins. He looked again. This time, alongside a pair of stained knickerbockers, an opening! He propelled himself forward, scuttling through and pulling himself upright. Then he felt a hand on his collar. Using his momentum, he was able to spin and break the grip, but it was only a matter of time. Seeing where the crowd was thickest, he plunged his way into the mass, ignoring the shouts and yells from behind. If he had been taller, someone might have caught him, but beneath the heads of the crowd, he became invisible – a fish that had slipped its hook and was safe beneath the surface again. Even so, he didn't stop until long after the cries of his pursuers had faded into the surrounding hum. This one had been too close, and he knew that for all his skill, it was only a matter of time. So, when the day came that he finally earned his chance at escape, he snatched it without a thought.

The King
(1632 – 1635)

It was the fifth of June 1632 and Sebastian was now twenty-four. He had grown into a man, or at least as much of a man as he would ever be. His beard was finally thick enough to conceal the recessive jaw and he could at last look at his reflection without revulsion. Indeed, from the neck up, he looked almost normal. His ragged hair and dark eyes lent him an intellectual bearing, offset by an amiable softness to the nose. It looked peculiar, such a serious face on a small frame, but *peculiar* still made a considerable improvement on *grotesque*.

He was sitting in the Place de Grève, his back to the Hôtel de Ville as he watched the ships unload, their nets bulbous clouds heavy with boxes as the hoists swung their loads onto shore. Then the scuttle of dockers pulling them away and the merchants descending on their cargo in a swarm, levering open the booty before carrying it to waiting carts or else secreting it among the honeycomb of barrels and boxes piled along the riverside.

He was distracted by a group of overdressed men striding across the square, all clothed in blue with golden fleurs-de-lis. With nothing better to do, Sebastian decided to have a little fun with them. It was one of the few advantages of living on the street. After all, those who have little have little to lose, and he had very little indeed. The man in front struck him as the most suitable target – heavy-chopped and swollen with his own importance – and, rushing out into his path, he promptly introduced himself by pleading for a sou. After making an unsuccessful attempt to brush him away, the man was forced to take a step sideways, much to his irritation.

'My stomach's only small, Your Grace. Your money will go further with me. Half a loaf and some cheese and I'll be full for the day.'

'I'm not Your Grace, fool. That's a duke … anyway do you have any idea who I am?'

'No.'

'I am a chamberlain of the King.'

The man halted and stared down over a puffed chest, expecting compliance. However, Sebastian had seen the back corridors of enough noble houses to have little respect for titles, least of all a glorified servant.

'Five sous, then.' This was enough to draw laughs and the men circled around Sebastian, enclosing him between walls of gold stars and blue sky.

'Bet his mother got the shock of her life when he popped out.' The whisper came from Sebastian's left and drew a rumble of laughter.

'At least my father didn't.' It came out before he could stop himself – but thankfully they took it well, even the recipient of his abuse seemed amused.

'You give as good as you get, don't you, dwarf?'

'That depends what I'm given ... on the subject of which ...'

'How about a room, board and two livres a week?'

The response silenced Sebastian, and he looked every bit as bemused as the dozens of employers who had refused him over the years. 'Are you offering me work?'

'We'll try you out first. And you'll have to mind your tongue. The King's court isn't the gutter, you know.'

Sebastian stared at the man, still not quite able to comprehend what was happening. But the face seemed sincere.

'What would the King want with someone like me?'

'To perform at court, of course. We have need of dwarfs. Go to the palace at sundown and ask for me. My name's Alain Bouchard ... oh, and your five sous.'

The chamberlain pressed the money into Sebastian's open hand and walked off. Sebastian, meanwhile, remained where he was, staring at nothing in particular, and it was some time before he allowed himself first a smile, then a snigger and finally a roar of delirious laughter. It seemed fantastic, almost ludicrous. That after so many years of trying to find work, it had been work that found him. And not simply any work, but work at the royal court. For he, Sebastian Morra, was now a servant of His Majesty King Louis XIII of France.

* * *

Sebastian had always tended to avoid the Louvre. Along with the Pont Neuf and the Île Saint-Louis, it was both popular with the watch and intolerant of peddlers. It felt very different to the rest of the city. The streets were paved and the buildings boasted high windows and classical flourishes. Passing by the waterfront, he even had enough space to enjoy a view of the Seine, or what he could see of it through the carpet of barges, rafts and ships. On reaching the palace, he found himself confronted by the largest building he had ever seen. Trudging round its walls looking for the entrance, he found it impossible to comprehend its dimensions. From whichever angle he viewed it, he could only ever see two edges, never the whole, and he remained unsure whether it was square, pentagonal or something in between. Eventually, after a walk that would have taxed a normal man, let alone one of his proportions, he came across a wrought-iron gate, painted black, its details in gold. Bouchard was waiting. He frowned over crossed arms and greeted Sebastian with a tut.

'You're late. Keep the King waiting and I'll have your bloody head, understand?' Leaning down, he snapped his fingers in front of Sebastian's eyes, demanding acknowledgement.

'It won't happen again.'

The reply seemed to satisfy Bouchard, who summoned a footman with a clap of fleshy hands.

'Take him to his quarters – third floor, room twenty-six.'

Inside, the palace seemed even larger, an endless sequence of huge and pillared chambers floored with marble and roofed in gold; its cathedral proportions possessing a serenity which seemed unnatural after the bustle of the streets outside. Sebastian found it difficult to keep up with the footman as he gaped at the painted landscapes, tapestries, and silhouettes of Roman busts – dazzled by the pomp and feeling utterly out of place.

Eventually they took an unmarked side door and walked into surroundings that were more familiar – rough plaster walls with long rows of plain doors, each with a name painted on in white. A few had Roman numerals, presumably the empty ones. His was at the end of the corridor – XXVI – yet to be assigned a title. After being ushered inside, he was informed, 'Privy's at the end of the corridor. Pick up your food and candles from the kitchen. You'll get work from the chamberlain.' Then the door closed and he was alone.

It wasn't much of a room (little more than a cot, chest and a grate), but he was overjoyed nonetheless. He was used to lodging houses and shared, dank cellars. This, however, felt like a home, with thick walls, a window and somewhere to warm his feet, and he immediately decided to make it his own, retrieving coins from various seams of his clothing as he mulled over what to buy. A wardrobe first, then an escritoire, perhaps with a silver inkwell and swan-feather quill like Père Jean's. A footstool, of course, to help him reach the window. Maybe new candlesticks, and some books to go with his *Gargantua and Pantagruel* (it had been the one thing he kept during his days on the street, something to sustain him during more difficult times). It would be expensive, far more than he had. But, with two livres a day and a bit of skimping here and there, not an impossible hope. He was still deciding where precisely to place the wardrobe when he was interrupted by a knock from outside.

Opening the door, Sebastian looked up to see who was there but found himself staring at empty space. It was only when he looked down that he saw what he momentarily took to be a mirror and then realised was another dwarf. In fact, not just one dwarf, but two. He continued to stare and it was some time before he managed to stumble out a greeting, at which point the first dwarf introduced himself as Jerome, the other as Claude. Jerome suffered the same affliction as Sebastian and it showed on his face, though his light hair was wispy and his beard less able to hide his chin. Claude was older, perhaps in his forties, but perfectly proportioned, with neat features and a bald scalp. Unfortunately, he also seemed to be moronically stupid and it only took Sebastian a few moments to conclude they had nothing in common beyond their height and sex. Jerome, however, showed more promise, though he was a little brusque in manner. Naturally, when the pair enquired how he had arrived at court, Sebastian was discreet, not wanting to air his past, and claimed to have arrived from Camoches only a few days before. Fortunately, they didn't probe any further and the conversation soon moved on to their performance that evening, at which point Jerome produced a costume and ran through the parts.

Any concerns Sebastian had about the difficulties of his post were dispelled when he heard his lines. It barely ranked as farce. The performance consisted entirely of making pyramids, tugs of war, along with a series of very bad impersonations, all the time wearing voluminous trousers, which only further increased his chances of falling over. Not that he minded, of course. If people wanted to pay to watch him make an ass of himself, then more fool them. It certainly made a considerable improvement on the street.

* * *

The performance took place during dinner in the great hall, a vast chamber overhung by heavy chandeliers. An avenue of candelabras tapered away to the far wall, where a table stood on a raised dais encircled by a sparkling patchwork of tapestries. Sebastian could just about discern a canopy amid the splendour, and beneath it what looked like a throne – as they drew closer, he continued to stare with growing fascination. After all, this was no normal person. This was Louis XIII, heir of Clovis and Charlemagne, chosen by God to command the realm and crowned in Rheims. And he did indeed look magnificent, with a cascading wig and brushed robes of ermine and velvet. However, he seemed ill at ease with his magnificence and was struggling to eat while keeping the wig out of his bowl and the food from his collar. He was seated at the centre of a long table, spread with gold plate. Members of the great houses of France sat on each side – all dressed in brocades, velvets and organza. Their clothes were iridescent in the candlelight, giving the illusion of disembodied heads floating in glitter. They seemed amused by the performance, Sebastian in particular, their faces bobbing as they tittered at the latest novelty come to entertain them. All except for the King, who observed the evening's events over a half-eaten chicken leg with the weary air of a man reliving an evening he had already lived far too many times before.

One thing Sebastian couldn't fathom was his silence. During the whole performance the King didn't say a word, as the others chattered amongst themselves. Even afterwards, he didn't speak, remaining mute as he picked his way through both the second and third courses. Sebastian assumed it was shyness. The man clearly loathed the formalities of kingship, and seemed visibly embarrassed by the bows and curtsies of others, shunning every servant's offer of help.

It was only during the final course that Louis finally spoke, and when he did, the reason for his silence became clear: a stammer that reduced all speech to a thick-tongued gargle. The voice was impossible to connect to the man. He was unable to utter even the shortest of sentences before collapsing into bumbling repetition. It was like listening to a bad imitation of an idiot, and Sebastian could see the frustration as he battled with his tongue, the faces of his listeners contorting as they tried not to laugh. Sebastian, however, found something inspiring in his impediment. Seeing such a powerful man struggle with infirmity provided hope and a comforting reminder that he was not alone.

* * *

Eager to find out more about his new acquaintance, Sebastian decided to go to the tavern with Jerome the following day. While the evening began pleasantly enough, it wasn't long before the atmosphere began to sour. Despite his young age, Jerome's features were puffed with drink, his nose veined red and purple. And after pickling himself with cheap wine for much of the evening, he let pour his indignation, raging at the injustices of the world until his grape-stained mouth finally ran out of expletives and he passed out on the table.

Hoping for an improvement, Sebastian tried again the following night. If anything it was worse than before. After being rejected by one of the local prostitutes, Jerome began drinking aggressively and grew ever more abusive. Rabid with indignation, he was barely more than an animal by

43

the end, drooling and incoherent. When Sebastian finally intervened, Jerome turned on him for being 'just like the rest of them, with your fancy words, thinking you're better than us', ending the evening shortly afterward by swinging a punch and leaving him with a black eye for his trouble.

After that, he gave up. It was pointless and dispiriting. Not so much because of Jerome's behaviour, but for what it implied. Sebastian was searching for wisdom and experience, to learn another's lessons. Instead he saw a man ignored by everyone around him – who had given up and stood isolated, screaming at a world of deaf ears. From then on, Sebastian kept his relationship with Claude and Jerome to polite talk or rehearsing whatever they were performing that day. He found no comfort from knowing them, only a reminder of his own frustrations.

*　*　*

Sebastian had never quite felt part of the society around him. As he saw it, there had always been two worlds: his own and another where everything took place two feet above his head. The court was no different, a foreign place ruled by tradition and etiquette. Every morning at nine-thirty precisely, the King would be led to his throne, where a queue of petitioners awaited him. He would then hold audiences for the remainder of the day, usually with a trusted councillor to assist. Meals were opulent, held at set hours and consisting of many courses. However, beneath this veneer of long-respected convention, there was another, more secretive domain, which unfolded in the shadows, in corners and whispered asides. Its mood followed strange tides, the courtiers inexplicably scuttling around like disturbed beetles or else flocking together, impassive birds of prey. Nothing was said openly, though occasionally he would catch a rumour, that such-and-such a person had joined a particular faction, or so-and-so was an agent of Richelieu. But there were only ever indications, suggestions, and inferences – nothing was certain. For Sebastian it was like looking at smooth water and seeing a track of ripples across the surface – a sense of not knowing what lay beneath.

However, a few truths were readily apparent: the principal of which was that the King only ruled France in name. Anyone could see he was no leader. Instead a child, but a child who had grown unchecked, without anyone to impose authority or make clear the realities of life – most clearly manifested in a hatred of formality and juvenile impatience which refused to accept being delayed a moment longer than necessary. And though he did possess gravitas of a kind, it was a teenage solemnity, the behaviour of someone playing the part of a man. Incapable of laughing at himself, he would instead make lengthy proclamations about justice and duty, all in a stammer that only further tortured his leaden prose.

*   *   *

Mostly Louis avoided the demands of court, preferring to spend his life hunting or playing war with his soldiers and travelling with a vast collection of harquebuses, which he kept like so many toys. Occasionally his sense of duty would compel him to attend a meeting of the *Conseil d'État* or to deliver a speech to the *Parlement*. Even so, he was always careful to keep his pronouncements suitably statesmanlike

– a few lines of fatuous rhetoric that no one could disagree with: defeating enemies, bringing glory or fulfilling the divine will of the French people. The task of actually living up to this bombast was left to the exasperated ministers seated behind him, all sunken-eyed with exhaustion. The people, however, loved him for it. To them Louis was not a ruler, but a symbol – the face on their coins, the name they were asked to pray for every Sunday, the son of Henri le Grand, and God's representative on earth. They never saw him govern or heard him speak. He was required to be little more than a cipher, and it was a role he filled to perfection.

Behind every symbol is the reality it represents: the laws, the taxes, the administration of state. And, as the people loved the King, so there was one man they loathed above all others – Armand-Jean du Plessis, Cardinal-Duke de Richelieu – also known as Chief Minister, the red eminence or the scarlet pest depending on the source. A man of formidable intellect, he had risen from the provincial bishopric of Luçon to the most powerful position in France. Always careful to act in the King's name, he kept to the shadows, leaving ample room for speculation, which his contemporaries were happy to fill. Rumours of murder and embezzlement were rife: that he had slaughtered his way to the top or that the entire *Conseil d'État* was in his pay; even that he had tried to seduce the Queen. Nevertheless, a few facts were known. His value to the King was beyond question, and he had served his master for a dozen years without interruption. Also there was Richelieu's network of spies and informants, rumoured to stretch into every cranny of France and beyond. Above all, as Louis wanted to be famed for his mercy, so Richelieu seemed intent on being remembered for his lack of it. Every opponent was either dead or arrested, every revolt crushed and every rebel put to death, without exception, to the point where Louis had been forced to exile his own mother when she tried to have the cardinal removed.

Despite his reputation, Richelieu made no attempt to counter it and seemed utterly indifferent to the ceremonies of court. In his first year, Sebastian only saw him four times. All were state functions, where he would sit in silence beside the King, dressed in his scarlet soutane. Sebastian would have recognised him even without his cardinal's robes. His face had a distinctive sharpness, with thin eyes, pointed beard and skeletal features which sat oddly beside those of his more pampered peers. He rarely talked and instead sat in quiet judgement, scrutinising, evaluating and re-evaluating, hunting for glints of truth in the murk.

As Louis was the child so Richelieu was the father. Louis liked to spite, all insolence and petty rebellion, referring to the cardinal as 'His Obstinacy' and mocking his prudence and propriety. Richelieu, meanwhile, responded as the long-suffering parent, smiling it off or correcting with gentle admonishment. The relationship was peculiar – inverted, yet understandable all the same. Louis had not only lost his father at a young age, but also a father regarded as one of the great kings of France, a ruler whose fame had only grown in death. Used to such a dominant figure, he naturally wanted to replace him, and few men were more dominant than the Cardinal-Duke de Richelieu.

Finally, there was the Queen, Anne. Born the Infanta of Spain, she was barely fourteen when she had been married to Louis in an attempt to bind the two countries together. Their marriage had proved a failure in more ways than one.

The rumours were many and varied, and it was obvious, even to Sebastian, that they had nothing in common. He only ever saw her from a distance – a pale-skinned figure always surrounded by her attendants, sometimes playing paille-maille, sometimes horse-riding or being transported round the palace within a cloud of damask, satin and taffeta, but always laughing in that refined, almost musical way unique to ladies of court. In short, a woman who was unlikely to be attracted to someone whose main interests were hunting and building forts.

Though there was no heir, there were reports of numerous miscarriages, including one notorious occasion when she lost a child falling off the banister while playing with her friends. It was said the King had never forgiven her. However, it was also said that the miscarriages were a masquerade and no physical relationship existed at all. People would support the argument with a list of favourites – Marie de Chevreuse, the Duc de Luynes, Barradat, Saint-Simon, de Hautefort, de la Fayette – all of whom Anne ignored with regal indifference, either from decorum or simply because she had no choice. And it seemed to Sebastian that for all her titles and finery, she was a lonely figure, and that the dances and the games and the ladies-in-waiting were not there for pleasure but instead for escape.

* * *

In spite of all his power, Louis spent an inordinate amount of time following rules – enduring grandiloquent introductions every time he met someone new, having to watch people shuffle backwards as they left his presence, or eating alone in silent splendour while everybody else stood, waiting for him to finish before they could begin. Understandably, he escaped Paris whenever possible, usually to Fontainebleau, where he would idle away the days riding and hunting in the forest. Often he journeyed further, touring his realm. 'A king's purpose is his people. To not be among them is to not be a king,' was a favoured phrase. Consequently, Sebastian spent much of his time travelling, and during his first year he managed to see Blois, Tours, Saumur, Angers and Nantes. Occasionally, when watching the pageantry – the guards' gleaming finery, the King waving to the crowds – Sebastian was reminded of his own performances at court and wondered if the King was no different, simply another actor putting on a show.

*   *   *

Over time, Sebastian came to find the court a place much like any other. His surroundings lost their fascination and he would wander the lonely corridors, aware of the empty mirrors and the distant hiss of his life passing by like so many grains of sand. It was the same purposelessness he'd felt during his days in Camoches – a life alone, adrift from humanity. He could disappear unnoticed; his existence changed nothing and mattered to nobody. He had no friends or confidants. Although he was on cordial terms with most of the servants, he had nothing in common with them. And when he spoke with the courtiers or the chamberlains, the most he could hope for was an amiable indifference, feigned interest along with a distant smile, acknowledging his presence with a humiliating *noblesse oblige*. He repaid them with silent contempt, watching them preen in embroidered splendour while he saw the view from below: the hairs sprouting in their nostrils, the slope of their paunches, the folds in their chins as they looked down at him.

Sebastian spent most of his time in his room. Now furnished with all the comforts of home, it had become his refuge from the world. A narrow window offered an inspiring view over Paris, its roofs a patchwork of fields in green lead and slate, the treetops reduced to bushes and the spires like firs. In the centre of this landscape rose the two stubby towers of Notre Dame, reduced to the status of parochial church amidst the weaving trails and low, country walls.

Below the window, Sebastian's messy desk and inkwell were angled to catch what little light there was. The rest of the room was plain. Its most elaborate feature was the escutcheon on the door, a whirl of leaves and tendrils. Aside from the desk, the only other furniture was a bed and wardrobe, both adult-sized (he refused to make any concessions for his stature) and a stool to stand on when necessary. Otherwise there were mementoes, mostly piles of books and pamphlets. Working for the King paid well, and he saved to buy works of a more heretical bent than Père Jean had ever permitted. Calvin proved particularly inspiring and he came to loathe the artifice and pomp of Catholicism, longing for a return to the simpler traditions of Christianity. Often he would read the great plays including Corneille's *Mélite* and *L'Illusion Comique*. Other favourites included the *Decameron*, Boethius and his copy of *Gargantua and Pantagruel*, now rebound for the third time. His copy of Montaigne he reserved for bleaker times, when he would comfort himself with the essays 'Of Solitude' and 'To Learn How to Die'. As a rule, he regarded books as a considerable improvement on human company. The words were more considered, the argument more structured, and when they weren't ... well he could always turn the page.

Otherwise Sebastian would busy himself with long walks around the gardens or writing letters for Père Jean to read to his mother. He enjoyed reciting the various goings-on at the palace, consoling himself that however lowly his position at court, how illustrious his life must seem to her. He would always end his missives with a brief invitation, imploring her to visit, while secretly hoping she wouldn't, squirming as he imagined the horrified expression of the chamberlain when he found some provincial standing at the gate.

The remaining hours he occupied by writing a play – a brutal depiction of an inverted society which rewarded only the feckless, idle and dissolute. It wasn't much to begin with, but with each passing night he improved it, painstakingly reducing each draft to a collection of beautifully crafted scraps before starting again.

* * *

Sebastian had spent the evening in a local tavern. It didn't matter which one. They were all the same in winter, dark and packed with people huddled together for warmth, trying to drink their way through to spring. After renting a cheap room upstairs, he was now lying beside a prostitute in the aftermath of crumpled linen. It had been a frustrating day.

He had been asked to perform in front of the ambassadors' wives in the Jardin des Tuileries. They seemed to regard him as some kind of child and made him join various games of hoodman's blind and hot cockles, during which they clucked over him, swaddling him in their mille-feuille skirts and petticoats. By the end, Sebastian was fit to burst and promptly made his way to a brothel – a favourite haunt from his days on the street. Surrounded by poverty and squalor, it was unpromising from the outside, standing just a few doors down from the Hôtel Dieu. Yet, despite abutting a plaguehouse, it remained well supplied by the desperation nearby.

Sebastian always had a weakness for his fellow Normans and had settled on a lady from Caen called Michelle. She was a recent arrival – naive, young, and fresh, one might even say chaste – and gave him the pleasant sense that he might remain in her thoughts for at least a moment after he walked out of the door. However, midway through reminiscing about an uncle who had once introduced himself by striding in and vomiting in the fireplace, Sebastian was interrupted by a voice from downstairs. It seemed to be shouting what sounded like 'Michelle'. Jolting upright, he listened again. Yes, it was definitely her name. He made his way to the door, inching it open to see an overdressed, red-faced fop beating the counter downstairs and giving the landlord a piece of his mind ... or, to be more accurate, his spleen.

'I don't care if she's busy. Bring her now. You know who I am.'

Sebastian knew exactly who he was – the Marquis de Cinq-Mars. While Sebastian had some respect for the great names of state, the petty aristocrats he could see for the chancers that they were – no different to the beggars he'd known on the street. Nothing but flounce and bluster, flocking to court in hope of whatever scraps came their way. Cinq-Mars was a particularly repellent specimen, acutely conscious of his undistinguished birth, for which he compensated by being louder, vainer and even more boorish than his contemporaries. In truth, the only reason he was still tolerated at court was because his parents had died and Richelieu was his guardian.

It wasn't the first time Sebastian had seen the marquis out whoring, though normally his kind kept to the establishments nearer the Louvre. Evidently, Richelieu's pocket money wasn't enough to cover a courtesan's rates.

Despite the landlord's best efforts to pacify the marquis, he was having none of it, demanding that Michelle be brought to him immediately and that he would be willing to pay double, even triple whatever rates the local scum could afford. It was only when the landlord explained she was currently with a gentleman and aimed a pointed glance upstairs that Cinq-Mars noticed Sebastian. As both men locked eyes, Sebastian sensed trouble and ducked behind the wall in the hope of remaining unnoticed. However, as he gathered his clothes, he could hear the marquis' footsteps approaching up the stairs, and barely had enough time to make himself decent before Cinq-Mars was stood in front of him.

Henri Coiffier de Ruzé, the Marquis de Cinq-Mars, was dressed exquisitely, in a discreet ruff with a short-waisted brown doublet, gold-embroidered with interlacing roses and thorns. Silk-lined knickerbockers ended in a pair of spotless white boots. Standing in the doorway, he checked himself a moment, taken aback by Sebastian's size. This was followed by a second jolt as he recognised his face from court.

'What are *you* doing here?' He seemed more amused than outraged.

'I could ask the same of you.'

'Don't be insolent with me.'

'I'm not the one barging in … besides, unless you haven't noticed, I'm a little busy at present.'

The marquis shook his head and stepped into the room, bewildered to be encountering resistance. 'Is this some kind of joke, dwarf?'

'I don't see why. I've paid for my hour. My money's as good as yours.'

Shrugging, the marquis tossed a few coins on the floor. 'Then take your money and go.'

Sebastian was no hero by nature but something made him stand his ground – partly some misguided sense of chivalry, the perverse desire to protect Michelle from this odious sot, but more his sheer dislike for the marquis. The man stood for everything he found contemptible: that expectancy in the curl of his mouth, the effete, loose-strung body, all lace and swagger.

'I'm not interested in your money. Now, my lord, would you kindly leave?' He added a sarcastic little bow and citrus smile.

'It wasn't a request.' The marquis strode forward and glared down at Sebastian, though even anger couldn't entirely remove the smirk from his lips. 'What would you know about satisfying a woman anyway, half-man?'

Sebastian met his eyes with a look of pure rat, his voice dropping to a goading whisper. 'Once she's had us both, maybe she can let you know … or are you worried she might choose me?' It wasn't his most elegant rejoinder but was perfectly aimed at youthful pride.

Dumbfounded by the dwarf's cheek, Cinq-Mars paused a moment before lunging downwards and slamming Sebastian against the wall, then hauling him backwards by the collar onto the landing outside.

'Throw him out and don't go lightly on the little bastard. He's got a mouth on him.'

Then Sebastian took his beating. He didn't have a choice. Three of the marquis' friends were waiting and there was no way out except down the stairs. He still fought as best he could, lashing out in all directions and managing to catch at least two of them in the face while they were pinning down his arms and legs. But once they dragged him onto the street and set at him, there was nothing to be done except curl tight and swallow the pain.

* * *

It could have been worse. For all its drawbacks, Sebastian's stubby frame had a resilience, carapaced with ribs and knobbled bone, and he always seemed to be left with bruises rather than breaks. Even so, it was four days before he could get out of bed, at which point, after emptying the chamber pot, he hobbled to his desk, grabbed a sheet of paper and unleashed himself.

✤ *I never met a nobleman who was noble*
  Or a gentleman who was gentle.
  Only the arrogant, the foolish
  The greedy and temperamental.

55

❧ *You think yourselves men but you are nothing but guts. Mindless and spineless – only stomachs to gorge and arseholes to speak with.*

❧ *Some say greatness is born from spirit, others say the mind. But true greatness requires a title, wig and manners most refined.*

❧ *Nobility = No ability*

It wasn't long before he'd filled three pages. Insulting Cinq-Mars and his kind was hardly difficult. After which he went downstairs for his meal and thought no more of the matter. It wasn't until later in the day that the possibility of revenge crossed his mind. Returning to his desk, he glanced over his outpourings and smiled. A few of them were surprisingly incisive, though not quite personal enough for what he had in mind.

*   *   *

Sebastian didn't usually enjoy his performances. He was never entirely at ease when standing in front of the King, and buffoonery could be exhausting work. Today, however, he left the stage oozing satisfaction as he made his way to the changing room. Naturally, Jerome was curious about his good-humour, but Sebastian politely refused all questions until Cinq-Mars made himself known, yanking open the door and ordering Claude and Jerome out of the room.

'Leave.' He was furious, to the point of trembling. And when he spoke, his words were framed by bared teeth. 'I want this one alone.'

Wordless, Jerome and Claude snatched their clothes and exited at once. Sebastian, however, continued to undress, fiddling with a button shirt and paying the marquis no attention at all.

'You just stood up in front of the entire court and said my family crest was a chicken.' Cinq-Mars was wide-eyed with disbelief.

'Yes. Yes, I did.' Sebastian repeated the word – either from malevolence or to make sure he was understood.

The marquis reached for the sword at his waist. 'That's it. I'll kill you, peasant.'

The threat met with a scowl of contempt. 'You'll do no such thing.'

Cinq-Mars checked himself, his fingers still resting on the half-drawn blade. 'How are you going to stop me, you brazen little bastard?'

'Marquis … when I insulted you, did you hear anyone laugh?'

'What do you mean?'

'When I referred to your family crest, did anyone laugh? Or react in any way whatsoever?'

'But you were looking right at me.'

'You think anyone noticed? I'm a dwarf. I fall on my arse

and wave my feet in the air. Nobody cares what I do, let alone who I look at. The only two people who know of this are you and I. Your precious honour remains intact. You've nothing to fear. And frankly, having been beaten to pulp by your friends, I think you've had rather the better side of the deal.'

'I swear, insult me again and I'll ...'

'You'll what? Kill me? This isn't some brothel out near the wall. This is the King's court, in case you hadn't noticed, and I am one of his servants. We dwarves are a rare commodity, you know, expensive to replace.' This was partly true, partly bluster. Not that Sebastian was afraid. He'd talked his way off the ends of swords before, and more dangerous ones than that of the marquis. Besides, he was good at reading people and Cinq-Mars was not a hard man to decipher – arrogant and terrified of anything that might sully his reputation. 'I wonder what they'll call you ... Giant-killer, I expect – something like that. It might suit you ...'

Coiled tight with frustration, Cinq-Mars couldn't stand it any longer and pressed Sebastian up against the wall, his right hand balled into a fist.

'This isn't over.' He leaned in, nose-to-nose, his face swelling into a single raging eye. 'You will pay for this.' And with that he thrust Sebastian down onto the tiles before striding out of the door.

Sebastian lifted himself up, sore but satisfied. It had been worth it. And for all his bluff, he knew the marquis was bluffing more.

* * *

Over the following month, Sebastian continued to take revenge on the marquis each and every evening, giving him the knowing stare while referring to him in turn as: a pampered, over-praised little guttersnipe; a jumped-up country squire leeching off his betters; a dim-witted layabout not even worthy of the ignominious title he lays claim to; a powdered, bewigged, scent-infused, embroidered, grandiloquent heap of excrement – because shit is still shit no matter how much perfume you put on it.

And each time his eyes would meet Cinq-Mars' glower from the lower tables, surrounded by a circle of indifferent courtiers as they chatted and joked among themselves, oblivious to their neighbour's nightly humiliation.

* * *

It was the knock of bad news – two voiceless raps, sharp and staccato. Sebastian's fears were confirmed when he opened the door to see the footman, his black doublet carrying the cardinal's coat of arms topped by its familiar red galero.

'Please accompany me. My master desires your presence.' The voice was as functional as the knuckle had been.

Sebastian tried not to show his panic but, like all the court, his fear of the cardinal ran deep. And with good reason, as it was generally agreed that a summons from Richelieu meant death, dismemberment or disgrace – occasionally all three. Sebastian asked the footman to repeat the name, hoping there had been a mistake. The man then repeated 'Sebastian Morra' in clipped tones – acid polite – adding that he was expected immediately and leaving Sebastian with no option but to put on his coat and follow.

The journey was short, only five minutes from the north wing of the palace. It was a beautiful evening. The first snow of winter had fallen, the crystals prismatic in the moonlight, layered with violet shadows that cut against the white. Not that Sebastian noticed in the slightest. His attention was fixed on the Palais-Cardinal, ever-expanding with their approach. Baroque, it was fronted with colonnades, which obscured the building behind so that all that could be seen were the columns and pediment, endowing it with the stark austerity of an ancient courthouse or amphitheatre.

The footman led Sebastian to a high metal door whose fleur-de-lis and curlicues had been transformed by the dark into writhing forms better suited to the gates of hell. A bell was rung, after which a guard led them up to the third floor. Sebastian followed automatically, still deliberating whether to brass it out or simply plead for mercy, neither of which possessed great appeal.

Then came the wait outside the cardinal's chamber. Time passed quickly, then slowly again. Sebastian found neither sensation pleasant, part of him wanting the meeting never to arrive, another wanting it over as quickly as possible. He was still caught between the two when the door swung open. He could see a row of flaming torches along the wall and a long, wooden floor, waxed to a gleam, leading up to a faraway dais. Knowing he had to walk forward, he took care not to look at the platform, preferring to concentrate on the floor as he inched into the room.

* * *

Armand-Jean du Plessis, Cardinal-Duc de Richelieu sat in his official chambers. The room was designed to awe the visitor and did so admirably. Its high-panelled walls were hung with pictures by Rubens, Poussin and Titian – above them, a cornice of interweaving gold leaf. Eight Swiss Guards ringed the room in perfect symmetry, each wearing a red coat with dark blue lapels and white embroidered cuffs, topped by a tricorn hat. On a rostrum at the far end, the cardinal reclined in a throne of papal proportions, high-backed with flaring armrests. Immaculately dressed, he wore a black soutane with starched collar, red skullcap and white-hemmed cardinal's cloak. On his finger was a single ring, a round chrysoberyl encircled by emeralds. The face above was anaemically thin, its narrow features ending in a pointed beard. Overworked, his eyes were buried in wrinkles; yet they gazed at Sebastian with crystalline concentration, two jewels placed in rumpled velvet.

Terrified and unable to meet the cardinal's stare, Sebastian stood with his palms locked in front of him, holding hands with himself for comfort. The room was rubbed clean and smelt of polished wood, over which he could detect his own animal odour. Richelieu glanced across at the guards and motioned them to leave, which they did in perfectly spaced single file. Then, after waiting for the door to close, he finally spoke.

'You, dwarf, have been mocking my ward, the Marquis de Cinq-Mars. Tell me why I shouldn't make an example of you.' The voice was flat and terrifyingly certain.

'Make an example of me, Your Eminence? I don't understand.' Instinctively, Sebastian pawed at his face, an ineffectual shield.

61

'I'm not a fool. Don't treat me like one.'

'I apologise, Your Eminence. Is this about my performance this evening? It's just that I didn't think you would concern yourself with such minor matters.'

'Minor? You insulted a marquis to his face while standing directly in front of the King. Duels have been fought over less ...besides, have you considered the consequences if anyone notices what you're doing?'

'Of course, I'll stop immediately, Your Eminence. But may I just reassure you this wasn't a fight of my choosing. I was provoked.'

'Likely enough. Henri can be ...insensitive at times. What was the source of this quarrel anyway? He insulted you, I imagine.'

'Yes, Your Eminence, something of that nature.' Sebastian had no desire to go into more detail than he suspected the marquis had done.

Sensing evasion, the cardinal peered closer and rubbed his beard. 'Hmmmmm ...well, I'd say whatever insult you've had to endure it's been more than repaid, wouldn't you?'

'I'm sorry, Your Eminence. Please forgive me. It won't happen again.'

'Indeed it will not ... which still leaves the question of what to do with you.' Richelieu paused and stared down at Sebastian. The dais magnified the difference between them and Sebastian stood open-mouthed, in awe of the sheer spectacle in front of him – the rostrum, the throne, the biblical scenes on each side. 'I've a mind to punish you. However, I have to admit it was somewhat humorous. What was it you called him last night?'

'A malodorous sot in love with the smell of his own farts.'

Sebastian grimaced out the words. They didn't seem quite so humorous when standing before a prelate of the French Church. Fortunately, the cardinal seemed entertained and slumped back into his throne with a chuckle.

'There's a certain eloquence to it. You're a literate man, I imagine?'

Sebastian nodded.

'But you've no title. You're clearly not rich. I assume you didn't educate yourself.'

Sebastian paused, unbalanced by the question. He wasn't used to people showing interest in him, let alone the Chief Minister of France.

'My local priest taught me,' he ventured.

'Where?'

'Camoches, in Normandy.'

'Camoches …' Richelieu paused and it took him a while to place the name. 'It's a long way from there to court, especially for a man like you. How did you manage it?'

'Through my wits.'

'Your wits?'

'Yes, it's hardly as if I've much else going for me.'

Richelieu croaked a laugh. 'I see, but why make the journey in the first place? It can't have been easy. You must have had good reason.'

'Isn't every subject's greatest wish to serve his King?'

Richelieu laughed again. 'A diplomatic answer … and hardly one I can disagree with.' Then he paused and leaned forward furtively as though about to impart a secret of great importance.

'My associates inform me that you used to be a beggar. Is this true?'

Sebastian was startled. The cardinal's reputation was clearly justified, and tempted to lie as he was, he knew there was no point and conceded with a shamefaced, 'yes, Your Eminence.'

His background seemed to fascinate the cardinal, who spent the following five minutes probing into his time on the street. The questions were both sequential and precise: what he had done; why he had done it; and what he had learned. He was particularly interested in Sebastian's tricks and insisted a guard was brought in for him to demonstrate on.

'So, how did you choose your victims?'

'Depends on the person. Generally, the drunk and the young are easiest ...women give more easily than men. Also those with scars often have them for a reason. But sometimes it's just a look or plain circumstance. You've got to keep an eye out for opportunities.'

'And this gentleman here? Would you try your luck with him?'

Sebastian smiled, observing the self-consciousness of the soldier as he endured their scrutiny. It gave him considerable satisfaction to cause such discomfort and he felt a reassuring sense of his own significance.

He examined his subject carefully. The man was no more than twenty-five, tall but with the hollow eyes of the infirm, a wan complexion and a sniff – not an intimidating prospect. 'I'd consider him, yes.'

'And you would attract his attention how?'

'Most likely arrange my path to cross his or else pretend I was lost. If he was trapped in a corner, I might use poor man's plague.'

'Poor man's plague? I've never heard of it.'

Now it was Sebastian's turn to be self-conscious, and he looked away, apparently rubbing an invisible speck from his cheek. 'It's a street trick, Your Eminence. Not appropriate for these surroundings.'

'Appropriate or not, I'd still like to see it.'

'I'd really prefer not.'

'I insist. And here ... why not some incentive?' He tossed the soldier a livre. 'Give it to him if he's convincing enough.'

Sebastian's desire for coin hadn't entirely diminished, certainly not when there was half a week's pay to be won, and he became markedly keener, nodding the soldier into position.

'If you'll just let me prepare,' he said, tucking his face into his right arm and emitting guttural noises while coughing into the crook of his elbow. The effect was peculiar and both soldier and cardinal looked on, baffled, unsure if he had fallen unwell. Then Sebastian looked up, transformed. Drool and mucus were pouring from his mouth and nose, sticking in his beard as he squinted out of one eye. Combined with his already peculiar proportions, it gave him a startling and rabid appearance that immediately had the soldier pressed against the wall in an effort to keep his distance.

'Money for a dying man ...' Sebastian gave a loud and hacking cough, stumbling towards the soldier, who promptly tried to step to one side. The dwarf, however, was too quick for him and managed to tangle himself up in his legs, tripping him over and then reaching towards his face with a leprous and glistening hand.

'Take it,' the soldier yelled, flinging the coin onto the floor. This produced the desired effect, and Sebastian immediately scuttled after it, snatching his prize and stowing it in his pocket before cleaning his face with a handkerchief.

'Poor man's plague.' The cardinal chuckled to himself, amused by this new discovery.

'Stick oats on your skin and you can make good welts if you want to be showing a rash.'

'It seems rather a lot of work for a few sous.'

'Excuse me for saying, but you've never really known hunger, have you?'

'I fast for Lent.'

'I think you'll find Lent ends.'

The response was abrupt and met with a sharp look from Richelieu.

'Forgive me, Your Eminence, I'm still new to the ways of court. I do not mean to offend.' Sebastian's apology was accompanied by repeated and anxious bowing. 'It's just the way money is. At the top, there's more than enough. Further down, there's less to go round. You have to fight.'

His contrition appeared to satisfy the cardinal, who waved him to a stop. 'The court has its own difficulties, I can assure you ...' He was interrupted by a knock at the door – a herald announcing an emissary from the Duke of Lorraine had arrived.

The change in the cardinal's demeanour was instantaneous. His voice reacquired its clipped command as he requested his visitor be admitted without delay. Eager to escape, Sebastian wished the cardinal a quick goodbye but was immediately stopped with a raised finger – the upward point of parent to child. 'I haven't forgotten.'

'My apologies, Your Eminence, I don't understand.'

'Your punishment.' Richelieu paused a moment, luxuriating in his power as he left Sebastian to wait out a brief eternity. 'Two weeks' pay. I'll have the clerk deduct it at the end of the month.'

'Thank you, Your Eminence.'

'Don't thank me. It's self-interest. I am meant to be a patron of the arts, after all,' the cardinal finished, twitching a nod farewell. 'Now leave, Master Morra. I've enjoyed your company. Perhaps one day we shall meet again.'

Before meeting Richelieu, Sebastian would have been delighted simply to walk out of the room alive. Now he left with mixed feelings – glad to have escaped unscathed, but also disappointed that the conversation had come to an end. The encounter felt unfinished. The words 'perhaps' seemed too vague. He had so many questions. What it was like to run a country? What the cardinal thought of the threat from Spain? Why and how he had first come to serve the King? But now they would pass unanswered. He would never speak to Richelieu again. The chance had gone. When he next saw the cardinal, the most he could hope for was a glance or nod, if indeed he was remembered at all.

* * *

The year 1636 did not start well. There were rumours of plague from the Low Countries and Germany. The peasants of Guyenne had risen in mass revolt. Worse still, the war had turned against France. Champagne, Burgundy and Picardy had already been laid to waste, and an army under Thomas of Savoy had been reported as near as Corbie, only two days' ride from Paris. Prayers were already being made to the bones of Saint Genevieve in the Pantheon. And while people hoped for safety from their fortifications, there was no denying that those of the left bank were three hundred years old and ready to topple at the roll of a drum.

The cardinal stood on a balcony in the Louvre, searching the checkwork of distant fields. He knew the enemy was too far away to see. But there would be scouts ahead, perhaps in the forest near Saint Denis. It might be worth sending a few patrols to check. No, the area was too large. It would be pointless, simply despatching a few soldiers to get lost in the woods. Rubbing his beard, he shook his head and returned inside, where a ledger lay open on his desk. The pages were divided into evenly spaced columns, each filled with numbers in neat script. After tucking his soutane beneath him, Richelieu sat down, waved away an errant fly, drew out his quill and continued his calculations in a slow yet meticulous hand.

He had completed six pages by the time the King appeared. There was no knock and the cardinal didn't need to look to know who it was. Immediately, he stood up and bowed.

'Good afternoon, Your Majesty.'

'Don't bother,' Louis motioned him to sit down. As ever, he was dressed magnificently, in a blue doublet embroidered with silver, full-puffed sleeves and cloak. His beard and hair were perfectly trimmed, apart from a single lovelock, which straggled over his right eye.

'You've heard the news?'

'About Corbie?'

'Sources inform me there may be scouts within sight of Paris ...' Richelieu halted mid-sentence as he noticed Louis peering at his ledger.

'Am I muh-muh-mistaken or are you going through the accounts?'

'As I do each month.'

'But why aren't you raising troops?'

'I am, Your Majesty.' Richelieu looked up at a still-sceptical King. He paused, awaiting a realisation, which didn't come.

'Allow me to explain.' The cardinal reached into his pocket and drew out a livre. 'What do you see?'

The King frowned and let out a sigh. 'Is this another of your riddles, Armand? Now is not the time.'

'Power, Your Majesty. What you are looking at is power.' Richelieu held up the the coin, winking it in the light. 'This is enough to pay one soldier for two months. Our enemies have fifty thousand troops. That means we require one hundred thousand of these coins. Without them, we won't have the numbers to fight. It is the rule of government. He who has the money pays the troops. He who pays the troops makes the law.'

'What use is money if we lose the battle? Muh-muh-muh-money alone doesn't win wars.' His stutter was particularly pronounced on the m's and b's. 'You need other things too. A good general, the right weapons and men, properly trained.'

'Yes, Your Majesty. There are many ways to lose a war, which is precisely why I endeavour to avoid them.'

'Nobody likes war, buh-buh-but it is a fact of life. War made this country and it is war that will protect it. We have enemies on every side. They have the advantage. They mean to attack.'

'You're right, Your Majesty. War is a fact of life. But so is money. We've increased our takings fourfold since I began office. And for one reason alone, to pay for war. Yet, if I raise too much, the people rebel. And if I raise too little, we can't defend ourselves. You ask me why I'm reviewing our accounts. It is only because of reviewing accounts that we are still in the fight.'

'Then I shall leave you to your studies, Armand, but bring me troops. In three days I shall march to Corbie, defeat the enemy and we shall continue this conversation on my return.'

Astonished by Louis' words, Richelieu opened his mouth, about to spit back a riposte and only managing to check himself at the last moment. Even when he did eventually speak, his voice remained uncharacteristically taut.

'You must not leave Paris, Your Majesty. Without you, the country is lost. Send one of your generals – La Fayette or Soissons. We can't afford such a risk.'

'No.' Louis waved him aside. 'You want me to sit by and do nothing? Rulers are remembered for the battles they win, not the taxes they raise. I will do as my position demands.'

'Your Majesty ...'

'Are you questioning me, Armand?'

'Of course not.' The cardinal restricted his exasperation to a tight smile. 'In three days, you will have an army. During your absence, I will stay in the city and ensure order is maintained.'

'Without troops that muh-muh-may be difficult.'

'I won't need troops,' Richelieu replied.

This time it was the King's turn to look surprised.

* * *

Before leaving the Palais-Cardinal, Richelieu completed his morning rituals. First, he applied his unguents and scents, next came the woollen stockings and vest, then his shirt and knickerbockers, followed by the soutane and crucifix. Last of all he waxed his beard and neatened its point. Each action was executed methodically: the oils massaged into the skin, the clothing pressed flat, the crucifix perfectly centred on his chest. Finally, after examining himself in the mirror, he made a few last adjustments and called for his horse to be brought to the courtyard.

As the cardinal rode to the gate, his guards tried to follow but were immediately dismissed. They didn't question him. In his regalia, he made a formidable sight, straight-backed as a statue, the red of his soutane against the white of his charger. Keeping the horse under tight rein, he advanced from the palace towards the Rue Saint-Honoré, then past the familiar sights: the duke of Vendôme's house on the corner of la Rue des Petit Champs, the unfinished arch in front of the Corps des Guardes. But they seemed different now. The streets were empty, cold and desolate. Virgin snow spread untrammelled along the avenues. It didn't feel like a city threatened by war – more as if the war was already over, the population dead and the buildings left to nature.

It was only when the cardinal neared the market that the first passers-by appeared. Their reactions were invariably the same. They would stop walking and stare at him, unable to believe that the most hated man in all of France was riding alone and unarmed through the middle of Paris. He smiled at a few of them, and all smiled back, but fearfully, suspecting a trick. It seemed odd to him that they should be so afraid. They had never met – to them he was no more than a name.

Once the cardinal reached Les Halles, the streets trickled back to life: merchants off to trade their wares, people returning home with their provisions, carriages and horsemen trotting the cobbles, relays of street-hawkers echoing from the walls. Signs in wood and metal overhung the street: the pen of the quill-merchant, the horseshoe of the farrier, the bloody rag and white post. Even so, the people's response was no different. The cardinal's arrival was like the coming of winter, all life and activity slowing then stopping as he rode by the frozen scene. And each time his eyes would flick from person to person, always holding an instant, just long enough to fix the memory in their minds.

The market square was as busy as ever, the deserting hordes trying to hawk the last of their chattels they could before fleeing south. Despite the throng, Richelieu made steady progress as people rushed out of his way, soon reaching the heart of the bustle where he reined his horse to a stop, dismounted and made his way up some nearby steps. Halting halfway up, he turned to face the crowd. There was no need to capture their attention. They were already watching him, silenced, an amorphous field of drab leather and staring eyes. He waited a few moments, maintaining his serenity in front of the mass, making clear he was not afraid.

'Yes, I am Richelieu, Chief Minister and scourge of France. I know what you think of me. That I'm the man who's taxed you, who has spies in every corner of the land, who drips poison in the ear of the King.'

He paused a moment, both to collect himself and allow the crowd to absorb what he had said.

'But today, my countrymen, I am not a minister of state, or even a cardinal. I am a citizen of France. Just like you. Like you, I will lose everything if Paris falls. Like you, I pray for the King's victory at Corbie.'

A further pause.

'I will not lie to you. These are difficult times for us all.

The future is not certain. However, we can be sure of one thing. We can be sure of today. Because today we are free. Our homes are safe. Thirty thousand men stand between us and our enemies. Today we are victorious. It is us who hold the field. And though we fear the worst, remember too that there may be better times ahead. We may look back at this not as a bitter moment in our past but as a great one, when we were put to the test and we were not found wanting. So I tell you this. Whatever tomorrow may bring, today let us rejoice. Because today we are free. Today we are victorious and we still have hope. Long live the King.'

The crowd was silent as the cardinal finished his speech, his voice resonating in the still air. Long moments passed before there was any reaction. However, when it came, it was like the collapsing of a dam, the trickle of applause growing stronger before bursting into a torrent of roars and cheers. *Long live the King. Long live the King. Long live the King.* Ill at ease with such displays of emotion, the cardinal acknowledged the crowd with a stiff bow before descending back into their midst. As he made his way back to his horse, he stopped to speak to people, whispering comfort and acknowledging fears. Then, with a final wave, he turned homewards and made his way back to the palace.

An hour later, he was back in the privacy of his bedroom and preparing for sleep. Without his soutane and hose, he was stripped of his authority – no more than an emaciated, old man sat on a plank of wood. His naked skin shivered from the cold as he wrapped his arms around himself and prayed under his breath, his ribcage jutting out beneath bony arms. The only light came from a half-extinguished candle and the large circular window behind him, offering a

73

view onto the moonlit roofs of Paris and distant woodland beyond. Richelieu gazed at the horizon as he prayed, awaiting news from Corbie. There was a fervency in his eyes – that of a pilgrim awaiting a sign.

* * *

The siege of Corbie had lasted three months. Like all sieges, it was inglorious – endless days of spadework and disease. Now it had reached the point where it was hard to tell who was being besieged. The earth round the town had been ground to sludge by the tread of feet. The attackers no longer patrolled, instead huddling in their tents for warmth, breathing air that was poisoned with the reek of excrement – both human and equine. Starvation and infection had become rampant. Sentries sat at their posts, homesick and waiting for an end. Illness and desertion had thinned their numbers, while the watches had lengthened for those who remained. Too tired to speak, they sat in the silence, looking out through sleepless eyes. Before them stood the city walls, an unchanging block of grey whose light pockmarks of cannon fire only reminded them of the impossibility of their task.

Gaston, Duke of Orléans, was walking among his troops when the King arrived. Alerted by scattered shouting and cheering of the soldiers, he turned towards the source of their excitement and saw two dribbles of silver winding down the distant hills. Ahead of them rode a dot of blue and yellow, the standard-bearer holding the royal colours. Rolling his eyes, Gaston swore under his breath before mounting his horse and trotting out to meet his brother.

Louis was on horseback near the front of a column, dressed for battle in full plate armour inlaid with gold. Joking with his lieutenants, he seemed relaxed, freed of the restrictions of court – even his stutter appeared to have subsided. He noticed Gaston approach and greeted him with the regal wave.

'Hello, I've come to relieve you of the burdens of command.'

Gaston's mouth soured and he looked away. When he turned back to face the King, he was smiling through taut lips. 'No need, brother. Your reinforcements are more than enough.'

'My country is at stake. I will take command.'

'Give me two days. Please. The town is about to fall. The sight of more troops will end it. Look ...' Gaston motioned at the city walls where a row of tiny figures peered down from above. 'They're already watching us. The news will be spreading. Right now as we speak. Forty-eight hours. Give me that. I've been here three months. I only need two days ...'

'Thank you, my buh-brother. You have done well and will share the glory. But this is not the time for argument. Our country needs its king.'

* * *

The King's command was a brief one. Events unfolded as Gaston had predicted. After seeing the new troops, the town put up one final show of resistance – a fusillade of cannonballs from the ramparts as a motley force of Dutch mercenaries appeared and tried to break the blockade. It was no more than the last twitches of a corpse. Exhausted from their journey, the invaders only managed a feeble charge before fleeing into the woods. Soon after there were rumours of a vote in the town centre and a few hours later the gates were opened to reveal a group of emissaries, shrunken beside the enormity of their protecting walls.

Joining the King and his guards to negotiate terms, Gaston looked out of place, his scuffed armour and ragged beard at odds with their coiffures and gleaming plate. Occasionally he glanced across at his comrades with weary exasperation but said nothing. Instead, his attention was drawn to the representatives at the gate. After ninety days they were hollow with starvation, their eyes sunken and their bellies distended. Despite their situation, they had still made the effort to dress and wore fine silks and brocade. All seemed determined to meet their fate with dignity, stiff-backed and high-chinned – except one who was stooped and pawing at his face in fear. Embarrassed by his cowardice, they stood apart from him, and as the King arrived, their leader even had the temerity to refuse to bow down, forcing one of the guards to punch him to the ground. They made a futile attempt to negotiate until it was made clear they were in no position to discuss terms. Instead, the King listened to their pleas for clemency before pronouncing judgement in his most solemn voice – the city walls were to be razed to the ground and the leaders executed. Sensing the significance of the occasion, Louis was particularly careful not to stammer and spoke ponderously, in silent battle with his own tongue.

Finally, the King completed his triumph with a speech to the troops. Gaston found the experience execrable, watching the men he had slept and fought alongside for the past three months being forced to listen to some stammered doggerel from a man whose only contribution had been a couple of nights in a tent and a light sweat from the ride. It was arrogant to the point of insult. Nobody had asked him to speak. They all just wanted to be home as soon as possible. Louis thought himself a warrior like their father, but he never understood that warriors are remembered for their battles not their words.

The Cardinal

(1636 – 1637)

Catching a whiff of the city gutter, Sebastian winced as the stink burrowed its way up his nostrils. Looking up, he caught a sign – *La Rue Merderelle.* Appropriate at least. He always loathed the crush of Paris. It had the relentless and unstoppable power of the sea. He would pry his way through the bodies but without any idea of where he was going. All he could see was bulk in every direction, towering and blocking out the light. No signs, landmarks or anything beyond shapeless, clothed flesh. Occasionally he would catch a chink of space – an empty street or square – and rush towards it only to be knocked off course. Other times he would be jostled down cul-de-sacs, squashed against the sides of buildings or else trapped behind a huddle of bodies, forced to wait for a break in the scrum before being able to move again.

The only alternative was to stay away from the main thoroughfares. However, keeping to the smaller streets brought its own problems. Aside from their twists and dead ends, they were unpaved, thick with mud, dung and whatever stinking foulness poured out of the tanners, which, while bearable enough during dry weather, became intolerable in the wet.

He had been intent on doing all his chores for the week – dropping off some clothes at the tailor, buying ink, visiting the barber and picking up his rebound *Gargantua and Pantegruel*, read and reread until it was little more than a collection of loose and dog-eared sheets. However, after visiting the bookbinder, he had decided to leave the rest for another day. The journey had been worse than pointless. He had spoken to no one and done nothing except be reminded of his own deficiencies. So it came as a considerable relief when, near the postern to the east of the palace, he was finally able to escape the stink and walk the last hundred yards in the open air.

Relaxing in the space and light, he paid no attention to his surroundings and only became aware of Cinq-Mars when he felt a tug at his elbow and noticed the book was gone. Turning round he saw the marquis staring back at him, standing among a group of friends.

'Well what have we here … The dwarf can read, can he?' There was a degree of surprise mixed in with the scorn.

'Can you kindly return it, my lord? That book is very important to me.' Mindful of Richelieu, Sebastian tried to restrain himself. It was difficult – the sneer and the puff of the clothes, the voluminous collar and broad-brimmed hat, that greedy stare pleading to be slapped off.

'And if I don't?'

'Please. It's mine.' Sebastian made a grab for the manuscript, which Cinq-Mars pulled out of reach then dangled, wanting Sebastian to jump. Instead he received a cocked head and rank disdain.

'I'm not going to beg.'

'Why? Don't you want it?'

'Yes. But making a fool of myself isn't going to help.'

'It might.'

'I don't see how. You won't give it back no matter what I do.'

'Who do you think I am, dwarf? I'm a marquis. I keep my word. I'll return this … thing when you do what I say. Now jump.'

If it had been anything else, Sebastian would have walked away. But it meant too much. It was the one thing he had kept from Camoches. Even when he was hungry and penniless, he'd never been able to sell it. The pages were smudged and barely legible in places, but he didn't care. He knew it all by heart anyway.

And so he jumped. And waved his arms and grunted and strained and did everything that was demanded of him. But it wasn't enough. The marquis seemed delighted with this new-found power and now decided he should try to bite his own ear.

'And not half-heartedly. Properly. Snap your teeth. Bend your neck. And I want you to growl like a dog.'

Sebastian obeyed, until he could barely look round after craning so much and had half-lost his voice from snarling. But it still wasn't enough. Now Cinq-Mars decided to amuse himself with discovering the truth of the rumour about *dwarves being compensated for their shortcomings elsewhere.*

'You mean my brain, I assume.'

'I mean your cock. Undress dwarf.'

So Sebastian did as he asked, pulling down his pantaloons and sullenly exhibiting himself to the amusement of all. Still it wasn't enough. Not content with having made a dog of him, the marquis now commanded him to put his face in the dirt and chew grass like a cow, and swallow it too, which he did until his belly ached and his mouth leaked green. Nevertheless, he suffered it out. He had been through worse. Tonight he would be back in his room, safe behind his locked door, and tomorrow this would be a memory. Cinq-Mars was already beginning to tire. He was talking among his friends now. It wouldn't be long. He took another bite and tasted the bitterness as the grass collected into a rough and indigestible ball, its blades catching in his throat. Then he heard the marquis' voice. It sounded mildly disappointed.

'Very well, dwarf. You've amused us long enough. You may leave.'

Struggling to his feet, Sebastian spat out the cud and held out a hand, expectant. 'The book.'

Cinq-Mars smiled before tucking the volume inside his doublet. 'You know what. I might keep it. Call it ... protection.'

'You promised.'

'I said I'd give it back, not when.'

'That's ridiculous. You call yourself a man of honour? You're nothing ...'

Sebastian was cut off by Cinq-Mars grabbing his shoulder and throwing him to the ground. Pinning him down with a foot, he watched him thrash, an upturned beetle flailing for escape. 'Hasty words, dwarf. What do you have to say now?'

Powerless, Sebastian lashed out with the only thing he had left – his tongue.

'Why don't you fight someone your own size? Or are you too frightened without the cardinal to protect you? That's the truth, isn't it? Without Richelieu, you're no one. Some jumped up squire who thinks himself a man.'

Frigid silence followed. This was the King's court. In 1636 servants didn't insult masters, let alone marquises, and certainly not in public. Shocked, the nobles looked across at Cinq-Mars, awaiting his response.

It wasn't long coming. Notoriously conscious of his ancestry, which was considerably less exalted than he made out, Cinq-Mars grabbed Sebastian and hauled him out of the dirt.

'Well, dwarf, it seems you're stupid as well as contemptible,' he said, locking his arm round Sebastian's head and marching forward, yanking him behind.

Barely able to keep up with the taller man's strides, Sebastian was pulled across the gardens and through a side door. He was in the main hall, though all he could see of it was the stone-flagged floor. Ahead of him was the fireplace, piled high and blazing, and momentarily he scrabbled, terrified of being hurled into the hearth. Instead Cinq-Mars halted abruptly, raising his head to face the heart of the flames.

'The book, it fell out of my doublet. Someone bring it here.'

'No. Don't.' His voice rose to shrieking panic as he realised what Cinq-Mars was about to do. 'Not that. You can't. My mother gave it to me. She saved for months. No, no, please God, no.'

'Nobody cares what you think, little man.' Cinq-Mars

bent down towards his ear, making sure he could hear every word. 'You're nothing. Something that should have never been born ...' And with that he tossed the book into the fire. For a brief moment, it remained intact and Sebastian scrabbled to rescue it but was held in place. Screaming, he struggled to break free as the paper first scorched then lit, disappearing in a matter of seconds.

It was as if his mother was burning in front of his eyes. The book had been his companion, shelter and sustenance – almost literally, considering the nights he had gone without food rather than sell it. The comforting feel of it inside his jerkin, warm as an embrace, now nothing more than ashes. He continued to watch the final few fragments cling to the logs before evaporating to dust. And then when it had all gone, his neck dropped as if cut and he stared slackly at the floor.

Now the excitement had passed, Cinq-Mars soon bored of Sebastian and let him drop to the ground.

'Anything else to say?'

Sebastian didn't seem to hear him, let alone reply.

'I thought as much. You brought this on yourself, dwarf.' The marquis strode for the door, marking his exit with an emphatic slam. Sebastian, meanwhile, remained where he was. Alone, he sat slumped, searching the fireplace with an empty stare.

Ignoring the chill of the stone floor, he continued to gaze into the flames before finally making his way upstairs, though he might as well have been sleepwalking, for he had no memory of how he got there. It wasn't simply the loss of the book but the reminder of his inadequacies – that talent and effort are not always enough, that not all obstacles can be overcome. And, closing the door behind him, he fell onto his bed, giving way to hot and shaming tears which only reminded him further of his weakness – though he did his best to fight them, refusing to give way to self-pity as he waited for the pain to subside. Eventually, with the sound of birdcall and the tread of feet in the corridor, the outside world made itself apparent and he composed himself once again. It was another setback – nothing more.

Besides, if nothing else, there was always the prospect of taking his revenge.

* * *

Sebastian's retribution was short and brutal. Cinq-Mars was not a hard man to mock, forever proclaiming his lineage despite the fact his title was unknown outside Auvergne. His crest, a phoenix with wings outstretched above a ring, was emblazoned on his armour, clothes, furniture – even on his underwear if rumour was to be believed.

He didn't indulge his quill with anything too elegant. He wanted Cinq-Mars to understand each and every word. The result was more fist than knife. The adventures of a knight called Sir Clucksalot, an over-dressed dandy whose crest was a chicken rising from an egg, boasting of his great deeds while in fact being terrified of everything and everyone. After twenty minutes of swagger and braggadocio, the play climaxed with Sir Clucksalot being publically humiliated and sentenced to eat ginger for a year in the hope it might instil courage.

The performance, if not the content, was one of Sebastian's finest. Jerome and Claude were terrified of offending one of Richelieu's creatures and refused to take part, leaving Sebastian to act out all the roles:

King Clovis: a wise and beneficent monarch
Sir Clucksalot: a cowardly braggart
Lady Clucksalot: his long-suffering and patient wife
Sir Morefed: Sir Clucksalot's portly and over-watered nemesis
Pierre Lickpenny: Sir Clucksalot's grasping yet unctuous servant

From the start, Sebastian performed the work with a hard edge born of violent hatred, glaring at Cinq-Mars throughout. Cinq-Mars stared back, first with amazement then with murderous, stewing fury. Sebastian continued, unconcerned. If anything, the marquis' anger spurred him on, his impersonation growing ever crueller and the laughter of the court ever more raucous. At the end, just to prevent any possibility of misinterpretation, he dedicated the piece to 'Henri Coiffier de Ruzé, Marquis de Cinq-Mars, the most honourable and courageous man in all of France', before the jeers of the entire court.

After the performance, Sebastian didn't even bother getting changed and took a stool in the changing room, awaiting his visitor. He wasn't long coming. Sebastian anticipated a furious entry, but it was careful, a creak of the door and click of the latch. The entrance of a man who didn't want to be noticed. And it was only once they were alone that the marquis let his emotion show – a face ugly with rage, at odds with his silk and lace.

'I thought you were a freak. Now I know you're a bloody abomination.'

Sebastian didn't move, staring back with verminous hatred. '*Henri.*' He pointedly ignored the title. 'Do you think I'm an idiot?'

'I think you're a corpse.' Cinq-Mars drew his rapier. It was a courtly thing, as much ornament as weapon, and was met with a laugh.

'God almighty, do you really think I'm such a fool?' Sebastian shook his head and drew a duelling pistol from his inside pocket. 'Didn't it occur to you that I might take precautions?' The gun was too large for him and he had to hold it in both hands, clearly battling with the weight, his short fingers barely reaching the trigger.

It was enough to stop the marquis, though not enough to make him sheathe his sword. 'Don't be ridiculous. You can't use that thing. It's not even loaded.'

'To be honest, I've no idea. I bought it from a pawnbroker a month ago. But considering you're four feet away, do you want to find out?'

'Runt. You're only making it worse for yourself.'

'Perhaps.' Sebastian was still struggling to hold the gun upright and it had started to wobble.

Cinq-Mars stayed where he was, eyeing the downward tremble of the barrel as it trickled down his neck and chest before finally halting over his heart, at which point Sebastian braced it with his one hand, holding it musket-fashion.

'It doesn't have to be this way.' His voice softened and he looked at Cinq-Mars with a smile, more rueful than pleasant. 'We've both suffered enough already. Can't we just leave it be?'

The marquis shook his head, taking a pace forward then another until the pistol was touching his chest. 'Do you really think you can threaten me, dwarf?' He glared down as he spoke. 'You're nothing. Besides, I've no intention of killing you now. I'm not going to be executed on your account. There'll be a better time. When you're out on the street, or in the courtyard, or at night in your room. All I want you to remember, when that moment comes and you're praying for death, is that it was me.'

Then with a shrug, he turned on his heel and left. Sebastian observed his departing figure with exasperation rather than fear. Pride had always struck him as a particularly ridiculous fault – most common among those least deserving of it. Besides, Cinq-Mars was bound to come to his senses eventually. Fool that he was, he had to realise he had no choice. The humiliation had been too public. He couldn't retaliate without everyone knowing it was him. Instead he would have to react as rank demanded – to show good grace, display the *noblesse oblige* and laugh it off as best he could.

Then, after a hot meal followed by a stroll round the gardens, Sebastian returned to his room and a life that seemed to have returned to its reassuringly normal self. And that night as he put his head on the pillow, snug behind his locked door, he even allowed himself a momentary grin – smug with the memory of what he'd done.

* * *

Carefully the woman pulled the sheet to one side before levering herself upright. Sitting on the side of the bed, she slipped on her dress and pulled on a pair of threadbare stockings. Then she turned to the mound alongside her. The bulk of it was hidden beneath the crumpled sheets, apart from a loose arm which hung as though from a corpse. A close examination revealed no movement beyond the slow rise and fall of ribs beneath the covers, and she promptly directed her attention towards the pile of clothes that lay in the corner of the room. Creeping over, she took another glance at the bed, then bent down and lifted the doublet, carefully feeling for each pocket and dipping a hand inside. Finding nothing, she moved onto the trousers. This time her efforts produced a candle stub and accompanying fragments, which she was sliding back into place when a voice emerged from the bedclothes.

'Lost something?'

She startled, narrowly repressing a shriek of alarm, then turned to face the voice – where Sebastian's head had now revealed itself from beneath the sheet. Still in the early morning fog, he stared at her through heavy lids.

'Don't worry. Stay a little longer. I've got coin.'

'How much?'

'Do we have to negotiate everything?' He sighed and rubbed his face. 'It does ruin the illusion somewhat.'

'I'm sorry, *my liege*. It might be pleasure for you, but it's work for me.' She noticed him wince and softened a fraction. 'Look, I'm sorry ...'

'God, is that pity? Please no.' Horrified, he cut her off instantly. 'I'm quite aware of the situation. I'm no woman's dream. Anyway I don't need your ... services. Just to talk.'

'It'll still cost you.'

'Four sous.' His remittance to his mother would have to be a fraction short this month.

'Six.'

'I'm short, not a fool. I advise you learn the difference.' The comment was followed by the chink of coin dropping onto the floor.

Sweeping up her prize, the woman smiled and returned to the bed. 'Is that a book in your bag? Are you some sort of priest?'

'Priests aren't the only ones who can read, you know. But I'll take your confession if you like.'

'You'd be here a long time.' She had a cackle of a laugh and he couldn't help smiling. 'Anyway, all this reading. What have you learned then?'

'Too much to tell.'

'That's no answer. This book here – what's it taught you?'

'Martial? That those who mock the rich will always be poor.'

'Don't need a book to tell me that.'

'There are whole civilisations in books. History. Philosophy. The minds of some of the greatest people who have ever lived. I can hear those very same thoughts Julius Caesar had sixteen hundred years ago – make those dead lips speak. Does that not amaze you?' He looked at her soft-eyed, seduced by his own words.

'Can't shag a book, can you?' She flashed a tit for effect.

'No … no, you can't.' A sadness fluttered across his face and he closed his eyes. However, it only lasted a moment, and he looked back at her with a drowsy smile. 'Tell you what. There's a baker opposite. How about you go and get us a couple of brioches for breakfast and we carry on talking then?'

'Give me the money then.'

He aimed another glance upwards. 'What about the four sous I gave you?'

'That's for working. Not to buy you breakfast.'

'Here's another two. Should be more than enough.' He placed the coins in her outstretched hand. Then, once she left, he changed into his clothes, flattening down the creases and fastening each button tight. Seating himself on the side of the bed, he retrieved his *Epigrams* and began to read while waiting for her to return. It wasn't until the fifth page that he glanced across at the door. He looked again on the eighth page, this time with a frown, and again on the tenth. However, it wasn't until the twentieth page that he took a deep breath, snapped the book shut and left the room, closing the door behind him.

* * *

Sebastian woke up choking and blind. The heat was unbearable and acrid smoke was burning his eyes. FIRE. Scrambling out of bed, he smashed his foot into the wardrobe. Then, sucking in a chestful of fumes, he choked again, this time coughing so hard that he bent double and barely managed to stay upright. Suffocating, he made another futile attempt to draw breath and stumbled to the desk, where he propped himself up and pressed his nightshirt to his mouth, straining for air that would not come. He couldn't see anything. The smoke was impenetrable and his eyes were flooded with tears. The only thing he could locate was the heat, which was now at his back, somewhere near the door. He needed another way out – the window. Groping round the bureau, he grasped the edge and pulled it to one side. The desire to breathe was overwhelming, pounding his chest. He was starting to lose consciousness. Feeling first the wall then the uneven glass and lead, he sucked against clamped lips as his fingers found the frame and then the latch. He gave a tug but it didn't give. Desperate, he forced the matter, hurling himself against the glass. Suddenly a crash followed by the thud of tile and the cold of the night on his skin. He was lying on the roof, heaving great, ragged breaths, then coughing again, the freezing air every bit as sharp as the smoke had been. For all the relief, it wasn't long before sense took hold. He was still in mortal peril. Whoever had just tried to kill him must be nearby. He needed to hide. A look around revealed a chimney pot to his right. Rolling onto his hands and knees, he crawled over and hid behind it, crouched and listening for approaching footsteps. Hearing nothing, he remained motionless, but there was only the distant crackle of his life being reduced to ash and he sat in his nightshirt, wrapping his arms round his legs as he sheltered from the wind as best he could. A short eternity passed before he picked out voices nearby. After satisfying himself that the sound was coming from his room and that help was finally at hand, he ventured out and crept back the way he had come.

Looking across the rooftop, he gazed dumbly at the scene. The fire had mostly burned itself out and he watched as the last of the flames were quenched, leaving his window soot-blackened and pouring smoke. It looked like some chimney turned wrongways, the surrounding wall stained with plumes of ash. Though what struck him most of all was the blackness of the chamber. He could see figures walking within, presumably servants come to deal with the mess. Unless Cinq-Mars was among them, checking if he was dead. The thought was enough to make him reconsider and he stole up to the ledge and peeped inside, checking the livery of each person in turn. And it was only once he had satisfied himself that he was safe that he finally climbed the sill and dropped into the room.

What had once been his life was now nothing but cinders. Everything he had ever read, written or owned: every book, every memento, every coin he had saved, all his clothes, his pen, his play – his refuge, the one place in the world that was created for him and him alone. Only the barest remnants survived: scraps of paper, half a bedstead turned to charcoal, the brass feet of his wardrobe laid in a perfect rectangle on the blackened floorboards. He had trouble recognising anything in the chaos and stared, half-expecting it to suddenly make sense, but nothing changed. He simply remained where he was, uncomprehending, until the soot overpowered his throat and he had to leave.

Out in the corridor, he lay by the stairs, exhausted. All he could taste, see and feel was smoke: stinging his eyes and chest, furring his tongue and throat and pouring in black streams from his nose. But he couldn't rest. Not yet. His attacker was still at large, and he would try again. He still couldn't understand how the marquis had managed it; his door had been locked and the window closed. It was only after stumbling back to the scene that he noticed the blot gouged into the boards by the door, where the fire had burned deepest. Instantly he realised what had happened.

Someone must have poured oil in from the corridor outside, then set it alight. Looking closer, he could even see a smear on the unburnt side of the door, tell-tale as blood. Quite simple, really – well within the capabilities of Cinq-Mars, or whichever stooge he had employed to do his bidding. The flurry of people was increasing. A number of servants had been woken by the noise and were tending to the mess, eager to finish and return to their beds. Some were carrying buckets of ash and soot, while others held mops to swab the walls and floors. Returning upstairs, he could see them filing in and out of the doorway at a steady pace, oblivious to his presence.

It was the chamberlain who first noticed him. A squarely built man of middling years, he was wearing an oversized wig, and his robe was unbuttoned, exposing the shirt and paunch beneath. He had been freshly roused from his slumber and didn't seem concerned by his appearance, or indeed anything beyond getting back to bed, judging by the near-permanent yawn as he shuffled down the corridor.

'So, you're the source of my troubles, dwarf,' he declared, without giving Sebastian the chance to speak.

'No, sir. It's the Marquis de Cinq-Mars. He tried to murder me.'

Sebastian expected at least a word of sympathy but instead met with indignation. 'What did you say?'

'The Marquis de Cinq-Mars. He tried to burn me alive.'

The chamberlain deliberated a moment, straining with thought. The effort was taxing and he soon gave up. Bending down, he pressed a stiff finger to Sebastian's chest. 'I am not a man who sleeps a great deal.' This was evident from a pair of bleary and wrinkled eyes. 'And what little rest I do get, I am thankful for. Consequently, I like my nights to be simple – making sure the palace is in good order, that the loaves are ready in the oven and that the guards are on watch, while occasionally returning a drunk student back to the Sorbonne. This allows me to catch what sleep God allows and to retain my good humour. But tonight, not only do you nearly burn down the palace and wake up half the staff, you now inform me that the ward of Cardinal Richelieu wants to kill you. Well, Monsieur Morra, I am not interested … in fact, I wish the man good fortune. He might at least make my life a little simpler.'

Sebastian stared in astonishment as the chamberlain turned round and strode back up the corridor. He felt an overwhelming desire to grab the man and scream, to make him understand he was dealing with a fellow human soul, no different to himself. But he knew it was pointless. The chamberlain could do nothing. Cinq-Mars was protected by the Chief Minister of France. And it was at that precise moment Sebastian realised what he needed to do. He had to see the only man who had influence over the marquis – Cardinal Richelieu.

* * *

As Sebastian trudged through the Louvre, he appeared out of place in the magnificence; a ragged figure set against jasper and marble, fluted pilasters and coffered ceilings. Not that he noticed the contrast. Deep in thought, he didn't even slow his pace as he walked barefoot onto the snow outside. He had more than enough to keep him occupied – principally, how to engineer an audience with the Chief Minister of

France at an hour past midnight when uninvited and dressed in a tattered nightgown. The best he could hope for was that the cardinal might somehow remember their previous meeting. However, bearing in mind it had been over a year ago and the subsequent invasion by Spain, it seemed unlikely to say the least.

Sebastian's first attempt to enter the Palais-Cardinal was abrupt, almost comical. Even before reaching the door, he looked ridiculous beside the edifice – an ant facing a cliff – and stood overawed for some time before venturing a knock. Shortly afterwards he heard the slow approach of footsteps and the sound of a bolt being pulled aside. Then a hatch opened, framing a mistrustful stare. The eyes were looking a foot above Sebastian's head and he was forced to shout for attention. Peering down, they narrowed with disgust.

'On your way, beggar,' a curt voice snapped as the hatch slammed shut. Having no alternative, Sebastian pounded the knocker again.

'I'm not a beggar. I need to see the cardinal. Let me in.'

After a brief pause, he heard the turn of a key in a lock and the door opened a slit. A face appeared in the gap – one of Richelieu's personal guards. He was plainly dressed, with the official insignia of three chevronels and galero.

'Begging your pardon, Sir, but can you let me in? I am hoping to arrange an appointment to see His Eminence, the Cardinal.'

'He's busy. State your business or leave.' The guard spoke in a military manner and was evidently more used to giving orders than asking questions.

'Please. My life is in danger. Someone just tried to burn me alive.'

'Your problems are no concern of His Eminence. He's got more important things to worry about.'

'But we've met before. Don't you remember? Last year he asked for me.'

The guard gave a rasping, abrasive laugh. 'I'd remember *you*.'

'Where I met him, the wallpaper, it was green. The floor was chequered black and white. Behind you, in the hall, there's a picture of a woman in a blue dress.'

The guard didn't speak and his face contorted as if being pulled in two directions. He glanced behind him, only to confirm what he knew was there. Then he looked back at Sebastian.

'Wait here – I'll check with the secretary,' he replied before slamming the door. Sebastian was left marooned on the step, not only shoeless but also pitifully underdressed, clad in only a scorched nightshirt; and it wasn't long before his feet grew brittle, forcing him to hop from one to the other to keep off the freezing stone. Hugging himself, he sheltered in a corner but the wind was in his face and soon he began to shiver uncontrollably as the cold sharpened to a blister then a burn. Resisting the urge to scream, he closed his eyes and withdrew into the darkness. And when the door did eventually creak open, he was too numb to hear what the guard said, only able to make sense of the arm beckoning him inside.

Barely able to walk, Sebastian was handed a blanket and allowed to warm himself for a few minutes before being led to an unfamiliar wing of the palace. It lacked the usual overbearing splendour, consisting instead of wood-panelled corridors which all looked much the same, so he soon lost all sense of his bearings.

He expected another overwhelming chamber and was surprised to be led into a pleasant but unremarkable room, hung with faded and badly rendered portraits. Perplexed, Sebastian took a few moments to notice the family resemblance and realise they were there for sentimental value rather than to impress. He observed other objects that appeared equally personal – a wooden pig, a flaking grandfather clock and a crewel-work tapestry crumbling to threads. The room felt private, unsettlingly human. Richelieu was not a man he associated with emotion and nostalgia, and it felt somehow inappropriate, as though he had walked in through the wrong door and found the cardinal undressed. His immediate instinct was to leave, but instead he averted his eyes and looked at the floor, trying to concentrate on what to say.

The wait didn't last long. After a few minutes Richelieu appeared from a side door, wearing a red biretta and plain cassock. The only hint of his station was the intricate silver crucifix shining out of the black of his soutane. Immediately he cocked his head and peered closer, intrigued by Sebastian's appearance. After a moment he appeared to reach some kind of conclusion and glanced across at the guard.

'Why haven't you given him some clothes? Money? Food?'

'You didn't ask, Your Eminence.'

'Isn't it obvious?' His voice had the hiss of acid. 'Look at his face and arms. The man's patently been in a fire and he's walked here in bare feet. I think he deserves a modicum of hospitality.'

The guard scurried to make amends and two minutes later Sebastian was in the kitchen holding a bowl of hot soup and a slab of bread with five livres stacked on the table top in front of him. The clothes took longer to find and he had to make do with a billowing shirt and sleeves rolled up to the elbow, along with knickerbockers that made him feel as if he was wading through a bog. However, his appearance was the least of his concerns. In five minutes, he was due to have an audience with the governor of France, and he hadn't the slightest idea what to say. Not only did he possess nothing of interest to the cardinal, but Cinq-Mars was the man's ward and the closest thing he had to a son. Nor did he have any hope of lying his way out of the situation, which left him with no alternative but to rely on Richelieu's compassion – not a quality for which the man was renowned.

Returning, Sebastian was led into Richelieu's private chambers, where he found the cardinal sitting on a small cushioned throne. Sebastian looked up at him, hoping for some sign of acknowledgement, only to find himself confronted by unblinking authority. He felt the same terror of breaking protocol as when they had first met, and shuffled forward, keeping his head bowed. He was unsure whether to meet Richelieu's gaze and his eyes flitted between the cardinal's feet and chin.

'I've come to plead for my life, Your Eminence.'

'I've no memory of ordering your execution.'

'You're the only one who can help me. Your ward, the Marquis de Cinq-Mars … he tried to burn me alive in my room. Speak to him, please, I beg you.'

'Henri.' Richelieu sighed and closed his eyes. 'Always so rash. He took offence to your play, I imagine. I heard it was somewhat unforgiving. Amusing but certainly unforgiving. You must have realised the consequences?'

'No, Your Eminence …'

'Dispense with the formalities. I'm a busy man.'

'Yes, Your ...' Sebastian narrowly managed to stop himself. 'I mean it was only satire. Nobody murdered Dante or Boccaccio.'

'They were wise enough to have patrons, and rather better suited to defending themselves than you. Anyway, it's beside the point. The fact remains that Henri is both my ward and a peer of the realm, whereas you are a court dwarf born of peasant stock. I must act in my own best interests, and much as I would like to help, I'm afraid it's not worth the price.'

'I will be forever in your debt.'

'Be that as it may, you still humiliated my ward in front of the entire court.' The cardinal shook his head, lifting a hand to end proceedings, only for Sebastian to speak again.

'I have a thought.'

'Make it brief.'

Sebastian hesitated, aware of the significance of the moment – his cornered mind searching for escape. But what on earth could he offer the Chief Minister of France? What use would such a man have for someone whose only discernible talents were as a trickster and beggar of coin? Then, as ever it came from nowhere – accompanied by that disconcerting sense that his mind was cleverer than he was, that he was no more than a mediocre rider fortunate enough to be saddled to a fast horse.

'I can serve you. Bring you information.'

'How? What do you know?'

'What do you want to find out?'

'Don't play with me.'

'I'm not, Your Eminence. But you'd be amazed what I hear. Nobody pays attention to me. I'm a buffoon, no threat to anyone. Besides, I'm already a known face at court. All I need is guidance and I'll find out all you care to know.'

The cardinal chuckled at his impudence. 'I somewhat doubt that. But go on … tell me about yourself. What languages do you speak?'

'Spanish, Latin …'

'Dicasne lingue Latina?'

'Satis agnoscare illa quaestio.'

'Very good. Where did you learn?'

'I listened in church.'

'An all too rare phenomenon …' The cardinal paused, and when he spoke again, his voice had fallen into a murmur. 'Very well. There's no harm in trying, I suppose. I'll tell Henri to keep away. For a month or so at least, if only not to draw suspicion over the fire. After that … well … we'll see.' He glanced across at Sebastian, his eyes two dots of pinpoint concentration. 'Now, you're an intelligent man. I assume I don't have to remind you that anything we discuss remains between you and me.'

'Of course.'

Richelieu nodded at Sebastian to leave, but the dwarf held his ground, drawing a raised eyebrow from the cardinal.

'Is there something else?'

'If you don't mind?'

'You're hardly in a position to make requests.'

'I know, but my books were burned. I'd like to borrow a few from your library.'

Richelieu's mouth convulsed into a smile. 'Is that all?'

'You agree?'

'I'm not going to stand in the way of a man trying to educate himself. There's some Lucan and Petronius you might enjoy. The *Bellum Civile* I find particularly entertaining. As regards the other matter, one of my representatives will meet you tomorrow evening by the north-west door at six.'

'How will I know him?'

'I wouldn't worry; I suspect he won't have difficulty recognising you. His name is Ambroise. He's a cousin of mine.' The cardinal glanced across at the clock in the corner, an elaborate affair with four dials: one timing the earth, the others astronomical, set to the sun, moon and stars. 'Anyway…it's late and I advise you get some rest. I'll have some men attend to your room.'

'Thank you, Your Eminence. I will repay your faith.'

'I've no doubt you will,' Richelieu finished, nodding at him to leave. The implication was clear enough.

Then, after taking a brief tour of the cardinal's library and picking out some Petronius, Lucan and Plautus, Sebastian returned to the palace, alone with his thoughts. He felt a certain sense of relief, of course, but tempered by the knowledge that he had not been saved out of compassion or mercy, but to serve a purpose. This was an agreement that once entered could not be undone. For better or worse, he had become the cardinal's man.

* * *

It was only on returning to the Louvre that the lateness of the hour became apparent. Sebastian had a dim memory of being led to the kitchens and shown a palliasse in the corner, draped with a sheet. He didn't care. He didn't even bother waiting for a pillow. The crook of his arm was comfortable enough, and after a long and dreamless sleep he woke up to find himself in what appeared to be a store room, complete with a pile of cooking apples in the corner. He could hear clanking and shouting from outside, the hubbub of people at work. Then, as he drew in a breath, he felt an ache in his chest immediately followed by the cold spike of reality. *It's all destroyed. You have nothing.*

Lurching upright, he ambled half-dressed through the kitchens and back to his room, hoping that it was some trick of the mind and everything would be its same normal self. In a way he was right. Everything was orderly and in its place, just not as he expected it to be. The room had been transformed. The same elements remained but the effect was entirely different. Plain walls had been replaced by oak panelling, the desk and wardrobe were walnut, the embroidered bed with its canopy looked more like a ship. On the bureau stood a stack of paper, quill and full pot of ink – all perfectly arranged. There was even a new library, complete with the works of Montaigne and Rabelais, gold-stamped and leather-bound. Indeed the only hint of what had taken place was a mild whiff of charcoal.

He continued to look about, bewildered. It didn't feel like his room any more, as if he had awoken to find himself in someone else's life. He prodded and poked, opening the wardrobe and lying on the bed, searching for something he could recognise. But it was all unfamiliar, and he continued to peer around while finding nothing to settle on.

Eventually, after a few trips to the corridor and a brief walk outside, he began to find the room if not comforting, then at least less disconcerting. He was able to think of other things: the blankness of the paper on his desk, the play already disappearing in his mind, the fact that he still had four hours until his meeting with Ambroise. And, after a deep breath, he marched to his desk and began to write. Desperate to save what he could, he didn't bother with details and paraphrased where possible, scrawling down the memories before they could fade away. However, it was dispiriting work and each half-remembered character and misplaced scene only reminded him of how much he had lost. The words seemed inadequate – dots and scratches, nothing more.

* * *

After walking to the rendezvous, Sebastian searched for Ambroise, but the corridor was empty. The only person in sight was a man in the garden outside, leaning on the edge of a fountain while observing the sunset. His back was to Sebastian but from what he could see of the man's attire, it appeared inconspicuous: well-cut but neither elaborate as a noble nor plain as a servant. Hearing his approach, the man turned round and stood up. If he was a cousin of Richelieu's, he was a distant one and, judging by his weight, he had none of the cardinal's discipline either. Aside from his girth, his face was plump as a pillow and his nose rosy from drink. Below it was a parody of a mouth, pinched at the top, with the lower lip sagging beneath. On seeing Sebastian, he introduced himself by chortling under his breath in a mildly insulting manner.

'I'll be damned. I thought I'd misheard.'

'I see you're amused by my size. Oddly enough, it seems quite normal to me.' Sebastian shook his head, more weary than annoyed.

'Sorry, don't mean to offend. But you look pretty different to the usual…people he sends. Who's going to spot you, eh?'

'Yes, I'm small. Yes, I'm unlikely to be noticed. Now are you going to carry on being an ass or can we discuss the business at hand?' Sebastian replied, amazed the cardinal would employ such an idiot. Clearly he prized loyalty over intelligence.

Ambroise was visibly taken aback. The grin disappeared and he replied with the only thing he could think of – his orders. 'The cardinal says I'm to take you to the great hall and give you your instructions.'

The hall was on the other side of the palace – a five-minute walk. Evidently uncomfortable with silence, Ambroise insisted on chattering the entire way, primarily about the cardinal. Despite being Richelieu's cousin, he admitted to knowing relatively little beyond childhood recollections. 'Armand doesn't like talking about himself. Thinks it's a weakness. He listens to what people tell him and he gives orders. Nothing else.' Sebastian reflected that this said as much about Ambroise as Richelieu. The cardinal wasn't the type to waste his time conversing with fools.

Aptly named, the great hall was a palace within a palace, its hammer beam ceiling engraved with coats of arms and interweaving ivy and honeysuckle. Long tables were lined in two symmetrical rows, leading up to a central dais and the King's table, complete with throne and canopy. Sebastian stood on the balcony that stretched across the far wall, listening to the chatter of the court as they ate, oblivious to the spectators overhead. From above, he had a better sense of the room. He could see the swarms of flies around the chandeliers as the insects caught the flames and fell onto the tables below. The room was of an imposing height, the candlelight fading into the gloom of the roof above; and rather than glorifying the King, the space diminished him – reducing him to a speck in the void. He considered sharing the observation with Ambroise but decided it would be pointless. Instead he waited, until eventually Ambroise produced a few scribblings from his pocket and peered at them for a moment, struggling to decipher his own words.

'The Duke of Saint-Simon, do you see him?' He nodded at the people below.

Sebastian spotted the man at a glance. Everyone knew Saint-Simon. Once a favourite of the King, he had long since lost his looks and now bore the effects of a life spent on the battlefield – his face flattened, shaped like clumsily-handled clay, his voice that of a soldier, blunt and terse. Yet Louis remained attached to him, finding his candour a relief from the usual timidity of his subjects. At present he was three seats away from the King, sharing a joke with his neighbour while rubbing the food off his moustache.

'Yes. He's on the royal table. Dressed in green.'

'Good ... now put this in his drink.'

Sebastian looked down to see a vial of clear liquid in Ambroise's hand.

'You are joking?'

Ambroise shrugged. 'No joke.'

'I'm not killing him ... besides, he's sitting right next to the King. I'd be struck down on the spot. I'm not doing this.' With that he marched downstairs and back towards his room. Passing through the hall below, he noticed the cardinal seated a few places down from his victim, picking at a dry-looking plate of vegetables and chicken. Richelieu's insouciance revolted him. That someone could eat his dinner a few yards away from the man he was about to have murdered. It seemed beyond callous. The cardinal seemed to sense his displeasure and glanced up. His eyebrows twitched with surprise; then he realised what was happening and the look hardened. Not with rage but intent. The stare of a man who had not just killed, but killed many times before – and would have no compunction doing so again. Still the eyes did not move. Sebastian remained trapped, paralysed through sheer will. Seconds passed before he was finally able to break the spell and look away. He had no time, only a few minutes at most. Long enough to scurry to his room, grab whatever possessions he could and flee before Richelieu's men arrived.

* * *

After stuffing a few clothes into a sack, Sebastian poured his remaining money on the table. Eleven livres and six sous – perhaps enough to reach Orléans. He could eke out some kind of living there, or at least find somewhere quiet to consider what to do next. Then came a knock knock from the corridor. Unexpected. Sebastian dived to hide beneath the bed. Too late. The handle dropped and he was still flat on his belly when the door opened to reveal a footman looking down at him, queer-eyed with puzzlement.

'The cardinal sent me. I'm to bring you to him.'

'How?'

'I don't know. He just ordered me to follow you. I'd advise you don't keep him waiting.'

Sebastian momentarily considered escape but it was too far. Even if he made it to the corridor, the entrance was three flights down and he always struggled with stairs. So, after pushing himself upright, he trudged behind, grimacing as he followed the man back the way he had come.

To the right of the great hall was a side-chamber – occasionally used for business when it required the King to interrupt his meal. Domed and colonnaded, it enjoyed an excellent view over the grounds. The cardinal stood by one of the windows, staring at the winter garden. Its blooms were now scaled with frost, the grass gleaming like upturned icicles, the moonlight catching the crystals and scattering into tints of violet and indigo. As Sebastian entered, Richelieu turned to meet him, his cardinal's cape purpled in the evening light.

'I like to come here in the evenings. Finding peace in Paris can be hard at the best of times.' The menace was not overt. Instead, the politesse of a functionary – a man in complete control of his manner and tongue.

Sebastian gazed back, his own fear magnified by the cardinal's lack of emotion. His guts seemed to have turned to water and his skin was damp with sweat. He remained silent a moment, too frightened to speak, then blurted out the only thing he could – the truth. 'Please, Your Eminence, you can't make me do this. He's done nothing wrong. You must understand. I mean, you're a man of God.'

'I am a man of God. And I fulfil his purpose by serving the King, his divine representative on earth.' The reply was mechanical and clearly a phrase he had repeated many times before. 'Like you, I take no joy in killing a man. Nevertheless, it is in the King's interest and therefore the Almighty's.'

'But why?' Sebastian couldn't meet the cardinal's eyes. The sweat was pouring now. His entire body seemed to be turning to liquid and he was straining from the effort of containing his bowels.

'Do you not understand the danger this country faces? We control barely half our domain and the dukes will betray us at the slightest opportunity. Our borders are weak. We have no natural defence, no Rhine to the north, no Pyrenees to the south. Our enemies are richer and more powerful than us. We have neither the gold of Spain nor the merchants of the Low Countries. Most of our land is forest and we are ravaged by starvation. Rarely has our country faced such a predicament. There is no time to waste. I need my orders carried out without question and to the letter. I cannot start debating the merits of my commands.'

'I understand what you are saying, Your Eminence, but you're asking me to murder someone. And magnificent as your words are, I need to know the reason.' The reply was gabbled and desperate, and so brief it seemed almost insolent. Mindful of the situation, however, Richelieu limited his reaction to a thinning of the eyes.

'You want to know the facts.' He nodded. 'Very well. Saint-Simon is the King's most trusted military advisor. He is also in the pay of Madrid. Unfortunately I don't have the evidence to prove it, and the King trusts him beyond reproach. He's already convinced Louis to send emissaries to King Philip and I believe in a matter of weeks we will be a dominion of Spain.'

'I don't understand, Your Eminence. Does that mean you don't know?'

'Of course. My work is based on uncertainty. I have to make choices even when I have next to no information – an intercepted letter, an interpretation of events, someone who could equally well be a spy. In this case I've received assurance from two sources who have been proved right a number of times before. Can I be sure? No. But it seems likely, and frankly the risk is too great not to act. Morality isn't worth losing a country over.'

'But you'll end up chasing shadows.'

'Yes, and I'll never know if what I did was right. It's something I live with. Be glad you do not.' The cardinal completed the remark with a flourish of the index finger and looked across at Sebastian, expecting the conversation to be at an end.

'Your Eminence.' The sweat was stinging Sebastian's eyes and he had reached the point of desperation. 'Forgive me but I must be frank. If there's something you're not telling me, I must know. I'm risking my life. I need to be sure I'm not killing an innocent man.'

Sebastian's suspicions were confirmed when the cardinal responded with a pinched, almost apologetic smile. 'There are many things I don't tell you, Sebastian. My work requires a choice – either to lie or not speak. I prefer the latter. Now I'm afraid I have another engagement. So I need an answer. Will you do what has been asked of you?'

It was the weight of Richelieu's face which betrayed him – that pendulous gravitas of a judge pronouncing sentence. It could mean only one thing. The simple fact Sebastian had known from the moment he entered the room – which had never once been mentioned. That refusal meant death. Saint-Simon was a close friend of the King. The cardinal would never allow himself to be connected to the murder. He hadn't summoned him to have a debate. He was giving him a final chance to save his life.

Two minutes later Sebastian left the room, shaking his head with self-disgust. However much he told himself Richelieu had convinced him, he knew it wasn't true. The cardinal had told him nothing of significance. From the moment he stepped into that room, he had been searching for some way to submit. His questions had not been asked out of courage but a desire to believe the cardinal. He was too weak to do otherwise. Richelieu would always be Richelieu and he would always be a dwarf.

Sebastian's unease only grew when he walked back into the hall and saw Saint-Simon smiling benignly, taking the occasional sip of his drink. The man didn't look anything like a Spanish agent. He was a retired soldier, a monument, cracked with age and sprouting tufts. The idea of him posing a threat to France, or indeed anyone, was beyond ridiculous. It felt like having to murder a well-meaning uncle and Sebastian looked away, forcing himself to concentrate on the task at hand.

Matters only became worse when he reached the table. An oaken construction of monstrous proportions, it was thick-beamed and level with his head. He could barely reach the brim, let alone Saint-Simon's glass. Initially he considered poisoning the drink while it was being served but didn't dare risk it for fear of picking the wrong cup, leaving him with only one alternative, to climb up and dispense the poison directly.

Sebastian chose an old routine, where he would hold a fork like a magic wand and pretend to be an ugly fairy with the power to grant warts. It wasn't one of his better acts, but it did allow him to tour the table, visiting each person in turn while bestowing or removing his gifts from increasingly amusing parts of his anatomy. And after clambering up onto the tabletop, he abruptly found himself concealing a vial of poison with a hundred pairs of eyes fixed on him. He felt exposed. Naked. As if each and every one of them knew what he was holding and what he was about to do. Cupping the vial in his left hand, he turned towards the Count of Soissons and muddled through the start of his act. It was enough to raise a chuckle, and he was soon able to progress round the table while all the time the vial sat in his palm, hot and ever-present. As he approached Saint-Simon, he found it impossible to look at the man, and concentrated instead on his cup. Thankfully, it was distinctive – a soldier's tankard, beaten and tarnished pewter which looked out of place among all the silver and glass. However, passing the duke of Anjou, he failed to notice a slick of grease and tumbled to his left.

Instinctively he slapped down an arm to brace himself. It was only then that he thought of the vial. Fortunately, a quick check revealed it to have remained intact, and looking round, he found himself at almost kissing distance from a bewildered duke. Then, giving the man a quick peck on the cheek to the considerable amusement of his neighbours, he stood up. Saint-Simon was no more than ten feet away, and after taking a few moments to pick up his thread, he turned his attention back to the cup. The act itself was surprisingly simple, a quick misdirection as he pretended to toss a shower of carbuncles in the air with one hand while emptying the vial into the tankard with the other. Much worse was the moment afterwards, those few sharp seconds as he remained frozen, staring down at the tabletop, listening to the hub-bub from the crowd and hearing his own death in every raised voice. But the chatter continued, and after reassuring himself that his crime had passed unnoticed, he drew the

111

performance to a close. Then, after bowing briefly and the usual round of scattered applause, he retreated as quickly as he had arrived.

Nevertheless, the ordeal was only half-complete. In spite of his desperation to escape, Sebastian knew better than to flee. Being seen leaving the hall just as the concoction took effect would be unwise in the extreme. Instead he tried to look inconspicuous while occupying his churning mind as best he could: counting the flies angling around the candelabra, calculating the number of chairs, the height of the ceiling and any other distractions within eyeshot. In between he would glance across at his victim, who continued his meal, unaware that he was already dead. However, the poison acted more slowly than he had anticipated, and ten minutes passed before Saint-Simon turned red in the face and began to splutter. Sebastian stared at him, transfixed, and time slowed as he watched, acutely aware of each and every moment: Saint-Simon grabbing his tankard, lifting it to his lips, the look of confusion as he felt it take effect, then the tranquillity of expression as he began to tire and weaken, sinking back into his seat as he entered his death throes … and then inexplicably leaned forward and took another sip of his drink before turning to his neighbour and resuming his conversation. Sebastian continued to stare, scrutinising the man with great intensity as he stubbornly continued not to die. Quite the opposite. Instead he appeared most content with life and looked about the table with the serene appearance of someone who knows his hard work is done and his rest well-earned, occasionally interjecting some bon-mot of military wit. There was no sign of discomfort, no choking or coughing, not even a reddening of the face.

Sebastian felt the vial, still warm in his left hand. Turning to face the wall, he inspected it. There was still some liquid at the bottom, and after a few moments' further examination, he tipped out the remains – three shivering droplets on his palm. He stared at them intently, sifting their translucence for colour, then sniffing for any sign of perfume, but to no avail. Glancing up at the balcony, he noticed Ambroise leaning over the balustrade, eating some pastry with a vacuous stare. He seemed bored, as though he was passing time rather than waiting for something to happen. Sebastian flinched as if slapped and choked back a scream.

Furious and cursing his stupidity, he strode up the steps as fast as he could manage before marching straight to Ambroise. His face was knotted with anger – locked so tight he could barely force out the words.

'Damn your eyes, that wasn't poison.'

Ambroise responded with a wide and braying laugh.

'You looked bloody terrified. Never seen anyone do it that way before.'

Sebastian flung the empty vial at Ambroise. 'I thought I was going to die, of course I was bloody terrified.'

'Don't be annoyed, what do you expect? We need to know you're loyal.'

'You lied to me, you bastard.'

'Yes, I lied, the cardinal lied, we all lie. You're in the King's court, my friend. We don't come here for amusement. We come for glory and money and we say whatever we have to.' Ambroise shrugged and retrieved the bottle from the floor.

'And if they saw me poisoning him? I could have been killed.'

'It's happened before. They would have made you drink the cup, nothing more.'

Sebastian hissed out a sigh of displeasure ... but also resignation. Ambroise was a hard man to be angry at. He meant no harm. Life was easy and simple to him. Like the pet of some wealthy master, he spent his days lying around and gorging himself, his only requirement to follow the occasional basic command.

'In any event,' Ambroise finished. 'I don't see what you're so concerned about. It's over. You wanted to serve the Chief Minister of France and now you do. Don't complain, rejoice.'

Ascent

(1637)

Sebastian had chosen the hour well. As he began his climb up Montmartre, the hill was deserted, silent apart from an indistinct chorus of fox and dog. Wrapping his cloak tight about him to keep out the cold, he plodded upwards to the rhythm of his panting breath. The moon was full and as he rose he could see Paris in the distance. Apart from its thin band of protecting wall, above which rose the silhouette of Notre Dame and the spire of Saint-Germain-des-Prés, he could distinguish nothing. Instead the different geometries of rich and poor merged into something that more closely resembled an eerie and tangled wood.

Monsieur Marchant's house was located halfway up, set apart from the abbey surrounds. Like its owner, it was respectable but not ostentatious, three narrow storeys of brick with bow windows overlooking the path. More interesting, however, were the five sacks of coal outside the back door, all lined up and ready to be taken in. One was even half-full, as though left especially for him.

Taking out enough coal to conceal himself, Sebastian squeezed inside the sack before covering himself with the remaining lumps. While restrictive, it was not uncomfortable, provided he took care not to disturb the dust that seemed to collect in every nook and cranny, particularly the nose and throat. It might have proved considerably more unpleasant had he been left there for longer than he was, but only fools left provisions out in the open, no matter how early the hour, and less than ten minutes had passed before he was lifted up, carried through a doorway and inside. Another door opened and he felt himself being heaved down a flight of stairs, then dropped summarily on a hard floor. A pair of feet shuffled into the distance and he emerged shortly afterwards to find himself in a cellar.

His next problem was finding some way into the master's room. The first floor seemed most likely, assuming he wouldn't want to walk up more than one flight of steps; and, after sneaking upstairs, Sebastian found himself confronted by three doors – all identical. Unsure which to try, he eased open the nearest and peeked inside, terrified he was going to find a pair of furious eyes glaring back at him – only to discover a pile of linen instead. The next door revealed a snug room, floored with matting, with a mullion window, warm hearth and thick walls to keep out the cold. More interesting was the figure asleep on a low four-poster bed, clearly identifiable from the prominent mole on his lower lip – Monsieur Marchant. Slipping inside, Sebastian closed the door carefully and searched for a hiding place. A cupboard stood on the far wall, offering a reasonable view of the room (albeit restricted by the four-poster) and he immediately wriggled beneath it.

His main memory of the following few hours was the smell of coal – omnipresent and so strong that he feared Marchant would notice. It remained a constant distraction, so much so that he found it hard to concentrate on what the man was doing. Not that there seemed to be a great deal worth concentrating on – he did nothing to indicate the fraud of which Richelieu accused him and instead Sebastian had to endure an hour of watching an old and sagging tax-collector eat breakfast then walk round naked, scraping himself clean. Then, after combing his beard, putting on his wig and dressing himself, Marchant finally left the room.

First taking a few moments to consume the remaining scraps of the man's breakfast (a crust of bread and some quail, both flavoured with a distinct tint of anthracite), Sebastian spent the remainder of the day searching the room and stealing what provisions he could from the kitchen downstairs. However, after emptying every drawer, and examining every surface and cubbyhole, he found nothing – not even under the carpet. He began to wonder if he had made the right choice, if it wouldn't have been better to follow Marchant as he carried out his daily rounds? Then he dismissed the idea. Aside from the fact he could hardly keep pace with the man, it didn't seem likely he would reveal his hand in public. Better a private place, and where more private than his bedroom? Besides, it seemed probable he would keep his valuables somewhere in his house, safe within reach.

It was three o'clock when Marchant returned. Sebastian only heard him as he grasped hold of the door handle. Thankfully he was near the cupboard and had just enough time to scrabble beneath. The man's guilt was plain to see from the moment he entered the room – the way he closed the door and locked it, meticulous and without making a sound. Stealing across to the bookshelf, he took hold of the end and slid it to one side. Then, reaching down, he pulled up a plank – from beneath which he retrieved a small ledger. Suddenly there was a voice outside and Marchant glanced round, startled. Nothing to worry about, though. Just the servant come to inform him the cheesemonger had arrived. Dismissing the man with a swift 'I'll be down shortly', he waited a moment before walking to the desk. Adding a new entry to the ledger, he drew a pouch from his pocket and carefully counted out five gold coins, taking considerable pleasure in the act. Then, placing both gold and ledger back in their hiding place, he returned the bookshelf to its former position, unlocked the door and left.

Now Sebastian's task was simple. And, after retrieving the book and a few coins, he slipped out of the door and down the stairs, intent on returning to the Palais-Cardinal as quickly as possible. Then, just as he turned into the hallway, he found himself facing an emaciated footman with a slick of brown hair. He stared at the servant, acutely aware of the ledger thrust prominently down the front of his doublet. The footman didn't seem to notice, gazing back with that look of repulsed fascination that he had come to know all too well, before thinking to ask who he was.

'Chimney-sweep.' Sebastian shrugged, almost dismissive. It seemed to make sense, considering the coal-dust and his diminutive proportions. Thankfully the servant, like so many before, showed no further interest, not thinking to ask why he had no tools or indeed giving him a further glance.

It wasn't to be the only time his size would prove of use. People never seemed to notice him and he overheard things others didn't. He could hide in the tiniest spaces, inside a chest or on top of an armoire. Occasionally he had to stoop to going through bins or stealing the post, but generally avoided such methods, finding them to entail considerable effort for little result.

The work was satisfying, at least to begin with. Success was not a sensation he was used to, and he felt an unfamiliar sense of importance, even power. He was, after all, influencing the fate of France, if only at its fringes. There was novelty too, as well as the opportunity to send his mother a few extra sous at the end of each month, and he worked with the enthusiasm of the new recruit, determined to prove himself and undertaking assignments without giving thought to the risks involved.

* * *

Mostly Sebastian was sent in pursuit of valuables of one kind or another, sometimes Spanish coin, more often unpaid tax or contraband. Tonight was no exception. A ring of Bretons had been smuggling untaxed goods from the coast to Paris. A few of them had been caught but the leader, known as *La Cravate* due to his penchant for tying a blue handkerchief round his neck (and discarding it when the time came to hide), remained at large. The man was notoriously secretive, restricting his meetings only to close friends and private places. There was a particular location he favoured – a small tavern, owned by a friend. In the back room of which an agent had discovered a small cabinet; reporting to the cardinal that it might be suitable for a person 'of particularly narrow proportions'.

Now Sebastian was behind that very cabinet, squeezed breathless as his cheek was pressed against the wood. At first he had assumed he would become used to hiding in small spaces. But he had not – if anything it became worse. Each time he dreaded it; concealing himself, compressed in some dark corner while thinking of all the occasions he had been in the same position before – always certain that this night would be his last.

The only thing which sustained him was the prospect of release. When, having heard each and every word they said, every name and every crime, when they had damned themselves utterly, he would finally be able to wriggle free. And that sense of accomplishment when he would walk out into the night, parched with thirst and dripping sweat, knowing his work was complete – for the time being, at least.

* * *

In spite of his initial fear of the cardinal, Sebastian came to admire him more as the months went by. Richelieu's mind was meticulous, logical and astonishing at storing detail, but lacking any spark of imagination or creativity. Information went in, was analysed and then dispensed with. He never spoke in metaphors or told jokes, except of the driest sort. Imagination was by nature a distortion of the truth and therefore a waste of time.

However, it was Richelieu's discipline and concentration which impressed Sebastian most. His capacity for work seemed near infinite, and he was forever meeting people, planning, signing documents or issuing orders. Sleep was a luxury and Sebastian became used to being summoned at ungodly hours to find the cardinal in full regalia, either having just woken or still completing the previous day. To begin with, he assumed it was simple ambition, but over time he noticed that the cardinal applied the same dedication to whatever he did, whether fussing over the plans for his town of Richelieu or simply arranging a feast for the King. And after a while Sebastian concluded it was conviction – an unshakeable and probably justified belief in his own worth.

Sebastian liked to think the respect was mutual, at least to some degree. Whenever they met, Richelieu found time to talk, and after issuing his commands, he would invariably digress onto a book, philosopher or even the affairs of state. Montaigne was always popular, hailed for his sense of understanding of what it is to live. Ovid also, though for his language rather than his philosophy. Oddly the cardinal showed less enthusiasm for religious works, doubtless having been overexposed to them at seminary. He always seemed interested in Sebastian's opinion, though invariably struggled not to interrupt with his own. Not that Sebastian minded; it didn't even concern him that Richelieu was probably flattering him, indulging him to ensure loyalty. After all, a man doesn't become Chief Minister of France without being able to manipulate and control.

The only difficult moment came when Sebastian asked if the cardinal would consider being his patron. He had spent much of the previous year rewriting his play and finally felt it ready. Perhaps no great work, but perfect in its way – crafted to the bone, precisely structured and clear in intent – certainly good enough for outside eyes. When he happened to mention it to the cardinal, Richelieu immediately expressed an interest and asked if he could see the manuscript. Naturally Sebastian was delighted to oblige, only to find he had condemned himself to a week of agonising over his master's response.

His next meeting with the cardinal took place in the antechamber adjoining the library. A model of his village of Richelieu, which the cardinal was inspecting with great interest, dominated the room. The model was perfectly rendered – square-walled, with gatehouses on each side, overshadowed by an ornate chateau and grounds. However, for all its immaculate detail, it was only half-finished – the castle semi-complete and without symmetry, more romantic ruin than fortress. There were gaps as well, conspicuous spaces between the townhouses from the hundred and sixteen plots that even the cardinal's offer of tax exemption had proved unable to fill. The overall effect was that of a fairy tale, a tumbledown castle overlooking a hamlet strewn across the snow.

Sebastian's attention, however, was focused entirely on the leather wallet in Richelieu's right hand. This fact did not go unnoticed by the cardinal.

'Your play, of course.' He nodded, returning the manuscript.

Sebastian took it, his eyes fixed on Richelieu. 'Does it meet your favour?' The vibrato in his voice betrayed his nerves.

'It's excellent. A really fine work. You have considerable talent.' Richelieu spoke taut-lipped, his solemnity of expression at odds with his praise. Sebastian knew full well what was about to follow.

'You'll pay for it to be performed?'

'I'm afraid not.'

'I don't understand.'

'You are a gifted satirist, Sebastian. But how can you expect me to support something that ridicules the state – however exquisitely?'

'I could change it, perhaps–'

Richelieu cut him off. 'Sebastian, excuse me for being blunt. While I recognise your abilities, you need to understand that not everyone can see beyond your size. By patronising you, I would be risking ridicule, and a man of my stature cannot be made a mockery of. Besides, it's not to my benefit. You're a good agent, I want you finding information – not idling away your days in the theatre. You'd be no use to me – or France for that matter.'

Sebastian looked away in an effort to conceal his disappointment. Richelieu, uncomfortable with emotion, grimaced and patted his own forehead as if trying to brush away something unpleasant. 'I understand your frustration, Sebastian. But your purpose is to be a buffoon. Like those two associates of yours, Jerome and ...' He paused and looked across at Sebastian.

'Claude.'

'Yes ... Claude. It already bothers me that you bring too much attention to yourself with that tongue of yours. You're meant to make a fool out of yourself, not other people.'

'Absolutely ... I understand.' Sebastian's tone was dutiful rather than sincere.

'You clearly have objections. Voice them.'

'My body causes me enough difficulties ... Must you take my mind as well? You are asking me not to be myself.'

'This is self-indulgence.' The cardinal shook his head. 'You ceased to be yourself from the moment you began working for me. That is what an agent does. He is not there to write plays, or be known for his wit or repartee. His purpose is to be anonymous, to not attract suspicion, to make others drop their guard.'

'Of course, Your Eminence.' The cardinal noticed Sebastian cast a sour glance at the model. The reason was not lost on him. He was asking someone else to let their name fade into posterity while building an entire town to carry his own.

'It's true.' He nodded. 'To ask you to make sacrifices in the face of such extravagance is unfair, I won't deny it. Just because I don't permit you the sentiment, it doesn't mean I don't share it. It's something we all aspire to – to be remembered.'

*　*　*

When the footman mentioned the word 'cabinet', Sebastian already knew its importance. He associated it with waiting: *the cardinal must not be disturbed as he is in his cabinet* or *a meeting in his cabinet has overrun and he will be delayed*. It seemed a mythical place. Somewhere that was spoken about but he would never see. He had no idea where the room actually was, though he imagined it to be on the top floor, some shadowed hall lined with faceless tomes, where secret papers, charters and the seal were kept in great chests. A place where all the cardinal's most surreptitious business was conducted, his sanctuary from the world.

The reality was somewhat different, and he found himself being led into a chamber that appeared little more than a cubicle, locked away behind a stateroom in the core of the building. The only light came from a single candelabra, and Sebastian could just make out the honeycomb of niches lining the walls and the cardinal lying on a small bed in the centre, reminiscent of a queen in her hive. He was propped up with pillows while an assistant passed him a stream of papers taken from random piles stacked across the floor. Not noticing Sebastian, he flicked through the documents and issued commands, ordering for various papers to be returned or filed or discarded as required.

Despite frequent announcements that the cardinal was unwell, Sebastian had always assumed they were simply excuses to avoid attending ceremonies and events of state. But this was no pretence. In the flicker of the candlelight, he resembled a corpse, his yellowed skin scaled and peeling and his hair lank with sweat, as he peered at the pages as if practically blind.

'Yes, I'm a sick man. We're more alike than we might first appear,' Richelieu croaked, looking up and observing Sebastian's shocked expression. 'I know what it's like for your body to be a curse. All my life I've suffered migraines, toothache, fevers ... ulcers, haemorrhoids, rheumatism. I may be one of the most powerful men in the land but I haven't been able to piss in two days.'

'Please don't refer to me as cursed, my Lord. Remember I don't look small through my eyes.'

'My apologies, I don't mean to cause offence. It's a compliment. I know how hard you have to fight.'

'There is hope of your condition improving,' a voice interrupted from the shadow.

'It hasn't improved in twenty years; I don't see why God should favour me now. Besides, it doesn't matter. Adversity makes us stronger. When all you've known are difficulties, you lose your fear of them. It's my ability to fight, to resist my urges that has given me everything I have. People say my fingers reach into every corner of France. They don't understand. I have power over nothing but myself – or at least what my body allows me. It is not through control that I have become a cardinal, but self-control.' Richelieu was speaking in a strained voice, glaring upwards, taut-faced. It occurred to Sebastian that his infamously cold manner wasn't intentional but rather the result of having to conceal perpetual and excruciating pain.

'Cardinal, you only have yourself to blame. As I've told you on repeated occasions, you must rest. You cannot continue to work like this.' The doctor's words were half-hearted. He knew he would be ignored but spoke up all the same.

'I am resting, doctor. I find peace in my work.' The cardinal turned back to Sebastian. 'I don't believe you've ever seen my cabinet.'

'No…it's plainer than I expected.'

'I don't like distraction when I think. Anyway, I've something important to show you.' Richelieu motioned his secretary to pick up a bundle of cloth from a nearby table. The assistant held it aloft then released the material – only to reveal what appeared to be a wrinkled calico sheet.

'I don't understand.'

'It belongs to the Queen,' Richelieu replied curtly, as if this would explain everything.

Sebastian flinched – and there was reason for it. A long circulated rumour that the cardinal had once declared his love for the Queen and been rejected. He had always claimed it was politeness misconstrued, but nobody believed him, not even Sebastian, who was now looking at the Queen's dirty linen with considerable embarrassment. Richelieu, however, remained too agitated to notice his discomfort.

'Don't you see? It's immaculate. The King and Queen aren't sleeping together.'

Sebastian shrugged. It seemed a statement of the obvious. The whole court knew Louis and Anne barely had anything to do with each other. Frankly it was a miracle they were still married. They had nothing in common. She lived a spindrift existence, following the wind with her gaggle of ladies-in-waiting, blind to the dangers of court. He, in contrast, was deeply serious, bound by his conscience and sense of justice, forever playing king. And it seemed to Sebastian that Louis' outrage at her miscarriage had only been a pretext to end a relationship that was already long-doomed.

'Don't you understand? France needs an heir,' Richelieu snapped, irritated by Sebastian's indifference. His voice was sparse and fired by certainty. 'From the day he was born, Louis has had above all one purpose. That purpose which falls on all kings – to continue his line. Without a successor, our country will tear itself apart. Thousands will die. This isn't just a sheet, it's the future of the realm.'

'What about Gaston? He's Louis' brother. Wouldn't he inherit?'

Richelieu gave a thin laugh. 'Gaston? He's reckless, a *bon vivant*. Able, perhaps, but far too weak. He's already botched two plots against the King – and been exiled twice. Hardly a record that augurs success. The man wants power but no responsibility. Who wants to be ruled by someone who can barely make it out of the brothel? Besides, even if he did become king, he'd never hold power, or at least only under the boot of Spain. Gaston's a distraction. The Queen needs a son.'

'I don't see how you can ask more of her. She's already had four and they all died.'

Richelieu considered the reply a moment, then ignored it. 'She must keep trying. She writes letters to her brother. I need them.'

'Her brother?'

'Philip of Spain.'

'I'm not quite sure I understand. How can you be sure about something you've never seen?'

'I don't need to see the letters.' The cardinal's voice was sharp with impatience. Fever had made him emotional and he had the consumptive eyes of a zealot. 'The woman is Spanish and staunchly Catholic – of course she writes to her family.'

'Even so, how can you be sure they're so incriminating if you don't know what's in them?'

'Philip's name will be quite enough. Now have you finished asking questions?' Sebastian knew better than to reply and after a pointed pause, the cardinal moved on. 'I've had her rooms searched, both here and in Saint-Germain. They found nothing, not even sealing wax. I think she's writing them in the Val-de-Grâce. She knows I can't go into a convent, and those nuns will do anything for her. No wonder, considering what she pays them.'

'How do you expect me to get into a convent?'

'I don't.' Then Richelieu turned to his secretary and requested paper, quill and ink. The assistant returned with a special tray, which slotted into the bedframe over the cardinal's lap, laying out the materials in neat order. Lifting himself upright, the cardinal proceeded to compose two brief introductions. As with everything he did, his work was meticulous, each letter perfectly distinct. For all his fastidiousness, he wrote quickly and without pause. After which he folded the pages, then applied wax and seal before handing them to Sebastian. One was addressed to the Queen, the other to her lady-in-waiting, Marie de Chevreuse.

'These should be sufficient to get you an audience. I doubt you'll see anything incriminating in plain sight, but look for signs or clues – maybe a place they mention … and beware of Chevreuse.'

Sebastian didn't need telling. He knew the name well enough. The courtiers always spoke of her in hushed tones, not as they did of others. Even the King referred to her rather sarcastically as 'the messiah'. Sebastian had heard the cardinal mention her a few times in passing, invariably followed by a hesitation and that slightly stiff expression he used when repressing strong emotion. It was obvious why. Whenever there was unrest at court, she was sure to be at the heart of it. Despite being married to the Duc de Chevreuse, she cheated on him repeatedly, though it wasn't her lovers that she was known for but what happened to them subsequently. Both Châteauneuf and the Comte de Chalais had ended up on the scaffold because of her. Her taste for traitors had also extended to Gaston and even an Englishman, apparently a close friend of the Duke of Buckingham. On top of this, she had been behind at least two attempts to overthrow the King. Even her family had disowned her and hadn't visited court in upwards of twenty years. Despite all this, or perhaps because of it, Sebastian was intrigued by the prospect of meeting her – much more so than the Queen – partly because of her beauty, but mostly the danger. She had the same mystique that the cardinal had possessed before he first met him, that lethal fascination of a spider or a snake.

* * *

Anne de Bourbon, Queen of France, Infanta of Spain and Portugal, Archduchess of Austria and Princess of Burgundy and the Low Countries stood on the balcony of the Château Neuf. Leaning over the balustrade, she looked out over the terraced gardens of carnations, violets and jasmine. Beyond them lay the Seine valley and forests of Marly, a patch of dark green fringing the horizon. She loved Saint-Germain every bit as much as she loathed Paris. The land, forest and open sky reminded her of Spain. Childhood days spent wandering the El Escorial with her brothers and sisters, horse-riding in the sierra, following trails through forests of chestnut and beech. Afternoons cooling in the cloisters and the gardens, devising games and word puzzles as they sheltered from the heat.

Her reverie was interrupted by a discreet cough from a footman, who presented her with a letter from the cardinal. Reluctantly she opened it, expecting a command to return to Paris, couched in the most polite and deferential terms. Richelieu was always careful to show obedience, never giving orders and forever using the King's name to disguise his own. False humility was one of his many repellent qualities. He meant to seem humble but it was blatantly political, no more than a charade so Louis could continue deluding himself that he still ruled France. Yet, despite her reservations, the letter turned out to be a simple note of introduction. One of the cardinal's representatives had arrived to discuss 'a matter of some importance'. And, after a moment's consideration, she asked the footman to admit him.

She anticipated an emissary, resplendent in embroidered livery and with a character as bloodless as his master's. Instead she was astonished to see a bearded and surly-faced dwarf, still dusty from the road, who bowed and presented himself in what seemed a mockery of protocol.

Having never seen the Queen at close quarters, Sebastian's only recollections were from a distance – a faraway sun, static and luminescent, around whom dandies and ladies twirled in orbit before being granted the briefest of audiences and moving on. However, the first thing he noticed wasn't her face, but her hands. He had heard of their beauty but never believed it. One hand had always seemed much like another to him. Up close he had to concede the rumour was true. They were ivory-skinned, without any hint of the Mediterranean, the fingers languorous, delicate and intensely feminine, the wrists accentuated with turquoise bracelets. Captivated, he stared before remembering the head above. When he did eventually look up, it was not a welcoming sight – instead a straight-backed figure, hands on hips, her face pursed with indignation.

'I have seen you before. You are one of those dwarfs at court.' She spoke with the curt, stilted speech of someone foreign-born. 'Explain yourself. Why is Richelieu sending some half-man to speak to me? Is this a joke? Is he mocking me?'

Sebastian blanched and stepped backwards. It was distressing enough to be faced by a queen, doubly so an angry one. He had no idea of the correct response and bumbled desperate apologies.

'Your Majesty, I'm sorry if my presence displeases you and I promise the cardinal intended no offence. My size is not meant to insult. It was God's choice, not mine.'

'The cardinal chose to send you nonetheless.'

'I assure you his intentions were honourable. He required someone to discuss your … marital relations with the King. He wanted the conversation to be as discreet as possible, so he chose me. I do not mix with the nobles of court.'

His answer seemed to placate her and her scowl softened. Then she conceded the slightest of nods.

'Very well.' A trace of Spanish remained in her v's. She did her best to hide it, but her lips couldn't quite stop rounding them into b's. 'What do you want from me?'

'The cardinal has observed your lack of relations with the King. He is concerned and worries there will be war if France does not have an heir.'

'He is concerned? What about me? You think I am happy? I love my husband. I want him to share my bed, I want to have his children. It is him you need to talk to. He despises me. I try to make him happy: I wear French clothes, I dismiss my Spanish ladies-in-waiting – women I have known since I was a girl. I put up with his favourites and his … appetites. It makes no difference. All he wants to talk about are his wars or the petitions he has received. I try to show interest but everything I say disgusts him. What makes you think my marital *relations*,' she spat the word, 'have anything to do with me?'

'I'm sorry, Your Majesty. I'm simply a messenger. Please be assured I know you're doing everything you can—'

'Do not insult me with your pity,' she interrupted. 'Go and tell your master the truth. It is perfectly simple. I love my husband but he does not love me. The fact is our marriage died a long time ago and all I have left are a few happy memories which become more distant with every day that goes by. I did not choose this situation, neither do I know anyone who would. I am trapped with a man who doesn't want me – a queen without a king.' She paused a beat. 'Now I have told you what you need to know, so leave.'

Sebastian hesitated, obliged to comfort her yet knowing it to be impossible. Then he observed her eyebrows drawing into a frown and realised his delay was being interpreted as further impudence.

In his hurry to depart, he almost turned around before remembering to shuffle backwards until out of sight, continuing his retreat long after the Queen had returned to the view, evidently keen to forget the conversation as quickly as possible.

Reaching the sanctuary of the adjoining room, Sebastian was about to leave when he detected an absence. Looking round, he took a moment to discern what it was – people. Checking more carefully this time, he confirmed there was no one in sight. The footman appeared to have left, presumably to his post by the front step. He had the palace completely to himself, for now at least. It seemed too good an opportunity to waste. Noticing an open door nearby, he peeped round. No good. It looked like a parlour of some kind. Far too public.

If she was concealing something, it would be somewhere private and out of the way. A reading room or study, perhaps? He crept down the corridor, peering through each crack and keyhole in turn. First a library, followed by a garde-robe and a ballroom which seemed to run most of the length of the corridor. Then, rounding the corner, he found himself in what appeared to be servants' quarters and instead tried a different passage, which led into an older area of the palace, stone-walled and draped with tapestries. Suddenly a noise, close by – the clack of approaching footsteps.

Sebastian's first instinct was to talk his way out of the situation but then he thought the better of it. He was on completely the wrong side of the building. It would be obvious what he was doing. He needed to hide and quickly. Looking round, he couldn't work out where the sound was coming from and scampered up a nearby flight of stairs to the upper landing, crouching by the baluster, from where he saw a group of ladies-in-waiting pass by. He remained frozen, holding the spindle as he listened to their chatter fade down the corridor. Then he became aware of a most peculiar scent – distinctly feminine, at odds with the surrounding scent of aging oak.

Looking behind him, he could see a door in pearwood, its lintel carved with fruited vines – their leaves so delicately wrought that they appeared soft to the touch. Approaching, he could detect the smell more clearly. Years of creams, unguents, and soaps built up layer on layer. A mix of jasmine, lavender, rosewater and vetyver that both repelled and attracted, its deep-soaked perfume heady and intimate. But also private, enough to make Sebastian acutely aware of the danger he was in. This was the Queen's bedchamber. There could be no explaining what he was doing beyond that door. He would be cut down where he stood.

Sebastian continued to stare, motionless. The door was ajar, enough to reveal what appeared to be an empty chamber behind. It was a terrifying prospect but also irresistible, and he knew he would never get the chance again. Taking another glance around the hallway, he inched forward and slipped through the door. Then, closing it carefully behind him, he turned to find himself inside a waiting room of sorts. After skimming through the dresser and a side table, he examined the adjoining chamber, which proved equally unremarkable. However, it was the closed door beyond which caught his interest, and he crept closer, bending down and then pressing his ear to the wood. Unable to hear anything over the beat of his heart, he took some time before feeling confident of the silence beyond. Drawing himself up, he placed one hand on the latch as if steadying himself to lift a heavy load. Next, and with a sharp exhale, he pressed with closed eyes, letting the door fall away under its own weight. Holding his breath, he tensed, waiting for a scream or cry. But none came. He squinted at the room in front of him. It was dazzlingly bright, walled almost entirely in a sparkling cloth of gold that made the ornate furniture seem drab by comparison. He stood in the doorway, transfixed, feeling as if he had wandered across some genie's cave or lost hoard. Jewelled bodices were draped over the backs of fluted chairs, while bracelets, diadems and necklaces were scattered across a dresser inlaid with ivory and tortoiseshell. At its centre stood a jewellery box that more closely resembled a treasure chest.

Eventually Sebastian was able to take his eyes off the

splendour long enough to notice the escritoire in the corner. Using a piece of charcoal he kept for such occasions, he immediately took a rubbing of the blotter. His efforts, however, revealed nothing more than a few invitations and brief replies. A search of the cubbyholes uncovered some loose correspondence and he was midway through deciphering a letter to a lady-in-waiting when he heard a whisper in his ear.

Jolting upright, Sebastian turned round. But there was nothing there. Then he heard the voice again. Curious. It didn't sound surprised or angry or as if it had noticed him at all. Bewildered, he remained frozen. It was only then that he noticed the open window. Of course! It was just the babble of conversation from the parterre outside. Still panting from the shock, he took a last glance at the dresser and then departed as swiftly as possible. There was no point continuing. Searching the palace was pointless: too many rooms, too many hiding places – impossible for any one man, twice as hard for him. There was nothing else for it. He would have to meet Chevreuse.

* * *

Marie de Chevreuse's house stood on a nameless street off the Rue de Grenelle, only a few minutes from the Louvre. Sebastian was grateful for the shortness of the walk. It was high summer and the dung in the streets was at its ripest, releasing a stink that both turned the stomach and stifled the breath. He, along with most of the court, was reduced to tipping perfume onto his handkerchief and keeping it pressed to his nose, while trying to waft away the swarms of flies attracted to his mouth and eyes. The scent, although still curdled by the reek, remained marginally preferable to the alternative. And at least the heat seemed to have kept the crowds off the streets, for once allowing him to move without enduring the usual clutter of knees and elbows.

As with all parasites, the nobles kept close to their king, and the buildings around the Louvre were inhabited by some of the greatest names of the realm: Lorraine, Montmorency, La Fayette. In spite of all the magnificence, differences still remained. Grand houses that would have been mansions elsewhere were dwarfed beside more extravagant neighbours, often with statuary, cupolas or even flags to announce the owner's presence. Though, for all their wealth, the streets were no less narrow than the rest of the city, the high walls on each side making them seem particularly restrictive. Sebastian had the impression of walking along a gorge, too deep for the sun to reach and with shadows that gave a sense of perpetual dusk. Peering through the thin light, he came across the house more through luck than design. It was three storeys of stone, lined with high windows and topped by a steep gambrel roof. Wide steps pooled down onto the street, bordered on each side by a fat-columned balustrade, their ends both crowned by a classical urn. The only indication of Chevreuse's reputation was the heavy door and barred windows, riveted and reinforced against any unwelcome visitors.

After receiving the customary look of surprise from her steward, Sebastian presented the message from Richelieu. Amused to receive this letter of introduction, the footman took it with a smile, expecting some parody of etiquette. Then he saw the cardinal's signature and his mouth plunged downwards. He immediately became as obsequious as if standing before Richelieu himself.

'Do come in, Your Emin ...' He narrowly managed to cut the sentence short. 'Would you care for a seat while I speak to Her Grace? Perhaps you would like a drink?'

Sebastian declined and waited in the atrium. Instantly he was struck by the lack of ornamentation. While respectable enough, the room was not opulent. The walls were simple panels and there was only one portrait of note, along with a few miniatures. The furniture was equally plain, comprising three chairs, a table and a chest of drawers, topped by two silver candlesticks. Hearing the steward retreat upstairs, he took the opportunity to examine the rooms nearby. Only a few were decorated. Fewer still were furnished and as he walked past, Sebastian could see slits of bare plaster and floorboard through half-open doors.

He returned to the atrium, unsettled. No duchess would ever live in a house like this. People like her flaunted their wealth whether they actually had it or not. Without the image, they were nobody. It had to be a trap. But if it was, then who had devised it? And why? Then came an image of Cinq-Mars waiting in an empty attic, sword in hand, followed by a stab of terror. But he could hear the servant descending the stair. It was already too late.

As the steward led him up to the duchess, Sebastian followed tentatively, leaning backwards, an unwilling body propelled by the legs beneath. On reaching the door, he paused and held his breath before grasping the handle, pulling and walking inside. Immediately he was enveloped by a sodden heat, sapping him of energy and drying his throat.

The brightness was intense, blinding him – a dazzle of gold, tapestry and light in all directions. Dizzy, he sucked in a gulp of air, only to find it soaked with bergamot and helichrysum, a rich and overpowering perfume that smothered whatever sense he had left. Drugged by the scent and befuddled in the glare, he searched for his bearings and saw Chevreuse lazing on a divan. She looked more like a portrait than a person. Attractive, though not as beautiful as her reputation led one to believe, she was groomed and sculpted with an artist's hand. Her make-up was applied expertly, the lips painted into crisp points, the skin smoothed to plaster white, her hair brushed back and fixed tight with a few loose curls left as a fringe. Below, she wore a bodice laced with silver and puffed sleeves slashed with velvet. She looked across at him, reclining aristocratically with a single arm draped over the back of the divan as her dress cascaded onto the floor in a tumult of luxuriant rumples.

'Your house is lovely, Your Grace,' he stammered, filling the silence.

'No it isn't, but it does allow a degree of mobility.'

Sebastian laughed, not so much at the comment as the sound. It was more a river than a voice, slow and comforting, with a rural flow that reminded him of his mother shushing him down. Against every instinct, he found himself warming to her.

'The Queen said you would be coming.' She waved him to the empty chair opposite. Her smile was unusual, tight and with closed lips – feline. 'So, who exactly are you and why are you here?'

Sebastian searched for a response, trying to think through the heat. 'I work at court, for the King. I'm the one who jumps out of the pie on his birthday.' He couldn't suppress a roll of the eyes.

'Yes, I remember you now. You made that play for Cinq-Mars.'

'*For* him?'

'He told me he commissioned it. That it was part of a bet, for rather a large sum of money, so I remember.'

'He may have been exaggerating somewhat.'

'Really? I'm amazed.' She smiled. Her reputation was such that sarcasm was not required.

There was a pause as Sebastian clambered into his seat. It was difficult but he approached it patiently. Adversity was something he had long become inured to: walking up steps, getting into chairs, using the chamber pot, waking up every morning in a world created for other people.

'You still haven't told me why the cardinal sent you.'

'I w ...' Sebastian was just about to say that he worked for the cardinal and checked himself, realising the error. The voice was making him forget himself. It made him feel safe, at ease. He wanted to talk to it, to pour out his hopes and fears, and it was a constant struggle not to surrender to the warmth. Instead he managed to evade as best he could. 'I was told by the cardinal I would be suitable. Because of the subject matter, I mean. I'm discreet and I don't have dealings with the rest of court.'

'And what precisely is this subject matter?'

'The cardinal is worried that the King and Queen aren't sleeping together and the country will be left without an heir.'

'Reasonable enough, I suppose, but it still doesn't explain your presence. The King's sleeping arrangements are no business of mine.'

'You have influence over the Queen. He hoped you might be able to persuade her.'

'She needs no persuasion from me. She loves Louis with all her heart, as you know full well. It's no secret.' Inquisitive, flittering eyes looked out from beneath heavy lids. 'No, that's not why you're here, is it? There's something else.'

'I don't understand, Your Grace. What possible reason would I have to lie?'

'Do you have a habit of avoiding questions?'

'Only when I've no wish to answer them.'

She laughed then plumped her lips. 'But, just between us, tell me why are you here, really?' She murmured the words, leaning forward into an area that bordered on the intimate. Sebastian was delirious, overwhelmed by the heat, her scent and colour and closeness and above all her voice. The words were on the tip of his tongue and he felt the relief of finally being able to unburden himself. Her mouth was so close, her eyes so open. Then he flinched at the thought. It was a dream, and dreams signified hope and hope brought nothing but misery. She didn't care about him. She was using him and he was letting himself be used. Instead, he leaned back in his chair, shook his head and smiled.

'There's a question I've been meaning to ask, if it's not too impertinent, of course. But your dislike of the cardinal, it's well known. I've never understood why you hate him so.'

Sensing resistance, she winced with displeasure. She wasn't used to being refused – least of all by a court dwarf – and when she spoke again, the voice had altered; it was no longer placid, its flow quickening into a sharper pace.

'I would have thought it was quite apparent. The man seeks only power. He's tearing the country apart.'

'You know that's not true. His only wish is to unite France.'

'Oh, I've no doubt of that ... but under whom?'

'The King, of course.'

'And who controls the King?'

Sebastian paused. He knew she was trying to turn him, but struggled to retaliate, deadened by the heat. All his words seemed to be mixing together, the thoughts boiling away before they could form. 'We're at war. We need to pull together if we're going to survive.'

'I'm not questioning the war, simply the cardinal. The man's a monster, can't you see? He's no servant of God, just a blackmailer – pure and simple. That army of spies he has. Everyone's too frightened to speak. Yes, he might be keeping the country together, but only through fear. And what's the point in that? Forcing his rule on people is only going to make them hate it all the more. He's not uniting the country, he's destroying it.'

'I don't see that he has any choice. You earn the people's love through prosperity and peace, not in the middle of a war.'

Chevreuse became ugly with disdain. 'But why fight at all? Why not just put this damned war behind us? The Queen is Philip of Spain's sister. We should be allies ... or consider the prospect at least.'

Sebastian was about to reply that she was blaming the wrong man, that it was the King's war and not the cardinal's, but checked himself instinctively. To insult Richelieu was dangerous, but to insult the King was treason. And so he found himself trapped. With every response, his answers were becoming more contorted as she penned him ever tighter into his corner. He needed to escape it all: the heat, the light, the scent, the voice. To find peace and solitude, to remember who he was. Changing the subject out of desperation, he blurted out the first thing that came to mind – her voice.

'Your accent, it's from Picardy isn't it?' The question was half-hearted and he expected it to be ignored. Her reaction, however, was dramatic. Visibly flustered, she snapped upright and drew her dress around her, wrapping herself in its folds.

'You must be mistaken.' The stream was gabbled, without its former flow. 'I grew up in Brittany. I've visited Picardy only once and then only for two days.'

She was lying. He knew the dialect well, primarily through Père Jean, who had spoken a particularly robust version of it. Incredulous, he asked again. 'Are you sure? You had a governess or childhood friend, perhaps?'

She was not enjoying the conversation and drew it to a rapid close. 'I've already told you, I know nothing of the place. Anyway, I have an appointment with the Duchess de Joyeuse, so I must wish you good day.'

Mystified, he thanked her for her time and left. It seemed a strange thing to be embarrassed about, no more than a rural softness to her vowels. Not that he gave it any thought once he reached the cooling shade of the stairwell. Delighted to be free of the place, he was hardly going to question why.

Outside, in the open air, Sebastian could finally reflect on what had just taken place. Now he understood Richelieu's fear of Chevreuse. The woman possessed a terrifying charm. That one brief moment when she leaned towards him, the closeness of her had been almost narcotic. Even now, recalling the memory, he closed his eyes and breathed in its warmth. The only thing that had saved him was his appearance. If he had been merely ugly rather than grotesque, he might have started to hope – and then he realised why it was he whom Richelieu had chosen to send.

* * *

Sebastian was skulking in a holly bush, trying to avoid prickles and suppress the pain in his thighs. He had been crouched there all morning, observing the Queen from a distance in the hope of some signal or clue. Knowing better than to return to the cardinal with nothing, he had spent much of the previous four days squatting in the dark, peering through keyholes, once even hiding inside a dog kennel. The experience was made worse by the conversation he had to endure: principally the latest fashions, who was in the King's favour, any handsome new faces at court, and who was sleeping with whom. In short, a world that didn't extend beyond the palace walls. At least they were pleasant to look at: so made-up, bewigged and frilled that it felt as if he was watching a play rather than real life, though it was third-rate drama – no more than banal pastiche.

The finale didn't come until that afternoon, when he found a rather more comfortable spot in the Jardin des Tuileries, from where he was able to watch them meander among the rose gardens, pools and elms. Chevreuse and the Queen were both in white taffeta, their long skirts spilling in folds around their feet. As the hours trickled by, his mind began to wander, giving him the peculiar impression that he was staring at angels – the serenity of the gardens, the whiteness of the dresses, the sunbursts through distant cloud above. A tiny Eden, self-contained, where these women idled in fantasy, oblivious to the miles of squalor and dung beyond the palace walls. Then he noticed a detail out of place. All the woman were picnicking and yet Chevreuse hadn't sat down. In fact, she had been standing the whole afternoon. It was a hot day and she was clearly tired, supporting herself on a tree while looking wistfully at the ground, occasionally forgetting herself and bending down before snapping upright again. Something was keeping her on her feet. His first thought was that she was injured, but she didn't appear to be in pain. Besides, if she was hurt, why would she be standing at all? Then he noticed something odd about her dress. The pattern of ripples was irregular, the disturbance of flow like a stone in a stream. It was only late in the day that he realised what it was, when she bent particularly low and he saw a point jut from beneath the fabric. She was hiding something in her petticoats. It was square and flat and the size of a folded sheet of paper. There could be no other explanation. What else would be worth spending an entire day on her feet for?

However, as with many discoveries, it simply gave rise to further questions – principally how to take possession of it. Not only was she a duchess, she was also lady-in-waiting to the Queen. Having her searched was out of the question. Also, considering its location, he had no way of stealing it. The most he could do was follow and hope.

*　*　*

Observing Chevreuse made a pleasant change from crouching in bushes and picking his way through thorns. When not with Anne, she spent almost all her time at her house by the Rue de Grenelle, allowing Sebastian to watch from the comfort of a nearby inn. As she rarely left the house, he was forced to draw his conclusions from her seemingly endless stream of visitors – a ragbag assortment to say the least. Some were male and well dressed – most likely admirers. Others looked shabbier and frayed at the edges – presumably tradesmen or spies. There were women too, a few of whom he recognised from court, as well as numerous servants despatched on chores and tradesmen trying their luck. Once her husband even appeared at the house, though judging by the brevity of the visit it was out of civility rather than love.

Most of the time there was nothing to look at except the building itself. Over time, he came to learn all its quirks. To begin with, it had seemed bland and unoriginal – a cube of square-cut stone. But slowly he started to see varieties in its greys: the darker shades at the base, where the blocks were wetter and sheltered from the bleaching effect of the sun, and the speckling of the topmost floor, which had evidently been mined from a different quarry. There was the lintel over the rightmost, second-storey window – skewed like some lazy eyelid. Most of all he enjoyed the colour of the facade as it changed with the ending of the day, the stones merging from afternoon yellow into sunset pink before the purpling of dusk and the abyssal blue of night.

On the fourth day, a surprise: the Spanish ambassador. Instantly identifiable from his dress and the point of his beard, he was trying to look inconspicuous and had dispensed with the usual coach and regalia. There could only be one reason for his presence. His master had sent him to pick up the letter in person to ensure absolute safety. A wise decision. Anyone else the cardinal could have ordered to be searched, but arresting a diplomat was too dangerous, the repercussions too great. So, having ruled out any chance of obtaining the letter directly, Sebastian decided on the alternative – to follow the clothes that held it, if only to confirm his suspicions before chancing anything too bold.

*   *   *

Winter in Paris was hard, long and cold, but worst of all were the windless days, when the smoke that poured from streetfuls of chimneys would gather into a vast, choking cloud that hung over the city, still in the dead air. The dangers were obvious and people would walk quickly, avoiding strangers and dark places, the fog catching their clothes, its tendrils like grasping fingers losing their grip. Even indoors there was no escape, and the vapour would wisp through cracks and keyholes, suffocating the candles and congealing the air.

Unable to see the house from the inn, Sebastian was forced to wait in the street, holding a handkerchief to his mouth as he gazed out from beneath an eave. The stream of visitors had slowed to a dribble and he spent most of his time shrouded in the half-light, surrounded by high and narrow walls that dissipated into the fog. His world was reduced to sound: the clip of a hoof on cobblestones in distant alleyways, the occasional drunken roar from the tavern, the chittering of invisible birds – all incongruous beside the unchanging nothingness. Unearthly, as though he was already dead and cast into limbo, only able to pick out echoes of the world left behind.

The laundress visited twice weekly, arriving at the side entrance with a handcart piled high with clean, folded clothes. After delivering these inside, she would be rewarded with an equally substantial sack of stinking laundry, which she would then dump back onto her cart before returning the way she had come. Due to the bulky load, she travelled slowly and Sebastian was able to follow at a leisurely pace as she trundled her way down the Rue Saint-Honoré and over the Pont Neuf. It wasn't until they reached the Seine that the view finally opened up before them, the space unfurling as he saw the cloud drifting over the river. Looking up, he had the sense of standing beneath an ocean of air. Cloudy light above, diluting an already muted sun and giving way to undersea yellows and greens before the oily sludge at city bottom, the darkness thickening with the drop. Occasionally he would see the chink of a house, its windows like chewed coral, as the woman struggled onwards, leaning forward as she battled her load. After a long and exhausting hour, she finally reached the Rue des Lavandières and the respite of her hovel, fronted by its washing board and barrel.

Drained from her journey, the woman tipped out the sack by the river, oozing fabric onto the bank, the silks faded in the twilight, broken by the occasional glint from a thread or sequin. Sitting nearby, she rubbed her feet and stared at the river with weary eyes before eventually rousing herself and returning to work, airing the dresses and bodices on a line while stuffing the hosiery to soak in the barrel. He watched them go in item by item: stockings, knickers, chemises and finally petticoats. All were unremarkable and it wasn't until right at the end that he caught a glimpse, a large pocket stitched above the knee and buttoned tight – more than enough to hold a document.

His suspicions confirmed, Sebastian left for the Louvre, eager to escape the street and return to the sanctuary of his room. Then, a few hundred yards beyond the Porte de Nesle, he was distracted by a swirl of movement in the stillness and looked up to see four figures approaching. Something about them seemed familiar, perhaps their shape or voices, or maybe their gait. He continued to squint as he neared but their forms wavered in the murk and he couldn't unpick one from another. Then at the point of recognition he stopped. The lace and the flounce. It could only be Cinq-Mars. What he was doing there, God only knew. Returning from some brothel or card game, no doubt. Alongside him were two friends and he was holding the leash of a large Alaunt. At almost the same time the marquis halted and stared back with incredulous delight. The dog was barking and straining at its lead, a mass of muscle and teeth. A second or so passed before the inevitable.

Cinq-Mars glanced down at the dog and then released it. The animal bolted forward at speed and Sebastian ran for the one visible shelter, a time-riddled shack by the river wall with a splintered but closable door. Within a few strides, he realised he wasn't going to reach it; the creature was virtually on him and his only hope was to grab something to hand. Noticing a broken rod in the dirt, he snatched it just as the dog crashed into him. Managing to deflect the blow, he ducked and fended the creature off as best he could, stabbing and screaming defiance, only for the stick to snap after a couple of thrusts. Then, as he turned to run, the dog knocked him over. He could feel its heat on his body as it lunged for his neck. Rolling away, he flailed for something to protect himself, grabbing a shard of wood and swinging in a wild arc. The response was immediate, a piercing yelp and spurt of wetness on his face. Opening his eyes, he caught a flash of thrashing head and an eye leaking muck, which rapidly disappeared somewhere to his right. Stunned, he stared at the empty space left behind before hearing the yell of approaching voices and remembering Cinq-Mars. Instantly he scrambled upright and fled – not once looking back.

The fog turned out to be his saviour. In daylight he would never have had a chance, but in the gloom it was impossible to follow even someone as slow as him, and after zigzagging across the street, behind a building, down an alleyway and beneath the third wagon to his right, he waited, panting and trying not to cough as the putrid air lodged in his throat. Then, after twenty minutes of dreading every passing foot-step, he felt his fear subside into relief and finally boredom. And so, with a final check of the surrounds, he nosed his way back out onto the cobbles, taking a long detour back to the palace, just in case.

*　*　*

Checking the letter was still safe in its pocket, Marie de Chevreuse took her seat beside the Queen for dinner. Exhausted from standing all day, she cursed her feet and forced a smile. The Comte de Soissons was staring at her again. He was handsome enough but she wasn't in the mood. Too tired to speak, she closed her eyes and listened to the conversation around her. It was nothing new – snatches of yesterday's rumours interspersed with the odd, cheap quip. At least there was entertainment to provide some distraction: first the acrobats and tumblers, followed by the dancers, then the dwarfs. Finally, a magician, who went around the table performing card tricks and making various items disappear.

The food was endless: pottages thick with meat and barley, quail, swan, blackbird, plates piled high with fruit, printed jellies, creamed fish that had been moulded into a gigantic fleur-de-lis, the usual profusion of sausage and black pudding, and a swollen capon, dripping juice. All of which she picked her way through, brushing away the flies and moths, finally making her excuses and escaping for some fresh air. It was only upon standing up that she sensed something was wrong. She could feel a breeze on her shins and thighs, an unexpected chill. Instinctively she reached for the letter and felt nothing. Then she looked down at the pocket and saw a slash of beige running down the front of her dress, flaring at the hem. Mystified, she prodded tentatively with a forefinger. The material yielded to the touch, widening until she could see the petticoat beneath. It was then she realised the cloth had been slit from top to bottom. She fled, horrified, to a nearby room, slamming the door behind her before scrabbling her way through her skirts, pulling them apart like petals down to the final layer where the pocket hung, buttonless and empty, a limp square of cloth. It was gone.

*　*　*

After leaving the dinner table, Marie de Chevreuse retired to the Queen's apartments, pale and tear-stained. She began by undressing, removing every reminder of what had happened and leaving a trail of splintered colour across the floor. Then, once she had scrubbed herself down, she put a drop of belladonna in each eye and dyed her hair with orris root. Ruffling through the wardrobe, she opted for defiance, a blaring skirt of red organza topped by a silver bodice. As she looked at herself in the mirror, a different woman stared back at her, and she puckered her lips into a kiss and examined herself from a variety of angles. Once satisfied, she called for a footman. The door opened a few moments later.

'The dwarf who performed tonight – bring him to me,' she commanded without looking round.

She had enough time to try on a short, pleated ruff and read an overlong and turgid letter from her husband before the footman returned and announced that Sebastian Morra had arrived.

Still dressed in the same harlequin costume from his act, the dwarf looked ridiculous – a sour-faced monstrosity. Worse still, he didn't have the decency to look guilty and stared her in the eye. Instructing the servant to leave with a curt thank you, Chevreuse waited for the door to close before making her fury apparent. When the change came, it was stark, her arms locked and lips twisted into a sneer.

'I know it was you.' Her voice had lost all its charm. Now the words were guttural, bubbled from the dregs of her stomach.

'I'm sorry, Your Grace. I've no idea what you're talking about. If you could perhaps enlighten me ...'

She shook her head. 'Don't waste my time. You think I didn't notice you skulking around all through the second course.'

'I still have no idea what you mean.'

'Nobody else could have possibly fitted under that table

except you – unless Richelieu's taken to engaging children for his dirty work.

'If you're so sure, why not call the guards.' He was actually smiling. The runt knew he had her trapped; she couldn't do a thing without incriminating herself.

'You admit it, then?'

'You expect me to apologise? You serve your master. I serve mine.'

'I don't want apologies. I want that letter back.'

'It's already with the cardinal.' He gave a shrug of such indifference that it bordered on disdain.

Chevreuse stepped forward, hand raised, but then thought better of it. Instead her arm returned to her side as she silently observed his discomfort. He was afraid, and with good reason.

'I don't think you fully appreciate your position.' Her voice was slow and at its most hypnotic. 'All I have to do is cry and rip my skirt, and your life is over. I'll tell the guards you laid hands on me and they'll kill you where you stand.'

Sebastian froze and repeated the threat in his mind. He was prepared for a pistol or knife, but not this. He was still struggling to make sense of what she had said, let alone the implications.

'Did you just say ...?'

'I did,' she snapped, not giving him a moment to think. Stepping back, she lifted a hand to her sleeve and pulled the material tight. 'I'll count to three.'

Sebastian stared back, muddled with terror. It wasn't just the words but the glibness with which she uttered them, without so much as a second thought. This was someone wholly amoral, unconstrained by belief or guilt – capable of doing anything to achieve her aims. 'ONE'. He opened his mouth, still without any idea of what to say, though he knew he had to speak or else he was going to die. Still nothing. He waited, praying that his cornered mind would somehow – as so often before – find some means of escape. 'TWO'. The prospect of death was now so overwhelming that he could think of nothing else, a lodestone in his mind that attracted everything to it. Every thought, desire, memory, everything that he was seemed distilled into this moment. The duchess in front of him. Her red dress. The scent of helichrysum – sweet and narcotic in the nose. 'THREE'. She smiled as she said it, triumphant. Momentarily he considered promising her the letter, if only to give himself some time – then recoiled. She did not strike him as the sort to be trifled with.

'Have you considered ...?' He murmured the words without any idea how to continue, seizing every last instant. But now there was no more. He met her eyes.

Suddenly inspiration struck him, that clarity at the moment before death, as the urge to live took over. The answer was obvious. His size, as ever, would be his salvation. He held up a hand to stop her. 'What makes you think anyone's going to believe you?'

'I'm a duchess, in case you were unaware of the fact.'

'You're also two feet taller than me. But if you're prepared to become the laughing stock of the entire court, then please go ahead.' His heart was thudding in his ears and he had difficulty pushing out the words. Nevertheless, it was enough to make her pause and her hand slackened, though it remained in place, hovering over the seam of her shoulder, maintaining the threat.

'I assure you I can be very convincing.'

154

'I've no doubt of that. I don't claim to read the future.' He was still struggling to conceal the fear in his voice. 'It's true I might die. But there might be a trial first. Maybe I'd even be pardoned and you'd spend the rest of your life humiliated. Or perhaps the guards simply won't believe you. I've no idea. All I know is that you've been exiled twice, and traitors usually don't get the benefit of the doubt ...'

With a snarl, Chevreuse whipped a palm across his face, knocking him into the wall. 'How dare you, you little bastard.'

Anticipating another blow, Sebastian backed into the corner, trying to protect his face. It didn't come. Instead she bent down until her face was level with his, and then she grinned. Sebastian had never seen her smile with open lips. Now it was clear why. Years of grinding had reduced them to a row of misshapen stumps, their wear a testament to the frustration inside. The symmetry of the surrounding face made their cracks and jags all the more apparent.

'Very well, little man.' Her breath smelled of meat. 'I'll spare you this time. And there are easier ways to have you killed. Poison. Digitalis. Wolfsbane. Bundled into a sack and thrown into a river. Maybe just a knife in the dark.'

Sebastian said nothing, his back pressed tight to the wall in his effort to widen the distance between them.

'At least tell me this. Is Richelieu really worth dying for? Do you actually think he cares about you in the slightest?'

Sebastian considered a moment. 'I've no idea, Your Grace. But much as you think I'm an abomination, I am at least a loyal one.' Then, and with the slightest of bows, he scuttled out of the room as quickly as possible.

Shutting the door behind him, Sebastian rounded the corridor before bracing himself against the wall and catching his breath. A spot of blood fell to the floor and he felt the cut on his cheek, pressing it with a handkerchief as he reflected on his good fortune. He had escaped unharmed – for the meantime at least. Her reputation was deserved. The woman was the opposite of Richelieu, but no less intimidating for it. Where he was supremely calculating, considering every possible permutation, she was an arch-opportunist. Logic, however mighty, follows clear lines. It can at least be predicted and foreseen. But she had no such restrictions; she did not pause to deliberate. Her preferred weapon was surprise – to be upon her opponent before he had time to respond. And Sebastian's fear of her took a different form – primal, the same sensation of being trapped with a bear or a tiger. Something that could not be negotiated with or bought off, something that would kill the first chance it got.

* * *

The reality is rarely as good or bad as one expects it to be; the dread can exceed the punishment, the hope surpass the reward. Even kings and queens are not exempt, and Anne of Austria had spent the entire morning worrying over her imminent meeting with the cardinal. Shame seemed certain, banishment probable, imprisonment possible – all were horrible. At first she hadn't even been able to get out of bed, refusing to face the day; each time hoping that when she woke up matters would somehow be different, but nothing ever seemed to change. Until, having no choice, she rose and dressed for the grand occasion, in a quilted gown topped with a ruby and diamond choker from her parure. Even then she didn't leave her apartments, instead striding up and down her parlour, venting frustration at the occasional servant unfortunate enough to appear at the door.

An hour before noon, the source of the Queen's fury made itself apparent, when a quailing maid announced the cardinal had just arrived and asked, 'Would Her Majesty care to grant an audience?'

'Do I have a choice?' the Queen spat back, her accent magnified with emotion.

The maid forced a smile and nodded.

'Very well, bring him to me,' the Queen finished. She paced to the window, then turned and assumed her pose – august, chin raised, shoulders back, her eyes fixed on the door.

When he entered the room the cardinal was, as ever, discreet. Wax-faced, he bowed deeply, gave a tight smile, then apologised for the intrusion. Anne loathed the way he hid behind his manners. Nothing was ever said directly, yet the meaning was always clear. Sometimes she almost pitied him, imagining how hard it must be to repress every emotion, every trace of the man inside – whether after so many years, any of the original self remained, like the shell of a beetle once all the flesh has gone, a perfect facsimile of something which has long since disappeared. Today, however, she felt no sympathy for the man, not after what he had done.

'How could you? To put a knife to a duchess? Have you no shame?'

'I am shocked you think I would countenance such an action, Your Majesty.' The words were meticulous, typical of a man who was careful not to lie, merely dissimulate. 'Nevertheless, I fear a more serious issue has since come to light. Naturally I have put every effort into retrieving the stolen document and I can reassure Your Majesty it is safe.

As you would expect, to check its veracity I was compelled to take a brief examination before returning it and could not help noticing it appears to be addressed to your brother Philip. Now, I am sure Your Majesty meant no harm, but you must understand any communication with the Spanish court poses a potential threat to our realm. And while I've no wish to show it to the King ...'

The moment Philip's name was mentioned, Anne looked away.

'Why are you doing this to me? Do you wish to destroy my marriage? To break the covenant we made before God?'

'There may be an alternative.'

'What do you want?' Her bluntness contrasted with his equivocation.

'Only what is the best for Your Majesty. For you to regain the King's favour and secure the future of France.'

'You mean have a son?'

'It would be a glorious event, Your Majesty. Our nation depends on you.'

'And the letter? You will not show it to the King?' Her hands had now dropped and were turned palms up, in the manner of a beggar asking for food.

'Knowing the happiness a son would bring him, I certainly wouldn't want to mar his joy.'

'But I do not understand. I have already explained this to your dwarf. The problem is with the King. He will not sleep with me.'

'I'm not sure you quite listened to what I said, Your Majesty. I didn't mention the King, merely that France requires a dauphin.'

She paused a moment, struggling to decode his words, then

let out a penny-whistle laugh and stared back, her mouth agape.

'Are you asking me to commit adultery?'

'I'm telling you to do your duty, Your Majesty. All France depends on you having an heir.'

The Queen looked away and paused, perhaps hoping for an alternative, or simply because the occasion demanded it. When she looked back, her face had hardened into its regal mask.

'Very well, cardinal. But remember that when the King dies I will be regent, and I will not forget this. One day you will pay for what you have done.'

'That is your prerogative, Your Majesty. Now I will intrude no further upon your valuable time.' As he left, Richelieu was careful to follow protocol, shuffling rearwards with eyes cast down, never once turning his back on her – formal to the end.

The Queen was left alone in a pastel hell, staring at the mirror opposite. Sitting down, she looked at herself framed in early baroque, a solitary figure on a fawn chaise longue. Her face looked featureless in the watery light, and her sex was buried under her dress. All that remained was a wilted posture: elongated and limp, hands on lap, her head like a drooping bloom.

Return to the Past

(1638)

Richelieu gazed at the rooftops of Paris through the circular window. Its glass was warped with age, twisting lines into curves, diminishing and magnifying space. On the streets below, people bubbled through its imperfections and the trees bent into unworldly forms. The cardinal was aware the illusion worked both ways, that to the outside observer looking up, he resembled some caricature, hook-nosed and axe-headed, clawed hands protruding from beneath his red soutane. Not that it concerned him. The view was as real as any other, the interpretation no more or less true. His musings were interrupted by a knock at the door. Cinq-Mars entered, without waiting to be called in.

Richelieu stared at the marquis tailored in velvet and lace, the material brushed to a liquescent shine. How could anyone waste so much time getting dressed in the morning? Did it give him pleasure or was it simply the result of having nothing to do? He thought back to the day Cinq-Mars first arrived, a shock-faced orphan, still trapped in the moment of his parents' death. It was months before he spoke, or did anything except walk through the house and stare at fragments of the past. They were arranged in his bedroom: a shrine of battered portraits, trinkets his parents had given him over the years. He would sit on the floor in front of them, torturing himself for hours. Richelieu had found himself drawn to the child's room, and would observe from the doorway, praying that the boy might find some way out of the dark.

But when he recovered, it was no better. As some people are strengthened by loss, others are destroyed by it. For Cinq-Mars, the void had simply grown until it consumed him, a bottomless and raging need. He had spent his whole life trying to fill it, always wanting more. Richelieu knew he was partly to blame. Pity had made him spoil the child, showering him with gifts in the hope it might somehow undo the past: clockwork dolls, musical boxes, toy horses and soldiers, a wooden sword, shield and bow, a suit of armour, books – more than he could ever hope to play with. He had the best private tutors and all the money he could want, and it had ruined him. Like so many before, he had atrophied in luxury. There was nothing to fight, nothing to strengthen him. Everything yielded to his touch and now there was none of that child left. Instead, a creature of privilege – soft, effete, and wildly overconfident. Like some pampered pet, surrounded by tamed nature and thinking himself master of the world.

'If this is about my spending, I promise I've been good,' Cinq-Mars declared. Their conversations over the previous year had consisted almost entirely of the cardinal berating him after being forced to pay his various debts.

161

'You've clearly been a model of frugality,' Richelieu remarked, making a pointed glance at his new doublet, fashioned from silver and black brocade, the cuffs and collar fine-worked needle lace. 'No, this is about another subject altogether. You may be interested to know that the King has taken an …interest in you.'

Cinq-Mars hesitated a moment, perplexed. Then he gave a slow and knowing smile.

'He has asked me to arrange a meeting in private,' Richelieu continued.

'What about de Hautefort? Isn't she his mistress?'

'De Hautefort is irrelevant. De Hautefort is not the King.'

'And is there anything I need to do? Beforehand, I mean.'

'Strangely, that's exactly what I wanted to discuss.' Richelieu did not sound surprised in the slightest. He motioned at the chair opposite. 'I assume you've time for a brief word.'

Cinq-Mars gave the slightest roll of the eyes before sitting down. His conversations with the cardinal tended to be anything but brief, invariably consisting of dreary and repetitive lectures that he was made to endure like some disobedient child, only ending when Richelieu seemed to bore even himself and would finally return to his reports.

'There is a possibility you may become close to the King, even discuss matters of policy with him. If such an occasion were to arise, I would like to be sure your advice is … sound.'

'Sound?'

'I would like our opinions to be in agreement.'

'You mean I should say whatever you tell me?'

The cardinal uncoiled from his chair and leaned forward, his thin features sharpening.

162

'Of course.' The marquis yielded with a dip of the head. 'But what exactly do I stand to gain in return?'

'You'll have my support – which you will need. If, and it is a considerable *if*, you ever do become his favourite, you may discover it to be less attractive than you think. You'll have great power, but only at another's whim. All it takes is for the King's mood to change. A beautiful face, an argument, boredom, and you'll be cast down again. It can be an unpleasant drop. There may be resentments. You will need protection.'

'And if the relationship doesn't end?'

'You are a young and beautiful man, Henri. One day you'll be an uglier but wiser one.' It was the sort of patronising remark that Cinq-Mars had become used to but still loathed. Not that he showed it, of course. There was no point arguing with Richelieu. The man was incapable of admitting fault. Better to nod along and wait for him to finish, which he proceeded to do as the cardinal explained in laborious detail how to answer anything he might possibly be asked, from the Croquants in the South-West to the removal of the state assemblies and clerical immunity from tax. Richelieu seemed to notice he wasn't paying attention and kept asking him to repeat things, which he did, thoughtlessly and mechanically. But this only seemed to further exasperate the cardinal, who finally gave up, announcing he was late for the *Te Deum* and taking his leave.

* * *

The King's son Louis was born on the fifth of September 1638, though the actual identity of his father remained a source of widespread speculation. Various noble names were put forward. A few people even suggested the Queen's old admirer, Buckingham, had been smuggled over from England. Above all, however, there was rejoicing. Bells were rung and fireworks lit. God had blessed France with an heir and the future was, if not secure, then at least less uncertain. If the King was aware of the hearsay, he gave no appearance of it. Like all monarchs, he had remarkable powers of self-delusion. And, as no one would ever correct him, he could afford to. In his world, the rumours did not and never would exist.

In contrast, the Queen was anxious to preserve her reputation and retired with her son to the monastery of Les Loges. Eager to show her piety, she passed her days praying in cloistered silence with the white-robed nuns. Occasionally she would be forced back to court, usually for state occasions: the King's birthday, festival days and the like. Regarding it as an opportunity to publicise her transformation, she would shuffle among the courtiers, plainly dressed in a wool bodice and long, matronly skirt. Seemingly aloof from the world, she only spoke when spoken to and even then restricted her conversation to Christian platitudes and quotations from the good book. Yet it was a virtue without passion and she fulfilled her duties with an empty gaze that was anything but divine. The austerity weighed on her like a suit of armour and every evening she would return to her bedroom and collapse in a jumble of giggles and tears, overwhelmed by the sheer relief of being able to shed the load, and every morning she would walk to her wardrobes and skim through fondly remembered damask and organza before turning back to the limp woollens draped over her chair. But she had no choice.

She was aware of the rumours and knew a queen must be beyond reproach. There could be no question of her son's legitimacy to the throne.

* * *

The Château de Blois wasn't really a château at all; it was three. The original Gothic castle in the centre, with two further edifices added as wings. One, dating from the Renaissance, had been added by François I. The other, classical in style, remained in the process of completion. The effect was to remove all symmetry, replacing it with a stew of styles on which the eye flitted but never settled. The most spectacular feature was an octagonal, spiral staircase that projected from the facade. A vast coil of filigreed stone, it dominated the view from the balcony where Gaston, Duke of Orléans, lounged, picking at some apple puffs with fried raisins. Opposite him, Marie de Chevreuse leaned against the rail, watching him sidelong while curling a tress around her finger. Despite her lingering glances, Gaston was either oblivious or else simply didn't care.

'I hear the cardinal's had you exiled again,' he remarked, in between mouthfuls.

Chevreuse gave a moue of displeasure and turned away, revealing a back of green velvet topped by a satin cap.

'Fifteen months I've been in Dampierre.'

'I would have thought you'd be delighted to spend so much time with your husband.'

'Dispense with the sarcasm. I'm in no mood for jokes.'

'Don't worry. Besides, I think Richelieu's got a soft spot for you. He could have charged you with treason.'

'But he didn't. And the fact is until we're rid of him, nothing's going to change. The people are too terrified to do anything. No one knows who to trust. It's ridiculous, the whole country wants him dead and not a single man will raise a hand against him.'

Gaston laughed and sipped his wine. Though young, his face was plump from excess, with a thin beard that didn't quite join up. He looked as if he would age fast and badly.

'What you're saying, it sounds like treason to me. Now, why do you think I'd be interested in overthrowing my brother?'

'I don't think it, I know it. But that's not what you're asking. You want to know if it's going to succeed.'

Gaston laughed again. Despite his cavalier manner, he possessed a restless charm, with curious flittering eyes. There was evidently a quick mind behind them, albeit unexercised.

'First, know this … I love Louis.' He looked at her, almost daring her not to believe him. But she knew he was telling the truth. Nobody would choose to have their own brother between them and the throne. 'He's just not meant to be king. He's no leader – too meek – he only does what Richelieu tells him to. Of course when I talk to him about it, he just takes the high ground. Gives me all that rot about Louis the Just. He really believes it, you know.'

Chevreuse nodded. 'I used to be his mistress – remember? He's been merciful, I suppose, but my God he lets everyone know it.'

'In some ways, I feel sorry for him. He's always worrying. Thinks everyone calls him an idiot. It's hardly surprising considering the stutter. Besides, he's always trying to live up to Father. Mother knew he was no good from the start. She always wanted me to be king.'

'And now Louis has a son, you never will be, or at least as long as that cripple stays in power.' Chevreuse sighed with nostalgia, as if they were old and discussing their regrets, decisions they could have made but hadn't.

'There's nothing I can do. Mother tried to remove him and he had her exiled. The woman's been in Holland for ten years. It's a disgrace, the man has no respect.'

'I'm not asking you to get rid of him. I've someone else in mind to do that.'

'Who? There's nobody left – Montmorency's dead, La Vieuville, Châteauneuf. He's even grooming that little brat of his to be favourite ...'

The remark captured Chevreuse's attention and she glanced across. 'Cinq-Mars, you mean? Now that is interesting.'

'Interesting? What's interesting about him? He's barely more than a boy ... hot-headed too. He'll most likely get himself killed duelling over some trifle.'

'But haven't you wondered why Richelieu's gone to so much effort?'

'It's obvious. He wants to control Louis.' Gaston replied dismissively, evidently viewing the question as an insult to his intelligence.

'Exactly, which means he doesn't have control now. Imagine it from his position. He still remembers Luynes. The man virtually ran France, banished Richelieu to Luçon. He's terrified of it happening again. Don't you see? He's worried a favourite could bring him down. And with good reason ... I mean, we'd both agree Louis isn't always the most rational of men.'

'What are you saying? De Hautefort could get rid of Richelieu?'

'He is just a man, you know. He can be persuaded. Put the right person in a room with him for a few days and … who knows?'

'Even supposing you're right – once Richelieu's gone, what then?'

'In Spain and the Low Countries, they speak highly of you. You're seen as a reasonable man, someone who would support their aims.'

Gaston paused, leaning on the balustrade and looking up at the dusk – the yellow and red fading into blue and purple. When he spoke again, the words were careful and non-committal. He knew what constituted treachery in a way only a traitor can. 'You're proposing a grand alliance, to overthrow my brother.'

'You already have their support. They want this war over – every bit as much as we do – and Louis is never going to end it.'

'I'm not convinced.' Gaston looked across and grimaced, shaking his head. 'I need time to think. What do you want from me anyway?'

'Nothing for the moment. I can take care of matters myself. And frankly the less you know, the better. I'll be in touch when the time comes.'

'I still haven't agreed to this.'

'You will,' Chevreuse finished, turning to leave. She liked Gaston in his way. Avaricious as he was, you could rely on his appetites. Hold out a juicy tidbit and he would take it. And yes, he might turn on you the moment something better was on offer, but providing you told him as little as possible, what was there to lose? Besides, it wasn't easy to be so close to the throne yet possess so little power. Condemned to waste away while waiting for a man to die – for no reason other than the date of his birth.

* * *

The Château de Ruel lay twenty miles west of Paris, a small country house but with gardens on a palatial scale. Its parterres were patterned with intricate hedgerows and perfectly raked pathways, intersected by wedge-shaped beds of catmint and marjoram. Long avenues ended in vistas across the grounds, from which fountains propelled water to impossible heights. Looking out from the house, Sebastian watched with bemusement. Beautiful as the view was, he found it sterile and unnatural – nature reduced to pretty ornament. He was interrupted by a cough from the cardinal, who had finished reviewing his reports and was now ready to speak. Walking to the chair opposite the bureau, Sebastian tried turning it to face Richelieu, only to find it fixed to the floor.

'The chair, I can't move it.'

The cardinal looked sidelong from his sickbed. He was ill again, this time with ulcers. It had been a week but his condition was improving and, despite the obvious pain, he seemed in relatively good humour.

'I prefer to see who I'm looking at,' he said through locked teeth. 'Liars never like being in the open. It's the feet that give them away – always moving. They can grip the chair but the nervousness has to escape somehow.'

'Ingenious, Your Eminence. It sounds like something out of *The Prince*.'

'Machiavelli? You like his work?'

'I thought it was well written, yes.'

'Perhaps, I find him a little naive myself.' The remark made Sebastian smile. Only Richelieu would call Machiavelli naive. 'It's obvious the man had no real power. To think you can run a country by following a few rules is ridiculous. You anticipate as best you can, but your control is always limited. You can only react to problems as they arise.'

'You say that, but surely you seek to control events? To prepare for the unforeseen as best you can?'

'Of course. I represent the government, I try to control everything.'

Sebastian laughed, disconcerted by the baldness of the statement, then rubbed his beard, not sure whether to admit he agreed with it.

'Don't be surprised. What is government except control? It might not be the kindest definition, but people don't pay taxes out of love for their fellow man. Or obey the law, for that matter. And without taxes, there wouldn't be armies, granaries, roads. You might even say that everything we have, we owe to government.'

Over the previous two years, Richelieu had become more open during their conversations. Sebastian wasn't sure why, whether it was time or respect or perhaps he simply had no one else to talk to. As their relationship became more equal, so Sebastian lost his reverence, to the point where he now found himself looking at the Cardinal, hollowed with disease, with an unaccustomed sense of pity. Unsettled, he replied with the first thing that came to mind, if only to fill the lengthening silence.

'But there's more to it than that. It's not just control for control's sake. I mean there has to be a purpose to it all?'

'The purposes change, the needs change, but the battle is constant. The presses never stop. Pamphlets, essays, periodicals – all fighting for the mob. Every rebel and heretic pouring poison into men's minds.' The cardinal spoke in a careworn voice, motioning across at the shelves, ceiling-high and toppling with papers and books. 'We try to suppress them of course, but it's like trying to ban thought. And they are appealing ideas, of course they are. Nobody likes the state. Everyone has a grievance. The poor see a boot on their neck, the merchants pay and get nothing back, the nobles all think they should run it.'

'But you have your own periodicals – the *Mercure*, the *Gazette*, the *Académie*.'

The words lifted the cardinal and as he looked up, the shadow fell from his face. Illness had deepened his sockets and given him wide and luminous eyes.

'True – the Académie Française, it will be our salvation, you know. To have one France, we need one language, agreed by all. Through it, we will create a single people, a single culture. We will change history, make people look back at a country that never was.'

Sebastian winced with disgust. He was from Normandy and proud of it – his language, his people and their heroes – Robert Guiscard, William II, Rollo – names he had revered since he was a child. The thought of being merely French unsettled him. It seemed a lifeless idea, a place designed by bureaucrats, somewhere that did not exist outside the words of treaties – an administrative convenience.

'I see you're offended. You probably think me arrogant. Perhaps you're right. I am one man against a nation. Such is the nature of control…it is fundamentally an illusion. It only works so long as people believe it. No more than religion, an act of faith.'

Hooked by a passing thought, Sebastian stared at Richelieu blank-eyed before noticing that the cardinal was waiting for him to reply.

'My apologies, Your Eminence.' He still referred to the cardinal as Your Eminence in moments of unease. 'It's just that ... well ... there's something I've been meaning to ask.'

'Then you should probably ask it.'

'Why me?'

'I don't understand. Would you care to elaborate?'

'The matters we discuss. They seem private. Things I wouldn't imagine you sharing with many people. And yet you tell me – why?'

Amused, the cardinal nodded, glancing across with a mildly patronising smile. 'I'm surprised you haven't realised. You've always struck me as intelligent.'

'I've a few suspicions, but I'd prefer to hear from you.'

'Very well. You're discreet. And wise to be so, bearing in mind your position. More importantly, I've put nothing in writing.'

'But you've still told me.'

'You've no proof, no records – only conjecture, another rumour at worst. And what's another rumour at court? No, only what's written is remembered, and people will know the history I tell them. You see that portrait.' Richelieu nodded at a picture in the far corner, a commanding depiction of him draped in a cloak of crimson silk with a glittering crucifix and scarlet biretta. The image of power, every inch the statesman, though the painter hadn't quite managed to hide the weight beneath his eyes. 'That is how people will remember me.' Richelieu snorted, aware of how different he looked in reality – a skeleton draped in skin, his beard barely concealing the gauntness of the face beneath.

Sebastian slid off his chair and walked to the window, his hands clasped behind his back. Then he turned round, a shadow against a background of sky. 'Since you're being so open, Your Eminence, there's one more thing I want to know. It's been bothering me ever since the dauphin was born. About the Queen … can you tell me if the rumour's true?'

'That depends on the rumour.'

'That you had Jules Mazarin smuggled into her bedroom at night. That he's the father.'

Richelieu nodded slowly and crooked a finger over his lips, fastening them like a staple. Eventually, he nodded at the wall opposite.

'You see that shelf. The paper tied with blue ribbon, bring it to me.'

Sebastian did as he was asked, though he found it awkward. The documents, like most things in his life, were out of reach. Climbing to the upper shelf, he was forced to pincer himself in place with one hand while snatching at the papers with the other. On the second attempt, he managed it and after teetering his way down, he passed the sheaf to Richelieu, who skimmed it before handing Sebastian three sheets.

'Put them in the fire,' he instructed. Sebastian instinctively glanced downwards.

'I didn't say read them.'

Sebastian turned his gaze to the hearth and scrunched the papers into a ball, tossing it into the flames where it erupted into ash – a blaze of brilliant colour, then gone. He looked back at the cardinal, hoping for an explanation.

'My cabinet has two types of paper. One half for me, the other for posterity. One half for the flames, the other to be filed. So, to return to your question, who is the dauphin's father? It's irrelevant. All that matters is that he is the King's son now, the rightful and legitimate heir of France.'

Sebastian didn't need ask any more. For a man who revealed so little, Richelieu could be remarkably clear. Instead he turned back to the window and looked out at the gardens. Again he was struck by their symmetry: the straightness of the clipped boxwood, the evenness of the paths, every flower pruned and in its place. It seemed magnificent and yet futile, a battle against the inevitable. One day the cardinal would die, nature would return and all this would be gone. Was it really worth spending so much time on something that was fundamentally no more than an illusion?

* * *

For all the beauty of the garden in autumn, there was no doubting summer had gone. The paths had become mosaics of fallen leaves as the fruit lay decaying on the grass and the nights grew ever longer. Sebastian paced the Jardin des Tuileries with mixed emotions. It might have been a paradise, but it was a fading one. Ever since Corbie, he had been aware of the uncertainty of his existence. The immediate danger had passed. The Habsburgs had been pushed back to the borders and now each side sat in their castles and keeps, content to wait. Nevertheless, the threat remained. Philip was paying down his debts, building his treasury as the gold continued to pour into Madrid. He would attack again and this time without making the same mistakes. Where or what his life might be in a year's time, Sebastian had no idea. Still deep in thought, he didn't notice the man approaching from behind. At the last moment, he caught a blur of yellow to his left and turned to face his attacker, raising his arms in defence. But it was only a footman, who startled and mirrored Sebastian's surprise.

'My apologies,' he said. 'A message from Marie Morra. She awaits your presence in Camoches.'

Sebastian paused. He expected almost any other name: the cardinal, Chevreuse, Cinq-Mars, but not that of his mother. In the eight years since he had left Camoches, she had never asked a thing of him. All he had received were a few short letters, thanking him for the money and telling him about Audrien and Charles. Always written in that self-conscious formal tone she used when speaking to people of education, viewing herself as a foolish old woman, a hindrance to his illustrious career. Yet now she was asking him to put his entire life to one side and make the seven-day journey to Normandy.

There could only be one reason. She was dying, and ill enough to know it. Then he noticed the footman still standing in front of him, his lips crimped with polite unease.

'The messenger was told he would be paid on delivery.'

'Of course.' Sebastian reached into his purse and unthinkingly handed over a wildly generous sum. Then he set about making preparations, ordering a coach and filling his pack with a few clothes and enough fruit to last the journey.

It wasn't until Sebastian had been on the road for an hour that he realised he had forgotten to inform the cardinal. Disappearing unannounced might seem suspicious. But there was no possibility of turning back now. Only three things mattered: himself, his mother and the distance between them.

* * *

Sebastian spent the first few hours in the carriage torturing himself with regret. It had been four years since he had last seen his mother. Despite his repeated requests, she had never come to the Louvre, forever giving excuses, all of which he had been happy to accept, not wanting to be humiliated in front of the court. Yet in all that time, he had never once made the effort to visit her. Even his letters home had become briefer and more infrequent as he dashed them off like an inconvenience rather than the comfort they used to be. And now, after all she had done for him, he was going to leave her to die alone. The thought was near unbearable, and he became more alarmed with every passing hour. His anxiety manifested itself in little tics: his head turning from side to side as he glanced out of the window, fingers drumming, feet tapping, the occasional glance upward in silent prayer. Occasionally he tried to distract himself in a book or by staring at the view, but no more than a few minutes would pass before his eyes returned to their inward stare.

As the coach journeyed deeper into the countryside, his frustration diminished. Free of the city, the crowds and the rush, he felt the world slowing down, and as he looked at the wooded hills, there was no sense of time passing, just the odd plodding farmer, cow or horse. Skeletal trees slumped in the dead air, their branches raking empty sky. He found himself thinking back to his youth and the boy he used to be. But there was no nostalgia. In truth, he could hardly remember himself, instead the mind of an animal: primal urges for food and warmth, crouching in corners for protection, the desire for escape. All he could pick out was a vivid image of that last day – standing on the prow of the cart, watching the village shrink into the horizon and vowing never to go back. In any other circumstances, he never would have.

* * *

As they approached Camoches, Sebastian began to recognise the scenery: the cathedral at Coutances, its double steeples reminiscent of devil's horns, the white streets of Lessay, and finally the lake of his near-demise. Bubbling with impatience, he stood up on his seat and leaned out of the window, eager for a sign of home. But all he could see were some derelict outbuildings with sunken roofs and collapsing walls, presumably stables of some kind. It was only when they passed the yew tree at the end of the village that he realised where he was. Yelling at the coachman to turn around, he looked again and this time was able to make sense of the mess. Most of the houses were unrecognisable but he was able to pick out a few, particularly the cottage of his aunt Adele. All seemed abandoned, most likely because of the plague. Scanning the water in hope of a clue, he noticed a ragged line of boats drawn up on shore. It took him a moment to work out why. Of course – the harvest – the whole village was inland, working the fields while there was good money to be made. Everything was precisely as it had ever been. It was only he who had changed.

The thought of his mother living in such squalor horrified

him and he prayed she'd finally taken his advice to leave. Over the years he had sent her six hundred livres at least, more than enough to buy somewhere warm in Caen or Coutances, with enough left over for a housekeeper as well. But he knew she hadn't, that she would regard it as an extravagance and had doubtless saved every penny for his return.

When the coach finally stopped outside the cottage, Sebastian wished the coachman a hasty farewell before grabbing his pack and rushing inside. Entering the house, he was immediately struck by the smell, a mildew reek that took him straight back to his childhood. A multitude of ghosts crowded around him: family, relatives, his father's dying face. Disoriented, he took a moment to recover his bearings before making his way to the back room. She was lying there, bedbound and shrouded in shadow. Moving closer, he could see she was indeed dying. The body whose vastness he once used to orbit was now reduced to a shell. Its flesh was in retreat: the eyes drawing back into their sockets, the gums nearing the bone and the skin hanging in crinkled folds. Up close, he could detect the sickly sweet odour of decay. Barely conscious, she didn't even notice him standing beside the bed, and it was only when he called her name that she turned to look.

She came alive immediately and tried to fuss over him, asking how his journey had been, whether he was cold and if he wanted a bowl of soup. Then she made a pitiful attempt to get up and even more pitifully apologised. Forcing a smile, he told her to rest and held her hand. It felt like meat – cold and stiff. Shocked, he massaged it back to warmth and continued to murmur words of comfort in her ear. After tending to her other hand and then her feet, he retrieved his belongings from the yard and gave her what food he had left, waiting for her to eat and fall asleep before turning his attention to the house.

His priority was heat. She needed warmth to stay alive and he remembered all too well how bitter it could become at night. First plugging the stones, he set about cutting firewood, a tedious business as he was forced to use a hatchet instead of an axe. Finishing just before dusk, he cleared the hearth and piled the fire as high as he dared. But it was no use. The heat seemed to rush out faster than he could add to it. Even beside the flames, it was barely tepid. And after a further hour of chopping, he was too exhausted to continue and paid a neighbour to take them to the nearest tavern.

It was a long journey, seven miles along rutted trails, all of which Sebastian spent trying to rub life back into his mother's limbs. Despite his efforts, she seemed to grow colder and slower by the minute, so that towards the end he felt as if he was the only thing left pumping the blood round her system, a substitute heart. Convinced she was going to die, he barely managed to restrain himself from grabbing the whip out of the driver's hand and beating the horse into a gallop. Nevertheless, they finally reached the tavern. Helping bring her inside, the innkeeper took her legs while he hoisted her trunk over his shoulder, all the time with the disquieting sense that he was already carrying her casket.

* * *

With the aid of thick stone walls, blankets and a hot fire, Marie recovered consciousness the next day. She managed a bowl of soup at lunchtime and by evening she was well enough to chastise him for wasting his money on her.

Laughing, he told her she was being ridiculous and it was *he* who should be sorry.

'You came as soon as you could,' she whispered.

'But I should have visited. Why did you never come? What about all the letters I sent?'

She still seemed to understand and her mouth split into a feeble smile. 'I did come once – on your twenty-third birthday. I meant it to be a surprise.' She paused, gazing in wonder at the memory. 'Then I saw Paris and the Louvre. And ... I never thanked you for that. To think ... my son working in such a place.'

'I don't understand. I never saw you. What happened? Did they not let you in?'

'I never asked. I couldn't go in there. The way they looked at me ... It's not my world.' Then she smiled again. 'I still saw you, though ... through the railings in the gate ... walking in the garden. You looked so happy. It was all I needed to know.'

Sebastian felt a stab of indignation, furious that she had never called out or at least told him what she had done, then guilt as he realised his hypocrisy, the succession of half-hearted invitations he'd sent, all the while hoping she would never come.

'Well, we're together now, at least.' He managed a grin and nodded. 'Actually, I thought you'd be harder to find. That's why I sent you the money, to buy somewhere nice for yourself.'

She flinched, glancing down in momentary penance.

'You spent it? On what?' Incredulous, he raised his voice before checking himself. 'Sorry, I'm not annoyed. I just want to know where it went.'

'Well, Charles and Audrien ...'

'But …no …you know what they're like. Where are they anyway?'

'Don't speak like that about your brothers.'

Sebastian smiled back through locked teeth, explaining that of course she was right and not to worry, while forcing down the rage. Nothing had changed. He already knew what had happened. They had come to her with some wild plan to make their fortunes and she had believed them. He doubted there had ever been a business at all. More likely they drank it away, arguing over how many fleets of boats they were going to buy in five years' time. He still nodded along as his mother told the rest of the story. How they had been going to repay her twice over and would have done so if some unscrupulous rival hadn't burned down their premises the week before it was complete.

What annoyed him most, however, was his brothers' absence. He could see the pain it caused her. Not that she mentioned it, of course, preferring instead to defend them, justifying their behaviour, more for herself than him: explaining how poor they were, their duty to their families, the length of the journey. Sebastian listened, wishing he could provide some consolation or advice, or even just fill the emptiness of the room. Instead, once she was asleep and the candles were out, he lay under a blanket on the floor, muttering furiously to himself as he stared up into the dark.

Despite her brief recovery, Marie's condition worsened the following day. Even moving her atrophied limbs became a struggle. She managed two mouthfuls of breakfast and a few sips of beer but could hardly lift her head from the pillow, forcing Sebastian to tip the liquid into her mouth. Then he told her to sleep some more while he attended to a few chores, intending to ride out to his brothers in Avranches, if only to let them know the suffering they had caused. But his anger was clear to see and Marie promptly called him back to the bed.

'Don't blame Charles and Audrien. They're good boys.' She spoke with that same voice he remembered as a child, the soothing hush of the sea. He didn't know if she believed what she was saying or was simply trying to protect him, still trying to keep him safe from the outside world. Either way, he was in no position to refuse. His place was at her side. So he returned to his seat and amused her with reminiscences and half-truths until she dropped back to sleep. Afterwards he took a short walk to occupy himself then reworked two scenes from his play before she woke again.

And so it went on, Sebastian's life following a clock whose hours were perpetually unwinding, the periods of consciousness growing farther apart. She didn't seem in pain, at least, or else was hiding it well, though her mind became increasingly febrile and he often had to repeat simple sentences four or five times to obtain a response. Even so, he didn't mind. She seemed happy and his days passed bearably enough. Quiet and straightforward, mostly filled with writing or reading Boccaccio (in his hurry he had forgotten to bring any other books) along with whatever pamphlets he could find in the local market. Occasionally his thoughts would wander back to the cardinal. Richelieu must have noticed his absence, though whether he cared was a different matter. After all, how significant could a single person be to someone who had an entire country to worry about?

*　*　*

182

It began with rumours of the *gabelle* – the salt tax. Sebastian overheard a huddle of locals discussing it by the bar while he sat in the corner, hidden in the shadow of the open door, safe from impertinent eyes. The voices were angry and the people clearly had nothing left to give. He could hear whispers of revolt and treason: that the money would only go to fund the war that had killed their children; that it would be better to make peace with Spain than go on like this; that if only the King could hear his subjects then he would change his mind. Richelieu as ever was the source of all their problems – the bane of France, sucking the country dry with his thirst for war.

The murmur grew over the following week, and the inn became busier as people gathered to talk. Self-appointed leaders stood up and made red-faced speeches. Words became stronger and by the Thursday, the murmur had escalated to a roar. There were reports of an uprising and a tax-officer being beaten to death. Nobody knew exactly what had happened and the meetings were thick with rumours of the cardinal's spies, of armies on the march and a great meeting near Rouen. By the weekend, people were gathering in packs and searching for enemies, culminating in the destruction of a local nobleman's house.

In spite of all the discord, the deaths were few and the violence sporadic, loose sparks that had yet to ignite. Nobody wanted war and after a few nights wandering aimlessly round the countryside, people lost interest and returned to their work, hoping the threatened tax would never come. It wasn't until the following week that Sebastian heard a hubbub from downstairs. It sounded like some form of altercation, so, after excusing himself, he ventured below for a look.

All he could see from the stairwell was a field of heads. A voice was bellowing hatred and rousing the crowd. Unable to make sense of the situation, he waited for a quieter moment before enquiring what was going on. Apparently the salt-workers had revolted the week before and begun the long march to Paris. They were due to arrive in a matter of hours and the townspeople were deciding whether to join them. His curiosity satisfied, Sebastian returned upstairs to tell his mother what had happened. Semi-conscious, she gave no appearance of comprehending, and he paced the room, thinking aloud. The revolt struck him as futile, bordering on suicidal. The *gabelle* was a local issue. It had no appeal beyond the coast. The moment they marched inland they would be without support, and with no supplies or reinforcements they didn't have a chance. They were all going to die.

*   *   *

The march arrived with a distant rumble. Sebastian could hear the sound from his room, a steady beat of feet on earth. Walking outside, he could see it approaching, the cloud of dust lifting from the dirt track. Unlike most armies, it grew less impressive the closer it came. To begin with, he had the sense of an unstoppable wave of humanity, glinting iron and steel. But soon the crowd began to fragment, replaced instead by broken forms, desperate-looking men holding farm tools or rusting swords. All were starving and their clothes hung from sunken frames. Coated in dust, they were indistinguishable one from another – grey-bodied and grey-haired. Most didn't even have shoes, their feet shrivelled to leather after so many years treading the salt. Nevertheless, despite their poverty, they carried themselves as soldiers, marching straight-backed and in formation.

He watched them stride past with a mixture of respect and pity, admiring their bravery while despairing of the life that had forced them into it. They didn't speak or sing as they walked, and their eyes were empty. As if they weren't marching to battle but returning from defeat after a long campaign, beaten soldiers with gaunt cheeks and limp beards, their weapons blunted, their uniforms worn to rags. One in particular stuck out; something about the man's walk seemed familiar, though he didn't know why. The face didn't look like anyone he knew, but the peg nose and the mole by the right ear reminded him of Audrien. God almighty, it *was* Audrien. The fool was going to get himself killed. He had to stop him. Thoughtlessly, he yelled his name and rushed into the crowd.

He did his best to battle the current of bodies but it was impossible, a pebble fighting a stream. Even so he continued elbowing forward as best he could until he was interrupted by a hand on his shoulder.

'Is that you, Sebastian?'

Sebastian's reply was short and urgent. Yes, it bloody well was him, and yes, he bloody well did need to get out. Amused by his brother's candour, Audrien let out a snort of laughter before pulling him from the crowd and accompanying him back to the inn.

Sebastian wanted to take Audrien straight up to their mother, but the man looked like he hadn't eaten in days – so first he bought him some food, a whole chicken with beans and ragout, and spent the following ten minutes watching him consume it right down to the bone. Afterwards they had a brief but unsatisfying conversation. There was so much to say that they ended up barely speaking at all, each summarising eight years in a few sentences.

Looking at the gnawed face opposite, Sebastian found it impossible to be angry at Audrien. His last memory of his brother was of a bearish man with a bushy beard, squashed nose and peephole eyes, but starvation had reversed his features. The beard had thinned, the nose sharpened into protruding bone and the eyes expanded as the face around them diminished. Even the person beneath seemed different. The arrogance had disappeared, silenced by repeated failure, and there was a wisdom to his voice that Sebastian had never detected before. Somehow it made the situation all the more painful – watching a seemingly decent man marching to lonely death. And it wasn't long before Sebastian leapt to the point.

'Audrien, you can't do this. It's suicide. You don't have a chance.'

Audrien's face tightened a fraction, though starvation had restricted his range of expressions and his pinched features strained to look anything other than austere.

'I've made a vow. I'm going to honour it.'

'What about me? I'm your brother. What about your family?'

'I said no. That's it.' The reply was firm, his accent thick as soil. 'Where's maman? I went to see her on the way over. The neighbour said she was here.'

Knowing there was no time to waste and how much it meant to his mother, Sebastian resisted arguing and led him straight up to the room. But it was too late. Audrien tried his best to elicit some reaction, holding her slack hand and wiping her forehead with a cloth, apologising for not arriving before. If she recognised him, she gave no sign of it. Dumbed by fever, she simply stared up in silence, her pupils motionless – lilies on still water.

Afterwards, Sebastian allowed Audrien time to grieve alone and went downstairs to finish the rest of his mead. But he'd never been good at holding his drink, and the alcohol only seemed to exacerbate his mood. So, after twenty minutes or so, he left his half-finished glass and returned upstairs to find Audrien gazing out of the window with an expression somewhere between boredom and exasperation. Eager to escape, he excused himself the moment Sebastian entered the room, explaining that he had to join his comrades before they marched too far ahead.

'But you can't leave yet,' Sebastian interrupted. 'You haven't told her what you're doing.'

'What?'

'You know – abandoning your family, going off to get yourself killed.'

Audrien stopped dead and stared back, dumbstruck. It was partly at the shock of the words, more so that they were coming from Sebastian.

'Don't you think you owe her an explanation? She spent fifteen years bringing you up. She's entitled to know why you're throwing your life away and leaving her grandchildren to starve.'

'Bastard.' Rigid with fury, Audrien brandished a fist and pressed it to Sebastian's face, the knuckle hard against the bone. He held it there a moment, struggling to control himself. Then, with a snarl of frustration, he stamped out of the door. After quickly checking on his mother, who appeared unaware of what had just taken place, Sebastian bolted down the corridor and caught his brother on the stairs.

'What the hell did you just do? Maman's dying and you go and tell her that? Have you lost your mind?'

'I can't let you do this. It's lunacy. You're going to die.'

'You think I don't know what I'm doing? You don't understand. I haven't got a choice. We've got no money, not a sou. If I stay at home, we won't last the winter. My wife, my children ... they're all going to die. But if I march, there's a chance. A small chance, I admit, but a chance nonetheless. So I don't give a damn about your opinion. And thanks for making sure maman dies thinking of me as a selfish bastard.'

'I can give you the money.'

Audrien grimaced and shook his head, that same expression as when they were young, trying to be polite though the embarrassment was clear on his face.

'You've no idea, have you? If I can't provide for my girls, what good am I? Just another mouth to feed. I know you're trying to help, but you're not my brother, not really. I haven't seen you in six years, and before that we hardly spoke. All we've left in common is maman and she'll be dead tomorrow.' Turning his back on Sebastian, he strode down the stairs – then stopped at the bottom step. Aware of the significance of the moment, he turned round.

'Look, if something happens, speak to Isabelle. She'll be outside church every day at six. She's tall ... with ginger hair. Besides, it's never difficult to spot a salt worker.' He smiled, holding up hands that were more like claws, their skin shrivelled to bark. 'Now go back. And if maman does wake up ... well, tell her I was here.' And with a nod, he turned and left.

Sebastian called him to stop, then tried to follow. But when he reached the street all he could see was a stream of anonymous faces and striding legs. Audrien had already disappeared somewhere deep inside the crowd, doubtless moving away at pace. It was an unpleasant way to part, but after calling his brother's name a few more times, Sebastian knew it was over. In some ways, despite all the time that had gone by, he felt as if nothing had altered. Audrien was still too proud to listen and too stubborn to change, the gap between them as wide as it had ever been.

* * *

The remains of the night's entertainment were still on the table: playing cards, half-drunk glasses of wine, a scattering of stains, crumbs and scraps. The faro players had long gone and only Gaston and Cinq-Mars were left, still drinking and gambling what money they had left playing alouette. It didn't last long. The stakes were absurdly high, more boasts than bets, and Gaston lost after only four rounds, at which point Cinq-Mars simply returned half of the pot and they began playing again.

They were in the library, a magnificent room panelled in walnut, its walls lined with imposing titles, all in Latin with the odd smattering of Greek. The books were pristine – in perfect order, their bindings unbroken, the gold leaf inlaid and crisp. A patina of dust glittered from their covers, sheened in the twilight. How long they had sat on their shelves was unclear – maybe months, maybe decades. It didn't matter; they had not been placed there to be read.

After spending a further hour or so displaying an

aristocratic contempt for money, both men settled in arm-chairs and discussed nothing in particular, at least to begin with. Gaston had a butterfly mind, settling but never staying, always fluttering off course. First a story about a bet that he could ride from Paris to Metz between sunrise and sunset, then a recent female conquest and the beheading of Montmorency, followed inevitably by his opinions on the dauphin – an incident recounted with acidic distaste.

'How can that child, which the whole kingdom knows to be a bastard, be declared legal? And for what? To appease my brother's pride? To spare him from what everyone already calls him behind his back?'

The marquis listened, head bowed as if in homage. Eager for every detail, he was continually nodding Gaston along, laughing or shaking his head when required, responding to every cue. Eventually Gaston seemed to tire of his own voice and lolled back in his chair, looking across at Cinq-Mars.

'So, Henri, what brought you to court?'

'I didn't have a choice. After my parents died, the cardinal was my godfather. He took me in.'

Gaston's response didn't extend beyond a nod. Like many of his contemporaries, he was well accustomed to death.

'And where were you born?'

'Clermont-Ferrand in Auvergne ... ever been there?'

'Has anyone? Your departure must have halved the population.'

They both laughed, the drink having long removed any awkwardness. Again Gaston looked at Cinq-Mars. This time he paused, pondering a dilemma. Evidently displeased with his conclusion, he gave a moue of annoyance and cocked his head as if examining the problem from a different angle. Finally, he leaned forward.

'So tell me, what do you really think of the cardinal?'

'I don't know. He's always looked after me, introduced me to the King. I can't speak badly of the man.'

Gaston brushed away the comment with a wave. 'Why not? I know how difficult it is living in someone else's shadow. I've done it all my life. Knowing what you could achieve yet never being given the chance – and worst of all, the endless lectures and moralising.' Gaston shook his head then looked up at the ceiling, blowing out a sigh. 'The King's no more than a child, you know. He's never had any need to grow up.'

Cinq-Mars listened, attentive to every word. It was heresy to speak ill of the King. Yet Gaston was openly insulting him and saying he was unfit for rule. This wasn't simply an indiscretion; it verged on treason. And like any secret, it drew them together; something had been shared, a weakness shown. However, it also left Cinq-Mars with a duty to respond. Now Gaston had revealed his hand, politeness demanded he do the same.

'You were telling me your opinion of the cardinal,' Gaston prompted.

And, after considerable obfuscation and qualification, Cinq-Mars finally gave way – the emotion spilling out in a gush of resentment: 'He's nothing but a hypocrite. Whatever I do, he declares it wrong, even when he does precisely the same himself. When I spend too much, he regards it as an extravagance. Yet he has one of the biggest palaces in France, Michelangelos and Raphaels, country estates, a whole army of servants. And no matter what my opinion, he simply ignores it. I'm sure he has his reasons. After all, he is meant to be the great statesman and I am only nineteen, but surely I deserve to be listened to at least.'

'So, what do you mean to do about it?'

'What can I do? Without him I wouldn't have money, couldn't even stay at court. Anyway, he's brought me up since I was twelve. No matter what I do, he treats me like a child.'

'Well, if you find your master unsatisfactory, why not take up with a new one?'

'You mean Louis?'

'I don't mean anybody. It's not for me to say how you live your life. You should be free to make your own decisions, the cardinal should respect that. He should give you the same chances he had.' Like his brother, Gaston used the regal form of argument. He didn't have opinions. Phrases like *I think* or *I suppose* were not part of his vocabulary. Anything he said was simply fact.

'But Richelieu is Chief Minister of France. He has the ear of the King.'

'Richelieu will say nothing. He knows better than to make problems for his master. Besides, Louis doesn't always do what the cardinal says – quite the opposite. He'll take any chance to spite him, if only to remind everyone who's in charge.'

Then Gaston stood up and strolled to the fireplace. On the mantelpiece stood an eighteenth-century fantasy clock. The base was a music box of ebony and silver, topped by a silver elephant with bronze tusks, which in turn supported a golden clock tower, intricately engraved. Above the four clock faces was a cupola ringed with arch windows – inside it, the desiccated husk of a fly on its back. Gaston had noticed the insect as a child, and had no idea how long it had lain inside the structure, maybe ten or even a hundred years. It seemed strange to him, thinking of this insignificant creature heading into oblivion, palaced in gold, silver and ebony, ruling its empire of one.

*   *   *

After worrying all night, Sebastian woke up determined to rescue his brother, only to find his mother had taken a turn for the worse. Her breath was ragged and shallow, while her skin had acquired the unmistakeable tint of jaundice. Barely conscious, she didn't seem aware of his presence, and let nothing pass her lips beyond the occasional sip of beer. He wanted to stay with her, yet there didn't seem any purpose to it. There was little hope of her waking or even being aware of his presence. Unless, of course, she recovered consciousness at the final moment and found herself left to die alone, spending her final hours staring at an empty wall, cursing the children who had abandoned her. But if he stayed, he would be condemning his brother to any number of potential horrors: an injury on the battlefield followed by slow death under a boiling sun, or a last minute change of heart when he was too exhausted to make his way home – or simply anonymous death and an unmarked grave. It seemed ludicrous to desert him for a woman who was already dead, and who, if she knew what was happening, would be imploring him to save her son.

He churned everything over for an hour or so, stamping his way round the field outside and swearing under his breath. Then, after changing his mind several times, he finally concluded his duty was to the living and not to the dead. He owed it to his mother to do what she would have done, to put the needs of her children before her own. And once he was on the road and in the saddle, he felt more certain of his decision – if only for having made it. After all, however deep the plunge, it's usually better than the brink.

The innkeeper had let him take his horse for a few coins. It was a dray, so large he could only mount it using a stump and felt more as though he was astride an elephant. Nevertheless, for all its size, it was a docile thing and simple enough to ride. And although he was quite aware how ludicrous he looked upon its back, there was no one nearby to mock or jeer. Indeed, there wasn't much of anything nearby at all. He was riding through the flatlands of Normandy. Around him the land had expended its energy and was oozing down to the sea, slow and level as an estuary. Autumn was ending and the skeleton of the world had become visible, the trees no more than bones, the land stripped of colour. All that remained was barren wood and bleached sky. He had no sense of motion, no houses or people to mark the way, not even a map or directions of any kind. But it didn't matter. He knew there was only one way they could have travelled: towards Paris and the King.

Four hours passed by before he first caught sight of them. The woods had thinned and given way to farmland, mile upon mile of orderly fields. Then the symmetry was broken, the hedgerows mashed by the tramp of a thousand marching feet. Something had steered the army off course. After scanning the horizon for clues, he continued to follow the trail, still searching for a sign. It arrived soon enough. A corpse, its broken form mottled with blood. The right hand was holding the broken staff of a pike, evidently used as a crutch to support weakening legs.

The next people he saw were moving. Peasants also, they

were stumbling forward on tired limbs. One was holding a musket and the other a sword. Both kept glancing over their shoulders, watching for pursuers. Looking at them, Sebastian felt naked by comparison. He was unarmed, and on a horse better suited to pulling carts than swift escape. Every instinct was telling him to turn around and follow them back to the safety of the road. Even so, he kept going, out of bloody-mindedness if nothing else. He'd left his dying mother to be here. There could be no turning back. More people passed by, all dressed in smocks or tunics, mostly injured: some hobbling, some bleeding, a few supporting others. None of them spoke. Only a few seemed to notice him. The rest stared into the horizon, battling forward without any thoughts where they were going, only what they were leaving behind.

The battlefield appeared as a dark blob speckled with gold. It jarred against the surrounding greenery and immediately he knew what it was. The brown was muddied soil and corpses; the gold was the King's troops wandering among the dead. As he approached, he could see them, soldiers looting the bodies and putting the wounded out of their misery – a sword to the throat, a spurt of blood, then on to the next. Nearby, women were screaming. Wives and mothers, their wails merging into a fountain of noise. The troops appeared not to notice and continued their business, hunting for sparks of gold or silver in the dirt.

Posing no danger, Sebastian was ignored, free to drift among the dead and the injured. It took some time to think through the horror, and even when he finally began his search, it was the living who troubled him more than the dead. The corpses he could simply pass by, but he had to return the stare of the dying as they pleaded for help, meeting their eyes while knowing there was nothing he could do. Until, like the soldiers, he too learned to look away – better that than to give them false hope. His search might have been considerably longer if he had not remembered an old pamphlet he had once read on the searching of battlefields:

❖ *Begin your hunt at the nearest corner of the site.*

❖ *Take the longest side, searching those bodies nearest the edge.*

❖ *Once the side is complete, move to the next row of bodies in the manner of a ploughman, walking the field in lines.*

❖ *Allow yourself rest to clear your thoughts and remember the face you are looking for. After a time, all dead bodies will look alike.*

❖ *Do not hope to recognise from the colour of the hair. Head wounds are common and the scalp will stain black.*

❖ *Do not hope to recognise from rings or weapons. Most bodies are looted upon death.*

✤ *Be wary of your emotions. Fear and hope can trick even the sharpest eyes. Always take a second look.*

✤ *If you do not find who you are looking for upon your first attempt, the body may be scattered. Consider looking for other identifying marks.*

Sebastian was making his second tour of the field when he noticed the arm. It was splayed out from beneath a body. Somehow he knew it was Audrien's without knowing why, perhaps from the withered skin or the crooked thumb. And when he rolled away the corpse on top, his fears were confirmed. The skin was white, the blood sunk to the back of the skull; not a peaceful expression but a face of lingering pain – the final blow a slash across the stomach, half-concealed by a grasping hand.

Sebastian stared at the corpse, struggling to absorb what he was looking at, and a full five minutes passed by before he reached down and attempted to drag it away. However, taking the strain, he felt deadweight and knew there was no point. Refusing to leave it behind, he spent the following half-hour scouring the field for some rope, which he then looped under his brother's armpits before using the horse to pull him to a nearby tree. After untying the cord, he tossed it over a branch and tried to hoist Audrien onto the saddle – only to find their difference in size made this impossible. Even when hanging by his full weight, he could only lift the body to a sitting position, where it dangled in a drunken slouch, seemingly taunting him. A problem he eventually solved by knotting a sack to the free end of the line and throwing rocks into it to make a counterbalance, until he was finally able to load the corpse and turn for home.

By the time Sebastian reached the track, the troops had already exacted punishment. A set of makeshift gallows stood by the roadside, their victims cut down and dumped in piles, leaving a row of severed cords shivering in the breeze. The executioners, now finished, were digging a mass grave. It was hard work, considering the number of the dead, and they hacked the ground, all the while cursing the toil, the bodies piled behind them. Noticing Sebastian, they stopped and stared, seemingly unaware that they appeared twice as freakish to him. Revolted, he looked away and moved on.

Sebastian was so preoccupied that he barely recalled any of the ride home. It wasn't just his brother, but his mother too. He had been gone eight hours at least. Eight hours without food or drink in her condition – that meant death or something close to it. Despite his impatience, he couldn't hurry the beast faster than a trot, and it wasn't until evening that he returned the horse to its stable and rushed up to her room.

The fear is often said to be worse than the fact. This was an exception. Her body was slumped half out of bed, arms clawing and spread like pincers as she had tried to drag herself to the door, either from thirst or a desperate wish not to die alone. Her bottom half was naked, the smock rucked up during her death throes – revealing a body that was scarcely more than skeleton and loose skin, any femininity long gone. But it was her face that eclipsed all else. It was ripped apart with pain: the eyes clamped shut, the mouth contorted into a single lip-splitting scream. There was no serenity, no peace. Instead it was the expression of someone who had spent her last hours abandoned in hell, and Sebastian knew the image would never leave him. Instinctively, he turned away, until her nakedness forced him to approach the body and pull down her dress. Heaving her back up onto the bed, he tried to close her mouth. But the face was trapped in rigor mortis. Instead he was forced to wrap her in the counter-pane, concealing her agony as best he could before returning downstairs to search for help.

*　*　*

The funerals took place two days later. Initially, he considered waiting a week to allow himself time to find Charles and Isabelle, but soon thought the better of it. He had no idea where Charles even lived, and no desire to go trailing after Isabelle while leaving her husband's body in the crypt, unblessed. In truth, he would have buried them sooner if he could. Although he had moved to another room at the inn, everything about the place reminded him of his mother – the smell of the corridor, the view outside, even the leek pottage the owner's wife made for lunch. Desperate to occupy himself, he set about organising the ceremony: arranging for pallbearers and a priest, incense and candles, flowers and coffins. He even tried inviting some people from the village, but gave up after knocking on a few doors, disgusted by the usual laughter and abuse.

The service itself was dour. An hour stood in a damp church listening to a bored and droning priest. It should have been longer, but everyone wanted the proceedings over as quickly as possible. The conveyance and cycle of prayers were ignored; the rites restricted to a brief mass, absolution and antiphon. It didn't even bring finality, if anything the opposite. Sebastian simply knelt in the silence, contemplating a life without the only person who had ever cared about him. They might not always have been together, but he had always known she was there for him – a refuge in time of need. Now there was no asylum or shelter – only her face screaming for release.

Once the bodies were in the ground and the pallbearers had gone, Sebastian handed the priest his money and made his final request. He had hoped for Père Jean, but he had died long ago and his replacement was some limp youth just out of the seminary and barely able to pronounce his Latin.

'I want flowers on her grave every Sunday for a year. There should be more than enough there.' Sebastian handed over a fistful of coins, which the priest checked before giving a nod.

'You are going to do this, aren't you? I will check one day.' Sebastian locked eyes with that same hard little stare which had so unsettled his predecessor.

'Of course.'

'Say it. I need you to say it.'

'I'll make sure there are flowers by her grave. Every week for a year.'

Sebastian held his gaze a moment longer, his pupils as emphatic as full stops. It was a lie, of course. He knew he would never come back. All he wanted to do was to return to Paris. To sit in the coach for seven days with the window open, feeling the sun on his face, staring into an empty horizon and letting the memories burn into the past. Now there was just one last piece of business to attend to and then he would be free of it all.

* * *

The first thing Sebastian tended to notice about people was their legs. But with Isabelle Morra, it was her hands. Over the years, her hands and feet had come to resemble preserved meat, all the water sucked out from tramping pools of brine or raking pans of salt. Their withered and crinkled skin sat oddly with her face, that of a thirty-year-old woman still pink with youth. She was dressed neatly in a woollen dress, shawl and headscarf, and the only evidence of her poverty were patches on the hem and elbows. Like many *nu-pieds* she wore sabots, the wooden soles being the only material capable of withstanding her feet.

On noticing Sebastian, she gave the usual look of confusion, but with a subtle difference. Most people greeted him with a sidelong glance, unsure if his appearance was some kind of joke or insult. But she looked upwards, trying to recall something forgotten.

'You're Sebastian, Audrien's brother.' She crouched down, conscious of her height. 'I've heard about you, of course, but I don't understand...Why are you here? I thought you worked for the King.'

Straight-backed, Sebastian nodded awkwardly, grimacing a smile in an attempt to disguise his unease. 'We need to speak somewhere quiet. Do you live close by?'

She seemed to guess what had happened and drew a sharp breath, steeling herself for the blow. 'There's an inn near here. They'll have a room.'

The only place available was the barrel store at the back. It was cold and draughty, but it was at least private. As they stood in the thin light from the open door, Sebastian was acutely aware of the need to speak and stared at her with vacuous horror. He had spent the previous three hours agonising over what to say. Nothing seemed right. Telling her that her husband was dead seemed far too blunt, but anything else struck him as affected or rehearsed. The man had not *passed over to the other side* or *joined our lord in heaven*. He was dead and that was the end of the matter. Then, and to his considerable relief, she pre-empted him.

'It's Audrien. He's dead isn't he?'

'I'm so sorry. It was quick,' he lied. 'I spoke to him the day before. He said how much he loved you.'

'Where is he now?'

'In Camoches, next to his mother. I paid for a stone. I'm truly sorry.'

'You've buried him already?'

'Forgive me, I thought it best. I mean if you want me to ...'

'Please no. I understand. It was good of you to look after him.' Despite their emotion, they were both trying to shield the other from their pain: faces locked in place, voices flat and without intonation, every passion contained. Sebastian tried to offer a comforting embrace, but couldn't reach her shoulder and ended up grabbing awkwardly at her wrist.

'Before he left, I promised to provide for you if anything happened. I'll send you money every month. But I'll need an address and a name.'

'Really, you shouldn't,' she began. Not that her protestations lasted long. She had no husband, two children and a senile mother who was more hindrance than help. Pride was a luxury she couldn't afford.

'It's not charity. I owe it to you.'

She asked him to explain but he refused.

'It's a personal debt. I'd rather keep the details to myself. Too recent. Maybe later sometime.'

She accepted, in return requesting that he eat lunch with her family. He was initially reluctant but she insisted, pointing out that he had an obligation to meet the two boys he was providing for, especially considering he might never see them again. In the circumstances, he could hardly refuse.

Despite dreading the meal, Sebastian was to recall it as one of the more illuminating occasions of his life. Seated at the head of the table, he did his best to exchange small talk with Isabelle over the screech of her squabbling children while trying to keep the stench of poverty out of his nose – a mixture of open cesspit, unperfumed skin and festering scraps. As he tried to force down his semi-edible slop he looked at her careworn, miserable eyes and remembered his yearning for normality as a child, to be just like everyone else. And now he was looking at that dream. If he had been born the same as his brothers, this would have been his existence. Perhaps slightly different, he might have been a farmer rather than a salt worker. His wife would probably have been considerably uglier and his children sicker. In other words, a marginally worse version of a less-than-bearable existence. And when it was time to leave, he gave Isabelle what money he could spare and meant it quite sincerely when he thanked her for a meal he would never forget.

* * *

Richelieu always saw the Château de Ruel as a misnomer. It was no castle; it was a garden. The two storeys of blank yellow stone, square windows and slate roof resembled something a child would draw. But he never meant it to impress. He already had more than enough places to awe his guests. Instead it served an entirely different purpose, a private retreat when he joined the King on his trips to Saint-Germain, free of the noise, congestion and foul air of Paris. There he could forget the world as he wandered the garden, its parterres planted with moresques, sunbursts and escutcheons – it was the house of Armand-Jean du Plessis, not Cardinal Richelieu.

Liberated from the necessities of court, he had dispensed with the usual finery and was dressed in simple brown pantaloons and a white smock, the sleeves rolled up to let his ulcers dry in the sun. He wasn't expecting visitors and was surprised when his steward announced that someone had arrived at the door.

'I said I wasn't to be disturbed.'

'It's the dwarf, Your Eminence. He's being extremely insistent.'

'Don't refer to him as the dwarf. He has a name. Use it.' His voice had the snap of authority. 'Very well ... Send him in.'

The oversized doors that led into the garden diminished Sebastian's already tiny frame, making him appear further away than he actually was. Purposeful, he marched towards the cardinal at a smart pace, eyes fixed on his host. Perplexed by Sebastian's unannounced departure the month before and his equally abrupt return, Richelieu watched him quizzically.

'My brother. He's dead. Your soldiers ... they murdered

him in cold blood.' Sebastian's voice grew louder as he approached. 'He was innocent. All he had was an adze, an adze for God's sake.'

Reaching the cardinal, he continued to vent his rage, describing in considerable detail both the horrors and the sheer futility of what he had just been through – not simply the murder of his brother but the slaughter of hundreds of people whose only crime had been trying to save their families from starvation. It was only once Sebastian ran out of words and was reduced to repeating himself that Richelieu motioned him to stop.

'Sebastian, I know what it's like to lose a brother. My brother Henri was killed in a duel.' Richelieu winced at the memory, evidently still not over the loss. 'And if I could have spared you the pain, I would have. However, you seem to be under the illusion that I had a choice. I take no pleasure in killing people. I agree the punishment was severe, that they didn't deserve to die. But the fact remains that I cannot allow rebellion – least of all against tax. All it takes is for one riot to succeed, then others will follow and all will be lost ...'

'But why kill them? You could have had them flogged, and sent them home with their tails between their legs. He didn't need to die.' Sebastian realised he had not only interrupted, but raised his voice at a man who could have him executed within the hour. Richelieu limited himself to a brief and pointed pause before replying, just long enough to let Sebastian stew in his mistake.

'I didn't choose to kill your brother. It was he who chose to fight.'

'That was no fight. That was a massacre. They were practically unarmed, for God's sake.' Sebastian spoke through bared teeth, struggling to suppress his anger. 'You say they were going to bring down the country, but they weren't. They were just some villagers with swords and scythes, nothing more. They weren't a threat.'

'I don't care if they were armed or not. Rebellion is no different to a plague. If you let one revolt pass, you will inspire another. It's virulent and a risk to the entire kingdom. I cannot allow it. People must fear the very idea. They need to know that even considering it will result in swift and merciless punishment ... I see you don't believe me. Well you're entitled to your opinion. You may even be right. But it does not change the facts. I must do as my position demands.'

'You still didn't need to kill them,' Sebastian repeated. 'What about a trial or evidence?'

'You aren't listening to me. This has nothing to do with innocence or guilt. It has to do with the threat to this kingdom. I cannot allow division. If we are not united as a people, we will not survive.'

Richelieu glanced down at Sebastian and paused mid-flow, noticing his face had changed, its furious angles replaced by something more settled. He had reached a conclusion, for better or worse, and nothing was going to change his mind. 'I'm sorry for your loss, I truly am. And I know there's nothing I can do to bring your brother back, but is there any way I can help?'

Sebastian didn't reply for some time. He knew nothing would make a difference but felt obliged to respond to the gesture. So he requested a tomb for them both, to replace their plots in Camoches. Observing his insincerity, the cardinal acquiesced with a sigh and gave him a stiff pat on the shoulder – the closest he could manage to an apology.

They both knew it was pointless and said nothing. Instead they wished their farewells and pretended everything was the same as it had ever been. It was six months before they spoke again.

*　*　*

Sebastian never experienced true loneliness until after his mother's death. She had been a constant, the thread connecting him with the mass of humankind. Strangely it hadn't mattered that she wasn't with him. Providing for her gave him a sense of purpose, along with the knowledge that whatever happened she would be there for him, a refuge of last resort. Even after her death he still wrote to her every Sunday, spilling his thoughts on the page in long unpunctuated streams of ink, the thoughts sometimes turbid and raging, at other times slower and more meditative. He told her of his life or lack of it, of how he missed her and Audrien, and that he knew she was with God – all the time trying to ignore the image of her death mask, still as vivid as yesterday.

Now adrift, he found himself confronted by the prospect of an existence spent completely and utterly alone. There would be no wife, no children or friends. And, as he watched life pass before his eyes, he was aware not so much of objects as the spaces that separated them: the distance between himself and the audience when he performed, the empty fields of clipped grass dividing the parterres, the blank wall opposite his bed when he woke up each morning.

With nothing else to occupy himself, Sebastian observed his own behaviour with increased fascination – how he had structured his days so as not to be noticed: always venturing out at quieter hours, avoiding busy places and keeping to the shadows. He even dressed in colours that would never catch the eye: choosing plain browns and creams. Not so much a life as a verminous existence shaped by the never-ending search for boltholes and cover.

By now so many years had gone by that it almost seemed normal. The idea of mixing with other people had come to revolt him. It wasn't simply their size and noise but their pointless, repetitive talk and their polite lack of interest. They were so predictable in taste and conversation, so desperate to fit in. He wondered if they died without ever knowing who they were, or if there were other times when they too would sit in the silence of their rooms, staring at their faces and wondering if anything was left beneath.

Time passed both quickly and slowly, each day never-ending, a succession of empty hours to fill. Soon they melted into a muddle of forgotten, unrecorded thought and he would look back over the flotsam without any idea what he had done or why he had done it. Even so, for all its solitude, he was later to recall the time with nostalgia, as a brief period when he had, if nothing else, experienced something approaching peace.

Decay

(1639 – 1641)

Sebastian looked out from his room at the ragged city below. He could make out the usual tide of carts, donkeys and traders, slowed to a trickle in the crush. From above, the mob lacked individuality, its colours and forms mixing together as they moved between one nowhere to another. He was glad of the distance. The streets grew more miserable with every passing year: the animals bonier, the stalls more dilapidated, the people sicker and their stoop more pronounced. For nearly two decades, he had been observing a country in slow decline, ravaged by war, the land wealed with battlefields and trampled by armies, whole towns decimated until only women and children remained. But over the previous six months, the descent had steepened.

Cinq-Mars was the source. Since Richelieu had first introduced him to Louis, his rise to power had been spectacular. The King was infected with love for him, to the point of fever. Within a week of their first meeting, both his old mistresses – de Hautefort and de La Fayette – were forgotten and dismissed. Within a month, the marquis had been made *grand écuyer*, obliging everyone to refer to him as Monsieur le Grand. Cinq-Mars responded with typical ingratitude, simply demanding more. Not that this seemed to bother Louis, who dismissed his insolence, infidelity and tantrums as foibles, seeming to find them somehow endearing. Even one notorious occasion when the marquis was too exhausted to meet Louis, having spent all night with the notorious courtesan Marion Delorme, went unpunished. If anything, his transgressions only seemed to increase the King's infatuation.

Their relationship came to follow a familiar pattern. Exasperated by Cinq-Mars' demands, Louis would lose his temper and scold the marquis, who invariably responded with breathtaking indignation, often insulting the King to his face and then disappearing for days on end. Wracked with remorse, Louis would then shower him with gifts and money in an attempt to win him back. Of course, whatever Cinq-Mars received was never enough: silks, braids, embroidered doublets, *Semper Augustus* tulips, coaches, servants, fireworks, chinoiserie, a pair of the latest flintlock pistols inlaid with mother-of-pearl, a stable of Fresian horses – nothing ever satisfied him for long. Until, having squandered away twenty fortunes, Cinq-Mars found himself with everything a person could wish for – except for one thing. Despite his fifty-two suits, he could never change the man wearing them – the world outside was simply not as large as the space within.

Now, six months later, the marquis' triumph was complete. Untouchable, he lorded over the palace with a retinue of associates and hangers-on, demanding audiences with and often insulting whomever his caprice happened to settle on, no matter how elevated their title or position. Unable to retaliate, his victims were forced to laugh along through locked teeth. Despite their fury, as long as Cinq-Mars remained the King's favourite, there was nothing they could do, and they were forced to invite him to every banquet, tournament or event they wanted Louis to attend.

Sebastian spent an increasing amount of time avoiding the marquis and his coterie. Unable to visit the garden or wander the palace, he passed most days shut in his room, only able to leave during the marquis' occasional retreats with Louis to Saint-Germain. One thing he couldn't escape were his evening performances. Previously, the marquis had tolerated them with unalloyed disdain, sitting stiff-backed in the audience and observing proceedings with the scorn of the impotent – Sebastian had even grown to delight in his sour stare. However, those same performances had since taken on an entirely different complexion. Cinq-Mars' scowl had now been replaced by the smirk of impending revenge, and whenever Sebastian looked across at him, he met the same disquieting grin. Trapped within the confines of the stage, Sebastian would try to ignore him, but the marquis remained an angry smudge in the corner of his eye, as conspicuous as imminent and violent death.

Richelieu remained Sebastian's only protection but he was rarely present at court, occupied instead with the recent revolts in Catalonia and Portugal. Ever fearful of the threat from Spain, he was doing all he could to support the rebels in the hope of tying down the Emperor's troops.

The cardinal's absence didn't go unnoticed by Cinq-Mars, who was continually grasping further, feeling for the edges of what the King would permit. It began with slight insubordination, just the odd remark, that the cardinal seemed overworked or that he seemed to take to his bed more frequently nowadays. Then more direct, that he was *old* or *not what he once was*. Soon he realised there was no check at all, except for the occasional admonishment from Louis, who clearly enjoyed hearing his chief minister being taken down a peg or two. Alarmingly, Richelieu remained either oblivious or simply didn't consider it worth bothering with. Like Louis, he seemed to regard the marquis' behaviour as youthful exuberance, no more dangerous than that of a child.

* * *

It was two days before the Assumption that Cinq-Mars finally made his intentions known. Sebastian had been performing a pastiche of the imperial general, Jean de Werth – considerably improved by the absence of the marquis, doubtless off debauching himself in the depths of the city. Then, after taking the opportunity for a brief walk round the garden, he returned to the sanctuary of his room, only to find the door ajar.

Sebastian knew immediately that something was wrong. After the previous attempt on his life, he was careful to keep his door locked at all times as well as sealing any gaps before going to sleep – someone was most certainly waiting inside. Turning back towards the stairwell, Sebastian abruptly found his path blocked by a guard, his arms crossed and defiant. The face was familiar, seamed by a scar that ran from

212

scalp to jaw, and he recognised him as one of the marquis' bodyguards.

'You've a visitor,' he stated, nodding him back towards his room.

Sebastian instinctively reached for the pistol in his pocket, then decided against it. Shooting a guard was a capital crime. If Cinq-Mars wanted him dead, better to make it as difficult for him as possible. Instead he let the guard put a hand on his shoulder and steer him to the door.

The marquis was slouched by the desk, his clothes glinting, liquid in the candlelight. Both his left eye and cheek were scooped in shadow, making his face appear half flesh, half skull, and his right hand rested on his rapier. He watched Sebastian, letting the silence hang.

'You've come to kill me.' Sebastian was oddly unafraid. Having spent so long fearing this moment, he found it almost dreamlike, as though acting a part he had played many times before.

'No, this is just for pleasure.'

'No pleasure for me, *Monsieur le Grand*.' He pronounced the title with mocking reverence.

Cinq-Mars shook his head with a smile, and when he spoke his voice retained its murderous serenity. 'Insolent to the last, dwarf. And you will suffer for it ... be certain of that. I'm a patient man, or at least patient enough. I'll wait until the right time, when I can work on you at leisure. A few days, maybe a week if you last that long.'

'That's what you came to tell me? Don't you have anything better to do? I was under the apprehension that you are a *very* important man.'

213

'In fact, I am here on business. Your room is required. I've had enough of your stink around the palace and I've a spare clerk I need lodgings for.'

Sebastian considered asking if the cardinal had been informed, then thought better of it. Why would the man need the cardinal when he had the King? 'Well, I'd best get packing.' He accompanied the remark with a pointed glance at the door.

'Don't play the hero, dwarf. It doesn't suit you,' the marquis replied, noisily drawing up a glob of mucus and spitting it at Sebastian's feet – a parting gift. And with that, he turned for the door.

Then Cinq-Mars was gone. Except he wasn't. The after-image remained in front of Sebastian as he stood, battling with the implications of what had just taken place. Cinq-Mars was right. It wasn't an *if* but a *when*. His thoughts immediately turned to escape – and with it came disorientation. His room was his refuge from the world and the prospect of being cast from it was profoundly unsettling; as though he had been ejected from the womb, some shivering newborn thrust into a cold and terrifying world. Where was he to go? For a moment, he considered the streets, hiding away among the poor and anonymous. But there was no safety there. It had been hard enough before, let alone now. Besides, he was too used to his comforts to go grubbing round the cobbles or sleeping in doorways again. Better to take his chances at court than die on some lonely corner with one of the marquis' brutes come to stove his head in.

To begin with, Sebastian tried the local area around Les Halles. It seemed a good place to lose oneself in as any, the beating heart of the city, if it possessed one at all: a hive of costermongers, bargain-hunters, fruit-traders, thieves, artisans, sharpers, metalworkers, beggars, soon-to-be-beggars and people simply looking to try their luck. However, the crush was intense and the stink almost unbearable – predominantly fish, transported from the coast and bloating in the August sun, mixed with fetid pickles and meat. Consequently, his search didn't last long. After a few minutes of wincing his way through the stench while lost in the dark and the scrum, he gave up and headed for the Porte Saint-Martin and the *faubourgs* – intent on finding somewhere quiet on the road towards Saint-Denis. He expected a long journey, but half a mile beyond the walls, he stumbled upon a sign advertising a cheap room. The house belonged to an ageing widow, clearly looking to support herself. She seemed amused by him at first, then gained sudden interest when he mentioned paying two months in advance. The low price was explained when she led him to a bare room overlooking Saint-Lazare prison. Not that it bothered him in the slightest. In the circumstances, anything that kept people away seemed an advantage, especially considering it was walking distance from the Louvre. So, after ordering a cart to fetch his things, he moved in right away.

It turned out to be one of his better decisions. Liberated from the urban chaos, he woke up to clean air, open sky and chequerboard fields flumed with barley. Cinq-Mars was no longer a distraction and he was able to leave the confines of his room, allowing him space to think and to concentrate on making final revisions to his play. Determined to make the most of what time he had left, he no longer listened to his doubts and his writing acquired the fluency and energy common to those near death, the last grains of life flaring like powder in a flame. One loose end still remained, however – the cardinal. Over time, Sebastian's anger towards Richelieu had faded, to the point where he wondered if it had simply been frustration, the need to blame. After all, Richelieu had treated the revolt no differently to any other. And loath as Sebastian was to admit it, there was truth to the cardinal's words. He had no more leeway than an executioner did with an axe. He was and had to behave as chief minister; it was impossible to expect him to be otherwise.

* * *

Richelieu sat in his official rooms at the Palais-Cardinal. He had been working much of the night and slumped on his throne, his hands laid on its oversized armrests, a heraldic canopy behind. To compensate for his condition, his attendants had dressed him in overwhelming pomp – a soutane of silver thread set against the deepest black. And rather than his usual biretta he was crowned with a mitre that rose a full two feet above his head. Instead of glorifying him, it made him look all the more exhausted, his face leeched against the splendour, its only lustre provided by a thin gloss of sweat. Conscious of his appearance, his guards stared ahead from their posts, eyes steady, refusing to acknowledge his condition.

Sebastian's arrival was enough to raise leaden eyelids and the cardinal leaned forward, peering down and allowing himself a smile.

'Hello, Sebastian. Last time we spoke, your departure was … emphatic. Has something changed your mind?'

'It's Cinq-Mars. He means to kill me.'

216

Richelieu dismissed the concern with a flick of his hand, as if being informed of some schoolboy prank. 'Is that all? The boy's a braggart. It means nothing. He knows I won't allow it.'

'Even so, if I do die, I want you to know who's responsible.'

'You exaggerate. If he meant to kill you, he would have done so by now.'

'He's already tried to burn me alive.'

'That was before I spoke to him. Besides, what harm has he actually done?'

'He means to kill me, Your Eminence.'

'You forget he's my ward. I've been responsible for him for the past seven years, and he is answerable to me. Whatever he may claim, the fact remains I am still Chief Minister of France and head of the *Conseil d'État*. He will not break his word.'

'Your Eminence, I'm not sure you quite understand the situation ...'

Raw from lack of sleep, the cardinal was in no mood to brook dissent and rose out of his seat – stiff-backed, glaring down from on high with his gemstone peer.

'Mind your words. I tolerated your previous outburst because of your brother. Don't assume I'll do so again. I understand the situation perfectly well. In fact, after twenty-three years at court, I might possibly understand it a little better than you.'

'Of course, Your Eminence. Please accept my deepest apologies. You know I would never mean to offend. But surely you agree the fact you're his guardian might affect your judgement?' Sebastian's frantic efforts to rephrase seemed to succeed and the cardinal nodded, dropping back on to his throne, seemingly too tired to maintain his annoyance.

'Perhaps, but what threat does he pose? What are you asking me to be afraid of? His intelligence? His political skills? His ability to persuade? Chevreuse or Philip of Spain I could understand, even Gaston. But Henri? He has ambition, and precious little else.'

'Louis is infatuated with him. He has the King's ear.'

'Yes, but I have his. You forget it was I who introduced him to the King in the first place. Besides, you say my relationship with Cinq-Mars affects my judgement. Don't you think the same applies to you? That your belief he's trying to kill you might make you think him more dangerous than he actually is?'

'Yes, Your Eminence.' Sebastian conceded, not because he thought Richelieu was right but because he knew any further argument was futile. At worst he would infuriate the cardinal, at best merely irritate him. Anyway, who was he to lecture the Chief Minister of France? The man had been at court as long as he'd been alive, longer even.

During the ensuing lull, the two men glanced at each other, both aware that the conversation wasn't over and of what had been left unsaid.

Richelieu ended the silence. 'The tomb for your brother and mother, it's complete.'

'Thank you.' Sebastian's voice was flat, acknowledgement more than gratitude.

'I had an extra plot put in. I didn't know whether you wanted to be buried alongside them.'

Sebastian didn't reply, then looked back at the cardinal with a baffled smile. He knew Richelieu was probably just being meticulous. Even so, it seemed a very human consideration

– and there was humanity in the cardinal's face. Tiredness had softened the veneer and a curl had wrinkled its way into the corner of his mouth, barely perceptible beneath his beard.

'Yes, I would like that very much indeed.' Sebastian nodded. Then they glanced at each other again and smiled, this time knowing the meeting was at an end. And long after Sebastian had begun the long walk home, he ambled at a contented pace, oblivious to the knocks and blows of the passing throng, pleased to have seen his master again.

*　*　*

Despite Richelieu's predictions, the rise of Cinq-Mars continued unchecked. He was made successively Master of the Wardrobe then Master of the Horse, given authority over the royal stables, along with the right to every horse and saddle in them upon the King's death. He had power over the retinue, ceremonies and even the royal coronation. Along with both titles came ample salaries as well as whatever tidbits Louis would throw his way. But it still wasn't enough. He wanted glory, military command, and above all what he could never have – the respect of others.

Richelieu, meanwhile, was content to tolerate the marquis' requests, viewing them as distractions, irrelevant to matters of state. It wasn't until the King informed him of his agreement to Cinq-Mars marrying Marie de Gonzague that he realised the gravity of the situation. Louis mentioned it casually as they were discussing some petitions for tax exemption. Unable to hide his shock, Richelieu reacted as if the King had announced he was marrying Cinq-Mars himself.

'You can't possibly do this ...'

Louis wasn't used to being given orders and was stunned by the cardinal's response. Richelieu seemed equally surprised at his own lack of control and gazed back, momentarily forgetting what he meant to say.

'By which I mean of course that you can do it, Your Majesty. However, in my opinion, it would not be the wisest course of action.'

With a sniff of displeasure, Louis nodded at Richelieu to continue. Due to his stutter, he often communicated using little more than a nod or shake of the head, preferring to avoid the embarrassment of speech.

'Marrying into the house of Gonzague would destroy our entire Italian policy. The woman governs Mantua. She's an ally of Spain.'

'You think it matters so muh-muh-much?' the King replied with an innocence that Richelieu found half-endearing, half-contemptible. Sometimes he felt Louis was like a man locked in a tower, to whom reality was nothing more than a hazy jostle far below.

'I'm afraid so, Your Majesty. Aside from the political considerations, there would be the risk of a royal favourite being intimately linked to our enemies.'

'But I would be breaking my word, and a king does not break his word.'

'You would not, Your Majesty. I would be unable to allow it on religious grounds.'

'What religious grounds?'

'A sign from God, Your Majesty, a vision that the children of the union would be cursed.'

Louis laughed at the flagrancy of the lie. 'You're a good man, Armand. He will hate you for it.'

'Better me than you, Your Majesty,' Richelieu replied, shuffling backwards out of the room before Louis had the chance to change his mind. Then, closing the doors, he snapped upright and requested the steward to bring Cinq-Mars to his chambers of state without delay.

* * *

Despite his magnificent surroundings, Richelieu dressed plainly in a black soutane sans biretta and lace. Now in his mid-fifties, he was forced to use a stick, but shunned it today and stood beside his throne, gripping the armrest as a prop and staring ahead with the conviction of a messiah. The impression was of an austere figure, shorn of decoration and dressed for purpose, determined to exercise his will, the only sign of weakness the shake of his hand as he struggled to support an ageing frame. Yet even his frailty somehow added to the zeal, each spasm and waver showing his will to fight.

Cinq-Mars entered the room with the air of someone who wants to leave as soon as possible. Disregarding the usual pleasantries, he gave a cursory bow before enquiring what precisely it was that the cardinal wished to discuss. Richelieu left a brief pause to express his disapproval, and when he spoke, the words were as slow and accurate as a chisel on stone, their sharp edges stressed by a voice that seemed to take grim pleasure in the task.

'This marriage cannot happen. It is not the will of the Lord.'

Cinq-Mars listened with inevitable disbelief then exploded into fury, screaming outrage and defiance. Richelieu ignored him, letting the marquis' anger exhaust itself before repeating himself in blunter terms.

'Nothing you say can change this. I will not question a sign from God.'

'But you can't do this.' Cinq-Mars was now reduced to a whimper. The cardinal looked back, still struggling to hold himself upright. Then he too softened.

'Henri, if I could spare you this pain I would. But Marie de Gonzague? Don't you see the consequences of that?'

'But this is the woman I love. This is my life. Does that mean nothing to you?'

'It means everything to me, Henri, and I rejoice in your happiness. But what I feel has nothing to do with the needs of France.'

'I want to forgive you, but I can't, not for this. I'm giving you a last chance – reconsider.' Cinq-Mars looked at the cardinal with an expression which reminded Richelieu of the moment he first arrived after losing his parents. A traumatised, consumptive stare, the eyeballs aimless and without moorings.

'There's no point, Henri. I can't sacrifice Italy for anyone, not even you.'

'Very well, but remember this was your choice not mine,' the marquis finished, pulling himself upright before turning his back and striding out of the room. Even the clack of his shoes sounded abrupt.

* * *

The situation was compounded a month later. After his humiliation by Richelieu, Cinq-Mars' first reaction had been to implore the King to change the cardinal's mind, pleading with him almost daily. Tortured, Louis was desperate to oblige and hunted vainly for a substitute bride, but not one of the noble houses was interested. His opportunity arrived with rumours of the Habsburgs approaching Arras and the raising of an army to meet them. Knowing the marquis' desire to command, Louis immediately offered it to him – to Cinq-Mars' delight – only for Richelieu to visit the following day and have it withdrawn.

This time Cinq-Mars' fury was unrestrained. Marching straight to the Palais-Cardinal, he demanded an immediate audience. Richelieu, however, was occupied in a meeting with the papal legate and left him to seethe for twenty minutes, and by the time the marquis was finally permitted entry he was in a state of murderous rage: striding in, cape over shoulder and hand on sword. Richelieu's guards responded in kind, lowering their pikes and taking a step forward. Unperturbed, the cardinal defused the situation immediately, motioning the guards back with a wave of the hand before asking the marquis if he would care to let go of his weapon in return. Cinq-Mars left a defiant pause before unbuckling his rapier and letting it clash onto the floor.

'Don't you dare take my command. The King gave it to me, you've no right.'

Richelieu shook his head, then raised an index finger, parent to child.

'A year ago I told you that being a favourite was one of the most difficult positions in France. You have no power, only what the King chooses to give you. I suggest you act accordingly.'

'Why? You serve the King just as I do.'

'Don't make an enemy of me.' Richelieu's voice was disconcertingly measured, the opposite of bluster. 'I know what you've been saying. That I'm an old man. That my judgement isn't what it used to be. That I need to be replaced. I've let it pass for now. But take this command and it will be the end of you.'

'No more lectures, Armand. Don't you understand? You can't just threaten me any more. I'm not afraid.'

The response was treated with a slow sigh and Richelieu shook his head, more disappointed than angry. 'That was always your problem, Henri – speaking without thinking. What do you suppose would happen if I asked the King to choose between you or me?'

'Probably you, but only probably. You'd be taking a risk, and if there's one thing I know about you, it's that you hate taking risks if you can avoid them. So why do it? Why gamble everything? You don't need to do this.'

'You're right, Henri, I detest unnecessary risk, which is exactly why I won't put our largest remaining army in the command of a man with no military experience. If we lose at Arras, the Habsburgs will invade. I can't allow that, not under any circumstances. So reflect on this – if you take command and fail, I won't just go to the King and ask for your resignation, I'll ask for your head.'

The axeman's shadow had a sobering effect on Cinq-Mars who paused and took an unusually long time to reply. 'I get nothing?'

'All I ask is that you prove yourself. First lead the cavalry. Fulfil your duties and then we can consider higher command.'

After a brief hesitation, Cinq-Mars acceded with a

petulant nod before turning heel and leaving the room. Richelieu remained a moment then forced himself upright and shuffled to an antechamber, closing the door behind him. Taking the nearest chair, he sat back, opened his collar and stared at the opposite wall, his face hollow with exhaustion. The mask had grown heavier in recent weeks. Time – it used to seem an ocean stretching from boundless past to boundless future. Now it had become a puddle boiling away in the sun, its waters growing more brackish by the day.

*   *   *

Arras was a triumph and Marshal Châtillon its hero. Cinq-Mars, lauded in the *Gazette*, played a supporting role, having his horse shot from beneath him after heroically charging the enemy guns. Yet on his return, far from boasting of his exploits, the marquis was curiously subdued, refusing to discuss what had happened except to bad-mouth the marshal to anyone who would listen. Mostly, he sulked in his room, only emerging to go hunting with the King or play the occasional game of faro with his friends. Some thought he had been changed after witnessing the horrors of war, others had less flattering explanations.

Richelieu, meanwhile, was becoming an increasingly peripheral figure at court. His age had become apparent to all, though he did his best to hide it, wearing wide-brimmed hats to disguise his hairline and using his crosier rather than a stick. More often he spared himself the embarrassment of public scrutiny by staying in his palace, restricting his official meetings to the *Conseil d'État* and his twice-weekly audiences with the King.

His one indulgence remained his village of Richelieu. He had spent nine years watching over it, hiring a legion of masons to work its stone. Too busy to visit, he had the model of the town moved to his private apartments: walled and quartered, a lavish gate centred along each side. Each house was carved in wood, with spaces left for the few remaining plots. Arranged in a perfect grid, the buildings were close-fitting, making the whole resemble a chequerboard dotted with missing squares.

At the very end of the town stood Richelieu's palace, three wings of colonnades and domed splendour set amid elaborate topiary and shaded avenues. Despite never having been there, the cardinal still knew its precise dimensions and the contents of every room, even the patterns on the cornicing. He visited it almost daily in his mind. Somewhere to escape the pressure of work and imagine the day when there would be nothing left to be done.

Currently he was by the circular window in his private apartments, seated at a table and idly tracing its swirls. The top was inlaid with ivory and mother of pearl, quartering into four separate designs meeting at a circle in the centre, also quartered and with the pattern rotated to opposing sides – a bewildering vortex of diamonds, vines, fleur-de-lis, and crosses. Staring at the track of his finger, the cardinal specified the measurements and decoration for a small gate-house to be added to the castle entrance at the head of the moat. Each part was described in detail, from the wood of the frame to the height of the portcullis and the spacing of the crenulation. His instructions were fluid, recited without notes, as if he was simply reading off a chart – the voice a tranquil monotone.

The cardinal's reverie was shattered into a thousand splinters as the door flew open and smashed a side-table into the wall. The only people present were a doctor and an amanuensis, who gaped at the figure advancing towards them. Even when it stopped, they remained motionless, unsure what it meant to do.

'Good day, Henri, do you have something you wish to discuss?' the cardinal remarked, not even turning to look.

Cinq-Mars didn't reply, scowling at the attendants and jabbing a finger at the open doorway. In their eagerness, they scampered for the corridor without so much as a farewell.

Long after the door had closed, Cinq-Mars remained silent. His face, initially creased with fury, changed now that they were alone, the wrinkles flattening into something far more calculating. Richelieu suspected he had realised there was nobody else present and was considering whether to kill him. Not terribly wise considering the two witnesses and the twenty guards between him and escape. Eventually the marquis seemed to reach the same conclusion and looked across at the cardinal, admonishing him with a gentle shake of the head.

'How did it come to this, Armand? You're my guardian. You took care of me, introduced me to court and to the King. I owe it all to you. But now you hold me back. You block me at every turn. My marriage, my command at Arras, you even threaten to have me executed. I'm asking you to stop. I've been understanding until now, but this must end.'

'Henri, you've risen a long way. Why risk it all now?'

'It wasn't me who chose this battle, it was you. You made a fool of me at Arras.'

'From what I heard you did that perfectly well yourself.

Ordering your troops straight into the guns, what were you thinking?'

'It would have worked if it hadn't been for Châtillon.'

'Really?' The cardinal stopped his meandering of the tabletop and glared at the marquis. He had a curious ability to look down on people even from a sitting position. 'I heard he told you specifically to stay in reserve. That one of your men was forced to shoot your horse from beneath you so he could sound the retreat. Not only that, but you made repeated requests to charge again and the marshal actually had to overrule you in person.'

'That's a lie. I saw a gap and charged to split the enemy. But Châtillon wanted all the glory and ordered me back. The man knows nothing.'

'Does it matter? We won. History will say you led the cavalry. Isn't that enough?'

'No. If you hadn't taken away my command, none of this would have happened. Besides, you've heard the rumours I assume? People are laughing behind my back. I'm being made to look an idiot.'

'You may be right, but it doesn't mean I was wrong. Do you really expect me to put an army in the hands of someone with no experience at all? It would have been insanity. You can't judge a decision through hindsight ... only context.'

'But all I've ever wanted were the same chances you've had – to prove my worth. You're on the *Conseil d'État*. You've led on the battlefield. Why can't I?'

'Henri, it's not the same. You're twenty years old. You've already had a military command and a senior position of state, and now you tell me you want to be on the *Conseil d'État*. I was thirty-one before I had that chance – and thought young for the post. It isn't fair, Henri. The nobles won't stand for it. And without the nobles, we can't raise the troops. You'd be bringing the temple down on our heads.'

'You disappoint me, Armand. Is that really the best you can come up with? That I'm twenty years old.' Cinq-Mars stood up and walked to the window, hands clasped behind his back. Looking out, he saw Paris through drunken eyes – roofs and streets pooled together in its whorled glass. 'Louis was sixteen when he became king. I didn't hear of anyone saying he wasn't old enough, least of all you. Just admit the truth. You don't want me on the *Conseil d'État* because you don't want change. You're the one who isn't ready.'

'You do yourself no favours with these outbursts. The more I listen, the more I know I made the right choice.'

'What in God's name is that supposed to mean? Are you losing your mind, old man?' Cinq-Mars jeered, turning round and tramping towards the door. He stopped by the model in the corner before picking up one of the dwellings and peering at it. 'Look at you. Is this what you do all day? Play with your toy houses? You might have been a great man once, but you're nothing now.' Then he placed the building down in the castle courtyard, upside down, as if blown there by a particularly capricious hurricane. 'Either way, remember this. I gave you a chance, Cardinal. Whatever happens, you were warned.'

* * *

Sebastian arrived at the Palais-Cardinal with a black eye and a split lip, having narrowly avoided being robbed the previous night. It wasn't the first time. He'd been returning from a pleasant few hours shared between Michelle and a bottle of wine when, despite his best attempts to keep to the shadows, two men had seen him silhouetted on the Porte de Nesle and grabbed him as he made his way towards the Pont Neuf, pulling him into an alleyway before he could reach for his pistol. He had only escaped by hurling a handful of coins into his assailant's eyes and vaulting over the wall into some canal-cum-sewer. After which he was forced to squelch the three-mile walk home slathered in stinking foulness.

Consequently, Sebastian had spent much of the morning trying to remove the stench from his clothes and was in the middle of his fifth scrub when one of Richelieu's aides arrived and announced the cardinal was expecting him. Naturally Sebastian accepted, while keeping his distance from the man's nose and managing to beg enough time to finish cleaning himself and apply some lavender water.

After being taken to the palace, he was led through a side door, up two flights of stairs and through a suite of rooms, finally emerging in the antechamber outside the cabinet. Its architrave appeared incongruous amidst the book-lined walls – the only hint of its importance was the soldier stood at each side. A few minutes passed before the quiet was broken by the ring of a bell from within, at which point one of the guards opened the door and nodded him in. Sebastian hesitated. It was not an appealing entrance – instead a slab of black, which swallowed what little light there was, while casting an unnatural shadow that appeared to spill out beyond the door. Eventually, after a few moments peering into the gloom, he inched towards it, wavering at the brink before daring to step inside.

As the door closed behind him, Sebastian experienced the

same unease he had felt walking up to his father's deathbed. There was no sound or light to guide, and he was forced to grope through the murk, spreading his arms in front of him as he made his way forward. Then he stopped, sensing the presence of someone nearby, straining for a clue but unable to hear over his own laboured breath.

'Who is it?' The voice came from his left.

'Me – Sebastian.'

There was a pause followed by a grunt of realisation. 'Sebastian Morra ... you sound different.'

'Perhaps because you can't see me. People often confuse my height and my mind.'

'My God, what is that stink? Lavender and ...'

'My apologies, Your Eminence. I fell into a canal.' Sebastian interrupted as the cardinal searched for a word to end the sentence. 'An accident,' he added, wanting to change the subject as quickly as possible.

'An accident? Odd that a man of your stature should fall over a wall. What sort of accident?'

'I didn't look where I was going. My apologies again, the surroundings certainly draw one's nose to the scent.'

'Quite so ...' the cardinal gave a chuckle. 'Anyway, do excuse the dark. A relic from my migraines. I prefer to be away from light and noise when I think. It clarifies the mind.'

'Of course. You asked to see me.'

'Yes, I would like your assistance with something. If you're still working for me, that is?' He glanced across at Sebastian.

It was a pointless question; Sebastian was hardly going to refuse the only ally he had left. Though out of respect for his brother, he did at least pause before replying.

'What do you need from me?'

'Nothing immediate, though considering the situation at court, I can't rule out a plot. I imagine later I'll need information relating to Henri … I mean Cinq-Mars.'

'Actually I've been meaning to ask. I was reading the *Gazette* and I noticed a favourable account of his … exploits at Arras. It seemed odd. I mean it's an open secret your relationship has soured of late.'

'I hoped to spare him embarrassment.' Richelieu's voice thinned and he drew a breath. 'I thought he might be grateful, but it only seems to have infuriated him.'

'Infuriated him? I think you've done considerably more than that. You know he wants you replaced?'

'I'm fully aware of Henri's intentions,' the cardinal snapped, curt with annoyance. His diminished situation appeared to have made him more sensitive – even to the slightest of quibbles. 'Rest assured I will do what is necessary.'

'But why are you allowing this? Cinq-Mars is just some glorified country squire. You're the Chief Minister of France. Can't you just remove him?'

'It would jeopardise my relationship with the King. I would have to threaten resignation. It's not a risk I care to take.'

'It's not a risk.'

'Disobeying a monarch is always a risk. Louis is ultimately a man, as capricious and unpredictable as anyone else. It's easier to wait. Cinq-Mars will slip up. He's too greedy, too rash.'

'And if you're wrong? If Cinq-Mars doesn't make a mistake?'

'Henri will make a mistake. To make no mistakes, you need to have no flaws. Henri has flaws.'

'But what if the flaws make no difference?'

This was followed by a long and considered silence.

'Explain.'

'I think you're underestimating the King's infatuation with Cinq-Mars.'

Another pause.

'Not relevant. If the King is so infatuated with Henri, there's nothing I can do in any case.'

'Also, Your Eminence ...' It was not the momentary pause for dramatic effect, but the longer silence of a delicate subject. 'Your position may not be as secure as it once was.'

'Don't be ridiculous. I'm still doing everything that's required of me. Our recent victory at Arras. Who do you think raised the men? Made sure they were equipped? Provisioned them? I still run the *Conseil d'État*, manage the King's affairs.'

'Didn't you once tell me the difference between image and truth?' Freed of his body, Sebastian's voice had become surprisingly bold, to the point where a listener might have had difficulty telling cardinal from servant. 'It's Cinq-Mars people see every day at court. It's Cinq-Mars who sits by the King's side, whom we all bow to and call *Monsieur le Grand*. It doesn't matter what the truth is.'

'I don't care what the court thinks. The only person I answer to is the King. Anyway, even if I were to be replaced, we've already made arrangements. A successor has been agreed.'

Sebastian didn't ask whom. He didn't need to. It had to be Jules Mazarin. For three years he had been the cardinal's deputy in all but name, and Richelieu had already pressed for him to be given a cardinal's hat. Besides, he was godfather

233

and probably actual father of the dauphin, trusted by both an oblivious Louis and the Queen.

Though Sebastian had never considered the possibility of Richelieu being replaced, it didn't surprise him that the cardinal had something prepared. Richelieu planned everything in his life. For all his intelligence, he was in many ways a profoundly predictable man, always thinking in straight lines with that undeviating and methodical logic. His own death was treated no differently – just another strategic consideration. In an odd way, the environment suited him – locked in his dark and silent chamber, removed from any distractions of humanity or morality, like some mind in a jar manipulating an imagined world. And it occurred to Sebastian that perhaps this was the only way he could govern the country, that the only way to make hard decisions was to divorce himself utterly from their results.

* * *

There had been a sense of things coming to a head for some time – shadow-talk and whispers mostly. Bereft of the cardinal's stabilising presence, France became a wheel without an axis. The court whirled with rumours, all unconfirmed: that the uprisings in Catalonia and Portugal had been crushed; that a Habsburg army of a hundred thousand men were waiting to burst across the Pyrenees; that a Spanish fleet was crossing the English Channel, sailing for Normandy; that another revolt against the *gabelle* was planned. Hysteria took hold and people gave way to abandon: wine cellars were emptied, courtesans exhausted, everyone cheating and being cheated upon. There was no tomorrow so there could be no regrets.

The cardinal battled the situation as best he could, trying to trace each rumour, or amassing piles of reports, documents and notes which he was perpetually poring over and reshuffling in an effort to uncover a link. Continuing to avoid the court almost entirely, he worked harder than ever – requiring the help of three scribes to keep pace with his commands. This lack of contact with the outside world only seemed to heighten his suspicions, making him keener for knowledge and more demanding of detail. Information would be sifted and judged, and anything important written in a small notebook he kept by his bed – the left pages reserved for questions, the right for answers.

To begin with, it wasn't apparent what the cardinal was looking for. The requests were broad and Sebastian couldn't see any pattern to the people he was being asked to observe: courtiers, Spanish residents, even some of his fellow spies. Over time, the demands became more specific and the names more familiar: Gaston, Chevreuse and the marquis. Not that this made matters any clearer. All three knew they were being watched and restricted themselves to small talk so dreary that it was obviously a masquerade. Anything deemed important would be scribbled, passed between them and thrown in the fire.

Richelieu's frustration at the lack of progress was clear. He was constantly irritable, and while he seemed to be having no problem finding questions for the left-hand side of his book, the right side remained infuriatingly empty. Until he reached the point when he was too tired to be angry any more and would ask for news in an exasperated drone, anticipating the inevitable answer – that nothing had changed.

The breakthrough, when it came, arrived from an

unexpected source – the principality of Sedan. A letter from the Count of Soissons, a former accomplice of Chevreuse, declaring he would invade through Champagne with the support of the Dukes of Guise and Bouillon. Richelieu leapt upon the information with rabid enthusiasm. Everyone was put to work amassing material to build a case: intercepting letters, searching for military movements and contracts, bribing people who might have been approached. Within a fortnight, Richelieu had all the evidence he needed and was able to bring charges before the King. The verdict was a formality but also meaningless so long as Soissons remained at large. Its only purpose was to bring the enemy out into the open. Now the count was left with no choice but to respond, and within three days there were reports of his troops marching along the river Meuse.

With battle imminent, the rumours were replaced by real and concrete fears. During the two weeks it took the royal troops to reach the border, people discussed little else. It was generally felt that though Soissons had the smaller force, he was the better commander, at least on open ground. Up against him was Marshal Châtillon, hero of Arras. Though respected, the marshal was known as a siege tactician, preferring defensive formations, and the consensus was that he would favour conventional battle, Soissons the surprise attack. What was not disputed, however, was that a defeat would make the cardinal's position untenable. With an enemy marching on Paris, France would need more than an ageing priest to lead the state. Richelieu knew this full well and became desperate for news from the field, requesting hourly updates on any visitors for the King or diplomatic business, the principal result of which was a succession of false alarms – riders appearing at the gates and being rushed through to the royal chambers, only to offer the greetings of a foreign dignitary or tax rolls from the provinces.

When the messenger finally did arrive, Sebastian was midway through a performance in the great hall. This time there could be no doubt. The man was dusty and hot from his travels, a smudge against the bright tapestry of court, so weary that he seemed unaware of the rows of eyes upon him, all searching for a clue. Then, without a glance in either direction, he marched up to the King's apartments and was gone. The room remained in utter silence for a moment before bursting into hubbub. Some were convinced they had seen a giveaway smile, others a frown of defeat – though most remained unsure – and the discussion roiled round the chamber for five minutes or so before a herald eventually appeared and announced a victory for the King.

A victory it might have been, but it was not a glorious one. Châtillon had been ambushed while negotiating muddy ground. Attacked on the flank, over six hundred royal troops had been killed and half the remaining army captured. Yet, having completed the rout, Soissons had gathered his officers around him to celebrate when one of them had shot him in the face – apparently one of the cardinal's agents. Left without a leader, the rebels abruptly found themselves marooned without orders and more importantly without pay. So, after looting the nearest town, they promptly disbanded. It was an unsatisfactory conclusion. The army was lost and the country left wide open. There would be more to come.

* * *

When discussing the conspiracy, both men began hesitantly, discussing the latest theatre along with recent news. Neither of them took comfort in the exchange and there was a sense of the unspoken, a mutual knowledge that they were merely passing time. Eventually the conversation ran out, replaced by pin-drop silence. Both men glanced around the room, each waiting for the other to speak. Gaston had chosen to meet in a rarely visited outcrop of the Louvre. A small guestroom, it was inconvenient to reach as well as bitterly cold at night, due to its crumbling windows and lack of a fireplace, and was generally used to house unpopular visitors. The oak panelling was broken by white covers and throws spread over the squares of furniture, combined with a black and white checked floor that gave Cinq-Mars the impression of sitting inside a folded chessboard. Gaston, who was more familiar with conspiracy, spoke first.

'I've heard there have been…differences between you and the cardinal.' He twirled a piece of card, perhaps to occupy nervous fingers.

'It's his fault, not mine. Whatever I do, he blocks it. He even vetoed my marriage. Claimed it was a sign from God. My army commission at Arras as well. The man's shameless. He clearly sees me as some kind of threat. I've no choice, I can't just let him carry on.'

Gaston listened while continuing to spin the card. His pose was relaxed, slouched, even submissive – awaiting an indiscretion rather than inviting one.

'Richelieu's been carrying on for fifteen years. I don't see that there's a great deal you can do.'

'I've been telling Louis to ignore him. Just to remind him who's in charge.'

'I see it's working well for you.'

'It'll take time of course ... but what alternative do I have?'

The card stopped moving and was placed on the sidetable with the same flourish Gaston used when laying down a winning hand.

'That depends what you're willing to consider ...' He didn't complete the remark, leaving it to dangle – unfinished. Cinq-Mars didn't take up the invitation, instead looking round at a door he already knew to be closed. There was no one nearby – nor was there any way of avoiding a response. He turned back to Gaston.

'I know what you're going to say.'

'Then it would seem I don't need to say it.'

'You want me to support a union with Spain.'

'What an interesting thought.' Gaston returned one of his more ambiguous smiles, keeping on just the right side of treason.

'I can't. They'd have my head on the block. It's easy for you. Louis is your brother. You won't be touched. No, it's too great a risk.'

'No more risk than you're taking already.' Gaston shrugged and raised an eyebrow. His indifference was persuasive.

'I don't understand.'

'Your fate's tied to that of the King, as I'm sure you realise. I mean if Louis were to die tomorrow ...'

This time it was the marquis' turn to shrug. His was sharper and more aggressive than Gaston's, dismissive rather than indifferent. 'That's ridiculous. Louis won't die.'

'I'm sorry to disillusion you, but you appear to be forgetting that both my father and grandfather were assassinated. Besides, Louis is hardly the picture of good health. Six years ago he was on his deathbed. I saw him given last rites. Frankly it's a miracle he's lasted as long as he has,' Gaston finished wistfully, recalling dashed hopes.

'But what can I do? I can't keep him alive.'

'You can make sure you're protected.'

'Go on.'

With the bored tone of a man explaining the obvious, Gaston pointed out that there were only two possible candidates for the throne – most likely the Queen as regent, if not the Habsburgs. Both loathed Richelieu and would clearly be well disposed towards any man who got rid of him. Cinq-Mars listened, observing him carefully. Gaston seemed convincing: the smile was sincere, the eyes wide, the palms open. But he had a reputation for being untrustworthy, and you don't acquire such a reputation without persuading people to trust you in the first place.

'It seems to me that you have more to gain by this than I do. Once Richelieu's gone, the Spanish will make you king.'

'Rather late for that I think. I had my hopes of course. What prince hasn't? But now? Do you know what it's like to stand outside a door with all the riches of the world behind it?' Drawing in a sigh, he shook his head and gave a smile, clipped at the corners. 'You stand there in the cold and the wet, waiting. But it doesn't matter. Not when you know all paradise is just a few inches away. And you wait and you wait, telling yourself it's going to be worth it, that at any moment that door will open, nursing that dream in your heart, sustaining yourself with it – while all the time you become sicker and wetter and older. Until the moment comes when you realise your best days are behind you and you've wasted your entire life away standing on a step.' He shook his head again and drew another breath. This time there was no smile. 'My chance has long gone. With just Louis maybe, but two children as well … no … the most I could hope for would be a regency.'

'I don't understand. So why do you want rid of the cardinal if you won't profit by it?'

'Aside from the fact that he's had me exiled twice, I think he's going to destroy France. This war needs to end – and soon, or it'll be the death of us all. We have to ally with Spain – it's inevitable. And Richelieu will not even consider it. I mean he's a clever man. No one would dispute that. But better to be right than clever.'

'And who to replace him?'

'Mazarin, Séguier … perhaps even yourself.'

Despite his reservations, Cinq-Mars had to concede that the argument had merit. He knew the perils of power well enough from Richelieu, that it would invariably end in resentment and revenge. And it *would* end. The King would not outlive him. Even for the eighteen months they had been together, he had noticed Louis beginning to grey, the colour leeching from his face, like a painting left too long in sun. But now he realised it was not a painting but a mirror. It wasn't simply the King's decay he was seeing; it was his own.

* * *

The table was set for fourteen, a cloth of purple velvet ringed with goblets and silver cutlery. The cardinal sat at the head, alone, dipping a crust into a bowl of bouillon. The chef had prepared something more elaborate but he sent it back. Like most older men of court, a lifetime of swan, port and lard had left his stomach unable to hold down anything but the simplest food. Even the brioche was a struggle and his lips writhed with disgust, as if trying to swallow earth. Midway through the torture, he was interrupted by Sebastian, flushed with haste. Evidently he had news – and news that was worth running for. Thankful for the break, Richelieu put down his bread and beckoned him in.

After the briefest of hellos, Sebastian burst into an account of how he had been visiting the Louvre for his evening performance when he observed Gaston walking with Cinq-Mars. Their body language had been odd – side-by-side and not speaking – and he could see they were searching for somewhere they wouldn't be overheard. Judging by their direction of travel, he'd guessed the most likely location – an antechamber overlooking the Tuileries with a lockable door. And after taking a short cut, he'd been able to hide a moment before they arrived. Then he related Gaston's attempts to influence Cinq-Mars, as well as their mentioning of Spain. Richelieu appeared interested but not surprised.

'It's inevitable. They're all joining together – the Queen, Cinq-Mars, Gaston, Guise, Bouillon. Chevreuse, of course. Every time there are more.' His voice was subdued, meditative and almost acceptant. 'It's the curse of power – enemies. Every decision you make, someone benefits and someone suffers. But the good is soon forgotten, the bad always remembered. Sometimes I wonder if there's a man left in France who doesn't want me dead.'

'Does it matter? You still have the King on your side.'

'Everything matters. Every change brings new possibilities, new uncertainties …' The cardinal left the sentence half-finished. It was unlike him to be distracted and Sebastian noticed it immediately. Disconcerted, he forgot what he was about to say and in the lengthening silence simply blurted the first thing that came to mind.

'I forgot to congratulate you over Soissons – a masterstroke. I don't know how you did it.'

The compliment met with an acidic laugh. 'But I didn't.'

'What do you mean? The whole court knows it was you.'

'I know, remarkable isn't it? One of the odder episodes of my life. I mean Soissons had a good mind, one of the best France had to offer. Yet this man, versed in Latin and philosophy, had a habit of opening his visor with the barrel of his pistol. I assume I don't need to inform you of the consequences.'

'He shot himself in the face?'

'I'm astonished it didn't happen sooner. Obviously his comrades weren't keen to disclose the fact, so they put about some rumour that I had him killed. Naturally I've no wish to deny it. If people choose to believe I have an all-powerful control over France, I'm not going to disillusion them.' Richelieu spoke with amused disbelief, but also satisfaction. He was proud, almost vain when it came to his reputation, his power over people and their evident unease in his company, the fact they could never hold his gaze, the awkward silences that were not awkward to him.

After talking a little more, the cardinal drifted into contemplation, seemingly forgetting that Sebastian was in the room before remembering to excuse him after a minute or so. Once alone, he stared at the soup below him and sighed. It wasn't the pain that hurt so much as the indignity. The greatest mind in all of France – a leader of armies, a prelate

of the church and advisor of the King – now defeated by a
bowl of bouillon and a few crusts.

* * *

As 1641 drew on, the revolts in Catalonia and Portugal continued. Determined to keep the Spanish occupied, the cardinal
did all he could to support the rebels, even providing a French
force to reinforce the Catalans and taking Roussillon along the
way. Nevertheless, they were few in number and fighting the
greatest power in Europe. It couldn't last and ultimately would
change nothing – no more than chaff in a gale.

Meanwhile, the triumph of Cinq-Mars continued una-
bated. Everyone had hoped the relationship would end, that
Louis would tire of his sulks and tantrums. But if anything
his passion seemed to have intensified. It didn't seem to
matter what the marquis did or whom he insulted, Louis
would invariably indulge him, admonishing, but with an
almost parental forgiveness. Many found it impossible to
watch, seeing the King of France, heir of Clovis, ridiculing
himself over young flesh while the marquis flinched at the
touch of Louis' wattled skin or crinkled his nose at the sickly
perfumes he used to mask his decay.

Richelieu was the most notable victim. Previously the
marquis had at least limited his insults to private conversation, but now he began to treat him with open disdain, most
memorably during the *Conseil d'État*.

While not officially a councillor, Cinq-Mars still managed
to engineer access as a guest of the King – though being a
spectator he wasn't permitted to speak. And for the first few
weeks he managed to remain silent, making his thoughts

abundantly clear through grimaces and eye-rolls, usually at the cardinal's appeals for caution or diplomacy. After a month or so, following a budget statement from Chancellor Séguier, he could restrain himself no longer and interrupted Richelieu midway through his response.

'So, *Armand*,' he said. 'Broadly, would you describe your administration as a success?'

The whole room glanced across at him, shocked by the unexpected voice – as if a piece of furniture had just spoken. But on seeing Cinq-Mars, they choked back their disapproval and turned towards the cardinal, awaiting his reply. And for that moment, the room was utterly still, its entire focus on Richelieu – the bewigged nobles and councillors gazing down the table whose perspective narrowed onto the bright crimson figure at its tip. The cardinal remained silent, looking upwards as multiple responses passed through his mind, all of which he suppressed. Aware of the eyes upon him, he restricted himself to a tight smile.

'Yes, I would say our administration was successful.'

'Then can you tell me, after seventeen years of your leadership, why the people are starving, the army is destroyed and the treasury is bare? Why France has suffered defeats to the Empire and the Spanish? In fact, tell me anything that has improved at all.'

The cardinal didn't reply. Everyone, including the marquis, knew the reason – the words that couldn't be said. *I did not choose this. I didn't want to drag this country into some insane war, wasting everything we have to pay for our people to be killed. This is not glory or honour. This is butchery, plain and simple. And every day I pray for it to end.* The only person who seemed unaware was Louis, who smiled then motioned at

245

the cardinal. 'So, what have you to say, Armand? It seems that the marquis has silenced you.'

Richelieu paused, his face puckered with frustration. 'Your Majesty, I'm sure you will concur when I say I have executed your policies with the utmost precision.'

'But, cardinal,' Cinq-Mars interrupted again. 'The problems we face must either be the result of the King's orders or your carrying out of them. If you say you executed them perfectly, then doesn't that mean the commands themselves were wrong? That the King was in error?'

'The King, as you know, is God's representative on earth. For him to be wrong would be for God to be wrong. The only possible explanation is that these events are preordained, that it is the will of the Lord and for the greater glory of his subjects,' the cardinal replied, ending the conversation. The marquis might have been able to argue with him on secular matters, but not spiritual ones.

Even so the damage was done. The cardinal's humiliation was total. He had been ridiculed in front of the King and every great person of state, and for the remainder of the meeting he remained silent, his head bowed as he contemplated what had just occurred. The distance between him and the rest of the table, normally a sign of primacy, now isolated him instead.

Spain
(1641 – 1642)

In mid-July, Louis fled the formalities of Paris. Fontainebleau was a particular favourite: close, yet surrounded by forest, teeming with boar and deer. Richelieu chose to stay nearby in his country house at Fleury. His health was declining and after lunch, once the midday swelter had passed, he would retire to the grounds, following advice from his doctor who recommended the heat to balance his excess phlegm. Today he was working at the small escritoire he had set up in the garden, overlooking a pond of goldfish and carp, flanked by statues and ilex hedges. Despite the peaceful surroundings, he appeared nervous, and spent much of the afternoon observing the view over locked hands, his fingers knotted together, whitened from the strain.

The cardinal's thoughts were interrupted by a cough to his left and he turned to see a footman who enquired if he was expecting a visit from a Monsieur Sebastian Morra. The cardinal assented with a nod and a few moments later saw a familiar misshapen figure appear from behind a tree to his left.

'You used the side entrance?'

'Of course, but I'm not being followed.'

'I know, but the man on the door works for Gaston and I don't want him informing Cinq-Mars of your whereabouts.'

'What? You know he's a spy? Get rid of him then.'

'No, better to have one's enemies in plain sight. If I removed him, Gaston would simply use someone else. Besides, I can always throw him the odd scrap of information when it suits...here...this way...I've something interesting to show you.' Richelieu turned and shuffled back towards his desk with the aid of his cane. His legs were barely able to hold him and the stick was taking most of the load, the back of his supporting hand a spider of bulging veins. On the tabletop was a paperweight of Murano glass, beneath it a scrap of parchment, blank apart from a few scribbles. He bent over the desk, smacking his palms face down on the surface as if fixing something in place. Though there was weakness too – the need to support tiring limbs.

'Looks innocent enough, doesn't it?' He shook his head with disbelief. 'But you could be looking at the end of France. This very moment troops are being raised in Spain. About eight thousand at the latest count.'

'How do you know?'

'Some things I can't tell even you. But it's as I predicted. A grand alliance – Chevreuse, Guise, Bouillon, Lorraine. They're going to support a Spanish attack and put Gaston on the throne. Cinq-Mars is involved as well.'

'Arrest them, then.'

'I can't. All I have is an unsigned receipt and information from a confidential source. It so happens I know it's the truth, but it's not enough to prove guilt – certainly not for a prince of the blood.'

'Your Eminence.' The voice came from their right and they both looked round to see a man in the King's livery – blue with fleurs-de-lis.

'Guillaume.' The cardinal welcomed the man with a nod. 'Am I needed at the palace?'

'The dwarf, actually.'

Of the two men, it was hard to tell which was more surprised. Richelieu was the first to recover, and when he spoke, it was with his usual interrogatory tone.

'How did you know to come here?'

'Your footman was kind enough to send word.'

'I'm sure he was.' The cardinal added a sour tut. 'And the King, did he give a reason?'

'I was not informed, Your Eminence. My instructions came from the chamberlain.'

'And what was the order? Precise words please.' Sebastian was always impressed by the cardinal's questioning: sequential and to the point.

'That I was to bring the dwarf Sebastian Morra to His Majesty's presence in Fontainebleau.'

He looked across at Sebastian. 'You understand what this means?'

Sebastian understood all too well. The King had no interest in him. There could only be one possible explanation.

'And if I was to say Sebastian wasn't here, and had … left Paris never to return?' Richelieu subjected the messenger to one of his more unreturnable stares.

Unable to meet the cardinal's eyes, Guillaume looked at his feet. 'I can't, Your Eminence. There are witnesses – the footman, the coachman too. The risk would be too great.'

'Guillaume,' he repeated. He was not a man who required threats.

'Please, Your Eminence.' Guillaume wriggled as though on a hook. 'You know I can't. The command came from the King himself.'

'Very well. Leave us a moment.' Richelieu snapped, first waiting for the messenger to retreat a respectful distance before bending down, his voice dropping to a whisper. 'Listen carefully, Sebastian, we don't have long. Understand that I can't protect you. No one can overrule the King's orders, not even me.' He spoke staccato, keen to make the most of what time they had. 'I've no idea what Cinq-Mars has planned. But rest while you can, eat what you're given, and if you see your chance at escape, take it and do not come back.'

'The first I can promise.' Sebastian's eyes were fixed on the cardinal, alert to his every word. 'But the second … I still choose your protection over none at all.'

'A noble sentiment. And your loyalty is appreciated.' He was interrupted by a cough from the messenger, and only had time to whisper a few final words. 'But no heroism, please. My brother was a hero. Died in a duel when he was only nineteen – utterly pointless. Do not risk yourself on my account.'

'I won't risk myself on anyone's account. That I can promise.' Sebastian was even able to raise a smile, albeit a rueful one. Then, kneeling down, he bowed and kissed the cardinal's ring before turning to leave. He didn't normally make the gesture and its significance was clear.

'Good luck, and whatever happens, remember you have achieved more than God intended for you.' It sounded more like an epitaph than a farewell.

* * *

Sick with fear, Sebastian was barely aware of the journey to Fontainebleau or indeed anything other than the desire to vomit. However, it wasn't until they pulled into the courtyard that his stomach got the better of him and he voided himself over the carriage floor and his shoes. Not that it brought any relief. Instead the nausea was replaced by a clammy and pungent sweat along with a keen appreciation of both his surroundings and his situation. Spitting out the last of the scum, he gazed down at the spatter of stains on his left shoe before remembering the footman and looking up to see a face pinched from irritation.

'You can't see the King in those.' The man glanced at his feet, tutting sharply. Marching Sebastian inside the palace, he immediately barked at the stable boy to clean the coach – and bring a pair of shoes while he was at it. Sebastian was then presented with a cup of water to swill out his mouth and wash off the mess. Then, once he had been reshod, his journey resumed.

He had never liked Fontainebleau at the best of times. It was too large and empty, a place without theatre, or brothels or people, where his only memories were of being lost in its passages as he searched for some way to occupy himself. But, disorienting as it had been before, it was doubly so now. An endless sequence of long, oak-panelled corridors, each door opening to reveal another passageway and a further

251

door behind, every one seemingly narrower than the last. He kept breathing but could never take in enough air. And still the doors kept opening, their perspective taking on ever more restrictive proportions. It was torture. And it would not end. The sickness returned to his stomach accompanied by a light-headedness. Then, and for no apparent reason, everything came to an abrupt stop.

He was standing in a large room. A pyramid of light shone down from a cupola above – bright at the top, diffuse at the base. The rest of the chamber was in shadow so that only its outlines were visible, no more than a loose-drafted sketch. Four figures sat in the light, playing cards: the King and the marquis, accompanied by the dukes of Vendôme and Rethel. The colour and sparkle of their attire drew the eye, at odds with the tepid shades around them. Seasoned players, they murmured the bets and flicked down the cards with a practised rhythm. Absorbed in their game, none of them seemed to have noticed him except for Cinq-Mars, who had forfeited the hand and was observing him with that familiar smirk of imminent revenge.

'Aren't you going to bow in front of your King?' The tone was crisp, each word pronounced with bite.

'Of course, Your Majesty.' Sebastian threw himself to the ground in front of Louis, who appeared visibly embarrassed and waved at him to stop.

'Please don't b-b-bother. Anyway, Henri, this is more your affair than mine.' Glancing across, he nodded at the marquis to continue – ever-eager to avoid the torture of speech.

'Delighted, of course. As His Majesty was saying, I was just speaking to him yesterday and he had the most wonderful idea. You really must hear it.'

252

Sebastian nodded with a curtness that indicated they had very different interpretations of what constituted a good idea.

'As you know, I've always enjoyed your performances. And I was just telling Louis how I'm going to the country and how much I'll miss them. Then he had the most marvellous thought. You could come with me for the week and keep me entertained – my own private theatre.'

Sebastian flinched. It appeared the marquis was going to do exactly as he'd threatened – 'to take his time', as he put it. For all its grand proportions, the room had begun to feel every bit as tight as the corridor had been.

'Marquis, thank you for your kind words. However, it is too great an honour.'

'I assure you the honour is entirely mine.'

'I must implore you, I have good reasons.'

'I'm sorry to hear that. Might you enlighten us as to what they might be?'

'It's a private matter.'

'But to overrule your king's command? Surely you're obliged to provide some kind of explanation.' Like Richelieu, Cinq-Mars had acquired the habit of using the King's name to disguise his own.

'It's a delicate subject.'

'You can rest assured that anything you say will remain between these walls.'

'It concerns His Majesty personally.' Sebastian was doing his best to obfuscate and could think of no better reason.

'Are you implying the King has something to hide?'

'Not at all.' Sebastian noticed the King's expression had changed from polite indifference to mild concern and that he was talking himself from a bad situation into an even worse one. 'I've been writing a special performance in honour of His Majesty and was hoping to surprise him this weekend.'

Louis responded with a laugh, evidently relieved it was nothing more serious, then informed Sebastian that he could always perform the following weekend.

'Besides,' he added. 'I promise I'll look surprised.'

Left with no alternative but to agree, Sebastian tried his best to delay, claiming he would need an hour to return to his room and pack. The marquis, however, granted him no such luxury.

'Actually I'm just going now. If you come with me, I'll have a footman fetch your things.' He stood up and beckoned Sebastian to the door.

'There's really no need. I can do it myself,' Sebastian responded hurriedly; but the players had already lost interest and were staring at their cards.

Cinq-Mars steered Sebastian out of the room, walking alongside him, his palm resting on the dwarf's back. To Louis, they seemed on the best of terms. However, as they turned the corner, all Cinq-Mars needed to do was twist the collar to yank Sebastian upright and have him tottering, a puppet in the grip of his controlling hand. Sebastian cried for help but found a palm clamped over his mouth.

'Fighting will only make it worse,' Cinq-Mars whispered in his ear, removing the pistol from his inside pocket before leading him down three flights of stairs, out of the entrance hall and into the courtyard beyond.

A coach was already set up and waiting, brown-lacquered and decorated with the marquis' coat of arms – the phoenix and ring. Through its open door, Sebastian could see silk wallpaper and tasselled blinds. An empty trunk sat on the centre of the floor, its open lid yawning over the pit below.

'I've already prepared your accommodation,' Cinq-Mars announced, allowing Sebastian an instant to view his fate before pressing him inside. Despite spread-eagling himself, he couldn't sustain the weight from above and only managed to resist for a few moments. Then the lid slammed down and he found himself entombed in the dark.

The space was tight, even for a man of his limited proportions, forcing him to crouch on hands and knees – the sides of the box pressing against his feet and downturned head. The waistband of his trousers was cutting into his torso, and finding himself unable to loosen the string, he was forced to compensate by straightening his back, placing further pressure on his limbs. However, it was an improvement on the alternative and slowly he became more aware of his surroundings, the musty air thick with the smell of sweat and moistened wood. He could just make out a prick of light beside his hip, presumably from the keyhole, though he had no prospect of looking through it. And, listening to his own laboured breath, he felt that familiar sensation of tight spaces and impending death, accompanied by the knowledge that this time there really was no escape.

As the journey continued, the pain in Sebastian's arms and legs steepened, forcing him to shuffle from one side to the other in order to ease the pressure. Soon the temperature began to rise as his body warmed the chamber from within. He became thirsty and his tongue started to swell, followed by a pain in his lower back, which again he could not reach. All he could think about was water in all its forms: snowy mountains, clear blue lakes, cups filled to the brim. The urge became overpowering and his mind erupted into furious thought, searching for anywhere that liquid might be found. He licked a rough tongue around his mouth, shoulder, even armpit – hoping for moisture – before remembering the scoop of his collarbone. Reaching up, he thrust a finger into the hollow only to find salted skin. His last hope gone, he choked out a few dry tears before slumping, exhausted against the side of the box. And he lay there listless, aware of nothing except the constant drum of the horses' hooves, altering with each kick, and every pebble and stone. As he sank deeper, only the sound remained, growing evermore intricate, rhythms within rhythms – hypnotic as the sea. By the end, he barely noticed when the hooves stopped, replaced by the rap of heel on stone. There were voices too, but dim and faraway. Better to remain where he was and return to sleep.

Pain. His forearms and knees were aching. His waist was in agony. Sebastian opened his eyes. He could see a shadow and wall in front of him – a cell of some kind. Next came thirst, overpowering thirst. Noticing a gleam of wetness nearby, he lunged for it – a bowl of brackish scum, still sweet to the tongue. Not enough. He searched for more. There was nothing, only darkness patched with slivers of dark brick. Suddenly noise, lots of noise, dogs snarling and scrabbling. He crouched, arms raised for protection. Then a roar and a strike from behind.

Bolting upright, he flung himself forward. The effort was considerable and the blood rushed from his head, sending the world into a spin – though he narrowly managed to keep his balance with the assistance of the wall. Taking a few breaths, he waited for the shock to pass while trying to ignore the chorus of dogs in his ears, until his thoughts slowed again. He seemed to be unhurt, at least. The animals hadn't attacked and were evidently behind some kind of barrier. Even so, they were close. He could smell their scent, a mingling of wet pelt, excrement and foul breath. Hesitant, he reached out and felt something cold and round on his fingertips – a bar. Another one next to it. Groping his way along, he reached the corner, then a small, grated window and a door. There was no handle, and when he gripped the underside, a rattle revealed it to be locked. Returning to the window, he squinted into the blackness and could make out a crescent of light scattering from under a distant doorway – presumably the way out.

Now apprised of his situation, Sebastian focused his attention on the lock. First he tried to pick it with his pocketknife, only to find the blade too large and clumsy. Next he tried his belt-buckle but it was too short to get any purchase. So, with nothing else to hand, he trusted to serendipity and fumbled on the floor for a substitute tool. But half an hour's search only produced some pebbles and a shard of chicken bone. So, all possibilities exhausted, he could do nothing except wait and hope.

With the dawn, light entered the distant corridor, enough to see by. He appeared to be in a cellar of some kind, entirely brick and ending in a long passageway. There were another three cells besides his own – one adjoining, the two others on the opposite wall. All contained a variety of hunting dogs which now seemed to have lost interest in him and had returned to scuffling among themselves.

Over an hour passed by before he heard footsteps. He

expected Cinq-Mars, but the visitor was middle-aged, near bald with a tufted beard – presumably the master of the hounds, come to feed and water them. On seeing the man, he pleaded for help, only to be met with the indifference of someone who had seen such displays many times before: striding into the cell, filling the bowls with water and scraps, then leaving without so much as a glance. Alone again, he stared at his food for a minute or so, considering whether to eat it. However, with no one around, there seemed no point in defiance, so he forced down what he could before curling up on the floor and returning to fitful sleep.

* * *

A hand grabbed Sebastian by the collar and pulled him up. The images that passed before his eyes were fast and jarring: bricks, iron bars, open door, a slit of sky, circles of teeth, a pointed ear, more bricks, another door, cobbles, light-splintered puddles, the spiral of the stairwell, a flash of Cinq-Mars.

'Lovely place you have here.' The words were choked rather than spoken. Then he felt the grip pull tight round his throat.

'Behave like a dog and I'll treat you like one. Anyway, the kennels are too bloody good for you. I should throw you to the damn pigs.' Cinq-Mars completed the remark by yanking Sebastian's neck, pulling him onto his hands and knees as he struggled to keep pace up the stairs – until finally they reached level ground. Then, after being walked along a corridor, he was led into a library and deposited by the hearth, too out of breath to notice the figure standing in front of him.

'Oh, you're still alive.' The voice was familiar, caustic and female. He stared upwards, struggling to make sense of the face. Then he recognised her – Chevreuse.

The marquis had taken his place alongside her. He was typically overdressed, wearing an overly elaborate ruff with a coiffure that was impossible to take seriously. Chevreuse, however, was the opposite: the embodiment of command, dressed like a queen with wide gauntlets and a bodice of purple velvet threaded with pearls.

'Well, give him something to drink then.' She looked across at Cinq-Mars, who stared back, confused.

'You want him able to speak, don't you?' she snapped. 'And let him relieve himself while you're at it. I don't want him soiling the carpet.' And so Sebastian was allowed two cups of water and to squirt the contents of his guts into the privy, though supervised throughout and with no possibility of escape.

He returned to the library to find the marquis and Chevreuse in animated discussion, seemingly over their relationship with Gaston, and for a brief moment he remained mercifully free of their attentions.

'What about when Gaston is regent? He won't need us any more.' The quarrel seemed to have been underway for some time and Cinq-Mars shook his head with the resignation of someone who knows he will go unheeded but still feels obliged to speak.

Chevreuse had no time for such doubts. 'Gaston won't care. He just wants to enjoy himself. To *play* the king, not be it. Can't you see? He and Louis haven't changed since they were children. Gaston's still the favourite. Always spoiled, getting away with murder. And Louis – poor, serious Louis.

The older brother trying to act grown-up. I don't think he's ever been truly happy a day of his life.'

'We could leave for Spain.'

'And spend our lives wondering what could have been?' She sneered at the mere suggestion. 'You know me better than that. Besides, who leaves a play in the final act? And on the subject of final acts ...'

She looked down, scrutinising Sebastian, her face lop-sided with revulsion. Raising a hand, she whipped it across his cheek. He winced but remained silent, denying her the pleasure of seeing him suffer.

'I'll deal with him.' Cinq-Mars stepped in, grabbing him by the collar and thrusting him down onto a chair. 'Lock the door. I don't want any interruptions ... and I'll need something to tie him with. That shawl of yours ... yes, perfect.'

Sebastian did his best to fight, kicking and clawing and biting and butting, even managing to land a blow on the marquis' shin and earning a kick in the ribs for his efforts. But once the marquis had a knee on his neck, it was only a matter of time, and soon enough his feet were lashed to the legs of the chair, his right arm bound behind him.

Satisfied with his efforts, the marquis took the opportunity to bend down, unpleasantly close. While gripping Sebastian's free hand, he licked his left cheek slowly and deliberately, leaving a trail of spit behind along with the odour of his breath, sharp as vinegar.

'I don't need to tell you what's about to happen.' His voice had dropped to a whisper. So if you wish to spare yourself a great deal of pain, I advise you speak now.'

Sebastian felt Cinq-Mars' squeeze tighten round his wrist, but said nothing. The marquis waited a moment, then a moment more – delighting in Sebastian's unease. Then he nodded, seemingly approving of his defiance. Striding across the room, he fetched a side-table from the far wall, which he placed in front of Sebastian before again grasping his free hand, slapping it down on the table as though upon a butcher's slab. Sebastian suddenly knew what was going to happen. He tried to pull away, straining against his bonds as his hand tried to scrabble free of the marquis' grip. Then he saw Cinq-Mars reach down and fetch something. He held it up, brandishing it – a hemisphere of pure glass, cannonball-solid. Lifting it up, he cocked his arm, ready to strike. His eye was fixed on Sebastian's hand – which was now clenched into a fist, awaiting the blow.

'Last chance.'

Sebastian didn't reply and closed his eyes. Time passed, drip by drip by drip. Long enough for him to feel the horror of the moment. Then the pain. It was immediate and like nothing he had ever felt. Hotter than fire. Sharper than a blade. Relentless and without mercy, it spared nothing. He tried to scream, but there was no air. He tried to open clenched eyes but could not see. Nothing existed except the agony and he writhed breathlessly, trying to think of anything else, anything that might bring relief. No good. Then through the pain, he heard her voice.

'Can you hear me, dwarf?'

Unable to speak, he managed a nod but it went unnoticed.

'Don't insult me.' She took hold of the injured hand and squeezed, this time drawing a cry as he arched back, trying to withstand her grip.

'I said, can you hear me?'

'Hurts too much.' The words were forced out through spit and locked teeth.

'That's no concern of mine. You'd better learn.' She squeezed again, drawing another scream every bit as loud as the first.

'You're an aberration, cursed by God.'

'We were …' Choking, he couldn't manage more than a few words between breaths, '…all dwarfs once …even you.'

'No. You can't survive without help, you're a parasite.'

'And you …who do …you live off? …Who works …your fields? …Cooks your food?'

The remark was repaid predictably. This time so hard, he felt a crunch in his hand and immediately retched. Vomit spewed from his mouth and nose, which he was unable to clear and instead sucked back in, blocking his throat. He tried to cough it out but had no air and began to suffocate – grasping for his windpipe, only to feel his hand being held in place. Thrashing for breath, he wriggled against his bonds, mouthing for help. The room was bleeding red and he could feel the pressure building behind his eyes as he sucked again, only to feel nothing there. Then the world took an abrupt tip sideways and he crashed to the ground, jolting the muck from his mouth and enabling him to take a strangled breath before spitting the leftovers from his throat and heaving for air.

They allowed him a few minutes to recover before taking hold of him and pulling the chair upright again. Cinq-Mars reached for his wrist, but Sebastian told them not to bother, and placed his crabbed and swollen hand back on the table. Preferring not to look at the injury, he stared back at Chevreuse as she resumed the interrogation – this time enquiring what he knew about the cardinal and his plans. Sebastian gave the question some thought before dismissing it with a shake of the head.

'I can tell you I know nothing, but you won't believe me ... Though there is one thing.' The words weren't uttered with hatred or spite, or even courage for that matter. Instead, in a voice that no longer cared. 'That first time we met, when I asked you if you came from Picardy and you denied it. I knew you were lying. It didn't make sense to me at the time.' He paused to catch his breath. Chevreuse was staring directly at him, expressionless apart from the slightest pressing together of the lips. 'And Rohan, it's in Brittany. I know why you chose him ... the Duke of Rohan ... You needed someone who never comes to court, who no one ever sees ... Some mad bastard, who you knew wouldn't recognise his own child even if he knew her. In fact, there's only one thing I don't know.' He drew another ragged breath. 'Marie de Rohan – was she already dead or did you kill her yourself?'

Chevreuse continued to stare at Sebastian and it was some time before she spoke. Standing up, she pressed down her dress and looked across at the marquis.

'Can you put the poker in the fire?'

* * *

Opening his eyes the next morning, Sebastian stiffened with pain. Everything hurt: his arms, knees, hand, waist, and his left cheek – now a wet and weeping strip. The memories of the previous day were still raw: Chevreuse holding the glowing poker in front of his open eye, the heat on his skin as he screamed, the marquis kicking him down the stairs, fighting off the dogs. Not that it served any purpose. He had told them nothing. They thought it was courage, but it was nothing of the sort. It was fear that stayed his tongue, the knowledge that as long as he kept silent, they would have reason to keep him alive. Because in spite of it all, despite the pain and the struggle, he still did not want to die. That verminous core burnt as strong in him as ever – born of the street, it would not give in, it would crawl through tunnels, eat scraps, endure any indignity just to survive another day.

Lifting himself up, he groaned in muffled agony as his face peeled from the pillow. Once the pain had dulled he was able to force himself into a marginally less excruciating position, from which he was able to look around the room. Not that there was a great deal to see. Only a small square of bare floorboard, four walls of crumbling plaster and his own palliasse – though at least there was no sign of Chevreuse or the marquis.

Some time passed before his mind turned to escape. The only window was barred, and judging by the treetop swaying outside, it was too high to jump. Noticing a door in the far wall, he lurched upright and stumbled across, propping himself up against the frame and briefly examining the lock. However, after fiddling with it for a while and giving the handle a few desultory yanks, he gave up and returned to his mattress, where he lay, trying to ignore the pain and keep his wound away from the sheet.

It turned out to be a considerable wait, long enough for him to be served two meals and reflect on his former life with an unanticipated nostalgia. Lately he had been too preoccupied to appreciate it, too busy with the cardinal's business and the intrigues of court. But now it seemed like paradise, scribbling away the hours and forgetting himself in country views. Let everyone else chase the money, power and glory: all he wanted was his own small space in the world.

Somewhere quiet with a pleasant view, to spend his days as he chose with enough money to afford the occasional visit to a brothel or theatre. And he promised himself that if by some miracle beyond imagining he was to escape this place, then all he would ask from this life would be a small but reliable pension, enough for his needs, and to be left to spend the rest of his days in peace.

* * *

The moment Sebastian heard the noise, he knew it wasn't the guard. His gaoler had a quiet way of unlocking a door, controlled and perfected through routine. This time the key scuffed the lock and he could hear the hinges creak from the weight of a body pressing from outside. The scratching continued briefly before the door flew open, sending a wedge of light across the room. It was Cinq-Mars. Clearly drunk, he tottered in, his shirt half-unbuttoned and wig askew. There was an object in his right hand, but silhouetted with the light behind so it was impossible to see – perhaps a club or baton of some sort? Wary, Sebastian stood up and edged towards the corridor outside, keeping his back to the wall, his fingertips brushing across the rough plaster. Cinq-Mars seemed distracted by what he was holding, waiting until Sebastian was a couple of yards short of the corridor before lifting the object and waving it in his direction.

'Any time I like,' he slurred.

'What do you mean?' Sebastian could see the marquis looking at him and stopped, aware of the gaping doorway just to his right.

Then he heard a twang followed by the thunk of a bolt

beside his head. Flinging himself to the ground, he crouched, awaiting the worst. But there was nothing – no flash, no blood, no sound except the unsteady clack of approaching footsteps. They circled his head and stopped.

Aware of the silence, Sebastian looked up. The marquis was standing between him and the corridor, the perspective enlarging him to titanic proportions. His body was silhouetted and all he could see was the arrowhead of the loaded crossbow, its point glinting and aimed directly at his forehead. Instinctively, he scrambled back crabwise on aching hands and feet, but the arrow followed him all the way to the corner, at which point he tired of the game and slumped back against the plaster, glaring up at his captor.

'I can kill you any time I like,' Cinq-Mars drawled, malicious with drink.

'For God's sake, just stop this.' Sebastian was desperate, almost outraged by Cinq-Mars' inability to understand. 'You're killing me over nothing. It's been three years since I wrote that play. Everyone's forgotten.'

'I haven't. And there's what you did to Marie. She was exiled because of you.'

'But you've tried to kill me ... twice. Destroyed everything I owned. You've burned my face, scarred me for life. What more could you possibly want?'

'Shut up, little man. You're nothing. I don't care what you think.' Cinq-Mars had tired of the conversation and grabbed Sebastian by the collar. Up-close he reeked of sex, an acrid mix of sweat and fluids, raw as fish. Leaning in, he examined Sebastian, turning his head so the slick of wetness was clear in the light. The sight seemed to please him and he grunted his satisfaction, giving Sebastian's windpipe a final squeeze before hurling him into the corner, clattering already bruised limbs and leaving him a groaning heap on the floorboards.

Once the door closed Sebastian lay in the dark, waiting for the marquis to return, but he didn't. He wasn't like Chevreuse. To her, torture was a means to an end. But Cinq-Mars was different. He gave no sense of wanting answers. For him it served no purpose except entertainment, something to feed the void.

The pain took some time to subside but eventually he remembered the arrow. It had to be wherever the marquis had fired it. Hobbling upright, he felt his way along the side of the room. It was higher than he recalled, about two inches above his head and planted tight into the wall near the door. The height caused him some difficulties, but after five minutes' waggling, he managed to release the barb from the wood. Immediately he set about the lock – first scratching a niche beneath the casing and next levering it up. The work was slow and hard on the hands, but his perseverance was rewarded when he finally prised up a corner and was able to reach the workings inside. After that, it was trivial; a quick twist of the tumblers, a turn of the handle and he was free.

Opening the door, he saw a round face pursed with shock as the guard stared back at him. An instant passed. First to react, he took to his heels. There was no hope of outrunning the man and he scurried down the first turning available, followed by the second passage to his right, then left before finding himself facing three different doors. Pausing momentarily, he heard the sound of pursuing feet and ducked into the nearest room where he hunted for somewhere to hide. Under the bed – no. In the chest – no. Behind the arras – no. The cabinet – yes. It was perfect: small, innocuous, unused and with a deep drawer in the base. Yanking it open, he tucked himself in and pulled it shut from the inside.

The rush of those first few minutes contrasted with the time that followed, squashed in the dark, unable to move while listening to his own breath. First there was the sound of his pursuer pacing the room; uncertain feet that walked with an anxious tread, first here, next there, soon followed by the sounds of cupboards being opened and the bed being searched. Despite his alarm, he took comfort in the drawer's narrow dimensions. It didn't appear human-sized and would pass first glance at least. The feet left and then returned again, this time with a partner. Now the search was briefer, soon followed by shouts as the alarm was raised. Then long silence as he waited for the hubbub to subside.

Damn – he'd forgotten to piss. A beginner's mistake. It wasn't serious now, but he already knew what was coming. When the fear had taken hold and he would feel first the tingle, then the burn, as he crouched in the dark, cross-legged and gripping himself as he tried to squeeze back every last drop. The knowledge was no use to him, however. If anything it made him more conscious of the need. He still tried to hold out as best he could, but couldn't resist forever and eventually had to yield. Wriggling onto his back, he aimed upwards and let the liquid spill over his belly and soak into his clothes. The smell was foul, but at least his efforts prevented any leaks, and after ten minutes he became almost used to it. More serious was the risk of the stench giving him away. Someone would notice, surely? He heard the sound of feet nearby.

Holding his breath, he listened for signs. This time the footsteps were slow and methodical. Marching to the far wall, they turned and came straight towards him, a loud clump. They stopped then moved away again and began to travel the floor, sometimes nearby, sometimes further away. In the background he could hear what sounded like swallowed tittering, but without speech or context. It made no sense. Someone was definitely in the room. Even so he couldn't hear the sound of anything being opened or lifted or moved, only the footsteps mixed in with the occasional snort of laughter. Then a crackling noise. Odd. A crunching, but accelerated and growing louder, like some ever-expanding paper ball. Soon afterwards he caught a gust of smoke and guessed that someone had lit a fire in the hearth. He wasn't sure why. It was late summer and the heat was uncomfortable enough already. As the smoke thickened he felt warmth beneath him, quite uncomfortable. It continued to become hotter, painful to the touch, now a burn. Then he realised the flames weren't in the fireplace, they were directly below him. The cabinet was on fire.

His reaction was violent and instantaneous. Grabbing the frame, he yanked himself into the open and sprang from the drawer, gasping for air as he scrambled to escape the blaze, only stopping when he became aware of the guffaws nearby. Through watering eyes, he could pick out a gaggle of figures wobbling with hysteria and pointing at him. Then he looked round to see a pile of smoking straw beneath his hiding place, which a servant was now extinguishing with a bucket of water. Realising he was safe, he collapsed to the ground and lay there a few minutes, too weary to move, until Cinq-Mars grew bored of the spectacle and ended it by having him dragged back to the kennels again.

*　*　*

The document itself was unremarkable – a vellum square, creased into quarters from where it had been folded. Its script was suitably stately: perfect calligraphy without error, every letter serifed and crossed, the black ink crisp against the white. The only disorder came from the five signatures at the base, each scribble separated by an accompanying red seal.

Sebastian lay trussed in the library once again. It was a favourite place for punishment, perhaps because the thick walls muffled any cries from outside ears. And for all his love of literature, the leather-bound books brought him no comfort. Instead his attention was drawn to the oversized furniture and a grotesque red marble fireplace which gave the room both a hellish appearance and sulphurous whiff.

'You see this.' Cinq-Mars held up the document with great care, as though exhibiting a masterpiece. 'This will change the face of France. Look at the signatures – me, Gaston, Lorraine. There are more too. Richelieu can't win this time. You've chosen the wrong man.'

It was at that exact moment Sebastian realised he was going to be killed. Cinq-Mars had just shown him something the cardinal had spent months searching for, a document whose discovery would mean the marquis' immediate downfall and death.

Instantly his mind turned to escape. There was no time to lose. His instinct, as ever, was to talk his way out of the situation. But he knew it was hopeless. He had nothing to offer Cinq-Mars. Besides, the man wasn't going to listen to him. No – it would have to be more direct, straight out of the castle and over the walls. But how? Whenever he left his cell, they kept him tied up or under guard. The only possibility was at night – but it would have to be a different room, at least without bars on the window.

'You're going to kill me, aren't you?'

'That depends. We're open to persuasion.'

'You've beaten me, burned me, put your bloody dogs on me. What makes you think I'm going to tell you anything now?'

The marquis shrugged. 'Then yes, you're going to die.'

Sebastian took a moment to absorb the words. Even though he knew they were coming, they were still not easy to hear. 'I believe I'm allowed a last request.'

'You want mercy? From me?'

'I'll not ask much. Just a night in a comfortable bed and a good breakfast to follow. To die with a bit of dignity, well-slept, well-fed. Besides, I'll put on a better show if I'm in decent shape. I mean, do you really want me passing out in the first minute?'

'Enough.' The marquis waved him to a stop. 'I'm minded to refuse you for cheek. However, since you seem to have discovered a degree of humility, I'll consider it.' He glanced down at his doublet, grimacing at a grain of lint that had made its way onto his chest. Extracting it with a nail, he rolled it between his fingertips before blowing it into space. Then he checked the spot again, brushing down the ruffle and restoring it to a liquid shine. Now satisfied, he looked back at Sebastian.

'I've put considerable thought into how I kill you. The rope, the sword, poison, do you have a preference?'

'If I do, I'll be sure not to say.'

'Probably wise. Recently I've been thinking that height might be appropriate, or should I say lack of it.'

'Very perceptive, *Your Lordship.*'

The marquis ignored the aside. 'I was wondering if there might be a way to shrink you somehow. If we bound you into a ball, then wound you tighter until you suffocated. Or maybe put you in a wine press. I wonder what liquid would come out first – mainly shit, I would imagine.' As Cinq-Mars spoke, he scrutinised Sebastian, searching for a reaction. But Sebastian remained mute in that manner of the powerless, when all they have left is scorn.

* * *

Even during his years training to be a priest, Sebastian never had much faith in the Almighty. Years of praying as a child had taught him that God might be omniscient but he is also deaf. Nevertheless, tonight he broke with tradition, murmuring the ritual *Pater Noster* under his breath, soothing himself in its familiar lines. *Qui es in caelis. Sanctificetur nomen tuum.* Latin constructions that could not be rushed. *Adveniat regnum tuum. Fiat voluntas tua.* Pronouncing each word carefully and with precision. *Sicut in caelo, et in terra. Panem nostrum cotidianum da nobis hodie.* It provided a sense of finality, the desire to leave a tidy life with no loose ends. *Et dimitte nobis debita nostra.* And now it was at an end. Quite possibly the last words he would ever say. *Sicut et nos dimittimus debitoribus nostris. Amen.*

The bedsheet was lying in the centre of the floor. Its ends had been knotted to make a sack, into which he had stuffed every piece of material he could find: curtains, tapestries, a small rug, his pillow, even his clothes. He tugged the knots again, satisfying himself that they were secure. Closing his eyes, he sucked in a deep breath, as if about to plunge to the bottom of the ocean. Then he crossed himself, lifted the bundle above his head and concentrated on the small chest he had placed in front of him. After the briefest of pauses, he ran at the window, using the chest as a ramp as he sprang at the glass, holding the cushion tight in front of him. The impact came in a spray of noise and splinters. Time slowed and there was a momentary stillness, long enough for him to notice the cold and the dark.

Next the drop. A shriek of air and sheer, blind terror. Gripping the sheet tight, he opened his mouth in a silent scream, clamping his eyes and bracing for impact. A moment passed. Pictures flashed through his head: his mother stood above him in Camoches; the cleft yew at the end of the village and the road to Créances; the view through the curtain while he stared at Père Jean; the cardinal gazing down from his throne; the sight of Michelle on the pillow as she slept; all those times spent crouching in tight spaces listening to his own breath. Then the images disappeared and he remembered that he was falling before smashing into the ground with a crunch of bone. Then black.

* * *

The pain was overpowering, this time from his elbow. But, while the agony in his hand had ended, now it was constant. Worse still, he couldn't make a noise and was forced to bite his lip as he bent double in his effort to contain himself. He lay curled, waiting for the torture to ease, but there was no relief. His stomach rose and he bent forward, hacking out

273

a pool of vomit. The cold sweat revived him somewhat and he became aware of the press of gravel beneath him and the muck in his face. Then, after wiping the scum from his cheek, he managed to struggle upright, took two steps and fell straight onto the damaged arm.

The pain was every bit as severe as before, and it was some time before he managed to uncoil and push himself up. He collapsed again almost immediately, but succeeded in keeping his elbow away from the ground. Standing up once more, he managed to reach the lawn before falling over yet again. Exhausted, he rolled onto his back and lay there a moment. Even so, tired as he was, he could feel the open air on his face, reminding him of the need to hide. It took all his effort to clamber upright and, noticing a blur of bushes to his left, he flung himself towards them, using his own momentum to carry his bulk the final few yards before tumbling into the copse.

Now safe in the undergrowth, he was able to recover and catch his breath. Propping himself up against a tree, he examined the wound. It was hard on the eye, impossible to look at without a wince. The forearm had sheered completely out of its socket and drooped at a sickening angle, hanging loose with the bone thrusting out beneath the skin. The elbow, meanwhile, had swollen to a tender bulb of flesh, too painful to touch. There seemed no break at least, and a hard tug appeared enough to pull it back into place – though it took him five minutes to build up the courage and a further fifteen to recover.

Eventually the pain subsided enough for him to remember the cold and he became conscious of his shivering and the phlegm pouring from his nostrils. Remembering his clothes, he hobbled back to the bundle, extracted his jerkin and trousers and dressed himself with slow and agonised care – paying particular attention to the elbow. Still cold, he draped one of the curtains over his shoulders – a makeshift blanket – and took the sheet to bind his arm. Then, returning to his hiding place, he spent the remainder of the night huddled beneath his cover while whittling two splints for his forearm and lashing them into place. It was hard work, only being able to use one hand – especially tying the knots. But he had both time and patience, and by dawn the limb was half-usable again. Now he could turn his mind to escape.

* * *

Sebastian observed the morning unfold with muted horror. It wasn't the fact he was going to die which terrified him, but rather that he knew precisely how it was going to happen. First, there would be the discovery of the evidence, then the searching of the rooms, followed by a hunt of the grounds before his inevitable capture and death. And yet he had to endure it in total silence, breathless with fear, hoping for an escape that was never going to come.

It began with a servant strolling out and walking the portico, taking in the light and the silence. On the return journey, he stopped, noticing the sack of fabric on the ground. Then he scuttled across, perplexed, and began picking through the rags. Looking around, he didn't take long to work out the source and stared up at the blank black windows which topped the house. One stuck out, splashed with a blot of white from the ceiling behind. The man looked down again, perhaps searching for a body, then called for help. A moment or two later, the doorway spat out three servants who clustered around him, muttering among themselves. A guard with a halberd appeared, and immediately began searching the vicinity.

Sebastian was sodden with sweat, breathing heavily and struggling to keep calm. It was only a matter of minutes now. He was too close for them to miss. The urge to run was overpowering. He had to do something – anything but sit and dumbly await his demise. Frantic, he glanced across at the front gate. One of the servants was walking towards it, probably to cut off his escape. Then he noticed something moving between the bars. Assuming it was simply a trick of the eyes, he peered closer, trying to make sense of the smudge.

A moment later the shape coalesced into horse. A horse? Then he realised it was a visitor waiting to be let in. Immediately he looked back at the servant, who was already undoing the bolts. It wasn't much of a chance but it was all he had – sixty yards, every step in full view. No point thinking. Just run and pray.

The pain was excruciating. Every jolt shooting fire down his arm. His eyes were tearing up from the effort it took not to scream. Still forty yards to go. Somebody had to have seen him. Resisting the urge to look round, he kept running, eyes fixed on the brown smear of the gate. Thirty yards. The pain was unbearable but he forced himself to keep going. He couldn't give up. Not when he was so close. Twenty yards. He could see it now. A covered wagon pulled by a single horse. Ten yards. For the first time it occurred to him that he might actually succeed. Then, as he slowed to turn the corner, there was a voice to his left.

'In a hurry, little man?'

He froze and looked across, steadying himself for the blow. But it wasn't a guard, instead a fat-faced local looking down from the wagon with a mildly bemused expression.

'Anything wrong? You okay?'

Returning a curt, 'Good day', Sebastian nodded and gave an iron smile. Then, rounding the gate, he unexpectedly found himself a free man.

From then on, the rat took over. Knowing he had to keep off the main road and away from the scent of dogs, he took the fastest way downhill, soon coming across a stream and following it to the nearest village. After that, a quick rummage through his clothes revealed two livres sewn into his waistband with another in the collar. And three coach rides, two taverns and six meals later, he was back in Paris and outside the Palais-Cardinal.

* * *

The moment he saw the steward, Sebastian knew matters had taken a turn for the worse. Richelieu's moods were always evident in his staff. The man was baggy-eyed and semi-conscious, exhausted from overwork.

Despite Sebastian's appearance – foul-smelling, injured, his clothes cracked with wrinkles – the man seemed too tired to notice and simply mumbled that the Chief Minister and his staff had already left for Lyons. However, when Sebastian explained it was urgent, the man conceded there was a slight chance the cardinal's carriage might still be in the courtyard at the rear.

Ignoring his arm, which remained a constant source of

pain, Sebastian made his way to the back of the palace, only to be stopped at the gate by two guards. One of them, a bent-nosed and lugubrious individual, lowered his halberd, his confusion further deforming an already homely face.

'Dwarf, this is the Chief Minister's palace. Try somewhere else.'

Sebastian glared upwards and rolled his eyes.

'I don't have time for this. I need to see the cardinal – now.'

The soldier didn't expect to be spoken to in such a manner, and gazed back, struggling to shape an answer.

'He's sick. He isn't seeing visitors.'

'Look, I've travelled three days and risked my life to get here. Now you can either let me in or you'd better pray Richelieu dies, because if he finds out what you've done, he'll have your head.' The guard continued to stare back, still unable to connect the voice with the figure standing before him.

'Say something, you idiot,' Sebastian prompted, hands on hips, before abandoning the enterprise and marching forward. 'Enough, I'm going in.'

The barb was enough to jog the man into a response, and with a disgruntled *follow me*, he beckoned Sebastian inside.

The courtyard consisted almost entirely of doors: high studded doors for the carriages, stable doors for the horses, weather-beaten doors for storing wood and coal, and plain doors that led into the palace itself. A few were entirely distinct. A solid metal door, bolted and barred, that clearly led to some kind of vault. A battered door, sunk deep into the walls and half off its hinges, probably either for refuse or a cesspit or both. Along with a portcullis through which a hidden garden, thick with roses, could be seen. The general impression was of a place full of comings and goings, the arrival of kings and retinues, the despatching of messengers – all the bustle of statecraft.

Today there was no activity, only silence, apart from a single carriage standing in the middle of the square, its horses ready and clinking in the harness. It appeared to be some kind of baggage wagon, dun and leather-clad. The only indication of its owner's importance was the vast pile of trunks bound to the top, doubtless packed with papers and diplomatic business. There was no sign of the cardinal's coach anywhere. Assuming Richelieu had already left, Sebastian was bemused when the guard stopped him at the rear wheel and told him to wait. He couldn't see any purpose to the delay and it took him a few moments to work out the reason. Of course – the cardinal would never use his state carriage on the open road. He didn't have walls or the King to protect him, probably no more than a few guards. It made sense not to stand out.

After a brief whisper through the window, the guard waved Sebastian forward. Richelieu lay inside, on a stretcher between two seats. He'd been sick before, but this was different. He looked halfway to death, already fading from the world. The surgeon had bled him near-translucent and his wraithlike skin contrasted with the grey of his beard. Sickness made him apostolic: his long hair sprayed on the pillow like a ragged halo, his feverish eyes fixed on some point in distant space, his gaunt features smooth and without earthly concerns. Hearing footsteps, he turned his head mechanically and stared at Sebastian. Then his lips drew back into a smile that was all tooth, no gum.

'The King's timing, as ever, remains impeccable. I can barely move and he's decided to join the siege at Perpignan.'

'Tell him you can't go.'

'I must. He's travelling with Henri the entire way. It's a fortnight at least. He's already turning the King's mind, I know it.' Instead of its usual monotone, Richelieu's voice wavered with emotion, taut as a bowstring, and for perhaps the first time Sebastian doubted his judgement, worried the fever had tipped him into delirium.

'Tell him to postpone.'

'He won't postpone. He lives for his troops, just like his father. Nothing will stop this.'

'Your Eminence, I'm not sure you're in any condition to ride. Trust me, I spent months travelling Normandy when I was young. It's going to get hot, you'll be knocked about. It's not something you can do on a stretcher. Besides, you've served the King for fifteen years. Louis won't abandon you.'

'You don't understand. Yes, I've served the King, lasted out his fads, seen favourites come and go. And you know how I've survived? I've never been complacent. I've seen how quickly things can change. My life, everything I've worked for, it could all be gone in a moment. You forget I'm at the mercy of a man's mood. All it takes is a poorly chosen word, a change of heart, even plain boredom – and I'll be gone. It's happened to me before. I was on the *Conseil d'État*, serving Concini, the Queen's consort. Then Louis took power and that was that. Within the hour, I lost my position, my pension, everything. Two years I had to spend in Luçon. I thought I'd never come back.' Richelieu's glazed eyes snapped into focus and he nodded at Sebastian. 'Now I need to catch the King. So whatever you want to tell me, tell me en route.'

Sebastian did as he was bidden and took a seat. Almost

immediately, he felt ill at ease, enclosed in the compartment. The proximity of the cardinal was unsettling and he didn't know whether to look at the withered body alongside him or out of the window. Both felt awkward and somehow rude; instead he examined the carriage studiously, observing the whorls and eddies of its bare wood, along with the seats, which appeared to be the one concession to luxury, quilted in oxblood leather and stuffed to near distension. Eventually he was interrupted by the cardinal's voice to his right.

'Your arm. I hadn't noticed. What happened? Cinq-Mars, I imagine.' The sentence emerged piecemeal, unmeasured, a flurry of thought. Evidence of a mind that had lost none of its speed, only the ability to judge and filter.

'It's a long story.'

'We have time.'

'We do,' Sebastian replied, struggling to hear the cardinal over the echo of the horses' shoes from the quadrangle as they left. Then he explained what had happened, as briefly as he could and without detail. Richelieu listened politely, though it was only when Sebastian mentioned the treaty that he became interested. His head jerked from the stretcher and he stared at the dwarf with wide eyes, pursing his lips in an effort not to interrupt – cutting in the moment Sebastian drew to a close.

'This treaty. You say it's signed by Henri, Gaston and Lorraine. Are you sure?'

'Why would I lie?' Sebastian replied with a shrug.

'And you know where it is now?'

'Across the border more than likely. I can't imagine Cinq-Mars keeping it. He must have known I'd tell you.'

'I assume Chevreuse didn't put her name to it.'

'How did you know?'

'We share an aversion for incriminating ourselves in print.' The cardinal gave a half-smile and shook his head. He always spoke of Chevreuse with grudging admiration. Perhaps he appreciated her talents better than most. Then he nodded at Sebastian and closed his eyes. 'You've done well but now I must sleep.'

The following half-hour ranked among the most awkward of Sebastian's life. Everything was so normal: the carriage, the view, the noise. It could have been a journey like any of the hundred others in his life. The only difference was that the most powerful man in France was lying asleep a few inches away from him. Every time he had met Richelieu before, there had been a guard or attendant or someone nearby. Now they were completely alone, just him and a shrunken and vulnerable body. He could see the veins threading his neck and the hollow beneath his ribs beating in time with his heart. Surreptitiously, he brushed a hand across the knife in his belt, perhaps just to check it was still there. The fact it was alarmed him and he stiffened at the thought. Then he looked away, trying to concentrate on the view. His hands were clasped on his lap, the fingers mottled red and white from the tightness of the lock.

* * *

As a result of the late start, they arrived at Angerville two hours after dusk. Sebastian was asleep, having long since succumbed to the rhythm of hoof and wheel, and he woke up to see fire – two soldiers holding torches, the shadows rippling across the quilted seat in front of him. One of them gave him a prod on the shoulder and motioned him to follow.

Standing up, Sebastian pressed his hands to his face, rubbing himself back to life. Outside, the night air was damp, and it smelt of furrowed ground, when the rind of the earth has been split and fresh soil left open to the air. Two rows of tents lined a field of scrubby pasture, all erected with military conformity, their doors facing inwards. The soldiers were eating dinner round various campfires, sitting on chopped logs or their bedding to keep off the wet grass.

At the end of the camp stood a pavilion. Aside from its cleanliness, it appeared unremarkable – a block of perfect white topped by a tasselled fringe and two pennants. The inside was a different matter. Walled and roofed with silk, it was floored with exotic carpet, thick as sphagnum and soft on the tread. In the centre stood a low table laid for six, its porcelain, cutlery and glass perfectly arranged, set around a fruit bowl and lighted candelabras. The cardinal and his doctor were eating soup, the doctor's bowl empty, the cardinal's barely begun. Ever conscious of his appearance, Richelieu had somehow mustered the energy to change into soutane, zucchetto and full regalia, disguising the wasted body beneath. However, even sitting was an effort and he was breathing heavily, his mouth crinkled from the pain. With the cramped movement of someone not entirely in control of his body, he gestured Sebastian to take a seat. Observing the cardinal's discomfort, Sebastian tried to tempt him into lying down, pretending to be exhausted from the journey and flopping onto a nearby cushion.

'It's been a long day, Your Eminence. Join me.'

'Thank you for your sympathy. However, I will eat as I

have always done.' As Richelieu spoke, the doctor glanced upwards with exasperation.

'Only the doctor and I are here – please rest.'

'I'll recover, Sebastian. I've spent the past thirty years being told to rest. If I'd listened to that advice, where would I be today? Besides, if this is the end, I'd rather die this way than on my back.'

The meal was four courses of small talk and protocol, interspersed with unbearable silence as Sebastian had to watch the cardinal struggle through the rest of his soup while he and the doctor made their way through venison, fowl and cherry pottage. Every mouthful was excruciating and before each swallow Richelieu would steady himself then force it down, his face crumpled with pain. Nevertheless, the merest mention of his illness would be met by silence, sarcasm or outright contempt. The doctor, meanwhile, seemed distracted throughout and was continually leaning towards Sebastian then checking himself. Judging by his facial contortions, he wanted to discuss a delicate matter but wasn't sure how to broach it, and it took three glasses of wine before he finally summoned the courage to open his mouth.

'I don't quite know how to say this.' He was picking at his moustache in an effort to mask his words. 'But would you consider ... well ... selling me your body ... I mean only once your soul has departed it? It's just that you are, well, such a unique specimen.'

Sebastian's immediate reaction was disgust. The thought of being anyone's specimen revolted him. However, he still had a beggar's instinct for coin, and thinking the matter over for a moment, he soon reconsidered. After all, it was free money, and what use is pride to a corpse?

'How exactly am I going to spend it if I'm dead? You'll have to pay upfront.'

'That's ridiculous. You could leave and never come back.'

'You can trust me. I'm a man of honour, as I'm sure the cardinal will attest.' Sebastian glanced at Richelieu, who concurred with a smile, either amused by the conversation or else simply relieved at being able to take a rest from his food. 'Now you have the guarantee of the Chief Minister of France. Is that enough?'

Left with no choice but to accept, the doctor flinched with dissatisfaction before sullenly agreeing. They had moved to haggling over details, specifically the cost of Sebastian's remains, when they were interrupted by the sound of raised voices and weapons being drawn. A moment later a soldier appeared at the door, announcing that the Marquis de Cinq-Mars had arrived and was demanding to speak to the cardinal. Richelieu steadied himself for the occasion, drawing himself upright, then wiping his face and locking it into place. Looking back at the night-sparkled entranceway, he instructed the guard to lead the marquis inside.

A few moments later Cinq-Mars appeared. He looked pointlessly handsome, sporting a flamboyant hat and black feather, his short ruff rising from a collar of Chantilly lace. Even his boots were ostentatious: crafted from the softest Swedish leather, their tops red with yellow trim. Glancing down, he noticed the cardinal – then Sebastian.

'Dwarf, what a pleasure to see you, and your master too. Truly, I'm honoured.' Striding in, he sat down – unasked.

'As are we,' Richelieu replied, brutally cordial. 'Would you care for some wine?'

'No, thank you, I've already shared a bottle with the King.'

The implication was clear enough. 'Doubtless Sebastian has informed you of his stay at the Château Dampierre.'

'Naturally, and be assured you'll suffer for it.'

'Do you really think you can intimidate me, old man?' Cinq-Mars enunciated each word to prevent any misunderstanding. 'Take a look at yourself. You can't even stand. Why not just give up and die?'

Sebastian stiffened, expecting an eruption. No one spoke to Richelieu that way: with anger perhaps, hatred even, but never contempt. Instead there was only silence. Curious, he looked around and saw a washed-out face straining for breath. 'I won't die, not for you, Henri.' The words were grated, forced out of the back of the throat.

'You know what offends me most. It's not what you've done, it's what you haven't. You wasted your power. You brought no glory to France, no victories worth the name – Arras and Soissons, a siege and a farce. You made cowards of us and now we don't even have the men to attack our enemies. Yes, we survived, but at what cost? Our youth is dead. Our borders are open. What was the purpose of it all?'

Richelieu rasped out a cough, then motioned Cinq-Mars closer. 'You're an idiot, Henri.' Despite the weakness of his voice, it had lost none of its snap. 'You think you're some modern Alexander, that you can somehow march out and conquer Europe. It's fantasy. We never had the men or weapons to protect ourselves, let alone invade. Even if we did, we'd simply be leaving ourselves open to attack. All I can do is keep the country safe – guard it. A lamp in the storm.'

'A lamp? That's the best you can come up with? You think I'll be impressed? There's no glory in a lamp. We're remembered for the wars we fight, for our boldness, our courage. Not giving up without so much as showing our claws.'

'What pretty words, marquis.' The cardinal's voice remained feeble and his face was flushed with the effort of concentration. 'However, had you governed anything of significance, you might have learned it's rather easier to lose a battle than avoid one. Unless you haven't realised, we're surrounded on three sides. We cannot possibly win. All we can do is keep our enemies occupied and away from us. There simply is no other way to survive.'

Cinq-Mars was barely paying attention and gazed at the tabletop, deep in thought. After a few moments he seemed to reach some kind of conclusion, nodded briskly to himself and stood up.

'You know what ...' he said, drawing his sword. 'It doesn't matter what you think. You're of no interest to me. I could kill you right now.' He took two paces forward, resting the tip of his rapier on the centre of the cardinal's chest. Richelieu looked down at the blade with mild disappointment, not afraid in the slightest. Sebastian, however, was transfixed, so concentrated on the weapon that he forgot entirely about the person at the end of it.

'Henri, please stop these cheap displays. There's nothing heroic about threatening an unarmed man, especially when you're never going to carry it out. You know as well as I do that there's an entire garrison of soldiers outside. You wouldn't even reach the door ... anyway, why kill me yourself when you've already paid an assassin to do it for you?'

The sword-point wavered before returning to position.

'Yes, I know you've hired someone to murder me ... which

is a treasonable offence, in case you were unaware. So if one of us should be making threats, it isn't you.'

The rapier remained horizontal a moment longer before flicking up and returning to its scabbard. On the way Cinq-Mars couldn't resist nicking one of the cardinal's sleeves, exposing a diamond of shirt below, as white as the pale skin it covered.

'You can't win. I'll always have time on my side.'

'Time is on no one's side. It defeats us all in the end.'

'Some more than others, and frankly I have no time left to waste on you,' Cinq-Mars finished, striding out of the tent without giving the cardinal a chance to reply. The remark was intended to be emphatic but instead appeared petulant, that he was leaving because he had nothing left to say.

Once the marquis had departed, there was a moment of unearthly silence, reminiscent of the interval between the last line of a play and the subsequent applause, as the audience waits, unsure whether to end the illusion. Sebastian was the first to speak, turning to the cardinal.

'How did you know? About the assassin, I mean?'

'I didn't.' Richelieu wheezed. 'It seemed reasonable they would try every possibility. Chevreuse put him up to it, no doubt.'

'You don't seem afraid.'

'Of course not. People will try to kill me. It's inescapable, a fact of power. I take what precautions I can, as those before me have done. They may work, they may not. But I'll worry about the things I have control over, not those I don't.'

The remainder of the night was subdued, barring the ongoing and heated negotiation between Sebastian and the doctor, which was completed shortly after dessert with his mortal remains being valued at three livres and four sous, a livre for each foot and a sou for every inch left over.

✳   ✳   ✳

The King had reached Valance. It had been a long and tedious journey. Every trip seemed more boring than the last. Having criss-crossed his realm over the years, Louis' main conclusion was that it was above all extremely flat – with the notable exception of the Massif Central where no one seemed to live. The hours spent on his horse would merge into the same view of sky and earth, until the journey was finally over and he could drop onto his mattress, drained from the heat and the saddle. This particular evening, he was staring at an expanse of ploughed fields, their emptiness broken by a lone elm in the distance. He was, however, unable to make out the two people beneath it. Both were trying to stay out of sight, keeping close to the trunk so that their forms merged with its shadow.

'How is he?' one asked. Hidden beneath a cowl, the figure was anonymous – though the voice was a woman's. She had a narcotic perfume, thick with helichrysum and neroli, and wore a ring of amethyst on her left hand.

'I left him in the tent, to think.' Her companion was taller – a young man, judging by his voice, still cracked from adolescence.

'Think what? Did you tell him everything I said?' The words were spoken sotto voce, the voice easy on the ear – that lullaby rhythm of fairy tales.

'Of course. You were right. His resentment of Richelieu. I'd never realised.'

'It's hard to live in another man's shadow – doubly hard if you're a king.'

'I know. When I told Louis to get rid of him ...'

'You did what?' The interruption was more stabbed than spoken.

'I told him to get rid of Richelieu.'

'Never tell a king what to do, never.' She was furious, jabbing a finger, the digit leading the whole body behind. 'You can't give orders to the ruler of a country. Don't you understand? The man's been brought up as a god. People don't tell him to do things, they suggest or imply. He'll think you're a fool. Your purpose is to put the ideas in his head, then let him decide ... What did he say, anyway?'

'He said I didn't understand. That the cardinal held the country together, kept control, that without him, it would all fall apart. Even so, he was definitely considering it. It won't be long now.'

'It'll be a damn sight faster if you do as I say. It's not difficult. Just use Louis' arguments against him. Tell him he's right, that the whole country depends on Richelieu. That no one can replace him and when he dies everything's going to fall apart. Then something casual. Maybe about how they'll have no problem in Madrid finding a successor for that fool Olivares. That'll sow the seed in his mind.'

'What? About having a successor? How's that going to make a difference?'

'I've told you before. We'll never get enough support as long as that bastard's in power. It doesn't matter how old and sick he is, people are still terrified of him. The name's enough.'

'So who should it be? Mazarin?'

'It doesn't matter. Once the cardinal's gone, the rest will follow. The moment there's a whiff of crisis they'll start fighting among themselves.'

The man moved behind her and cupped her breasts. She lay against him, resting her head on his shoulder. Then her hood fell back, revealing a face made young in the evening light. The man was younger still, his features blank from their lack of years. Uncomplicated, early love – two innocents starting on a life together. After a moment or two, she broke the illusion, pulling away from him. Much as she was attracted by his youth she also found herself repelled by it. With the spontaneity came a thoughtless idiocy. He remained a constant frustration, following instructions but without elegance, like a cheap and shoddy puppet. No matter what she did, the strings would tangle and every movement seemed to jar and stutter.

'One thing I've been meaning to ask,' he added. 'What the dwarf said; it's true isn't it? That you were born a commoner?'

The reaction was immediate. She spun around, rigid and indignant.

'How dare you? Listening to that dwarf's lies. If you ever repeat that … I swear …' Then she caught herself mid-sentence, realising her anger had given her away. He observed her with a schoolboy smirk – the master outwitted.

'Don't worry. I won't tell.'

She paused and looked away. 'Don't talk about what you don't understand. You've no idea what it's like to be cold, hungry, covered with lice every night. All the time looking for shelter, your next meal. Like some … animal. Then to see a life like this. Who wouldn't give everything for such a chance? I worked for that woman for four years. Watching her try on beautiful dresses, eat off silver, play paille-maille. And when she was dying, I did all I could. No, I did nothing wrong.' Unsettled by the memory, she flinched and looked back at him. 'Now look at me. We will never discuss this again, do you understand?' And Chevreuse angled her head, peering into Cinq-Mars' pupils, searching for light in the dark.

* * *

As the journey continued, its futility became increasingly obvious. Every day the cardinal grew sicker. What was once a man had now become little more than a husk, cratered with bedsores and flaked dry. Even so the spirit remained. He was determined to catch the King, insisting on early starts every morning and urging the coachman to use the whip. But the body couldn't keep up and he would invariably pass out or vomit within the hour, forcing them to stop. Eventually he would recover enough to speak, then pronounce himself fine and order them forward – only to collapse a few miles later, at which point the whole performance would begin again. Towards the end, it bordered on pathetic. They couldn't even keep pace with their retinue, who had already slowed to a dawdle, forcing them to spend nights incognito in cheap inns, huddled alone in their beds, trying to keep out the chill. Looking at the cardinal's skeletal body in the dank, unfurnished rooms, Sebastian was often reminded of his mother's final days and inevitably her death – the screaming mouth and naked body scrambling for escape.

A few miles before Narbonne, Sebastian decided he'd had enough. It wasn't simply the pointlessness of the journey but the indignities the cardinal had inflicted on himself: the vomiting, the exhaustion, the incessant commands to keep moving, clinging to moribund hopes. He couldn't see that a determination that had once seemed admirable now simply appeared desperate. The guards had even started a lottery, betting on the day he was going to die. It was an insulting end for a great man; twenty years of serving France deserved more than ridicule.

They had just finished the tenth stop of the day, brought on by the cardinal spewing into a bucket which Sebastian kept nearby for use at a moment's notice – holding the pail in place while trying to keep his nose away from the reek. Eventually, after half an hour of intermittent retching, Richelieu recovered enough to demand they get back on the road, only for Sebastian to interrupt.

'If you don't mind, Lord Cardinal, I'd like a word in confidence.'

'In case you hadn't realised, I'm in a hurry. We can discuss this in the coach.'

'I'm afraid it can't wait.'

'It's going to have to.'

Sebastian didn't reply, instead fortifying himself with a deep breath before turning to face both doctor and coachman.

'Leave us,' he demanded, pointing them out of the carriage without giving either one the chance to reply, then closing the door. The cardinal remained speechless throughout, glaring across from his stretcher.

'Do not defy me.'

'Forgive me, Your Eminence. You know I would never disobey you without good reason, that I've risked my life for you many times. But I can't let you do this. You're killing yourself. This has to end.'

Without the strength to sustain his anger, the cardinal fell back and yielded with a sigh. 'You forget there's an assassin out there, waiting for me to stop.' He motioned at the wilderness. 'We must keep going. I have no other choice.'

'What about the paper? The one Cinq-Mars signed.'

'I sent an agent but he arrived too late. It's already in Madrid, locked in the King's cabinet. There's nothing anyone can do. It's over.' Then he paused. 'Though you know what annoys me most. I've seen the back of so many – Chalais, Marillac, La Vieuville, Marie de Medici, Montmorency. So many giants, brilliant minds, and to be defeated by an idiot ...' His voice tailed off, rueful yet resigned.

'The treaty, I'll get it for you,' Sebastian responded with a shrug. At the time it seemed a perfectly reasonable suggestion. He'd never failed the cardinal before. There seemed no reason why he should now.

'You're a good agent, one of the best I have. But this? No. It's in the King's cabinet in the *Royal Alcázar*. It's the most secure place in the most powerful kingdom in Europe. An army couldn't get it out.'

'Thank you, Your Eminence, but please understand I'm not doing this on your account. If I don't find some way to stop him, Cinq-Mars is going to kill me. You say you don't have a choice, well neither do I. I'm asking you, please let me go.'

The cardinal winced. Ill or not, he was not accustomed to losing arguments. 'Hmm ... perhaps ... and in truth you'll probably be safer once you're over the Pyrenees. I'll send a letter by horse. I've a man at court. He can arrange work when you arrive.' He was about to call for assistance when Sebastian interrupted.

'One thing, Your Eminence.'

'Yes.'

'If I do manage this, I'd like a pension, about four hundred livres a year … with no duties at court.' He wasn't used to making demands of the cardinal and the words were hesitant as he tried to gulp them back down his throat.

Richelieu seemed more amused than surprised by the request and shrugged agreement. 'Not much to ask, I suppose … but I'll need his signature. And don't try to pass off some forgery, I'll know.' Then he called for the guard. It was an awful noise to hear, the voice guttural, as if crying out of torn flesh.

'Bring me a coach and a hundred livres.'

* * *

The cardinal took treatment in the abbey near Narbonne, where each day he was carried out into the garden to bake away his sores in the midday sun. Otherwise he would lie in bed, nibbling on dry crackers to suck up his phlegm, which resulted in raging thirst and endless bouts of coughing as the flakes caught in his throat.

His room was medieval, walled in a patchwork of mortared stone, the only light from a small window, which offered a view onto ripening vines. After centuries sheltered from the elements, it had acquired that undercurrent of ancient places – a scent of baked earth waiting to be released by the rain. Mostly he would sit alone, contemplating his accelerating

295

decline as his world grew smaller and smaller, now nothing more than the sixty square feet of his cell and the lawn outside. Soon he wouldn't even be able to go outdoors and just the chamber would be left; after that only his bed and the ceiling above, his domain forever retreating as his senses continued to fade. Until that day when his universe would extend no further than the confines of his body – before the final indignity when he would lose control of even that. First the bladder and last of all the guts, when he regressed to worm; a tube with a mouth and an anus, immobile and abandoned to solitary, stinking death.

His one solace remained the town of Richelieu, which he commanded to be brought from Paris and reassembled in his chamber. After twenty years it was finally complete, the bare spaces now replaced by houses, shops and families, civilisation where once there had only been grass and soil. At the centre of it stood his palace, now finished in every detail bar one – its owner. Twenty years had gone by and still he had never found time to visit it. Except in his mind, when during quieter moments he imagined a secluded retirement in contemplation of its arcs and symmetries.

The model pleased him to look at: clean, straight, orderly, his to control – so unlike the outside world. This would be his legacy. Somewhere not built along Norman, Breton or Parisian lines. Instead, a logical grid, where everything was in its place, its people united by shared belief and culture, that showed France as it could and should be. Above all, a place that would survive.

*　*　*

Spain looked different – stern and imperial. It lacked the freedom of France – that fevered atmosphere of a country under siege. Instead it was conservative and enduring. A country which had given itself up entirely to God, its capital lined with abbeys and churches, where every stone and window seemed dedicated to the Almighty – whether through inscription or stained glass. Women wore huge ruffs known as devil's cartwheels and the men tightly buttoned doublets. They stood still as ravens, lined before the altars as they waited to confess their transgressions and submit themselves to Christ. Even when they walked the streets, it was as if they had never left the pew. Sedate and silent, they kept every emotion contained; the men holding out a stiff arm, their wives' limp hands resting in the crooks of their elbows.

Yet, for all the displays of piety, the decadence was there for all to see. The country was overflowing with gold from the New World. It was everywhere: painted on walls and cornices, threaded into clothes, moulded into garishly proportioned brooches and altar-screens, and in such quantities that it seemed almost tawdry and Sebastian became nostalgic for the simple sophistication of silver and semi-precious stone.

With nothing beyond a promise from Richelieu that he would be looked after, Sebastian had no idea what to expect when he first arrived at the *Royal Alcázar*. He had no friends, no patron – nothing beyond a reasonable memory of Spanish from his years with Père Jean. However, the moment he stepped off the coach he was astonished to be greeted by a royal footman who, after checking his name, announced that he was expected and his letter of introduction was exemplary. Unsure whether the man was a fellow agent or not, Sebastian limited his conversation to a brief thank-you and followed him inside.

The *Royal Alcázar* turned out to be every bit as stifling as its surroundings, if not more so – choked by protocol and tradition. In their oversized ruffs, embroidery and dour colours, the courtiers looked as if they were from a bygone age. Pinched and squeezed, they stood in file before the throne, waiting for the herald to call their name, the royal chamber utterly silent except for the drone of petitions and responses. The building was no more welcoming than the people it contained; its rooms vast, lightless and lined with stern-faced forebears, wound together by a labyrinth of twisting corridors.

Other aspects of court were more familiar. Much of his time was still spent enduring the indifference of people with an unwarranted sense of worth, and he was still required to perform the same moronic pastiches, though for considerably better pay at least.

He was also able to spice up his act with a wicked impersonation of his master, performed with all the cruelty that familiarity brings. He took particular pleasure in mocking the cardinal's pomposity, adopting his most pedantic and ponderous voice, along with a few smaller touches – his stiffness of movement and taste for the dramatic pause. For all its taboo thrill, though, there was always the nagging suspicion that somehow his every word was reaching Richelieu's ear.

Remarkably, it never once seemed to occur to anyone that he might be an agent of France. Despite the fact he spoke with an unashamedly French accent and had only arrived a few days earlier, they asked him no questions – even giving him a room and allowing him to wander the palace at will. Yet again his appearance seemed to have had its desired effect. He was rendered invisible to them, defined by nothing other than his size – an amusing insignificance.

Sebastian devoted his spare time to Philip's cabinet. Like Richelieu's, it was hidden away and hard to find – a small, plain door in an unremarkable corridor on the second floor of the palace. The only indication of its importance were the guards flanking each side, along with the occasional officer of state waiting in the corridor or emerging with a suitably grave expression. A circuit of the area revealed the room to be windowless. Its ceiling and floor were reinforced, preventing any access from above or below, and it seemed to be almost permanently occupied.

Initially, Sebastian was overwhelmed. Richelieu was right – there was no way in. Not that he let this put him off, partly from innate stubbornness, mostly from a lack of choice. With the alternatives exhausted, only one option remained: to enter directly, straight through the door. Clearly there was no obvious reason for a court dwarf to go inside, so it would have to involve some kind of deceit. Various outlandish schemes came to mind – creating a form of diversion while the door was open and sneaking in, concealing himself in a box and being carried inside, hiding beneath a large object as it was transported into the room – none of which held the slightest promise of success.

At a complete loss, he trusted to chance and spent his spare hours wandering the corridor, observing the cabinet and hoping for inspiration. It made for dispiriting work, repetitive in the extreme: trudging the same sixty yards, looking at the same portraits and the same people walking in and out – the King, his secretary, the Count of Olivares, Don Baltasar de Zúñiga. After a while it felt like a prison, locked between narrow and windowless walls with no one to talk to, nothing to do and no hope of an end. Despite the toil and tedium, he persevered, no longer sustained by hope but simply the absence of anything else to do. Until on the sixth day a new visitor arrived. It took Sebastian a while to believe his eyes, but he appeared to be looking at a four-foot-tall knight dressed in a full suit of armour.

* * *

The cardinal awoke in the dark, devoured by pain. He knew he was going to die. The agony was excruciating, a blade churning in his gut. He couldn't get up, couldn't think and writhed in his sheets, praying for a death that refused to come. Remorseless as crucifixion, the pain continued. It reached the point where he couldn't bear it any more, and still it did not stop. Eventually he gave up and broke down, weeping and pleading for mercy. He hadn't cried in forty years but it made no difference. Finally, out of sheer desperation, he scrabbled for the pistol beneath his mattress, intent on putting an end to his misery with a bullet to the head. It was futile, of course. He barely had the coordination to find the gun, let alone fire it.

Respite arrived only with morning, by which time he was simply too tired to feel anything. Instead he lay prone for half an hour, numbing himself in the silence before at last being able to open his eyes and take in the light, after which he managed to roll into a sitting position and call for his doctor. The physician, always close by, appeared in moments.

'I can't move. I'm dying.'

'Rest, you're ill. You need time to heal.'

'I'm dying, you idiot. I don't need rest.' Despite his condition, Richelieu had lost none of his disdain. 'Now fetch me ...' He halted mid-sentence and his body stiffened with pain.

'It seems to be an obstruction of some kind. Now if you'll let me examine your phlegm ...'

'Bring me a priest.' The words were hissed through gritted teeth.

'Don't give up, Your Eminence. There's still hope. Many times I've seen patients recover from your circumstances – often worse.'

'You've seen them die too. Fetch me a priest.'

'There is no priest here.'

'Père Joseph.'

'Père Joseph has left for the Holy See, Your Eminence. He has an audience with the Pope. I would have to go to the local village.'

'Then go.'

'But ...'

'Go. I will not enter the next world unblessed.'

*　*　*

After putting on the armour, Sebastian walked out into a different and more unpleasant world. His vision was restricted to a thin slit and all he could hear was the pant of his own breath. Moreover, the suit was too large and exceedingly uncomfortable, digging in from all directions, the iron bitter in his nose. The helmet was particularly cumbersome, far too roomy and threatening to topple off at any moment. If it hadn't been for his hours spent pacing the corridors he would have found it impossible to find his bearings, but even with only a sliver to navigate by, he knew which way to go.

As he moved forward, he could feel the metal still slippery with the boy's sweat. It had been a devil of a business to get hold of, three days of trailing after Prince Balthasar and his nurse until finally the weather became hot enough for the wretched child to remove his prized possession. Even now, it could be only a matter of minutes before he realised it had disappeared.

Rounding the corner, Sebastian tried to advance in a straight line while keeping his balance. Only at the door, when he caught a glimpse of the guard's panache – a dazzling white feather reminiscent of Henry the Great – did he fully comprehend the danger he was in. But the guard was staring at him and it was too late to turn back. He had no choice except to lumber forward, aiming for a space between the sentries while praying to God that the door was going to open. Miraculously it did, and the room revealed itself before him: a sepulchral twilight in which a single figure was hunched over a desk beside a guttering candle.

Suddenly he felt a sharp strike on top of his helmet and jolted to a stop, terrified he'd been discovered. Unable to see, he steadied himself to run, planning to fling himself out of the nearest window in the hope the armour might somehow break his fall. Then he heard an echo of laughter and realised the sentry was simply patting his head. Staggering forward once again, he could now see recesses and shelves lining the walls of the chamber, and above all, documents. Documents on the desk, stuffed in alcoves, piled in corners, stacked on ledges. Documents on documents, documents in documents; half-open, locked away, scattered on the floor; some labelled, some torn, some that seemed to contain nothing at all; more documents than he could count, let alone read. It felt like staring into infinity, a lifetime's work when he only had a minute or two at the most.

*   *   *

Richelieu spent the morning refusing to die, concentrating ruthlessly on his work while trying to withstand the pain. After calling in his secretary, he managed to dictate two despatches and respond to a report. The words came slowly, in short sentences through taut lips. However, as the day wore on, he showed a few signs of recovery, managing to sign a backlog of documents and even drinking a cup of water. Then, at a few minutes past noon, the priest arrived.

After being let in by the guards, the clergyman waited in the corner as Richelieu completed his review of the King's accounts. Once satisfied that the books were in order, the cardinal turned to his visitor. He was dressed simply – in cassock and collar – but it was his shoes that drew Richelieu's eye. They were clean and sharp-toed, made for silence and comfort, not the weather-beaten boots of a man who spent his days trudging a parish. Then he noticed a tell-tale glint from inside his robe.

'Quid defluis?' he asked, only to be met by a baffled smile. 'You're no priest ...'

'But I'll bring you closer to God,' the man replied, producing a pistol and motioning the secretary to the corner. 'The gun under your pillow. Throw it on the floor.'

'You've been well informed.' Wincing from the effort, Richelieu managed to pull out the weapon and toss it onto the tiles before collapsing back onto the mattress. When he finally spoke it was with closed eyes, concentrating only on what he had to say.

'I've done as you ask. Now, since you're about to kill me, at least tell me why.'

'For money.'

'If I pay you double?'

'I've given my word.'

'And you know who I am?'

'Who doesn't? You're Cardinal Richelieu, the most hated man in France.'

A smile passed across the cardinal's lips. Despite the situation, he still took pleasure in his notoriety. 'Be that as it may, you realise what you're about to do?'

'Don't try your clever words on me.'

'I won't, but at least assure me you understand the consequences.'

'I know the consequences. I'm not afraid.'

'I'm not talking about you. I'm talking about your family, your town, your country.'

The man nodded, his pistol still levelled at Richelieu's forehead.

'This is a kingdom at war, and it is not a war we're winning. We've been attacked mercilessly. Four years ago we almost lost Paris. If our enemies hadn't run out of money, we wouldn't be talking now. Since then they've attacked us from the south-west, and remain a threat from both north and east. Make no mistake, they will invade at the first opportunity. But there is hope. The people are tired of battle. Both Portugal and Catalonia have rebelled against Spain – revolts that I am paying for, that would not survive without my help. If these uprisings continue, even spread, there could yet be peace. After twenty-three years, this war that has ravaged our continent might actually come to an end. But if I was to die unexpectedly, ask yourself what would happen then?'

'You're saying we'd be attacked.'

'I can't read the future. But we've survived until now, and if you kill me, we may well not. You hold the fate of an entire people in your hand. The people you serve, Gaston and Chevreuse, they mean to ally with Spain – have no illusion about that. We will be ruled from Madrid. Our taxes will go to Philip and we will suffer the inquisition. Now you may still choose to fire that pistol. All I ask is that you give it the consideration it deserves.'

The cardinal's response was met by a conspicuous pause, then his eyes snapped open.

'Hurry. You still have time.'

Once the room was empty and the footsteps had receded into the faraway hum, Richelieu turned to his secretary, who was still staring at the spot where the assassin had just been.

'I imagine that's the first time you've been at the wrong end of a weapon?'

The secretary gave a jolt, seemingly having forgotten the cardinal's presence, then mumbled his agreement in a still-shocked tone.

'A word of advice, next time you face an armed man, remember he's every bit as scared as you. Murder is a hanging offence, slow death at the end of a rope. You can be sure he's looking for an excuse not to do it. Any reason will do, just give it to him and he'll do the rest.'

'But why not kill him? What if he comes back?'

'He won't. Not once Chevreuse finds out what he's done. I give him a week at best.'

* * *

The chess set was from the Far East, ivory-carved with one side stained black. Its pieces were sculpted in human form, with peasants for pawns and men-at-arms for the bishops and knights, the king and queen fine-carved in their robes of state. Each had been created by a different craftsman and there were subtle variations even from pawn to pawn – some carrying cleft staves, others scythes, some clubs and hatchets.

Each man's play reflected his personality, both searching for glory and the heroic attack – the double Muzio Gambit, with white sacrificing a knight and bishop in the first eight moves. Louis, now with king exposed and under attack from queen and rook, decided against any hasty response and chuckled to himself before looking across at Cinq-Mars.

'This will leave one of us looking like a fool.'

'Better foolish than forgettable.' Then Cinq-Mars hesitated a moment. 'I'm sorry,' he added. The apology explained the pause. Remorse didn't come easily to him. 'I've spoken harshly about the cardinal. It's not fair, he's done great things for France.'

Louis stared back in astonishment, momentarily silenced. It was the first time he had heard the marquis express regret.

'My only worry is that he's too great a man, too important, irreplaceable.' Cinq-Mars paused again, tiptoeing forward, giving Louis every chance to respond. 'To the point where his death would put us under immediate risk of attack.'

'Guh-guh-gathering an army that quickly is difficult.'

'But it can be done. I believe the cardinal himself has managed it before.' The reply was too quick, too rehearsed and Louis sensed it. He looked away, his eyebrows accented with suspicion.

'Perhaps. Buh-buh-but as we have established, the cardinal is an exceptional man.'

'I agree, but he's going to die. The whole court knows it, and so will Spain. They must have something planned.'

Louis didn't respond and considered the marquis' words while adopting a suitably regal pose: rubbing his lower lip, head turned away a fraction, gaze fixed on the far distance.

'The thought had crossed my muh-mind.'

'All I'm suggesting is relieving him of a few powers, just to reassure people that something's in place. So there's no confusion when Richelieu goes. Wasn't it you who told me of the need for continuity?'

'And if the cardinal recovers?'

'What of it? All you will have done is highlight his successor. Anything you've handed over you can return. But I can't imagine it happening. The man hasn't left his bed in months. Last time I saw him he could barely speak. In truth, I'm amazed he's lived as long as he has.'

'I too am sick.'

'Don't be ridiculous ...' The marquis dismissed the remark with a smile. 'But even if that were the case, wouldn't it be doubly important to put someone in place? I mean if you were both to die ...'

'That still leaves the problem of telling the cardinal,' Louis murmured. It was a vague reply but the change in the conversation was concrete – *if* had now become *how*.

* * *

With a deep breath, Sebastian skimmed the documents in front of him. Despite the impossibility of the task, he didn't have time to waste being despondent. His only chance was to look and hope. None of them resembled the treaty. He remembered a stamp of lapis blue and gold leaf, but all he could see were piles of bare parchment and plain wax seals. Then he noticed movement to his left and glanced round to see the man at the desk. He was wearing a gold-stitched doublet and pantaloons. The face was familiar: a beard, plump lips, the palest of skin and bulbous eyes. He couldn't put a name to it at first, but then he remembered the portrait from the corridor outside. God almighty – he was looking at Philip IV, ruler of Spain, Portugal, the Netherlands and the New World. The most powerful man in Christendom was two yards away and staring directly at him. Philip's mouth moved, producing a phrase which the echo of the helmet rendered completely unintelligible. He remained paralysed, overwhelmed by the sheer magnitude of the situation. His mind had emptied itself and though he knew he had to do something, he had no idea what. Fighting the urge to flee, he stumbled forward and hugged the King's leg. It was at that precise moment, as he turned his head, that he caught a flash of blue. The treaty, or something similar to it, was lying beside the desk. His instinct was to grab it and run, but he had no chance of passing the guards on the door. Looking back at Philip, he could see the King's mouth emitting a further stream of gibberish. Then his surroundings transformed. Noise, light and air – the world outside was rushing into his head. It took him a moment to comprehend it. Philip was pulling off his helmet, no doubt to kiss him. Stiffening with panic, he flung up his hands and managed to haul it back in place. Hurriedly he glanced across to check the King's reaction. But he was smiling, seemingly amused by this act of petulance, and had already returned to his work. Then, as Sebastian was tottering for the door, his moment came – and during the instant his back was to Philip, he managed to grab the paper, sliding it beneath his breastplate before escaping the room.

* * *

'Is that what I think it is?' the cardinal's voice sharpened with interest. Sebastian had found him in the steam-room in Arles, where he was currently being treated with a series of hot baths. Surrounded by smoke, he appeared half-dead, floating midway between heaven and earth, his arms out-stretched along the ledge behind him. A man who had made peace with the world and whose mind had turned to less earthly matters. However, as he caught sight of the paper in Sebastian's hand, the torpor seemed to lift and the bridge of his nose crinkled slightly as he peered through the mist.

Sebastian nodded.

'I would say I'm surprised, but you'd probably find that offensive.'

'I would.'

'It has his signature and seal?'

'Of course.'

309

As the cardinal reached out to take the document, he smiled with an unfamiliar innocence, forgetting himself in delight. Unfolding it carefully, he examined the contents while shaking his head with disbelief. The seals and the names were all there, in a neat line: Lorraine, Gaston, Fontrailles, Bouillon, Philip and, right at the end – Henri Coiffier de Ruzé. He continued to stare. Something had to be wrong – the text could be inconclusive, the signatures could be false. However, after checking and rechecking, there was no doubt: the words were explicit, the meaning clear, the crest of every signatory present. He turned back to Sebastian and asked to hear the story from the beginning. Delighted to oblige, Sebastian regaled the cardinal with his various triumphs and failures, finishing with a spectacular account of a hailstorm while crossing the Pyrenees on his return. After which Richelieu drew the performance to a close.

'Thank you, it appears I'm going to have a rather busier day than I had anticipated,' he said, lifting himself upright with some difficulty and calling for the steward to bring his clothes. Within the hour the building was frenetic with activity: people packing, giving orders, carrying boxes and trunks, horses being fed and coaches being prepared. The order had been given; they would be returning to Paris immediately.

*　*　*

The design of the chapel was simple, almost stylised – its nave without aisles, flanked by rounded arches leading to the altar. A single beam of light shone down into the

310

transept from a window in the dome overhead, while the only decoration consisted of the candles in tall sconces, one placed in each of the eight corners. A solitary figure knelt at the chancel, head bowed, deep in prayer. Dressed in a white shirt and loose trousers, he resembled a priest of some sort, and Sebastian suspected it was either Père Joseph or Mazarin. It was only when they were a few feet away that the man turned around to reveal the face of Louis XIII. Sebastian had spoken to the King before, but this time was different – it was just him, Louis and the cardinal. He thought back to his encounter with Philip and felt the same sense of awe, knowing he should do something but not sure exactly what. Then he noticed his eyes were at the same level as the King's and realising the breech of protocol, flung himself to the ground.

'Your Majesty, I had no idea it was you.'

Smiling, Louis got up off his knees and shook his head, motioning him to stand. The cardinal remained upright, head lowered, evidently unable to bow and clutching his crosier for support.

'Armand. I wasn't expecting a visit so soon. The marquis told me you were breathing your last.'

'He may come to wish that I had.'

'What do you mean?'

'This treaty has recently fallen into our hands. I was wondering if you would care to take action.' Sebastian noticed a difference in the cardinal's voice. It sounded meek and nasal, bereft of its usual snap. Servility didn't suit him. It felt wrong – as though he was looking at him undressed, nothing but grey and sagging flesh – and he stared down at his feet. Louis, however, seemed well accustomed to flattery

311

and took the document without a word. Examining it briefly, he grimaced and shook his head.

'Have them all arrested and Gaston exiled.' His voice was calm, a hush of disappointment, nothing more. Sebastian was surprised by the lack of reaction. It seemed callous bordering on blasé. With a glance and a couple of words, he had condemned his favourite to death. A man he had been infatuated with for the previous two years, who had dominated his every waking hour, was now facing torture and the executioner's block. He didn't even seem surprised, so used to people being corrupted by power that he had simply come to expect it.

'Your Majesty, I would also like to introduce the agent who uncovered the plot.' Richelieu motioned at Sebastian, who continued to scrutinise his toes, alarmed the King might somehow find his gaze impertinent. He could hear muttering, no doubt Richelieu confirming to Louis that his saviour was indeed a dwarf.

'You are allowed to look at me. I'm not so repulsive, you know.'

Sebastian was too nervous to observe Louis' joke. 'It truly is an honour, Your Majesty ...'

'I remember you,' the King interrupted. 'You're the one who jumps out of the pie on my birthday ... How did you get hold of this?'

Sebastian began to explain but could see the King lose interest after a minute or so. Though he was nodding along, his stare had drifted into the middle distance and his smile was thin and forced, similar to the boredom of a child being introduced to an unknown relative. Understandable enough – the man probably spent half his life having to be polite to complete strangers. So, after cutting his story absurdly short, Sebastian departed as quickly as was possible while both walking backwards and adding appropriate salutations and bows.

Richelieu had clearly intended the meeting as a reward, for him to be acknowledged by the King for his services, but he found the experience profoundly unsatisfying. He had hoped that three years of ridiculing himself in front of the man might have left some impression, but evidently not. Instead, it was merely another reminder of his own unimportance, as though he had met God only to be mistaken for someone else.

*　*　*

Richelieu approached the cell prepared for confrontation, head and chin lowered for the charge, his crosier clanging the stone flags to the rhythm of his walk, its echo plangent as an iron bell. Dressed in his black soutane, collar and wig, he looked more like a judge than a priest as he stared fixedly at the metal door in front of him, his eyes if not as bright then at least as hard as they had ever been.

After being let in by the guard, he advanced into a low-ceilinged chamber of oppressive proportions, its stone walls glossed with slime, the damp thick in the nose. A figure sat crouched beneath the slit window at the far end, chained by its left ankle to the wall. Hearing the visitor's footsteps, it looked up sullenly. The face was not immediately recognisable as Cinq-Mars. Roughened with beard and whitened from the dark, he was already succumbing to the conditions and greeted the cardinal with a hacking cough.

313

'Come to gloat, I see.'

'I take no pleasure in this.'

'Why don't you sod off then?'

The cardinal shook his head, his nostrils pinched in disgust. 'Do you know why I wear this soutane?'

Cinq-Mars didn't reply.

'It doesn't stain. I reserve it for those occasions when blood may be involved.' Despite his assurance to the contrary, Richelieu lingered over the words with considerable malice. 'Do you think there will be blood involved?'

'Judging by the fact I'm not going to tell you a damn thing, then yes, I'd say there's going to be blood involved.'

'Don't play the hero. You're a traitor. If you don't co-operate, you'll regret it – at your leisure and in considerable pain. Confess quickly and you may just survive.'

'And Gaston? Is he being tortured too?'

'Gaston? The man's an irrelevance. He betrayed you long ago. Not that we needed him to. We already have all the evidence we need.' The cardinal drew the treaty from his soutane and held it in front of Cinq-Mars.

'Are you going to talk at me all day or get this over with?'

'Very well.' The cardinal turned to walk away, then paused and looked back – his eyes softer now. 'At least tell me this. What possessed you? You were the King's favourite. You had money, power … Why?'

'You never understood …' Cinq-Mars clenched a smile. 'What it's like to be powerless, to mean nothing. Knowing you'll be forgotten, an addendum – not even that. This was my chance. You would have done the same.'

'No, I would have waited. That was always your problem, Henri. You were always too greedy. You never had the patience.'

314

'What was the point? I would have waited forever. You never believed in me.'

'Don't blame me. It was your choice to rebel. I'm here because of you, not the other way round.'

'So tell me … If you don't feel responsible, why are you trying so hard to justify yourself?'

There was enough truth in the statement to make the cardinal flinch, and he glanced away, stung. When he looked back at the marquis, the mask had returned, rigid with authority.

'It appears this conversation is at an end. Make your choice.'

'I've already made it. I'm not going to confess.'

'Don't be so naive. It's just a matter of time. Breaking a man isn't complicated – time-consuming perhaps, but not complicated. First the rack, then the whip, then the rope, then fire. Then if necessary I'll have you nailed to a wall and let you hang by your palms … Now understand that I don't want to do this. Spare yourself. If not for you, then for me.'

'You call that an offer? Why should I care what you feel?'

This time the cardinal remained silent.

Richelieu expected Cinq-Mars to crumble in a matter of moments. The man was all bluster, no heart. However, he kept his word and even seemed to find nobility in suffering. Perhaps it was all he had left. The rack was normally sufficient to break a man, but after wavering at the beginning, he grew stronger – hurling insults through locked teeth – intolerable to the end. Even the lash couldn't silence him, and it was only when they started ripping out his nails that he could no longer hide the pain. It wasn't enough to make him confess, however, and after running out of fingers and toes they moved on to the flaming torch. The work was all smoke and heat, noisy in the extreme. Nevertheless, the gaoler went about his business with grim purpose as the cardinal sat on a stool and endured the spectacle while rubbing his face in silent frustration. Until, after two hours of screams and burnt flesh, Richelieu couldn't stand it any longer and told the gaoler to stop. There would be no confession and, without that, it was nothing more than gore and revenge.

Only two parts of the marquis' body had escaped the fire, his palms and the soles of his feet, and he crouched naked in the dark, unable to lie down. Blackened and scabbed, squatting on all fours, he seemed more animal than man – panting for breath and reeking of sweat and burned hair. Richelieu looked at him through weary eyes, planting down his crosier and hauling himself from his stool before yelling at the guards to 'give the man some food, water and a comfortable bed'. After which he shuffled for the door, never once looking back.

*　*　*

Sebastian had no desire to see the marquis' trial but went nonetheless. Having been responsible for his arrest, he felt obliged to see the matter through to the end. Besides, he didn't have anything else to do, no work at the palace – or for Richelieu either. The cardinal had been as good as his word, rewarding him with a pension of four hundred livres a year, to be collected from the court bursar every second Thursday. Not a fortune but more than sufficient for rooms, furnishings, food and the odd luxury – with enough left over to send

316

something to Audrien's family at the start of each month. Mostly he spent his time reading, continuing to make his way through the cardinal's library, beginning with Plato and working through the Greeks before progressing onto Rome. However, having recently become bogged down in Aristotle, he was secretly glad of the break.

Despite his hatred of Cinq-Mars, Sebastian found himself developing a certain respect for the man as the proceedings wore on. The atmosphere was intimidating – an oak-panelled chamber, its far wall dominated by a vast coat-of-arms – below it, an empty throne reserved for the King. Seventy peers sat in rows, dressed in full pomp, all stern-faced and ermined, observing the defendant over crossed arms. Their disapproval was clear and the result never in doubt, but Cinq-Mars didn't appear to care and leaned back in his chair with scornful indifference. When questioned, he immediately admitted his guilt, showing no remorse whatsoever. His audience made a dutiful attempt to appear outraged – as if the thought of seizing power had never once crossed their minds. With tuts and cries of 'Shame! Shame!', they commanded the marquis to show contrition and behave as his rank demanded. Naturally, he refused, revelling in his defiance and accepting his punishment with equanimity, even forgiving the judge on the grounds of having no part in the matter despite being forced to deliver the final blow.

* * *

The execution itself took place in Lyons. A thin city, it bristled with tall, anaemic buildings that looked too slender to support their weight – geometric and functional constructions, a place for business but not to live. So, after walking the narrow streets and finding little to do, Sebastian gave up and decided to join his fellow travellers in the tavern, drifting through the days between drink and sleep, until the end arrived with an overcast sky and slight drizzle.

As with most executions, the beheading drew large crowds, particularly as it involved the spilling of noble blood. Keen to avoid the tumult, Sebastian took the precaution of renting a balcony, where he could sit and observe the spectacle over a bottle of wine. He had never seen a public execution before and it was every bit as dispiriting as he had imagined. There was no doubt what the people had come to see. Some even brought their children. They stood row on row on row, munching cakes as they ogled the block – a lone altar, its significance made clear by the expanse of bare platform around it.

Cinq-Mars didn't die until early evening. Determined to extract as much money from the audience as possible, the organiser insisted on having the prisoners executed one by one, finishing with the marquis. Each was led by cart to the stage, then permitted a lengthy speech begging forgiveness. The majority were desperate affairs that their victims were too inarticulate to express: crimes forced by hunger or poverty, starving families left behind, drunken mistakes, a sixteen-year-old pleading he was too young to die.

To his credit, Cinq-Mars remained arrogant to the end. Before even stepping onto the scaffold he demanded a higher rostrum on the grounds of his lineage. The mob, by now mostly drunk, enjoyed this show of rebellion and cheered him on. Next he refused to remove his hat, furious at having to bare his scalp before an executioner of such low social rank. This only further excited the crowd, who continued to roar their support as he struggled against the increasingly frustrated guards. Then, as his hat was about to be ripped from his head, he managed to break free and toss it into a sea of outstretched arms. The people had now stirred themselves into such a frenzy that Sebastian worried they might actually storm the stage. Sensing the danger, the soldiers ended it immediately, marching the marquis straight to the block and ordering the axeman to begin.

The beheading itself was vile to watch, a protracted and visceral death. The executioner had been taken ill, replaced by a novice who in his panic had forgotten to sharpen his sword. After a few ineffectual blows that had left his early victims howling in agony, one of the soldiers had been despatched to find a substitute blade. The best he could manage was an adze. A farmer's tool, it was better designed for chopping wood than necks, and it took thirty bludgeons to remove Cinq-Mars' head, each one spraying blood over the roaring crowd. Sebastian endured it with a repelled fascination, forcing himself through every crunch, spurt and gurgle. Finally he turned away and worked through the remainder of his wine, not finishing until long after the body had been taken away and all that remained was a few people huddled in the sheen of the square.

Sebastian had hoped to find redemption in the marquis' trial and execution; a satisfaction in the knowledge that what he had done was right, that he hadn't shied from the consequences of his actions. But he felt no different – if anything, worse. It was his fault the marquis was dead. And however much he reminded himself that if Cinq-Mars had succeeded, the cardinal would have been the one facing the axe, it still didn't soothe his conscience. Then he understood why Richelieu had chosen to stay in Paris. It wasn't out of cowardice, but the knowledge that while heaven might bring salvation, it rarely comes on earth.

*　*　*

Freedom was a novelty for Sebastian and his first few months back in Paris proved pleasant enough. He managed to find an unused room in a church garret on the Île Saint-Louis. The rent was low despite the central location, primarily due to the formidable climb. He didn't mind. The view provided ample compensation – a sweep across the river and the weave of streets beyond. He could see all the bridges onto the island: the neat-cut stone of the Pont Neuf; the high-arched Pont Saint Michel, clumped with teetering houses; the lopsided Pont aux Changes still sagging from its load. It gave him a sense of being part of, but also removed from, the city. Every day he could see subtle changes: pillars of wooden scaffolding sprouting above the skyline, the charred blots and scabs from innumerable fires, pyramids of crates rising and shrinking along the jetties by the Place de Grève. Bewitched, he would often lose himself in its intricacies and end up having to turn his chair round, forced to use his bed as a desk in an effort to get anything done.

With autumn, the problems became apparent. First there was the cold. The room had no fire or heating of any kind and he was reduced to a life spent under blankets and layers of tightly knitted underwear, all of which had to be tailor-made at considerable expense. Far worse was the boredom. After a while what once had seemed like freedom became a prison cell. He had a better view, perhaps, but his existence was no different. Every day he would sit alone, with nothing to occupy himself except drawn-out meals, ablutions and sleep. And over time he came to detest his drab walls, and the once-inspiring view now seemed to taunt him, an unending and fantastical universe of which he could never be part. Often he would simply give up, grab his coat and spend a few sous getting drunk in the local tavern, if only to provide the illusion of heat to cold-gnawed bones.

He tried to address his situation by filling his days as best he could, busying himself with long walks; touring the churches of Paris; studying both mathematics and the basics of clock-making; even rowing (something of a struggle as he could barely hold both oars at the same time). Once he had dreamed of stability, but now he viewed it with horror – a life mapped in front of him, inevitable as the clock, flat and unchanging normality as far as the eye could see.

Often he thought back to his time serving the cardinal, remembering some near-disaster or close-escape, and he would find himself smiling. Part of him sensed there was more to come and that he would see Richelieu again. There had been no final farewell, and loose ends were against the cardinal's nature. Though, as the months passed by, even Sebastian began to have doubts. So when the day finally arrived and the cardinal's servant appeared at the door, he couldn't be sure whether it was an invitation or simply a messenger announcing his death.

Retrieving his coat from the stand in the corner – adult-sized of course – he made the slow descent to ground-level and then out onto the street, where a carriage waited by the step, its door held open. He recognised it immediately: the mottled sheen of its leather, the gravel-pocked mudguards, the seats between which the cardinal had lain in his stretcher, even Gilles the coachman. Exchanging a cordial *salut*, he hoisted himself up, closed the door and sat down. It was only with the crack of the whip that he thought to ask why Richelieu had chosen to summon him. By then, of course, it was already too late.

*　*　*

At night, the Palais-Cardinal was at its most imposing – a block of shadow on shadow, its vast and looming wings suffocating in their embrace. In the silence, all Sebastian could hear was the chatter of wheels and the iron clack of horseshoes on stone, the tempo slowing from gallop to canter to trot. Finally, the coach rocked to a stop and a footman appeared at the window, opening the door before leading him through a back entrance, up a steep flight of wooden stairs and down a portrait-lined corridor. The journey ended in a ballroom, dominated by a long wall of swag curtains, rumpled by the weight of their luxuriance. Behind them, threads of light filtered in through the shuttered windows, catching the cloth in glints and sparkles. The waxed floor was empty apart from a chaise longue and a table with a single chair. A blanket had been placed over the couch and a shrivelled head was poking out of the end. It was, of course, Richelieu – no one else would justify such a setting. Then Sebastian was aware of something else, the absence of other life. There were no guards, attendants, not even his physician. It was as if, like some grand old creature, he had wandered into the desert to die alone, too proud to endure the embarrassment of his indignities. And in truth he did not look dignified. He looked old and crumpled with age, as though left in water too long, his eyes the yellow of a stagnant pool.

'You look well, Sebastian. It appears retirement has done you good.'

'Thank you, Your Eminence. You too are looking better ...'

'Don't bother. I'm dying. There's no need to pretend otherwise.' The voice was thin and vaporous, more like a sigh.

'There is hope. A thousand people in Notre Dame are praying for your recovery.'

'I doubt it will offset the million who want me dead ... Anyway, I have a question for you.'

'Certainly.'

'How is it that I've risen to the highest office in the land, yet I look back at my life and see only failure?'

'You haven't failed. You've spent your life working for the people of France.'

'Dispense with the flattery. The truth is that nothing has changed. We're still at war, still one battle away from defeat. The people are still poor, still suffering.' He stared up at the ceiling, his jaundiced eyes confronted by a life that offered little more than a vague wash of disappointment. 'I had dreams once, but ... I can punish. I can tax. I can kill, but only destroy, never create. The truth is that I've steered the ship, but we're no closer to land. And soon what little I've achieved will be forgotten. Every day a little less ... until all that's left is a name.'

'How can you say you've achieved nothing? We're still here. You've kept us safe for twenty years.' Sebastian sounded almost indignant, as though he was the one being belittled.

'Yes, but what is safe? I've kept control, I've run the King's affairs. But is one person happier because of me? Or richer? Or wiser? Is one more person alive because of what I did?'

'I'm sorry, Your Eminence, but if you want pity don't look to me. You've had a life I can't even imagine – power, money, command. You'll be remembered forever. What could you possibly have to regret?'

'You're right. It's probably just self-pity. I've never thought of myself as the self-piteous kind, never had the time for it I suppose, but what else is a man meant to do on his deathbed? What's left but the past? Anyway, enough of this maundering. This evening is for your benefit, not mine.' He chuckled to himself for no obvious reason – apparently a personal joke. 'I thought all those years of service deserved some kind of reward.'

'You've already given me a pension for life. What else could I need?'

The cardinal raised his eyebrows and clapped his hands together smartly. A moment or two later, a side door opened and a man appeared wearing a soldier's tabard, Greek helmet and holding a sword. Mystified, Sebastian stared, unsure what to say – if anything at all. Then to his amazement, the man performed the opening soliloquy from his play. He looked across at Richelieu.

'I hope you don't mind, it took a little longer than I anticipated. I had one of my agents borrow the manuscript while you were away at the trial. And …I …well …affairs of state.'

Sebastian nodded, barely paying attention as he watched in delighted bewilderment, still unable to believe what was taking place. Slowly the story unfolded before him, scene by scene – featuring props, a backdrop, even a small ocean of rippled silk. A vicious satire of court, it portrayed an inverted society where only the feckless, idle and dissolute prospered – and Sebastian expected it to have suffered the censor's pen. But not a line had been removed, even the few that bordered on treason, though the actors couldn't help the odd hesitation under the cardinal's unforgiving eye.

Sebastian watched with mixed feelings. Pleasure, certainly – the satisfaction of observing his own talent and knowing it was being watched by perhaps the greatest mind in all of France – but frustration too. And during the final speech, he wept silently to himself. Not at the words, but the knowledge this would be its first and last performance – an orchid, blazing into bloom one night only to be gone the next, unnoticed and without purpose.

'It really is excellent,' Richelieu concluded as they clapped the players off the stage. 'As good as anything Molière produced. You should write another of these dramas of yours. It would be a shame to see such talent go to waste.'

'Then let it be performed in public. Nobody need know I wrote it.'

'I'm dying, Sebastian. If I recover, I will gladly support it. Frankly, I've little else to do nowadays. But I won't lie to you. Expect nothing. I've no wish to make promises I can't fulfil, I admire you too much for that.' Then the cardinal reached out and grasped Sebastian's arm. It reminded him of the hand of his dying father, and he flinched, but said nothing, instead forcing a smile and giving another round of applause.

* * *

325

A week later, the cardinal was dead. The news travelled fast, and over a distance commensurate with his reputation. First his palace, then Paris, then the Île de France, then Normandy, Picardy, Burgundy and out into the border regions of Lorraine and Limousin – even through Spain and the Low Countries.

Richelieu had been hated by so many for so long that initially a manic joy took hold. Bonfires were lit all over France and bells rung. People believed a poison had been removed from the King's ear, and whatever their desire, the cardinal's death seemed to answer it: the poor thought taxes would be lifted, the church prayed for unity, the nobility saw a chance to regain their rights. However, in spite of all their hope the King did not suddenly come to his senses. No *Parlement* was convened, no edicts were made, no laws rescinded. And slowly the joy ebbed into uncertainty. Richelieu had been in power so long – for many, nearly all their lives. To them, he was the government, and without him, the country seemed to be drifting, a feeling that only deepened when the King became mortally ill.

Flight

(1643)

The King first fell sick in February, during one of his many retreats from Paris to Saint-Germain. Despite recovering briefly, he soon suffered a relapse and was forced to his chambers, where he lay in bed making preparations for his death: summoning his councillors, writing his will, apologising to his wife for any pain he had caused, and blessing his children. The doctors treated him as best they could, with a course of enemas and bleeding, which he endured with the royal dignity demanded of him – though it did no good. Every day he more closely resembled the marble figure that would mark his tomb: lying on his back, his body hardening and growing ever colder while his skin lightened into a preternatural white, his hands locked in never-ending prayer.

As the King's illness worsened, the court became consumed by worry and inaction. Without their monarch, the nobles had no purpose and wandered the Louvre aimlessly

– queenless bees, milling about the hive in hope of their ruler's return. Strangely, there was little conspiracy, no reports of plots or scheming. People wanted certainty, not intrigue – for life to return to the way it had been. Nobody disputed the succession. Jules Mazarin was already serving in the cardinal's place and Louis made it clear his wife would be regent during his son's minority. Without rumour or dissent, instead the court was dominated by silence, and though Louis was still alive, it felt as if the funeral had already begun.

Concerned as Sebastian was for the health of the King, he was far more worried about his own. Anne would be regent, which meant the return of Chevreuse, who would undoubtedly want to finish off what she had failed to achieve the first time round. France was no longer safe for him – which immediately raised the question of where to escape. He knew nobody in Flanders or Italy, leaving only one alternative; to flee for Madrid. Fortunately, his stealing of the treaty seemed to have passed unnoticed so he could be sure of finding work at court, a necessity as he could no longer claim his pension. The only real obstacle would be the cost of the journey, a ruinous undertaking as he needed to travel by coach and alone due to the risk of being robbed. What little money he had left would barely cover a quarter of it, and after visiting the court bursar he was politely informed his next payment wouldn't be due for another four weeks. Having no choice but to wait, he spent the intervening time unobtrusively, hoping to be forgotten and left to make his escape. To make every sou go as far as possible, he lived frugally: only venturing outside to buy food and the occasional necessity, and making do with tallow candles which made his room stink of beef fat – not even spending money on paper and ink. He kept his mind off the confines of his room by working furiously, rereading all the books in his collection and writing short compositions on chalk and slate. Without even the money to spend on pamphlets, he lost all sense of the city outside except for the bells of Notre-Dame as they called the faithful to prayer and rang out the ends of each hour. He came to chart his day by them, beginning his work after matins before taking a meal on the stroke of lauds and finishing his day at vespers. Over time he was able to decipher their code – which occasions merited all five bells and the ones when the great Emmanuel tolled alone. Then one night, long after compline, he heard it: dirge-like, a slow vibration through the midnight air, repeating its single unchanging note. The time was so unusual and the pace so leaden that he knew instantly what it meant.

The King was dead.

After a momentary pause, Sebastian transformed into a flurry of motion, flinging whatever he could find into a hessian sack: money, books, clothes, even his blankets. Scampering downstairs, he reached the side entrance just in time to see a couple of soldiers arrive at the door. In his desperation to escape, he barely noticed and only looked round when the larger of two shouted something, then grabbed him by the collar. Bewildered, he gazed up to see a florid face with a cratered nose, the mouth gaping mid-guffaw as the man shared some inane joke with his colleague – doubtless about his height. It didn't make sense. How could they be arresting him already? It was too soon.

329

'I don't understand.' The words were muttered, not spoken – his mind thinking aloud. 'The King's only just died.'

Still laughing, the soldier choked out an unintelligible reply that Sebastian eventually deciphered to mean the King had died that afternoon and the Queen had dispatched them before issuing the announcement.

'And where are you taking me?'

This time the words were all too clear.

'The Bastille.' The soldier steered him forward and out onto the street. 'I see you're already packed,' he added, noticing Sebastian's sack. While the man's colleague seemed amused by the remark, Sebastian barely registered it. The world had suddenly acquired an unreal quality, as if he was already looking at it through the eyes of the dead, and he plodded forward unaware of the hubbub around him while people spilled onto the streets, all agog with the news.

Sebastian's abiding memory of the journey was the front of the Bastille. Previously he knew nothing about the prison beyond its reputation as a fortress. It was a place of rumour, by necessity as no one had ever escaped its walls and its guards were the king's finest, not the type to talk. All the stories followed the same broad theme, of a place without hope, its prisoners locked away until the end of their days – never to emerge again. And while Sebastian tended to be sceptical of hearsay, walking through the gate he was confronted by an impregnable cliff of stone and cement, its windows narrow as squinting eyes, its turrets jutting upwards – a crown of sharp horns. Each block of its ramparts weighed at least a ton, hewn to resist cannonballs, let alone men, and there were many, many blocks. The single entrance comprised a needle-thin doorway, flanked by sentries on each side, dull-eyed from the monotony of guarding its unchanging walls.

Despite the imposing entrance, the interior was relatively comfortable. His cell was clean, with space to walk and sleep. There was a small window, though far out of reach and offering only the tiniest crack of blue. In the corner was a mattress – filthy, but no worse than his childhood one in Camoches, along with a chamber pot deep in the corner, bulging out of the gloom.

After examining his new home, Sebastian threw himself on the bedding, trying to make sense of his situation. The Queen meant to execute him, of that he had no doubt. Her choice to imprison him as one of her first acts was a clear statement of intent. Memories of the marquis' execution flashed through him: the crunch of the adze, the spray of blood, the dangle of his half-severed head. And for a moment he could feel the breeze of the axe on his neck. Jolting upright, he began to pace the room in furious circles, pawing at his face as he listened for the approaching footsteps of his executioner.

But no one came. And as the hours slipped by, he started to tire and his terror subsided into a morose acceptance that there was nothing to do but wait – for the moment at least.

It wasn't until Sebastian's eyes became attuned to the dark that he noticed the graffiti. The writing was everywhere, etched into the rock like a thousand tiny fossils, ranging from simple, scratched initials and dates, to chiselled epigrams – one even in ancient Greek. He couldn't look at them without imagining the history of each one, though they were all sad stories and always with the same unpleasant conclusion.

Out of obligation, he added his own name to the list, rather unobtrusively, low down in the darkest corner. The work was slow as, having nothing sharp to hand, he was forced to use the side of a coin to wear away the stone. It took him over a day but he found the toil pleasantly absorbing. Forcing himself to concentrate on something, however mundane, allowed his mind to drift and his worries were replaced by an unexpected calm. He wasn't sure why. And though he knew he should be frightened, in the silence and the emptiness it was hard to feel any sense of danger. Besides, he had nothing to fear from death. As the cardinal once said, he had achieved far more than had ever been expected of him. He had been born a malformed peasant boy, ignored and laughed at, unable to use even a net or a scythe. Yet he had lived. He had met, even crossed swords with, some of the greatest names of state, stayed in palaces beyond his childhood imaginings, received the thanks of a king. Because of him, France had a dauphin and had been spared civil war. His name might not go down in history, but he was one of the great anonymous: the negotiators, the diplomats and the spies who comprised the hands of state. He had still made his mark, every bit as indelible as the letters carved in front of him.

And yet...

Something didn't sit comfortably. It seemed a poor death, to meekly accept his fate and whimper his way to the grave. He could still run, scream, love, hate, argue, punch, bite. And as long as he was alive, wasn't there some chance of escape, however small? Admirable as nobility seemed, surely it was better to fight, to be heard, to end life as he would like to be remembered – with an exclamation mark rather than a full stop?

The thought inspired him, the chance to write his epitaph,

his final cry before departing this earth. But what to say? What he had learned or remembered? Perhaps it was better not to discuss himself at all. And what emotion to instil? Pity, in the hope of being spared? Or defiance to the end? Intrigued by the possibilities, he immediately set to work and circled the few yards of floor, muttering alternatives under his breath.

His greatest problem was finding a way to take notes. Eventually he improvised, grinding the handle of his wooden spoon into something approaching a nib. For ink he used a thimbleful of blood, and a corner of his bed sheet for paper. Due to the limited size of the material and the pain of bleeding himself, he was careful not to waste a word and spent at least an hour composing and refining before putting spoon to cloth. It took him three days in all, but eventually he managed to write a speech that was, if not perfect, then at least the best he could make. His remaining time he devoted to his performance, rehearsing each gesture and pause, when to impose himself on his audience, when to pull back and allow them to consider what had just been said. Until, with the last of the light, he would flop back onto his palliasse, calming himself in the distant slit of stars or else reciting some *Gargantua and Pantagruel* – murmured, maternal as a lullaby.

* * *

Walking into the hall, Sebastian looked up to see columns so high they appeared to bend space. Above them, thin windows slit the darkness. Below, the emptiness was amplified by an expanse of bare stone floor, unfurnished apart from a single candelabra in each corner, their flames burning fatly in the still air. He advanced towards the distant throne, aware of the doorway disappearing behind him and suppressing the urge to flee. Ahead he could see the silhouette of the Queen, her jewels like a constellation, the crucifix glittering from her neck, her dress threaded with beads of pearls. Beside her stood another figure. Contempt personified, it was tilted back on one foot, chin up and glaring down over crossed arms.

After making the long walk to the dais, Sebastian stopped and bowed deeply, hands stiff at his sides. Both women were dressed with imposing formality, Chevreuse in a long dress of taffeta, its sleeves lined with fox, along with a velvet cap and curling feather. It had only been a year since he'd last seen her, yet she had aged – still attractive, but robbed of what innocence she had left. Clearly aware of the change, she had compensated with make-up and was masked in white, flattening her already soft features and removing all expression from her face. Anne, meanwhile, appeared every inch the queen: chin raised, eyes fixed, mouth downturned with gravitas. Previously, her only power had been through her husband, and now that her time had come, she was determined to make the most of it.

'Plead for your life, dwarf,' she declared.

Maintaining decorum, Sebastian responded with another deep bow.

'If it pleases Your Majesty, I would prefer to be called Sebastian.'

The Queen arched then peered forward, narrow-eyed.

'By God, are you being insolent?'

'Not at all, Your Highness. I am a dwarf. More than

that, a dwarf who was born in poverty. People laugh at me. They've laughed at me all my life. And for what? Because of something I never chose. And I've endured it these past thirty-three years. I've been kicked, beaten, insulted, spat at and pissed on. And here I am in the grandest hall of the royal palace, in audience with the Queen of France herself. I would like this one time to be called by my name.' He looked at the Queen with bravado, the strength people acquire when they know they are going to die – not because they have no fear, but because they have nothing left to lose. The Queen met his stare with distaste, the same way a fox might eye a limping shrew. There was no enthusiasm for the kill.

'Do not play the innocent with me. I suffered at your hand. So tell me, why should I not have you executed?' Her accent still had an undercurrent of her native Spanish, that precise diction of a foreign tongue.

'You've every right to execute me, Your Majesty. It's your prerogative. But I never meant to harm you. I didn't have a choice. I've never had the power to choose. Caught between Richelieu, yourself and Cinq-Mars, what chance did I have? The fact is that I'm a dwarf and I live in a world of titans.'

'Small you may be, but you still have the power to refuse. You could still have said no.'

'You're right – I had the power to refuse the cardinal. We all have the power to commit suicide, Your Majesty. Just because we choose not to exercise it, it doesn't make us evil men.'

The Queen seemed amused by Sebastian's candour but restricted her smile to a twitch of the mouth. She paused and Sebastian sensed indecision, as did Chevreuse, who immediately bent down towards her ear.

335

'You could always exile me,' he interrupted.

'And if I did, then where would you go?'

'To Spain, Your Majesty. They would take me at court.'

Anne cocked her head. 'You would join our enemies?'

'I doubt I'll be too much of a threat.'

This time the Queen's smile was accompanied by a nod and Chevreuse, now concerned, whispered to her behind a cupped hand. Anne considered a moment then responded with a shake of the head. 'You must,' Chevreuse muttered, the words hissed and barely audible.

'I am regent. I shall do as I wish.' Anne drew herself upright and stared down at Sebastian with rarefied disdain. Luxuriating in her power, she made him wait a moment before announcing her verdict.

'You are sentenced to death. Guards, take this creature outside and hang him from the nearest tree – without delay.'

Sebastian gazed back, disbelieving, as large bodies burst from the shadows, bulbous with muscle and glinting iron. This was the end. He remained rooted to the spot as one of them grabbed him by the neck and hauled him back the way he had come. Within a few strides he was already at the doorway, squinting to keep out the dazzle of the sun. Disorientated, he stumbled forward, the arm shackling his head like a yoke.

Eventually they stopped, though the soldier kept his head fixed in place, leaving him unable to see much beyond his feet. There was a brief silence followed by the hiss of rope being pulled over a branch and a twang as it was pulled taut. His death would be crude and inexpert, a slow dangle as he flailed under his own weight. Perhaps his size would make it impossible, forcing them to pull down on his legs as he kicked furiously for escape. It seemed somehow fitting, that after a lifetime of outsized chairs, cutlery, furniture, saddles and clothes now even his noose wouldn't fit him properly. Then he remembered his final words. In all the drama, he had forgotten them completely. But before he could speak, the rope was already round his neck and drawn tight, leaving him unable to manage more than a rasp.

A pair of hands reached from behind, lifting him for the drop. He attempted to break free but his hands were tied behind his back. He could hear the rattle of a carriage approaching, doubtless the Queen come to watch his demise. It slowed then clattered to a stop, until the only sound he could hear was the horses' lathered breath.

'Gentlemen, you know who I am.' The voice was unfamiliar – foreign, but only faintly so. It was male.

Male?

Sebastian felt a rush of hope. This was not the Queen or Chevreuse. This was someone new. Someone passing by who had decided to stop, a person of authority.

'Yes, cardinal.' Mazarin, it was Mazarin – the cardinal's protégé. But it made no sense. What was he doing here?

'Release this man immediately.' Sebastian felt himself being placed on the ground and the grip loosen from his neck. He tried to look at his saviour, though it took his eyes some time to recover from the glare of the sun.

'But the Queen said ...'

'The Queen will not know. This man will be placed in my care and taken to the border immediately.' The cardinal was dressed in soutane and skullcap – no different to his predecessor – though his beard still had a trace of the Italian fop, a curled and trimmed moustache, the chin below broken by a single flared line. Above all, he had that same command, his dark eyes emotionless as glass, and the guards were fixed as targets in his stare. To Sebastian, however, he resembled some kind of deity. Not the cold, imperial almighty of a Richelieu, instead the face of a kind and welcoming divinity, a parent come to rescue a child who was lost but not forgotten.

'As far as anyone knows this man will be dead, unless either of you is intent on telling the Queen?'

'Of course not, Your Eminence.'

'Good, then release him.'

As the hand let go its grasp, Sebastian looked round at the guards, still uncertain whether it was some form of trick. However, observing their fear, he knew it to be true. He was a free man. He immediately turned to Mazarin.

'I don't understand.'

'The cardinal – before he died, he asked me to look after you. You'll find two thousand livres under the seat and the coachman will take you wherever you wish to go. Now much as I would like to talk, we must leave. You're meant to be dead and I don't want any prying eyes bringing you back to life.' With a flourish of the wrist, the cardinal motioned Sebastian inside. Then with a kick of the hooves and a few turns of the wheels, it was over. And though he was never to see Mazarin again, Sebastian always remembered him with overwhelming love, realising in that moment that whatever happened to him in the future, he would never truly be alone – because a god was watching over him.

And so Sebastian Morra became Don Sebastian de Morra – born 1610, died 1672 – court dwarf for Philip IV of Spain, painted by Diego Velazquez circa 1645. Known today only as an image in a gallery on the first floor of the Prado in Madrid, he hangs among more illustrious subjects – the King of Spain, Isabella of Bourbon, the Count-Duke of Olivares and the god Mars. But amid all those great portraits, his is the one that catches the eye.

His face stops passers-by, as they find themselves confronted by thick and steepled eyebrows from under which black irises glower, refusing to be ignored. He makes no effort to impress – unbuttoned, his robes hang dishevelled while his beard has been left untrimmed. It doesn't interest him that he is being immortalised by the greatest painter in Spain, or that his image may one day be seen by millions. He knows why he is being painted – because he is regarded as a freak of nature without any purpose beyond the entertainment of others.

So he sits, meeting every stare that has settled upon him since, always responding with the same brutal truth.

'I may be a dwarf, but I am a greater man than you.'

Author's Note

Except for Don Sebastian de Morra, about whom nothing is known, the remainder of this story is broadly based on historical characters and events. However, I've taken a few liberties with events and timing for the sake of dramatic interest, principally:

Cinq-Mars was not an orphan. His father Antoine died when he was young and Richelieu was closely associated with the family.

Cinq-Mars was not romantically involved with Chevreuse.

Chevreuse was from the House of Rohan and was not born a farmer's daughter.

The paternity of Louis XIII's children is a subject of historical debate. However, Cardinal Mazarin is one of the many people touted as the possible father.

Richelieu gave the Palais-Cardinal to Louis in 1639, and it was known as the Palais-Royal thereafter.

In the Oxford edition of *The Three Musketeers*, David Coward states that Richelieu was in fact an admirer of Machiavelli, and therefore did not think him naïve.

Richelieu did not stay in Paris during the siege of Corbie, but in fact took the town on 14th November 1636.

The siege of Arras took place before Richelieu's vetoing of Cinq-Mars' proposed marriage to Marie de Gonzague.

Spain was far more deeply in debt than the book implies and had largely ceased to be a threat by 1640. The Spanish were finally defeated by the French in pitched battle at Rocroi in 1643, ending a century of dominance. Cardinal Mazarin was to continue Richelieu's work centralising the state, under Louis XIV – the Sun King and builder of Versailles.

Many books have been written on this period of history. Two I found particularly useful were *Cardinal Richelieu: The Making of France* by Anthony Levi and *Louis XIII* by A. Lloyd Moote.

Acknowledgements

I want to thank my wife Shula – for everything. Also our two daughters, Talia and Shira, for being generally splendid.

Also my mum, Miranda Seymour, and dad, Andrew Sinclair – for their guidance, example and encouragement.

Hugh Fasken, Karl French and Sallie Seymour for their wise advice.

Martin and Yochi Goldberg for all their help in looking after the children and giving me time to do this.

My agent Charlotte Seymour - to whom I owe multiple thanks for not only being a magnificent agent, but also for spending I don't know how long whipping it into shape, as well as having the faith to take me on.

Finally my publishers, Black & White, in particular Chris Kydd, Lina Langlee and Campbell Brown – without whom this book would not be here.